KT-434-562

Foreign Affairs and Other Stories

Sean O'Faolain was born in 1900 and educated at the National University of Ireland. For a year he was a commercial traveller for books but gave it up to fight on the side of De Valera in 1921. He was a member of the Irish Republican Army for six years, taught for a further year and then studied for three years at Harvard University. For four years he taught at Strawberry Hill Training College for Teachers, after which he turned to writing and went back to his native Ireland, where he now lives in Dublin. He has written some twenty books, including travel and literary criticism, novels, biographies, and several books of short stories. He has also contributed to many well-known periodicals in Great Britain and the United States. His other publications include an autobiography, *Vive Moi!*, and a history of Ireland, *The Irish*, which he calls 'a creative history of the growth of a racial mind'. *Foreign Affairs* is the third of three Penguin volumes that together form the first full paperback collection of Sean O'Faolain's short stories. The first two volumes are *Midsummer Night Madness* and *The Heat of the Sun* respectively. Penguin has also published several of his other books, including the novel *And Again?*

Sean O'Faolain is a D.Litt. of Trinity College, Dublin.

Sean O'Faolain

Foreign Affairs
and Other Stories

Penguin Books

Penguin Books Ltd, Harmondsworth, Middlesex, England
Viking Penguin Inc., 40 West 23rd Street, New York, New York 10010, U.S.A.
Penguin Books Australia Ltd, Ringwood, Victoria, Australia
Penguin Books Canada Limited, 2801 John Street, Markham, Ontario L3R 1B4
Penguin Books (N.Z.) Ltd, 182–190 Wairau Road, Auckland 10, New Zealand

First published under the title
The Collected Stories of Sean O'Faolain, Vol. 3 by Constable 1982
Published in Penguin Books 1986

Copyright © Sean O'Faolain,
1968, 1969, 1970, 1971 (*The Talking Trees and Other Stories*),
1971, 1973, 1974, 1975, 1976 (*Foreign Affairs and Other Stories*),
1982 (*Unpublished Stories*)
All rights reserved

Made and printed in Great Britain by
Richard Clay (The Chaucer Press) Ltd, Bungay, Suffolk
Typeset in Pilgrim

Except in the United States of America, this book is sold subject
to the condition that it shall not, by way of trade or otherwise, be lent,
re-sold, hired out, or otherwise circulated without the
publisher's prior consent in any form of binding or cover other than
that in which it is published and without a similar condition
including this condition being imposed on the subsequent purchaser

Contents

The Planets of the Years

I confess that I did not enjoy that winter of 1967 in Cambridge, Mass. My husband had too much to do and I had nothing to do: a common complaint, I have since gathered, with visiting professors' wives. Every morning while I faced an empty day he could go off happily to Widener Library researching for his biography of Henri Estienne, a character about whom I knew nothing except that he was a sixteenth-century French wit whose most famous *mot* is 'If youth but knew, if age but could.' I never got to like H.E., as we called him. His *mot* is out of date anyway, and his equally famous observation, that God tempers the wind to the shorn lamb, is complete baloney. I far prefer the man or woman (*Anon.*) who said that God never opens one door but he shuts another. And I like the other sad one, too, that says we are all as God made us, and some of us even worse.

When my happy man left me in the morning I rarely saw him again until dinnertime, and after dinner he so often buried himself in the study with H.E. that before the winter was out I took to calling him The Man Who Lives Upstairs. To be fair, he did, early on, introduce me to Boston, especially to its museums, and to two or three other disoccupied foreign wives. (American wives are never disoccupied.) But after that, apart from airily recommending me every morning to the delights of Boston, the only thing he did for me was to take me on Saturday nights to the Symphony, occasionally to a play, and, to my surprise – Are all newlywed wives constantly making these surprising discoveries about their husbands?— I found that not even H.E. could keep him away from a Western in Harvard Square or a Humphrey Bogart revival in Brattle Street. The only other way I could seduce him from H.E. was to make love with him – I will *not* tolerate the phrase make love 'to,' it is a ridiculous preposition – and as we were only four months married we made love a lot. It is my happiest memory of Cambridge, Mass. Still, no matter how much in love you are you cannot fill a whole winter's days that way. Certainly not in Widener Library. I was often lonely and mostly idle.

And then there was the house. It belonged to a friend of my husband, a professor in M.I.T., who in his turn was spending a sabbatical in Europe with, I am sure, his not at all disoccupied wife. I ought to have loved it, and in many ways I did. It was well furnished, well heated, well lit, contained lots of books, and it was delightfully roomy, far too big, really, for two people – it ought to have been full of noisy children. It was almost too quiet, tucked away on a side street flanked by a large if rather dank garden which I chiefly remember for the way its tall elms used to float up like seaweed every evening at twilight during those exquisite moments when the lights of the city are slowly turning the sky into a sullen, iridescent pink. I loved the house for its agreeably old-fashioned air of having been lived in for generations. I even liked the dust, the discarded matches, the lost coins, the bits of Christmas or Thanksgiving tinsel shining at the bottom of the hot-air registers in the floor. In fact, I liked everything about it except its situation – a long way up Massachusetts Avenue, bordering, across the railroad track, on the garish, noisy shopping centre of Porter Square, and the crumby neighbourhood behind it that looked anything but salubrious by day and, so my Cambridge friends warned me, was not particularly safe at night. Not being an American I suppose I dare mention the word Negroes. I do not mind mentioning Greeks, Italians and Syrians too. Like everybody in the world, I am nothing if not a racist – insofar as I accept every race but prefer my own. And I do not always trust the Irish either.

Now, I am not a nervous woman, but whenever The Man Who Lived Upstairs left Cambridge for a night to give a lecture elsewhere, and I lay in bed, reading myself to sleep, longing to have him by my side, hearing nothing but an occasional late car whistling along Mass Avenue, or the snow plopping softly from the roof, I could not help remembering that even back home in crimeless Ireland my parents' home had already been broken into three times in the previous three years. I could not also help thinking that the front door was partly glazed and that the downstairs windows were protected only by the weakest of hasps. Anybody who wanted to could, as the police say, have 'effected an entrance' without difficulty, and, the house being so tucked away, he could have done it unheard and unseen. Was that shuffling noise really the snow? On dusky afternoons I sometimes found myself rather shamefacedly putting the chain on the door.

Late one such snowy afternoon in November, I was alone in the house, writing home to my sister in Ireland. 'How I wish,' I had just written, 'we were together now, Nancy, gossiping over a drink or a pot of tea . . .' On the impulse, I had just risen to comfort myself with a solitary tea tray when, as I passed through the lighted hall towards the kitchen, I was startled to see two dark figures outside the glass door, outlined against the far street lights. I stood still and watched them. For quite a while they did not stir. Then the doorbell rang tentatively. I went forward, and saw through the muslin curtains what looked like two women. One was very small, the other was rather tall. I removed the chain and opened the door.

The small woman was ancient. Whenever I think back to her now I always see an old peasant woman wearing a black coif, bordered inside with a white goffered frill that enclosed a strong, apple-ruddy face netted by the finest wrinkles. I know this is quite irrational. She cannot have been dressed that way at all. I am probably remembering not her but my old grandmother Anna Long from the town of Rathkeale who came to live in our house in Limerick city when I was a child, and who was the first person I ever heard talking in Irish. The tall woman was middle-aged, and dressed conventionally. It was she who spoke first.

'I am sure,' she said diffidently, in unmistakable Boston-American, 'you will think this a very strange request that I am going to make to you. This is my aunt. She lives with me in Watertown. I brought her in to lunch in Cambridge for her eightieth birthday, and I promised her as a special treat that I would show her this house. You see, she got her first job here when she came over from Ireland sixty-three years ago . . .'

Here the old woman interrupted her niece. She spoke with a surprisingly rotund voice as if she were an oracle intoning from within the recesses of a cavern; but an oracle with an Irish brogue as thick as treacle and as rich as rum.

'We meant, ma'am,' she rumbled, 'only for to look at the outside of the house. But when I saw the lighted hall I made my niece ring the doorbell. For thirty-five years this was my door. It was a door-knocker we had. I'd love, ma'am, for to have wan tiny little peep into the inside of the house.'

I at once took her hand and drew her into the hall. At that moment nobody could have been more welcome.

'I was just putting down the kettle,' I said to them both. 'We'll have a nice cup of tea and be talking about home.'

When they had banged the snow from their boots I led them into the front drawing room. Tea, however, the old woman would not take, perhaps out of pure politeness, or from the delicate fear that I was only trying to compound her intrusion. She would not even sit on the chair I offered her. (I thought afterwards that in all her years as a servant she had never sat down in that house except in her kitchen or her bedroom.) Peering around her like a cat in a strange room, she started to talk about herself – again out of politeness? to cover her peering? – interrupting her flow only to say, every so often, like the warning croak of a bird, how much it had all changed:

''Tis changed entirely! We never had rugs on the floor like that. Carpets we always had, all over the house. Of course, when I landed in Boston it was the year nineteen-oh-four, and that is sixty-three years ago, and sure the whole world is changed since then! I was just turned seventeen. It was the month of January and I will never forget to my dying day the snow falling and falling. I never seen the like of it in all my life. From behind Slieve Callan I came, in the County Clare, and many's the time I seen Callan white with snow. Ye have the electric. Gas we had. But that Boston snow beat all I ever saw. It was like snow that started falling a long time ago and didn't know how to stop. Oh, dear! The blinds are changed too! It was my uncle Paudh met me off the boat, God rest his soul, and glad I was to get shut of it until I saw where he took me. To his home in South Boston. And a black, dark place South Boston was in them days. I was frightened out of my wits at all the rattle of the horsecars, and the trams, and the railway roaring like thunder and lightning all night long. I didn't sleep one wink with the fright and the strangeness of it all. Ma'am! Could I have a little peep at the back drawing room, if you please?'

We moved into it.

'Oh, no!' she said disapprovingly, peering down over the hummocked snow, indifferent to the beautiful sunset in the rusty sky, 'Look at the garden! Flowers we had, all the year round. We had a glasshouse. I can see no glasshouse! Have ye no glasshouse? The way I got the job was through my uncle Paudh's son, Patsy Coogan, my own first cousin. He was a coachman that time to a man named Newsom, a Quaker man, had a big country house out in Arlington. He had the job all lined up for me in this house with the three Misses Cushing. Are you sure there is no glasshouse? He came for me with the carriage the very next morning, and if I was frightened before, I was five and forty times more frightened the way we drove, and we drove and we drove. I that never saw any but the wan street of Miltownmalbay until I took the train straight down to the Queenstown docks ten days before. I was lost! There was no end to the streets. I was sure Patsy was lost too and was only taking me around in circles. I kept saying to him, "And where are we now, Patsy?" And Patsy kept saying, "In Boston! Where else?" I never in my life felt so cold as I did in that old horse carriage. It is very warm in here, God bless it! And no fires! It is the way ye have the central heating. The three Misses Cushing always insisted on a roaring log fire in every room. I was so cold I began to cry with the cold until Patsy said, "What the devil ails you and you going off to live in the finest house in Cambridge, Mass?" I said, "And where on earth is Cambridge Mass?" He got right cross with me. "Where is it?" he roars at me, "but in Boston! Where else?" Ma'am,' she pleaded, 'the one place I really wanted to see is my old kitchen.'

I led them into the kitchen.

'Oh, glory! Mind you, ma'am, I'm not faulting it. It is very nice. But somehow it is gone very small on me. God bless us, all the changes and innovations! I wouldn't know it at all, at all! Tiles on the floor we had. And where is my kitchen trough gone to? An electric stove! But where is my old kitchen range? Oh, the grand meals I cooked on that old range! For all the dinner parties! Yards long it was. And as bright as a battleship. Where can it be gone to? Am I in the right house at all?'

I showed her where I could only presume it must once have been, behind a walled-up part of the kitchen lined now with shelving.

'It was at that black divil of a range I learned how to cook. Oh, you have no idea of the kindness of the three Misses Cushing teaching me how to cook. The goodness of them! The patience of them! Though, mind you, many's the rap of the rolling pin I got on the knuckles from Miss Caroline when she'd be bad with the megrim. The best of good food they had! Would you believe it, this was the first house where I ever ate fresh meat. And is it how ye have the table and chairs for to eat in the kitchen?'

'Like we have ourselves,' the niece said crossly. 'At home in Watertown.'

'Three breakfast trays I took up every morning, winter and summer, to the three Misses Cushing. At half past six I would rise, and it was dark and cold them winter mornings, to light the range, and the divil of hell it was to light sometimes, and clear out the three fireplaces, and set and light the big log fires, and make the three breakfasts and, while the kettle was boiling, to steal up like a mouse so as not to waken my ladies, and put a match to the three fires in their bedrooms that I set the night before, and come down then and carry up the three trays at the tick of eight o'clock. Oh, the three loveliest, kindest ladies you ever met! Saints they were! I never in my life met such goodness. They thought nothing was too good for me. When I think of the darling little bedroom they gave me up under the roof, it was like a babby house, only for being like an icebox in the wintry nights.'

'You must have been very happy here,' I said comfortably, and realized at once that I had made a mistake by the way her head jerked like a bird cocking an ear to a worm underground. I had used a word she would never use. I was being sentimental about an experience that had been outside, and apart and beyond all sentiment. 'I mean,' I said hastily, 'you were contented here.'

'Ho!' she smiled. 'I was contented all day and every day as I never was before or since. I found my first and only home in this blessed house.'

'You have a nice home now,' her niece said. But once more the old lady paid no heed to her.

'Ma'am! There is one last thing I'd love to see. The stone trough in the basement.' (She pronounced it *throw*, as if she was still living in the wilds of County Clare, or in Anglo-Saxon Wessex.) 'Oho, then, the baskets and baskets of washing I did in that old black trough! And no hot water either only for what I'd drag down the stairs from the kitchen range.'

Was there a stone trough in the basement? I could not remember. Or had there ever been? But this time the younger woman rebelled, looked at her watch and looked out at a neighbouring house pouring two beams of light between the black trunks of the elms.

'It is too late, Auntie. The dark is falling. And there will be more snow. Don't encourage her,' she whispered to me. 'She could never make her way down those stairs.'

'Maybe I could help her?' I whispered.

The old lady was not listening. She had gone to the window, her mouth breathing moist patches on the cold pane.

'Marmee, her name was,' she whispered.

'Who?' I asked.

'The cat they gave me.'

It was only when she turned and began to sway, and we both ran to support her to a chair, that I realized the tiring day they must both have had.

'I won't let you go without the cup of tea!' I ordered, and put on the kettle, spread out the supermarket oilcloth, the rented china, the American biscuits and the Danish spoons, while her niece knelt beside her and looked worriedly at her pallid face and rubbed her knobbly hands. 'I only wish,' I laughed, 'that I had a nice hot slice of soda bread for you, cooked in the bastable, and tea smelling of the turfsmoke.'

They looked at me uncomprehendingly. Had they never seen a bastable pot or smelled turfsmoke? The old woman's eyes and mind had begun to stray away from me on the long journey homeward.

'Did you never go back to Ireland?' I asked. 'Didn't you ever go home?'

'Home?' she asked, and dropped her voice a pensive octave. 'Home?'

'I took her home,' the niece said curtly, 'in 1957. When my husband was killed working in the subway. It was my first visit to Ireland. And,' she said bitterly, 'my last.'

'Didn't you enjoy it?' I asked the old woman, and wet the tea, and sat beside her while she sipped it. I so wanted her to talk to me about Ireland!

'Slieve Callan,' she murmured, and I saw its whiteness rising like music under the low clouds moving imperceptibly from twenty miles away across the wrinkled Shannon. 'Letterkelly,' she whispered, and I saw a dozen roofs huddled under the white mountain. 'Miltownmal-bay,' she said, and that would be her nearest market town, with every slate in its one street rattling under the wind across Spanish Point, where, I had so often been told, three ships of the Armada went down under tons of sea. 'County Clare,' she sighed, and I saw its grey lava, its tiny lochs, and its cowering white cottages with their pigs' eyes of windows glinting in the sun.

'No, girl,' she said, 'I did not enjoy it. It was not the way I remembered it to be. Whenever you go back to any place,' she said, and

I marvelled at the phrase, 'across the planets of the years, nothing is the way it was when you were young. Never go back, girl! I thought when I was going back that, maybe, I might stay there and end my days there. But it was not me they wanted. I took home all my savings. One thousand dollars I had. The savings of fifty years. They were dragging it out of me and dragging it out of me until it was all but gone. Ayeh! God help us! They were poor and they couldn't help it. When it was all gone I said to my niece here, "Now, we must go home."'

I looked at her niece, she looked sullenly at me, we both looked at the old woman.

'You are Irish,' the niece said after a while.

'Yes,' I said. 'I am Irish.'

She nodded, and the three of us looked out at the falling night and we understood everything.

We rose. The niece carefully muffled the old woman against the cold. As we went to the door they thanked me again and again for showing them the house. The farewells ended when I said, 'Goodbye, now, and come again any time ye like,' and closed the door, and replaced the chain.

I watched them through the muslin curtains cautiously descending the wooden steps to the brick pavement. They moved away carefully and slowly, arm in arm, towards the bright headlamps flying along Mass Avenue, and the bright windows of Sears, Roebuck across it, and the friendly telephone kiosk that I liked so much because it remained bright all through the night. At the end of the street they halted, turned for a moment and looked back. I saw with their eyes this lighted door behind which I stood unseen. The whole house behind me would be dark against the city's glow. I knew better than to fancy that the old woman would be rejoicing at her last backward look. She would be uttering her vatic croak, 'All changed!' Or the exhausted niece might even be saying crossly, 'Are you sure it was the right house at all? It didn't look so very grand to me!'

As they moved out of sight large flakes were sinking silently through the penumbra of a street lamp. I saw a black mountain mourning under a white veil. Somewhere there had been a lost childhood. Somewhere, at some time, in some house, there had been a vision of home. I returned to the letter I had been writing in the drawing room.

'How I wish we were together now, Nancy, gossiping over a drink or a pot of tea . . .' I wrote on quickly. 'I could be telling you my great news. I have suspected it for weeks but I only heard today from the doctor that it is true. Oh, Nancy, the spring will be here soon, and after that the months won't be long passing until it comes, and then the four of us will all be together, in Ireland . . .'

How gently the lighted snow kept touching that window-pane, melting and vanishing, and, like love, endlessly returning across the planets of the years.

A Dead Cert

Whenever Jenny Rosse came up to Dublin, for a shopping spree, or a couple of days with the Ward Union Hunt, or to go to the Opera, or to visit some of her widespread brood of relations in or around the city, or to do anything at all just to break the monotony of what she would then mockingly call 'my life in the provinces,' the one person she never failed to ring was Oweny Flynn; and no matter how busy Oweny was in the courts or in his law chambers he would drop everything to have a lunch or a dinner with her. They had been close friends ever since he and Billy Rosse – both of them then at the King's Inns – had met her together twelve or thirteen years ago after a yacht race at the Royal Saint George. Indeed, they used to be such a close trio that, before she finally married Billy and buried herself in Cork, their friends were always laying bets on which of the two she would choose, and the most popular version of what happened in the end was that she let them draw cards for her. 'The first man,' she had cried gaily, 'to draw the ace of hearts!' According to this account the last card in the pack was Billy's, and before he turned it she fainted. As she was far from being a fainter, this caused a great deal of wicked speculation about which man she had always realized she wanted. On the other hand, one of her rivals said that she had faked the whole thing to get him.

This Saturday afternoon in October she and Oweny had finished a long, gossipy lunch at the Shelbourne, where she always stayed whenever she came up to Dublin. ('I hate to be tied to my blooming relatives!') They were sipping their coffee and brandy in two deep saddleback armchairs, the old flowery chintzy kind that the Shelbourne always provides. The lounge was empty and, as always after wine, Oweny had begun to flirt mildly with her, going back over the old days, telling her, to her evident satisfaction, how lonely it is to be a bachelor of thirty-seven ('My life trickling away into the shadows of memory!'), and what a fool he had been to let such a marvellous lump of a girl slip through his fingers, when, all of a sudden, she leaned forward and tapped the back of his hand like a dog pawing for still more attention.

'Oweny!' she said. 'I sometimes wish my husband would die for a week.'

For a second he stared at her in astonishment. Then, in a brotherly kind of voice, he said, 'Jenny! I hope there's nothing wrong between you and Billy?'

She tossed her red head at the very idea.

'I'm as much in love with Billy as ever I was! Billy is the perfect husband. I wouldn't change him for worlds.'

'So I should have hoped,' Oweny said, dutifully, if a bit stuffily. 'I mean, of all the women in the world you must be one of the luckiest and happiest that ever lived. Married to a successful barrister. Two splendid children. How old is Peter now? Eight? And Anna must be ten. There's one girl who is going to be a breaker of men's hearts and an engine of delight. Like,' he added, remembering his role, 'her beautiful mother. And you have that lovely house at Silversprings. With that marvellous view down the Lee...'

'You can't live on scenery!' she interposed tartly. 'And there's a wind on that river that'd cool a tomcat!'

'A car of your own. A nanny for the kids. Holidays abroad every year. No troubles or trials that I ever heard of. And,' again remembering his duty, 'if I may say so, every time we meet, you look younger, and,' he plunged daringly, 'more desirable than ever. So, for God's sake, Jenny Rosse, what the hell on earth are you talking about?'

She turned her head to look out pensively at the yellowing sun glittering above the last, trembling, fretted leaves of the trees in the Green, while he gravely watched her, admiring the way its light brought out the copper-gold of her hair, licked the flat tip of her cocked nose and shone on her freckled redhead's cheek that had always reminded him of peaches and cream, and 'No,' he thought, 'not a pretty woman, not pretty-pretty, anyway I never did care for that kind of prettiness, she is too strong for that, too much vigour, I'm sure she has poor old Billy bossed out of his life!' And he remembered how she used to sail her water-wag closer to the wind than any fellow in the yacht club, and how she used to curse like a trooper if she slammed one into the net, always hating to lose a game, especially to any man, until it might have been only last night that he had felt that aching hole in his belly when he knew that he had lost her forever. She turned her head to him and smiled wickedly.

'Yes,' she half agreed. 'Everything you say is true but . . .'

'But what?' he asked curiously, and sank back into the trough of his armchair to receive her reply.

Her smile vanished.

'Oweny! You know exactly how old I am. I had my thirty-fourth birthday party last week. By the way, I was very cross with you that you didn't come down for it. It was a marvellous party. All Cork was at it. I felt like the Queen of Sheba. It went on until about three in the morning. I enjoyed every single minute of it. But the next day, I got the shock of my life! I was sitting at my dressing table brushing my hair.' She stopped dramatically, and pointed her finger tragically at him as if his face were her mirror. 'When I looked out the window at a big red grain boat steaming slowly down the river, out to sea, I stopped brushing, I looked at myself, and there and then I said, "Jenny Rosse! You are in your thirty-fifth year. And you've never had a lover!" And I realized that I never could have a lover, not without hurting Billy, unless he obliged me by dying for a week.'

For fully five seconds Oweny laughed and laughed.

'Wait,' he choked, 'until the lads at the Club hear this one!'

The next second he was sitting straight up in his armchair.

'Jenny,' he said stiffly, 'would you mind telling me why exactly you chose to tell this to *me*?'

'Aren't you interested?' she asked innocently.

'Isn't it just a tiny little bit unfair?'

'But Billy would never know he'd been dead for a week. At most he'd just think he'd lost his memory or something. Don't you suppose that's what Lazarus thought? Oh! I see what you mean. Well, I suppose yes, I'd have betrayed Billy. That's true enough, isn't it?'

'I am not thinking of your good husband. I am thinking of the other unfortunate fellow when his week would be out!'

'What other fellow? Are you trying to suggest that I've been up to something underhand?'

'I mean,' he pressed on, quite angry now, 'that I refuse to believe that you are mentally incapable of realizing that if you ever did let any other man fall in love with you for even five minutes, not to speak of a whole week, you would be sentencing him to utter misery for the rest of his life.'

'Oh, come off it!' she huffed. 'You always did take things in high C. Why are you so bloody romantic? It was just an idea. I expect lots of women have it, only they don't admit it. One little, measly wild oat? It's probably something I should have done before I got married, but,' she grinned happily, 'I was too busy then having a good time. "In the morning sow thy seed and in the evening withhold not thine hand." Ecclesiastes. I learned that at Alexandra College. Shows you how innocent I was – I never knew what it really meant until I got married. Of course, you men are different. You think of nothing else.'

He winced.

'If you mean me,' he said sourly, 'you know damned well that I never wanted any woman but you.'

When she laid her hand on his he understood why she had said that about Billy dying for a week. But when he snatched his hand away and she gathered up her gloves with all the airs of a woman at the end of her patience with a muff, got up, and strode ahead of him to the levelling sun outside the hotel, he began to wonder if he really had understood. He even began to wonder if it was merely that he had upset her with all that silly talk about old times. A side-glance caught a look in her eyes that was much more mocking than hurt and at once his anger returned. She had been doing much more than flirting. She had been provoking him. Or had she just wanted to challenge him? Whatever she was doing she had manoeuvred him into a ridiculous position. Then he thought, 'She will drive to Cork tonight and I will never be certain what she really meant.' While he boggled she started talking brightly about her holiday plans for the winter. A cover-up? She said she was going to Gstaad for the skiing next month with a couple of Cork friends.

'Billy doesn't ski, so he won't come. We need another man. Would you like to join us? They are nice people. Jim Chandler and his wife. About our age. You'd enjoy them.'

He said huffily that he was too damned busy. And she might not know it but some people in the world have to earn their living. Anyway, he was saving up for two weeks' sailing in the North Sea in June. At which he saw that he had now genuinely hurt her. ('Dammit, if we really were lovers this would be our first quarrel!') He forced a smile.

'Is this goodbye, Jenny? You did say at lunch that you were going to drive home this evening? Shan't I see you again?'

She looked calculatingly at the sun winking coldly behind the far leaves.

'I hate going home – I mean so soon. And I hate driving alone in the dark. I think I'll just go to bed after dinner and get up bright and early on Sunday morning before the traffic. I'll be back at Silversprings in time for lunch.'

'If you are doing nothing tonight why don't you let me take you to dinner at the Yacht Club?'

She hesitated. Cogitating the long road home? Or what?

'Jenny! They'd all love to see you. It will be like old times. You remember the Saturday night crowds?'

She spoke without enthusiasm.

'So be it. Let's do that.'

She presented her freckled cheek for his parting kiss. In frank admiration he watched her buttocks swaying provocatively around the corner of Kildare Street.

Several times during the afternoon, back in his office, he found himself straying from his work to her equivocal words. Could there, after all, be something wrong between herself and Billy? Could she be growing tired of him? It could happen, and easily. A decent chap, fair enough company, silent, a bit slow, not brilliant even at his own job, successful only because of his father's name and connections, never any good at all at sport – he could easily see her flying down the run from the Egli at half a mile a minute, the snow leaping from her skis whenever she did a quick turn. But not Billy. He would be down in the valley paddling around like a duck among the beginners behind the railway – and he remembered what a hopeless sheep he had always been with the girls, who nevertheless seemed to flock around him all the time, perhaps (it was the only explanation he ever found for it) because he was the fumbling sort of fellow that awakens the maternal instinct in girls. At which he saw her not as a girl in white shorts dashing to and fro on the tennis courts, but as the mature woman who had turned his face into her mirror by crying at him along her pointing finger, 'You are in your thirty-fifth year!' How agile, he wondered, would she now be on the courts or the ski runs? He rose and stood for a long time by his window, glaring down at the Saturday evening blankness of Nassau Street, and heard the shouting from the playing fields of Trinity College, and watched the small lights of the buses moving through the blueing dusk, until he shivered at the cold creeping through the pane. He felt the tilt of time and the falling years, and in excitement understood her sudden lust.

As always on Saturday nights, once the autumn comes and the sailing is finished and every boat on the hard for another winter, the lounge and the bar of the Club were a cascade of noise. If he had been alone he would have at once added his bubble of chatter to it. Instead he was content to stand beside the finest woman in the crowd, watching her smiling proudly around her, awaiting attention from her rout (What was that great line? *Diana's foresters, gentlemen of the shade, minions of the moon?*) until, suddenly, alerted and disturbed, he found her eyes turning from the inattentive mob to look out broodily through the tall windows. The lighthouse on the pier's end was writing slow circles on the dusty water of the harbour. He said, 'Jenny, you are not listening to me!' She whispered crossly, 'But I don't know a single one of these bloody people!' He pointed out the commodore. Surely she remembered Tom O'Leary? She peered and said, 'Not *that* old man?' He said, 'How could you have forgotten?'

Tom had not forgotten her, as he found when he went to the bar to refresh their drinks.

'Isn't that Jenny Rosse you have there?' he asked Oweny. 'She's putting on weight, bedad! Ah, she did well for herself.'

'How do you mean?' Oweny asked, a bit shortly.

'Come off it. Didn't she marry one of the finest practices in Cork! Handsome is as handsome does, my boy! She backed a dead cert.'

Jealous old bastard! As he handed her the glass he glanced covertly at her beam. Getting a bit broad, alright. She asked idly, 'Who is that slim girl in blue, she is as brown as if she has been sailing all summer?' He looked and shrugged.

'One of the young set? I think she's George Whitaker's daughter.'

'That nice-looking chap in the black tie looks lost. Just the way Billy used always to look. Who is he?'

'Saturday nights!' he said impatiently. 'You know the way they bring the whole family. It gives the wives a rest from the cooking.'

It was a relief to lead her into the dining room and find her mood change like the wind to complete gaiety.

'So this,' she laughed, 'is where it all began. And look! The same old paintings. They haven't changed a thing.'

The wine helped, and they were safely islanded in their corner, even with the families baying cheerfully at one another from table to table, even though she got on his nerves by dawdling so long over the coffee that the maids had cleared every table but theirs. Then she revealed another change of mood.

'Oweny! Please let's go somewhere else for our nightcap.'

'But where?' he said irritably. 'Not in some scruffy pub?'

'Your flat?' she suggested, and desire spread in him like a water lily. It shrivelled when she stepped out ahead of him into the cold night air, looked up at the three-quarter moon, then at the Town Hall clock.

'What a stunning night! Oweny, I've changed my mind! Just give me a good strong coffee and I'll drive home right away.'

'So!' he said miserably. 'We squabbled at lunch. And our dinner was a flop.'

She protested that it had been a marvellous dinner; and wasn't it grand the way nothing had been changed?

'They even still have that old picture of the Duke of Windsor when he was a boy in the navy.'

He gave up. He had lost the set. All the way into town they spoke only once.

'We had good times,' she said. 'I could do it all over again.'

'And change nothing?' he growled.

Her answer was pleasing, but inconclusive— 'Who knows?'

If only he could have her in the witness box, under oath, for fifteen minutes!

In his kitchenette, helping him to make the coffee, she changed gear again, so full of good spirits (because, he understood sourly, she was about to take off for home) that he thrust an arm about her waist, assaulted her cheek with a kiss as loud as a champagne cork, and said fervently (he had nothing to lose now), 'And I thinking how marvellous it would be if we could be in bed together all night!' She laughed mockingly, handed him the coffee pot – a woman long accustomed to the grappling hook – and led the way with the cups back into his living room. They sat on the small sofa before his coffee table.

'And I'll tell you another thing, Jenny!' he said. 'If I had this flat twelve years ago it might very easily have happened that you would have become my one true love! You would have changed my whole life!'

She let her head roll back on the carved moulding of the sofa, looking past him at the moon. Quickly he kissed her mouth. Unstirring she looked back into his eyes, whispered, 'I should not have let you do that,' returned her eyes to the moon, and whispered, 'Or should I?'

'Jenny!' he ordered. 'Close your eyes. Pretend you really are back twelve years ago.'

Her eyelids sank. He kissed her again, softly, wetly, felt her hand creep to his shoulder and impress his kiss, felt her lips open. Her hand fell weakly away. Desire climbed into his throat. And then he heard her moan the disenchanting name. He drew back, rose, and looked furiously down at her. She opened her eyes, stared uncomprehendingly around her, and looked up at him in startled recognition.

'So,' he said bitterly, 'he did not die even for one minute?'

She laughed wryly, lightly, stoically, a woman who would never take anything in a high key, except a five-barred gate or a double-ditch.

'I'm sorry, Oweny. It's always the same. Whenever I dream of having a lover I find myself at the last moment in my husband's arms.'

She jumped up, snatched her coat, and turned on him.

'Why the hell, Oweny, for God's sake, don't you go away and get married?'

'To have me dreaming about you, is that what you want?'

'I want to put us both out of pain!'

They glared hatefully at one another.

'Please drive me to the Shelbourne. If I don't get on the road right away, I'll go right out of the top of my head!'

They drove to the Green, she got out, slammed the car door behind her and without a word raced into the hotel. He whirled, drove hell for leather back to the Club, killed the end of the night with the last few gossipers, drank far too much and lay awake for hours staring sideways from his pillow over the grey, frosting roofs and countless yellow chimney pots of Dublin.

Past twelve. In her yellow sports Triumph she would tear across the Curragh at seventy-five and along the two straight stretches before and after Monasterevan. By now she has long since passed through Port Laoise and Abbeyleix where only a few lighted upper-story windows still resist night and sleep. From that on, for hour after hour, south and south, every village street and small town she passes will be fast asleep, every roadside cottage, every hedge, field and tree, and the whole widespread, moonblanched country pouring past her headlights until she herself gradually becomes hedge, tree, field, and fleeting moon.

Arched branches underlit, broken demesne walls, a closed garage, hedges flying, a grey church, a lifeless gate-lodge, until the black rock and ruin of Cashel comes slowly wheeling about the moon. A streetlamp falling on a blank window makes it still more blank. Cars parked beside a kerb huddle from the cold. In Cahir the boarded windows of the old granaries are blind with age. The dull square is empty. Her wheeling lights catch the vacant eyes of the hotel, leap the useless bridge, fleck the side of the Norman castle. She is doing eighty on the level uplands under the Galtee mountains, heedless of the sleep-wrapt plain falling for miles and miles away to her left.

Why is she stopping? To rest, to look, to light a cigarette, to listen? He can see nothing for her to see but a scatter of farmhouses on the plain; nothing to hear but one sleepless dog as far away as the moon it bays. He lights his bedside lamp. Turned half past two. He puts out his light and there are her kangaroo lights, leaping, climbing, dropping, winding, slowing now because of the twisting strain on her arms. She does not see the sleeping streets of Fermoy; only the white signpost marking the remaining miles to Cork. Her red taillights disappear and reappear before him every time she winds and unwinds down to the sleeping estuary of the Lee, even at low tide not so much a river as a lough – grey, turbulent and empty. He tears after her as she rolls smoothly westward beside its shining slobland. Before them the bruised clouds hang low over the city silently awaiting the morning.

She brakes to turn in between her white gates, her wheels spit back the gravel, she zooms upward to her house and halts under its staring windows. She switches off the engine, struggles out, stretches her arms high above her head with a long, shivering, happy, outpouring groan, and then, breathing back a long breath, she holds her breasts up to her windows. There is not a sound but the metal of her engine creaking as it cools, and the small wind whispering up from the river. She laughs to see their cat flow like black water around the corner of the house. She leans into the car, blows three long, triumphant horn blasts, and before two windows can light up over her head she has disappeared indoors as smoothly as her cat. And that, at last, it is the end of sleep, where, behind windows gone dark again, she spreads herself under her one true lover.

Neither of them hear the morning seagulls over the Liffey or the Lee. He wakes unrefreshed to the sounds of late church bells. She half opens her eyes to the flickering light of the river on her ceiling, rolls over on her belly, and stretching out her legs behind her like a satisfied cat, she dozes off again. He stares for a long time at his ceiling, hardly hearing the noise of the buses going by.

It is cold. His mind is clear and cold. I know now what she wants. But does she? Let her lie. She called me a romantic and she has her own fantasy. She has what she wanted, wants what she cannot have, is not satisfied with what she has got. I have known her for over twelve years and never known her at all. The most adorable woman I ever met. And a common slut! If she had married me I suppose she would be dreaming now of him? Who was it said faithful women are always regretting their own fidelity, never their husbands'? Die for a week? He chuckled at her joke. Joke? Or gamble? Or a dead cert? If I could make him die for a week it would be a hell of a long week for her. Will I write to her? I could telephone.

Hello, Jenny! It's me. I just wanted to be sure you got back safely the other night. Why wouldn't I worry? About anyone as dear and precious as you? Those frosty roads. Of course it was, darling, a lovely meeting. And we must do it again. No, nothing changes! That's a dead cert. Oh, and Jenny! I nearly forgot. About that skiing bit next month in Gstaad. Can I change my mind? I'd love to join you. May I? Splendid! Oh, no! Not for that long. Say . . . just for a week?

He could see her hanging up the receiver very slowly.

Hymeneal

1

Away back in 1929, a few months before they got married, Phil and Abby Doyle had bought a red-and-yellow brick house, semi-detached, with a small garden in front and a useful strip for vegetables at the rear, on the North Circular Road. It stood about halfway between the Dublin Cattle Market and the entrance to the Phoenix Park – to be precise a bare 1300 feet, or 80 perches, from the Park Gate, as Phil had once carefully established in his schoolmasterish way by means of a pedometer attached to his left leg. All in all it was a pleasant quarter, so convenient to the city that Abby could be down in O'Connell Street by tram within ten minutes, and yet sufficiently remote for almost unbroken quietness. On still summer nights she could sometimes hear the morose growling of lions from the Zoological Gardens, the crazed laughter of monkeys. Early in the morning, if the wind was from the east, she might hear the mooing of cattle and the baaing of sheep from the Market. Otherwise the only obtrusive noise was when an occasional freight train from Kingsbridge came trundling along the loop north of the city down to the quays and the cargo steamers for England. But the greatest attraction of the North Circular for Abby was that when her sister Molly married Failey Quigley in the following year, they had bought an identical house next door. Abby, it soon transpired, was to have no children, so that when Molly's family got too long-tailed for their little terrace house, and Failey became a Member of the Dail, and ultimately a Cabinet Minister, she was all the more relieved that they moved only five minutes away, to a larger house, at the corner of Infirmary Road.

There they all remained, then, close together for more than thirty-five years, as much familiars of the North Circular as its postmen, busdrivers, doctors, shopkeepers, milkmen, dustmen, priests, beggarwomen, policemen and park-keepers; co-citizens of Oxmanstown, veterans of the Arran Quay Ward, seasoned Dubliners. Abby could have walked blindfold between Doyle's Corner and the Park Gate. She knew every dog with its nose out through the bars of its garden gate, every crack in every pavement, every step up or down, as well as she knew every vagary of her house – the secondhand Frigidaire that grunted up to her so comfortingly during the night, her one-bar electric stove that warmed her toes in the morning (if she remembered to stick the scrubbing brush under its loose wall-plug), the four permanently stuffed jets of her gas stove, the electric bulb in the middle of the kitchen ceiling that she knew how to light and put out with a tap of her broom handle, or the plants in her tiny glasshouse outside the kitchen window, all stolen from the People's Gardens or the Botanics and dropped into the pouch of her umbrella with the quick sideways look of a born babysnatcher, every one of them to be palm-touched afterwards with maternal love in their tiny indoor garden. Outside and inside number 26 Saint Rita's Villas, she had put down her roots for life in the North Circular.

Unfortunately, when his retirement was about a year away, Phil had been forced to make some unsettling observations. Of these the most inexorable was that Abby was getting a bit beyond housekeeping; and on his modest pension he could never afford a full-time servant. On the other hand, as the cost of living went up and the value of his pension went down, the house had quintupled in value. Now, if ever, was the time to sell it and move out of Dublin to some place cheaper.

After much searching he found exactly what he wanted west of the Shannon in County Clare, about a mile from the tiny village of Corofin, some thirty-five miles from Limerick, and less than twenty from the Atlantic coast. It was a small old whitewashed cottage, standing on a quarter-acre of reedy ground, with a stout slate roof (only a few of its slates were missing), two and a half rooms, cement floors, and an open turf-shed leaning against the gable under a rusty corrugated iron roof. Without saying a word to Abby he bought it. He had the holes in the floor filled in, the broken glass in the windows restored, the walls whitewashed, the woodwork painted blue, a dry closet built at the end of a path to the rear, and a cold bath installed in the half-room. The fine new zinc cistern that he raised outside, level with the roof, would supply plenty of soft rainwater. For drinking water there was a well about a hundred yards away. For heat they had two fireplaces. In the nearby bogs turf abounded. For light they would use petrol lamps. Absolute perfection!

When it was all done he took some coloured photographs of it and for months he kept them in his wallet to peep at as secretively and happily as a youth might peep at a picture of his first girl. Then, at last, one night, like a conjurer, he whisked them out of the air and fanned them out on Abby's lap.

'Our new home!' he cried triumphantly, standing over her – six foot two and thin as a rake handle— 'Isn't it the perfect answer? Isn't it lovely? You will garden. I will fish, and shoot, and take long walks. Every night we will sit on each side of a blazing turf fire, you with a cat, me with a dog, as cosy as two kittens in a basket. You will be sewing or knitting. I will be writing my Autobiography. And when the night ends we'll fall asleep lulled by the lovely pattering of the rain on the tin roof of the turf-shed. Perfect peace. Philosophic calm. Fresh air. Lovely country. Content and serenity without end.'

Abby slowly put on her specs and looked carefully at the pictures, one after the other. Then she went through them again. When she had looked at them several times she held them between her palms without raising her head or saying a word. She was forcing herself to remember that whenever Phil got some lunatic idea into his head there had always been only one thing to do – let him alone and he might, he just might begin gradually to forget it. Cross him and it was stuck in his head forever.

'Well?' he cried at last. 'Isn't it wonderful? Isn't it what the doctor ordered?'

She slowly lifted her head and looked at him with eyes as moist and humble as a dog so old that even its whiskers have gone white.

'It looks very nice, Phil. Very nice. For the summer. But the rain, Phil? The rain battering on the tin shed?'

In a fury he snatched up the pictures.

'Chalk and cheese!' he roared, meaning that that was what they always were.

He roved up and down the room like a caged cheetah. He kicked the chair. He kicked the table. He took up a cushion from the sofa and hurled it to the end of the room. Then he stood in front of her with his ten fingers splayed flat against her.

'Say no more!' he said. 'I understand! You have made yourself perfectly clear! Don't say one other single word! But for God almighty's sake will you tell me what it is that you don't like about our cottage?'

'You haven't even told me, Phil,' she whispered meekly, 'where it is.'

''Tis in West Clare! And please don't try to tell me that you, who were once a National School teacher, don't know where West Clare is.'

Abby had been reared in Dublin. Anywhere beyond the Liffey, or west of the Phoenix Park or south of Bray was, to her, a wasteland.

'Oh, of course, Phil,' she wailed humbly, 'I often *heard* of West Clare! I even heard a song about it. *Are ye right there, Michael, are ye right? D'ye think that we'll get there before the night?* All about some queer railway they have that has to balance itself on one track like an acrobat. Phil! Will we have to travel to West Clare on that awful railway?'

He sank into his armchair and bowed his head in his hands. Bloodshot he looked up at her. He spoke to her gently.

'Abby! The railway that you are trying to describe was called the Artique railway. It was an engineering experiment made by a Frenchman in 1889 away down in the County Kerry. It was abolished twenty-five years ago.'

'But, Phil, in the song they have the railway in West Clare. I'm almost certain of that, Phil! I can sing it for you.'

Which, pipingly and inaccurately, she began to do while he contemplated her, undecided whether to admire the power of female stupidity or the profundity of female deceit. At the end her voice broke and she was singing croakingly through a veil of tears.

'*And as the train draws near Kilrush / The passengers get out and push . . . Are ye right there, Michael, are ye right / D'ye think we'll get there before the night? / Oh, it all depends on whether / The ould engine holds together . . . / But we might, then, Michael . . . So we . . .*'

He went and sat beside her and touched her wrinkled paw, remembering how sweetly she used to sing for him long ago.

'Abby,' he whispered, 'that old railway was broken up, donkeys' years ago, too. Listen to me, Abby! Let me tell you, calmly, simply and quietly, about West Clare. County Clare is one of the loveliest counties . . .'

She dried her eyes with one hand while he held the other and talked and talked about County Clare – to her as he thought, to himself as he was despairingly to discover, both that night and on every other night that he tried to interest her in Clare's fauna and flora, its archaeology, its geology, its ecology, its methods of husbandry, and all the wild sports of the West. Her trouble, he realized in the end, gazing at her opaque eyes, was not that she could not take in what he was telling her. It was simply that she thought that the less she knew about Clare the farther she kept it away from her. He might, he saw, as well be trying to sell her an unfurnished shack in the Great Mohave Desert.

2

For some twenty-five years before Phil had been due to retire from his post as Inspector of Schools he had planned his pensioned years around The Book as exultantly as an executioner sharpening his axe to wrap it around the neck of his favourite enemy.

'On the night,' he would say to Abby, 'of the day that I hand in my gun, to whatever half-witted idiot will at that time be Minister for Education, I am going to sit down on that chair, by that window, at that table, and I'm going to start writing The Book.'

Unmuzzled at long last, he was going to expose, in his Autobiography, all the miseries and humiliations, botcheries and bunglings, all the chicaneries, evasions and general lunacies that he had had to suffer in silence at the orders of one fool of a Minister after another through forty years of serfdom.

'Mind *you!*' he would roar at her. 'This book isn't going to be just any old book. There never was, there never will be a book like my Book. It's not going to be a Book at all! It's going to be a landmine. It's going to be an atom bomb. The day my Book comes out you will hear an explosion like the Trumpet of Judgment reverberating from one end of Ireland to the other, and the next thing you will see,' spreading his arms like wings and letting his voice fall to the gentlest whisper, 'will be the entire Department of so-called bloody Education floating over Dublin like black snow.'

It was all ready. It was all waiting, locked in his bookcase. Two hundred and fifty blank pages of it, bound in black cloth, with the words *Chapter One* written on the top of page one, and the title neatly typed and pasted across the black cover: *I Was Speechless for Forty Years.* On nights when he felt particularly hard pressed by some harder-to-bear-than-usual ministerial folly he would run his fingers lovingly down the spine of it, sigh expectantly and feel calm again.

Not that Abby ever heard him utter all these wild words of his in one breath. Normally Phil was a staid, disciplined and good-humoured man, who had made countless friends all over Ireland and enjoyed countless happy days with them. All the same, over the years, and over and over again, Abby had heard every one of those separate words, always in total and tactful silence; having learned by experience that if she uttered as much as one word in reply, even if she did no more than sigh a gentle 'Oh, Moses!' – her one and only expletive – he would at once start reciting what she called the Pome. And the Pome was even harder to bear than his wildest guff about the Book.

This poem was a set of satirical verses entitled *The Patriot* which she privately called 'That accursed ould rawmeysh of a thing by Frank O'Connor that started it all off.' These malevolent verses Phil – if crossed, or imagining he was crossed – would recite at her in a voice like a tuba at full blast, slowly goose-stepping up and down the worn carpet of their little sitting room in the North Circular.

BEJASUS! (*forte*) Before ye inter me (*maestoso*)
I'll show ye all up! (*fortissimo*)
I've everything stored in me memory, (*con brio*)
Facts, figures enough (*veloce*)
Since I first swore an oath of allegiance (*spiritoso*)
As a patriot boy (*diminuendo*)
To avenge me maternal grandfather (*sforzando*)
They hanged at Fermoy... (*vibrato*)

On down to the last sibilant bellow of,

Ye think ye'll escape me? (*capriccioso*)
Ha! 'Tis true that me sight's a bit shook, (*scherzo*)
I was never no hand with a pen, (*allegro*)
But I'll write One Terrible Book (*pianissimo*)
Before, with gun-carriage and pipers – (*affettuoso*)
Ye dastardly crew! – (*parlante*)
Ye bring to his grave in Glasnevin (*legato*)
The ONE man that was true! (*tremolo*)

The only time Abby had ever spoken out about the Pome was one night after she had complained to her sister Molly that he must have recited that accursed pome to her at least once a month for the last twelve years, which made some one hundred and forty-four times in all – enough, Molly commented, to make even a gravedigger get a bit fed up with *An Elegy Written in a Country Churchyard*.

'But it's your own fault!' Molly had flashed at her out of her black gypsy's eyes. 'You're too soft with him! I tell you, if my Failey did that to me I'd soon put a stop to his gallop. Why don't you just tell him to put a sock in it? The man must be mad. But, sure, those fellows in the Department of Education are all mad. 'Tis well known! 'Tis given up to them! Every one of them is half-crazy from having to deal with priests and bishops from morning to night. You can't tell me anything about those fellows. If I didn't put my foot down on Failey at least once a month he'd be making speeches at me every night of the week – speeches that he'd never dare to give out in public but that I have to listen to just to let him blow off steam. The next time Phil Doyle recites that old stuff to you just tell him to put it where the woman told the monkey to put the nuts.'

Three nights later, like the fool she was, Abby took Molly's advice. When Phil had completed the Pome she gazed up at him pensively, allowed him his marital due of one minute's silence, and then gave a babyish little titter.

'Phil! Do you know what I think whenever I hear that pome? I think that it's a very nice pome. But somehow it always reminds me of that other lovely pome, "*The curfew tolls the knell of parting day, the lowing herd . . .*"'

'That thing,' he roared at her, 'has no guts in it!'

'Maybe,' she persisted tremblingly. 'But 'tis apt, Phil! 'Tis very apt. I mean if you ever do get around to that book of yours, and I'm sure, Phil, it will be a very nice little book too, it will be our parting day with a lot of old friends. That is if, God help me, I ever live to see it.'

'See it?' He charged at her with his finger pointing at her like a bayonet. 'You wait! And you know, too, who's going to get the worst lash of my whip in it – your lovely brother-in-law. Our longest reigning so-called Minister for Education. Ireland's beardless Palmerston! The original inventor of Total Inaction and Absolute Non-intervention in Anything Whatsoever! The blind boshtoon! The total botch! The braying polthacawn! Oho! If I was never to write another word but that fellow's obituary I'll show him up for the eedjut he is, was and always will be. He's going to be the linch-pin of my Book. The core, and kernel, fulcrum and omphalos of it! You just wait and see!'

Shaking like a poplar leaf, she still dared to persist.

'Oh, Moses! Is it poor Failey? Who was always and always so fond of the pair of us!'

'Fond?' At that Phil laughed in three descending, mocking brays, like the devil in *Faust*. 'Ho, ho, ho! That's a new one. Fond? I don't want fondness! I want action. But will I get it from Failey? Any more than I ever got one spark of it from any single one of his rubber-stamp predecessors? Let me give you one simple example. Look at this frightful case that cropped up only last week in Mullaghabawn East over a teacher named Hooligan! A fellow that, as every living soul in Mullaghabawn East, and West, well knows, hasn't been sober since he switched from his mother's paps to his father's poteen. And his wife as bad as him. Fighting in the schoolroom, the pair of them. Before the children's eyes. Throwing mollyers of stones at one another in the schoolyard. Calling one another bitch and bastard at the tops of their voices! But do you think your fond, and fair and lovely Failey will take any action about that? And why not, pray? Answer me! Why not?'

Wishing to the Lord God she had never opened her mouth about either the Pome or the Book, or that she had Molly there to talk up to him, she moaned:

'Phil! What do I know about any Hooligan or Booligan? You're the one who knows everything about these things.'

'You know damn well why Failey won't take action.'

'I don't, Phil. I'm sure it's some awful reason. I suppose 'tis because her mother is his aunt, or his cousin is his nephew, or his sister is the Reverend Mother of Mullinavat, or her uncle is a titular bishop in Africa, or...'

'Failey will take no action because he hasn't the GUTS, that's why, and he never had, nor never will have, and that's why!'

At which point in their sad comedy – where any normally intelligent member of the audience would have begun to roll up his programme and fish for his coat, and the doorkeepers would be signalling out to the cloakroom girls – what must Abby do but produce her last little weapon, pull the trigger, and let her feeble fan of protest puff out of it:

'Failey,' she whispered, 'is *kind!* It's through his kindness,' she began to weep, 'that you weren't retired like everybody else at sixty. And that leaves the pair of us with our one last year of peace and comfort here in Dublin. *And leaves the world to darkness and to me.*'

Curtain! With Phil falling back into his armchair behind his shivering newspaper; gassed, silenced, chokingly whimpering to himself at the insoluble mystery of why in God's name he had ever married a woman who knew nothing whatsoever about Education; and, if *she* was like that, in spite of listening to him day in and day out, how could he ever hope to liberate anybody or anything at all in Ireland? It was not, however, the end of their row. It never was. That always came as a final apotheosis, showing Phil deep in hell, growling through Greek fire and blue smoke – that is to say, locked upstairs in the bathroom, obscening at her as he never in his life obscened at anybody in public, strangling her with his two fists, shoving her head down into the W.C. and pulling the chain on her for good and all. That done, he straightens his four-inch stiff collar, tidies his thin dust of hair, and emerges on the landing to call amiably down the stairs, 'Abby! What about a nice little cup of tea and a few of those old arrowroot biscuits of yours?'

'Well,' Molly duly asked her, 'did you shut him up about the Pome?'

'I did,' Abby lied. 'I said the reason Failey kept him on, and every lunatic like him in the Department, was out of sheer kindness and nothing else.'

'And what did his Royal Irish Lordship say to that?'

'He said, "He kept me on because he knows I'm the best Inspector of Schools in Ireland."'

The two of them smiled wisely at one another. They knew that Failey had kept Phil on only because he adored him. The best storyteller, the funniest yarner, the only decent bit of company in the whole Department, the one man who knew the country inside out and from edge to edge, every parish priest in it, every jarvey, every tinker, every taxi driver, every bush in every bog, every sparrow on every telegraph wire, a man always ready with a comical tale about every one of them, a man to be welcomed with open arms whenever he came into the office in Marlborough Street, shaken heartily by both hands, ordered to 'sit down there, my old pal from far-off days and tell us the latest lunacy from the hinterland,' and straightway given a generous jar from the bottle of Irish that Failey kept in his bottom drawer for the few, the very few visitors that he could more or less completely trust. The sisters knew furthermore, having told him of it themselves, that Failey knew about the Book and that he did not like the smell of it at all.

'Not,' he once privately confided to Abby, 'that I care a damn what he puts into it. Give and take, I'm used to hard knocks. But Phil isn't. And he'll get plenty of them if he ever writes that book!'

To the end Abby built high hopes on those words. Maybe, she innocently hoped, Failey might extend Phil's retiring age to seventy, and by then all this lunacy about leaving Dublin would have 'frizzled out.' She spent her last few months pleading with him not to take her away. He spent them reassuring her that it was best to go. Then, his time up, he led her westward across the Shannon.

3

It took them a whole day to get from Dublin to the cottage. They went by taxi, by train to Limerick, by bus to Ennis, by a second bus to the village of Córofin, and finally by a hired car from the village to the cottage, the month being March, the day misty and windy, the daylight barely holding its own against the shrouds of the sun. When she got out of the hired car and stood under her umbrella on the roadside, cold and stiff, she saw a white box in a field, oblong, one-storied, wet-slated with two blank eyes. It was backed by a low wall through whose lacy chinks she saw the sunset. She saw rocks, she saw a dark lough blown into froth by the wind. She could barely discern the limestone-grey uplands that she was to come to know as the elephant's hide of the Barony of Burren. That night, from their bed, she listened for hours to the rain pattering on the tin roof of the turf-shed.

A couple of days later, during a dry, windy hour, she ventured alone on her first walk. She saw a small village huddled below the corrugated uplands. She followed a slim road. On a low rise she came on a ruined castle with six motionless goats on the tiptop of it, their beards blown by the wind. In the far distance she saw a broom of rain gradually blot out a tiny belfry. She saw two cottages whose smoke streamed sideways like two small ships in a gale vanish under the broom. When she got back to the cottage she went into their bedroom to weep in secret. Nor was she converted in May when the entire expanse of lava became lit up by millions of tiny gentians that brought the blue sky down into every sheltering furrow. She was not even comforted by the one blessed hot spell the Burren enjoyed that August when she could watch scores of small black cows wandering slowly over it to lick the tender grass from its marrowbones. Cows to her had always meant only two white bottles tinkling on her front step in Saint Rita's Villas.

She had nobody to consult except Molly. She did not write to her until the grunting September wind under the door warned her that winter would soon be counting her bones. Even then she wrote only because of a fright she got one frosty night, hard with stars and silence, when she was sitting on one side of the fire gazing into it, and Phil was at his table on the other side bent over the terrible Book. Hearing that vast autumnal silence of the Burren, broken only by the faint hiss of their petrol lamp and an occasional purr from the great fire of burning peat, it suddenly came to her with a pang of regret, as if for one other precious thing she had left behind her in Dublin, that he had never recited the Pome to her since they came to Corofin. She turned to him to ask him to recite it to her, and was startled to find him staring blankly into the globe of the lamp. She stole another glance, and yet another glance. Each time she looked he was still staring fixedly at the white globe. At last, as if he felt her eyes on him, he turned his head towards her, threw down his pen, said, 'I think I'll go for a stroll, it's a fine frosty night for a ramble,' put on his long greatcoat, took his stick and went out.

She waited until his footsteps faded down the ringing road. Then, she dared to peep at the Book. In his minute but beautiful handwriting he had, so far, covered only four pages – all, she gathered, skimming quickly over them, about his youth in Dublin. She also found, pasted inside the front cover, a calendar of dates and events. These she read with as much fear as if she was reading an account of his death in a newspaper:

Philip Ignatius Doyle, MA, D.Litt. Born in Dublin, February the fourth, 1901. Educated at the Christian Brothers' school in Synge Street, 1914 to 1918. Studied at Saint Patrick's Training College for teachers, Drumcondra, from 1918 to 1921. I taught school in Drumcondra from 1921 to 1926. I met Failey Quigley there in my last year. He was then aged twenty. Already balding, ingratiating, devious, ambitious, convivial. I attended evening courses at University College, Dublin, for my BA and MA, 1922 to 1927. In my last year there I met Failey again, studying for his BL. I duly completed my doctoral thesis on 'The Folk High Schools of Denmark.' I became Inspector of Primary Schools in 1928.

She looked a long time at the next three entries:

Met Abby (Abigail) Goggin with Molly (Máire) Goggin at the Gaelic League in Parnell Square. Striking contrast. Molly dark. Abby blue-eyed, Danish hair, the colouring of a young seagull. She sang sweetly in Irish. A small but perfect voice. I married Abby in 1929. Failey married Molly in 1930.

In, she remembered, the University church on Saint Stephen's Green, with Phil as the best man. But that was in their good days when they were all still on warm terms with one another, before Failey went into politics.

She closed the book and returned, shaken, to the fire. He came back from his walk as silently as he left. On the three following nights exactly the same thing happened. She bore with it for a few more days and then she wrote to Molly. This place was getting them both down. The Book was a flop. He had not spoken to her for a week. What in God's name was she going to do?

4

Another week passed and then, to her delight, he told her, grumbling mightily about it, that he had to go to Dublin to clear up some damnfool remnant business in the Department. 'The change will do you good,' she said, but he only huffed and puffed at the very idea. On his return, three days later, she was hurt to notice how much good it had done him, how talkative he was again, full of gossip and guff, relaxed, looking ten years younger. Then the lone walks and the silent nights came back again, unless he had met somebody on his wanderings, even if it was only the breadman, or a tinker, or even a child herding cows – he, who had always been used to travel and company of every kind.

One bright Sunday evening, in the last week of October, he returned from one of those walks, full of excitement because he had come on a few late gentians among the rocks.

'Look!' he cried, holding out the pallid blue flowers. 'Autumn gentians! I never knew they even existed. I came on them by pure chance up there on the hill behind Kilnaboy. Shining in the full moon. Aren't they miraculous?'

She looked indifferently at the pale flowers, and for the first time since they came there she summed up her feelings about everything.

'They make me feel like one myself.'

Startled, he looked at her pallid eyes and at her white head, hearing far away a young girl with gentian eyes and fair hair, singing a fluting love song in Irish. Slowly he laid the few flowers down on the black cover of the Book. He said, 'I must go back to the village, I forgot my tobacco. I'm forgetting everything these days. I'll soon be forgetting my own head,' and went out again.

He did not rightly know where he was going, or what he was remembering, until the little road brought him to the side of a moonlit lough where he paused to rest. There, he remembered that one of the things he had been looking forward to doing in Clare was fishing, and that another was shooting. He had done neither. And yet, when he used to be telling his colleagues in the Department about all the things he would do when he retired he had always boasted that 'that wrist' could drop a dry fly lighter, longer and later than any fisherman he ever met on Corrib or on Mask; and what a marvellous place Clare was for wild duck, planing down on their orange legs to the lakes at evening. He looked about him. What exactly was he remembering? He slashed a ghostly head off a ragweed. What the hell exactly was he trying to write about in his book? Why wasn't it blazing? Why wasn't he getting on to Failey? And leaning his two hands on the stick, he recalled that absurd talk he had with him three weeks before, in Dublin, about those two teachers in Mullaghabawn East.

'Failey!' he had said. 'I can call you Failey now, not "Minister" as I used to have to. I don't quite know exactly why you asked me to come back up here to talk about these two people. Unless it's just that, as usual, you want to find some pleasant way out of a nasty problem! If that is what you want, there is no way out of it! Because what that report of mine is really about,' tapping the grey folder on the desk, 'is

Love. And as an old fellow in Kerry once said to me, all love is just "shteam" condensed by the cold air of marriage.'

Failey had ruffled his grey poll and laughed delightedly.

'Phil! You haven't changed one iota since the first day we got to know one another. Always the same old cynic!'

'I am not a cynic. I am a stoic. Look! All that is wrong with those two stupid and thoroughly worthless people is that they got married before they knew one another. They found out their mistake too late. Live with me and know me, as the old Irish proverb says. This clod Hooligan is forty-one. His fool of a wife is thirty-five. I knew that fellow when he first came to that school at the age of twenty-three. A decent poor hoor of a fellow with no other interest in life bar football and his occasional pint. The first time I knew her she was a junior teacher in Blackrock. She wasn't bad-looking. In fact she was quite good-looking. And all she was interested in was golf. They were perfectly happy with their football and their golf until they fell in love – whatever the hell that means – and got married. Now look at them! He's drinking like a fish. You could cut cheese with her nose. And they hate the living sight of one another.'

Failey had scoffed.

'Come off it, Phil! Married people don't live like that. Squabble? Yes! Have a row? Sure! We all have rows. But married people don't hate one another to that extent, not anyway in Ireland! You know that!'

'I know it's the way with these two people. All marriage ever did for the pair of them was to ruin their lives.'

'It gave them five sturdy children,' Failey pointed out sensibly, and insensitively, to his childless friend.

'I wouldn't know anything about that side of it. How many have you, Failey?'

'Eleven.'

Phil noted how proudly he threw out the figure. That for the Book. 'Our beardless Palmerston, active in only one Department!'

'Phil, what are we going to do with these two unfortunates?'

'It's in my report. Dismiss them. And at once!'

'My God, I can't sack a man of forty-one with five children?'

'It's up to you. It is a question of principle. Or are you more interested in cohabitation than in co-education?'

(That for the Book, too – a darling phrase.)

Failey put a ministerial look on himself, calculating, would-be wise, his mind plainly as restless as his ten fingers. He got it out in bits:

'I was thinking. Principles are one thing, Phil. Human beings are another. What may be wrong. With those two unfortunate people. Is the place where they're living. Suppose now we could shift them? To some big town? Or even to some place like Galway city? You see, it must be very hard for any city girl, born and bred to the sights and sounds of the streets...'

And while he went on expatiating Phil had got so angry at the absurdity of the proposal that it never occurred to him what Failey was aiming at until now, by the glittering lake, savagely whipping the heads off stalk after stalk of ragweed. So mistress Abby had been conspiring against him with this unprincipled botch and boshtoon. And Molly, no doubt, with her!

He whirled for home, a thousand angry snakes writhing in his head, so possessing him with hatred of all three of them that he scarcely noticed the boy cycling away from his cottage gate. He strode down the moonlit path and with a bang flung the door open. Abby's face was twisted up with tears as she handed him the telegram.

'It's Failey,' she wept. 'Killed in a car crash!'

He snatched it from her and read it down to ' ... funeral eleven on Tuesday morning to Glasnevin Cemetery.' Glaring at his own dim face in the window, hearing Abby behind him, weepily talking and talking about the old days when they used to be so happy together in Dublin, all he wanted to say was, 'This is the ultimate interference. This is logical, a botch in life and a botch in death.' Quietly he said, 'Ah, well! Another poor devil whose dancing days are done. The Lord be kind to him. This means, I suppose, that we must put on our hats and coats tomorrow morning and go up to Dublin for another miserable jaunt to Glasnevin.' And to get away from her whining he went into the back room, took down his suit of clerical charcoal, removed the mothballs from its pockets, and started to brush the dust from his black homburg that he had worn for the interment of so many other public men whom he had neither liked nor admired.

5

The next morning ghost after ghost of mist went sheaving past their crucified window. At every pause on the journey it caressed their ankles, wrists and throats. They went by taxi (late and smelling of fish), by bus (late and damp), by another bus (so prompt that they barely managed to board it), by train (slow), finally by another taxi in Dublin shrouded by the same mist. They did not talk much on the way, yet, by the little that was spoken, each could guess at the unspoken thoughts of the other. Abby had talked again about their young days in Dublin. Once she was so frank as to say expectantly, 'I hope it won't look much changed.' He spoke twice about Failey's latter-day career, drily and ironically. Once he said outright, 'Everything can come out now! All will be revealed.' It was like him at his solitary worst and his sensitive best to insist that they must not stay with Molly. 'The house will be full of his country relatives.' She was disappointed at first, but she liked the small hotel he chose, on the Liffey, near the station and the old North Circular. After supper they called on Molly to pay their respects, and as he always did on such occasions he said all the proper, kindly things. He even said, 'Happy the corpse the rain falls on,' though he made up for it to his conscience the following morning by adding to Abby as the cortege moved slowly through the mist to Glasnevin, 'And miserable the mourners!'

The sky was low, wet and matted. It darkened every headstone, cobwebbed every yew and made the massed umbrellas about him look like barnacles. He had to stand at the graveside in line with Molly, and Abby, Failey's nearest relatives and his family of eleven, ranging from a middle-aged man of about thirty-five down to a young woman in her first twenties. With one glance from under his umbrella he ranked this as a Class B funeral. It was understandable that the President had not come; it was a bad day and he was an old man. But there were only three members of the Cabinet, including the Taoiseach. The leader of the Opposition had managed to rally only two members of his party. The Labour Party was not represented at all. He discounted the six priests, the three Franciscans and the two nuns. Relatives. The general public was small. The usual flock of civil servants, glad to take the day off. He frowned at the tricolour clinging wetly to the coffin. He lifted his eyebrows wearily when the surpliced priest, conducting the burial service from under an umbrella held by a mute, said the last few prayers in Irish – a language that, to his knowledge, Failey had never spoken in his life. He had to lower his umbrella to hide his amusement when he saw, among the wreaths that the gravediggers were now strewing on their wet hummock, a garland of bays. (What scoundrel, what embittered clerk, had the wit to think of that one?) He bowed his head in agony as the Taoiseach began the formal words of farewell.

' ... a colleague who did Ireland and me the honour of accepting without demur the arduous duties of a post of the greatest import to our country's future. Yet when he did so, Phelim Patrick Quigley did no more than he had always done, in the same spirit of devotion that, from his earliest years, inspired him to serve and suffer for Ireland. A man who ...'

Suffer? The reference, he presumed, could only be to the occasion when Failey, by the greatest stroke of political good luck, had been arrested on suspicion during the Civil War, at the age of twenty, and detained for three nights in the Bridewell. When the oration finished, he glared quickly around to see if there was going to be a firing squad or a bugler sounding the last post. Seeing that there was not, he relaxed; and then wished there had been – it would have made a lovely chapter ending for the Book, which he was at last free to write without quarter.

It was all over. The crowd began to dissolve with a seemly slowness that did not conceal from him their eagerness to regather in The Crossed Guns for the usual elegaic hot toddy. He was peeping at his watch, about to drag Abby away to the afternoon train for the west, when he felt her softly pulling his sleeve and whispering that Molly wanted them both to stay with her for a night or two. If she had not known him so well she might have mistaken his fright for anger.

'I will do nothing of the kind!' he was growling down at her. 'Stay alone in a house with two wailing women for two nights? I have no more to say, to Molly. Anyway it isn't me she wants, it is you. You can stay if you like, but I am going home.'

'She does want you. She's worried about the future. Failey had some investments. There's the insurance. And the will. The house will have to be sold. All sorts of money matters. And the relatives will be all gone, Phil. She will be left all alone. You must come.'

'She has lawyers. She has a son of thirty-five. Why pick on me? Am I never to be shut of that man?'

'She trusts you. And Failey was always kind to us. You can't refuse her.'

With a groan he surrendered.

'Alright. But I'll stay only one night. I want to get back to my Book.'

Abby recoiled.

'Oh, Phil! What a time to be thinking of that!'

After the funeral the feast. They found the house on the Infirmary Road crowded with half a hundred people enjoying, as the old sagas loved to say, 'the freshest of every food and the oldest of every drink'; secular priests, the three Franciscans, country relatives, greying politicians, lots of young people whom he took to be the Dublin friends of the family, and a gaggle of civil servants who welcomed him so eagerly that he forgot himself in their cascade of talk, argument, and gossip whispered behind palms with sidelong glances towards the politicians. It was four o'clock before the crowd began to thin out. By six all that remained were Molly, Abby, himself, two unmarried daughters and a young man who was obviously courting the older of them. When the young man took her away, the three women began to tidy up the house and prepare the usual Dublin supper of 'Tea and Something' – the Something tonight being the remains of the funeral feast. It was eight o'clock before the remaining daughter went out. To the chapel? Or to meet another young man? Molly and Abby sat reminiscing before the drawing room fire. By nine o'clock he was deep in gloom.

'Where are those papers, Molly?' he finally asked, glad of any excuse to get away by himself for the rest of the night.

'I'll show you,' she sighed. 'They're all in the engine room. It is what Failey always called his study. Where he did his homework at night. I have the fire lit for you and a bottle of Irish on the table.'

She led him upstairs. In the return room he saw an old rolltop desk, a green-shaded reading lamp on top of it. He saw shelves of books, a table, an old-fashioned mahogany wardrobe, a couch with a plaid rug on it and an armchair by the turf fire. As she closed the long rep curtains he saw raindrops gleaming on the windowpane. The wet wind was still blowing from the west, down the Liffey. Tonight the sea would be covered with white horses.

'Pay no heed to me,' he ordered her. 'You two can go off to bed when ye want to. I'll stay up until I finish this job.'

'Ayeh!' she sighed. 'As poor Failey often did until three in the morning. He was as strong as a bull. If it wasn't for that damned accident he'd have lived to be ninety.'

6

There was no doubt whose room he was in. The wall above the fireplace was covered with black-framed photographs of Failey, massed shoulder to shoulder and head to tail. Failey, with a face like a boy, dressed in cap and gown, holding a scroll. Failey wearing a barrister's wig. Failey in a cutaway coat, holding a grey topper in the crook of his left arm, standing beside Molly in a wedding dress whose train curved in a white stream about her feet. Failey as Parliamentary Secretary to the Minister for Roads and Railways opening a factory. Failey as Minister for R. and R. opening another factory. Failey as Minister for Education opening a new school. Failey grinning on the golf course. Failey addressing Rotary. Failey in a Franciscan robe with a white cincture roped around his belly recalled the press announcement of his death. 'Phelim Patrick Quigley, B.L., T.S.O.F.' Third Order of Saint Francis. To what other order, association or society had he belonged? The Knights of Columbanus? Probably. The Knights of Malta? But you'd have to be at least a doctor to get into them. There were at least a hundred of those black-edged pictures. Vanity? Or just a cool awareness of the value of publicity? The bookshelves were untidy, disorderly, and wholly predictable. Rows of the official records of parliamentary debates; books and pamphlets about railroads, canals, and aeronautics; paperback thrillers, *A Portrait of the Artist as a Young Man*, books on religion, the odd Yeats, a book entitled *How to Make a Million Dollars a Year*, a rhyming dictionary.

He rolled up the hood of the desk and found what he expected. Chaos. He filled himself a stout glass of malt, lit his pipe, seized a pad of writing paper and set to work. The first pile he made was of the unopened letters, most of them from constituents. He read them all conscientiously: begging letters, abusive letters, grateful letters. It took him an hour to sweep them one by one into the waste-paper basket. He wrote on his pad the word *Investments* and started to search for them. He found only five in all. He humphed as he noted that Failey had not invested a penny in Irish Government Stock or Irish Industrials. He had favoured English gilts and equities. Unaccustomed to such matters, it took him another hour to work out whether Molly should keep or sell them, poorly helped by a three-day-óld *Irish Times* that he found on the floor beside the desk. If Molly kept them they would not bring her in £200 a year, though the real wonder was that the man had been able to invest anything with such a long-tailed family and the modest salary of a Minister.

He was just about to pass on from Investments to Insurance when he came on a wallet containing a broker's contract notes of sales and purchases. These showed that, at one time, Failey must have invested much more. Only two weeks before he had sold over £4000 worth of stock. He looked for and found the bank sheets, and there it was duly credited, and on the same day a corresponding debit of £4310. He tumbled everything about in his eager search for Failey's cheque book, found it, riffled the stubs, and there was what he was looking for. The sum had been made payable to a well-known Dublin firm of solicitors. But what on earth was it for? Debts? The sum was too large for debts. A property purchase?

Thoughtfully, he wrote down on his pad the word *Insurance* and started to look for the policies. There were two, each for £1000, each taken out many years ago. He added the sums to Molly's credit. He next wrote down on his pad the word *Property* and started to search for the indentures, if any. He found two. To his relief the first one was for the house. This, at least, would be something of real value for poor old Molly. What Failey had paid for it he had no idea, and he would have to wait until the morning to find out precisely, but he had guessed ever since last February, when he had sold his own house at 26 Saint Rita's Villas, that this place, standing in an acre of land, must be now worth at least £12,000. He wrote down the sum £12,000, followed by a cautious query mark, to Molly's credit, reached ior his glass, and found it empty.

He rose, stretched himself, and looked at his watch. Past midnight. He refilled his glass, went to the curtains, and parted them. The windowpanes were still speckled with rain, the sky over the city a sodden pink sponge. He returned to the desk, picked up the second grey document, also headed in large decorative gothic letters with the word INDENTURE, relit his pipe and puffing easily began to read it. Abruptly he laid down his pipe and began to reread. There was no question about it. The document did witness that in consideration of the usual this, that and the other 'the Lessor doth hereby DEMISE unto the Lessee ALL THAT the plot of ground known as 26 Saint Rita's Villas, North Circular Road, in the City of Dublin . . .'

For a while he sat as rigid in his chair, staring as fixedly in front of him, as if he had suddenly died there. Galvanized he whirled to the last page to see the date. Two weeks ago. He grabbed the cheque book again and compared the stub. The dates agreed. Two weeks ago? Molly must have known of it. If Abby had not known of it before the funeral she did now. But why the secrecy?

He strode to the door, opened it, and listened. Not a sound from downstairs. The two of them must have gone to bed. He opened the door of the bedroom allotted to Abby and himself, and seeing it empty bethought himself. She would, naturally, be sleeping tonight in the same room as Molly. He moved down the corridor to its door and bent his head to listen. Through the door he could hear a soft whispering, lifted now and then to an audible feminine murmur. He was about to put his hand on the doorknob when he heard the sound of one or other of them crying. At the same moment he thought of the will. He hurried back to the desk to look for it. Two hours ago he would have blandly assumed that there would, characteristically, be no will. He now knew better. He went carefully through every pigeonhole and drawer again. It was not in any of them. Then he saw what had earlier seemed to him to be a long, slim horizontal panel, slightly protruding along the top of the pigeonholes, eased it forward, and there was the buff envelope, duly inscribed *My Will*. He drew out the document. In the usual benignant legal language of all wills everything had been left 'to my dear wife Molly for her own use absolutely.' He added everything up and found that if she sold the house well, she would enjoy an income of about two thousand pounds.

The pictures over the fireplace, the shelves of books, even the old-fashioned furniture suddenly possessed an ominous solidity. He had belittled Failey. This room, this home that he had created, the family he had reared were all about him. The man had been a rotten Minister, but he had been a good husband. To reassure himself he looked again at the massed photographs over the fireplace. He felt humiliated to notice that the wedding photograph hung in the middle of them.

When he came to himself he found that the hour was approaching two o'clock. To be certain that he had performed his task completely he returned to the desk, now tidily in order, and checked off each of its seven small drawers and eight pigeonholes, running his fingers back into their recesses to be sure he had missed nothing. He had missed nothing. The last central compartment had a small door like a tabernacle. It was empty, but as his fingers groped in the rear of it they entered a crevice, and at once a small upright panel to the side of it moved slowly forward a half-inch. He drew it towards him, one of those so-called secret receptacles that are sometimes to be found in old desks. He pulled it out and turned it upside down. It was empty. He did the same with the opposite crevice of the tabernacle, drew out its second panel, turned it upside down, and out of it fell a book. It was a small black book. Inside it was an envelope marked *Private*. On its black cover was pasted a white label bearing the written words:

THE DARK AND FAIR
1930–1935

A Sequence in Quatrains
by
PHELIM PATRICK QUIGLEY, BL

He found that it contained a gathering of verses, each one a numbered quatrain, each on a single page. Between embarrassment and pity he took it to the armchair by the sinking fire, threw on a few sods of turf from the turf-basket, relit his pipe and started to read the first verse.

Think not, who reads these tortured lines, I pray,
  Of Dark or Fair. To me they symbolize
Lost dreams of love or none, night after day,
  A dream I dreamed, a forfeit prize.

He turned the leaf indifferently. Unprepared, he felt the knife slip in:

This fool once suffered eyes of midnight hue,
  And gypsy-coloured ringlets to betray
A heart that burned for eyes of gentian blue,
  And virgin smiles, and primrose-coloured hair.

He tautened too late. He felt his skull crawling as he ran through the third, the fourth and the fifth quatrains to find out for certain who was who in this farrago.

Until, with gypsy smiles and wiles, she wound
  Her hair about my eyes and drew me deep
Into her gypsy flesh where passion crowned
  Desire, and Love cast out could only weep.

He was sweating when he came to the eighth quatrain. He read it several times, reliving every single one of those nights of his betrayal:

> Yet, every night as that last train drew out
>   For Bray, two girls backward waving, someday,
> I swore, I'd hold her in my arms, and mouth
>   To mouth on fire, my Fair would whisper, Stay!

Forty years ago. On the platform of Amiens Street Station smelling of midnight dust, fish, steam, petrol. The two of them joking upwards to the two girls in the lighted carriage, holding their hands until the very last moment when the engine shook itself and chugged slowly out. Then two white hands waving back through the steam until train and lights and hands vanished around the curve like falling cards. Out, then, mocking one another's ardour, into the empty streets for the slow walk back to their lodgings on the North Side, and the usual prolonged last talk or argument on the canal bridge, often not parting until two in the morning with cheery backward calls of farewell.

Did she? Ever? Let her hot mouth stay? He had to read on to the thirteenth quatrain before he knew.

> At last, the moonlight on the waves' soft sigh,
>   We kissed. Then bracken-deep in love we lay,
> Until 'Too late!' I heard her sobbing cry.
>   'Last night, in bed, he said, "Our wedding day!"'

The one secret of his life! His one lovely, imperious, flaming passion shared with that lying clod!

'The poor bastard!' he said, and laid the book aside. 'What have his private sins to do with me?'

It was only when he found himself standing in the rain on the pavement outside 26 Saint Rita's Villas, peering at the TO LET sign pasted inside the lamplit window that he knew that he was out of control. He was carrying Abby's ridiculous blue umbrella. He was wearing no overcoat. He removed his hat, looked at it, and found that he had taken Failey's. He had no key to let him back into the house.

He began to return quickly, but after walking for half an hour stopped dead. He was lost in a suburban maze. Not a soul in sight, nor a sound to be heard except the rain spitting into him like arrows. Had he been making for Glasnevin? He listened. A sighing wind down the concrete avenue made him turn in fright. He halted and listened again, and again he heard that sifting sigh. He started to run, gripped himself, and hurried as quickly as he could walk, back on his tracks. He calmed only when he had found his way to the door, shocked to see that he had left it so wide open that the rain was blowing into the hall as if it were a deserted house.

He closed the door silently behind him, and crept carefully up to the engine room, halting at every creak of the old stairs. The fire had melted into grey ash. With the box of firelighters beside the turf-basket, a bundle of Failey's discarded papers and fresh turf he made a blazing fire, and stripped to his skin; he hung the shirt by its sleeves from the mantelpiece, outspread like a crucifix, and sat naked before the fire watching the steam begin to rise from the clothes that he had strewn to dry on the brass fender.

It was then that his uplifted eye saw, peeping down at him over the corner of the mantelpiece, the envelope that he had found in the black book. He snatched it down and ripped it open. It contained two letters. He had at one time smiled at her handwriting for being so simple and childlike. Later he had frowned at it for being quavering and old. But, for years now, everything she said and did had made him think of her as somebody who had never had any proper womanhood between her girlhood and her age. The first letter was dated December 20, 1934, five years after they had married. As he read it, in spite of the fire mottling his shinbones, his whole body began to exude cold sweat.

Dear Fay,

How kind you were to write to me in my great unhappiness. I have read your letter so many times that I have it all off by heart. I will never forget one word of it as long as I live. I am sure you are right in everything you say about Phil, and there can be nobody living or dead who knows him better. You are right in another thing. He is not an unkind man by nature and he can be very warm, and giving, and loving. But there is something in him, or maybe in me, that brings out the worst in him and turns him into what you call an irate man full of cold principle. But it is all very well for you, Fay, to say that that is what makes him the most honest and reliable civil servant you ever met. You do not have to live with him night and day. God knows I don't ask much. If only he would not be so contemptuous of me. If only he'd make a few allowances for me. If only he would not turn all his anger on to me. The way he is I just can't go on with it. I feel I will have to leave him or have the life crushed out of me. I am terribly sorry Fay to have poured all this over you but I have nobody else to confide in. Molly is so strong and so dominating that whenever I have tried to hint any of this to her she just laughs and tells me to slap back at him. I can't write any more tonight, I am so miserable. God bless you for trying to understand. I pray that you and Molly and the children may have a happy, happy Christmas.

Ever,
Abby

He tried to remember that Christmas, but it was too long ago. The second letter was dated New Year's Day, 1935.

Dear Fay,

Thank you and bless you for all you said to me yesterday in Wynne's Hotel. I have thought it over and over and as always I see that you are dead right. I must stick it out. I will always remember specially two things you said. I hope it *is* true that he needs me, though I'll never know what he saw in me to want to marry me at all. The other thing you said was how wonderful he is with the schoolchildren and how tough he is with their teachers. I wish I could have given him children. It might have made him a bit more kind to me. As it is I must look on him now as my only child. I will not bother you any more, Fay. I promise. Not a word to Molly about any of this. And may you and yours all have a very, very happy New Year.

Abby

The letter fell from his hand, he closed his eyes, crumpled into his armchair and swooned out of the memory of man.

He woke, shivering. It was six o'clock. With a groan he remembered, rose, stiff in all his bones, laid another couple of firelighters into the seed of the ashen fire, the two letters on top of them, then the book of verses, then a pyre of turf, and watched until the flames embraced them all. Then he opened the wardrobe door, found a worn woollen dressing gown, and an overcoat, and put them both on. He went to the window and drew the curtains apart. The rain had stopped. By the city's glow and the presence of a few stars he could see that the clouds were breaking up. Once, for a moment, between their torn edges, he saw the moon, a steaming rag hung there to dry. To the north east the sky was becoming paler. Inside an hour morning would be creeping in across the plain of Swords, over Drumcondra and Glasnevin. After that it would soon be touching the city's spires.

A mile away, up there, he was lying where they had left him, a man he had never known, a life he had failed to share. He did not feel guilty. He felt only the barrier. Of late years he had noticed that his old friends no longer died. He would ask casually after one of them and be told in some surprise, that it must be a year or so since the poor chap had disappeared around some corner. Looking out at the paling sky he felt the pain of loss, the brevity of life and its challenge that never stops. He turned to the couch, lay and wrapped the rug about him.

When he woke again it was ten o'clock, the room filled with blinding sunlight, nearby roofs exuding a faint steam more soft than pity. A Saint Martin's summer? He found the bathroom, gave himself a cold shower, shaved, put on his dried clothes and went slowly downstairs in search of the Dark and the Fair. He found them in the kitchen, two white-haired old ladies talking quietly over their late breakfast. Molly got up to greet him. She was hooped even when she stood.

'Come in, Phil,' she said warmly. 'I hope you got some kind of a sleep on that old couch. Sit down there by Abby and we'll all have a fresh pot of tea. And you are going to eat a good plate of bacon and eggs, Master Philip, and none of your old arguments about it, if you please!'

'I will eat them,' he said obediently and watched her gather the soiled china on a tray. 'Anyway, I deserve them. I've done a good night's work for you. And to be shut of it at once, you are going to be alright, Molly. That is if you can live on fifteen hundred a year, tax-paid. Failey looked after you well.'

'Thank you, Phil. It's a great relief to me.'

As she lifted the tray and turned to go out to the scullery he held her.

'There is one thing I must ask you, Molly. Did you know that Failey had bought our old house on the North Circular?'

She half-turned.

'Yes, of course. He bought it two weeks ago when he saw it was up for sale again. He was going to write to you about it. He told me I should rent it. But he did say that if you and Abby want it you should have first call on it. At,' she added briskly, 'a nominal rent of five pounds a week,' and went out.

Abby was staring at the milk jug. Her left hand was trembling. He laid his hand on it and spoke as slowly and softly as if he were talking to a child.

'Abby! Do you want very much to go back to that house?'

Still looking at the milk jug she whispered, 'Yes.'

'Very well. Let's do it.'

Her hand closed tightly on his. He could see her throat gulping, and then the tears were creeping down her face, and she was sobbing into her palms. She raised her wet face to say, 'Oh, Phil, how soon can we go back there?'

'Right away, I suppose. We should be well settled in by Christmas.'

Molly came bustling in with the teapot.

'You can start on that, the bacon is sizzling, how do you like your eggs, basted or turned?'

'He likes them basted,' Abby said comfortably. 'And he likes two. With a nice little slice of fried bread, and a touch of parsley on it.'

'Ha!' Molly said sourly, but with a grin to take the harm out of it. 'You've spoiled him,' and bustled off again.

When she came in and out again with the toast he felt it to be sure it was not too crisp. 'She makes good toast,' he said and buttered it and began to eat, vaguely aware that Abby was babbling on and on about the house.

'We'll be doing it up,' he heard her saying, 'between now and Christmas. I'll be sitting on one side of the fire making new curtains. And you will be sitting on the other side writing the Book.'

'The what?' he said, startled. 'Oh! That? Pour me out a cup of tea, will you? Milk first. You always forget it. I see she has lump sugar. Why don't we always have lump sugar?'

'You will, Phil,' she said as she poured, forgetting the milk again.

'You'll have the best of everything. And peace, Phil. And calm, Phil. And philosophical content, Phil. And serenity without end.'

He munched silently, looking at the sun in the back garden. Saint Martin? He sniffed at the absurd legend: a soldier-saint who saw from horseback two beggars shivering in the snow, took off his cloak, cut it in two, and gave half to one beggar; then looked at the other beggar, took what was left of his cloak, divided it with his sword and gave half to him – so that now all three of them were shivering, until God, in pity, sent back the summer. And people believe things like that can really happen! Staring out he did not hear one word of the childish prattle by his side. He sniffed again. He smelled the rashers frying.

The Talking Trees

There were four of them in the same class at the Red Abbey, all under fifteen. They met every night in Mrs Coffey's sweetshop at the top of Victoria Road to play the fruit machine, smoke fags and talk about girls. Not that they really talked about them – they just winked, leered, nudged one another, laughed, grunted and groaned about them, or said things like 'See her legs?' 'Yaroosh!' 'Wham!' 'Ouch!' 'Ooof!' or 'If only, if only!' But if anybody had said, 'Only what?' they would not have known precisely what. They knew nothing precisely about girls, they wanted to know everything precisely about girls, there was nobody to tell them all the things they wanted to know about girls and that they thought they wanted to do with them. Aching and wanting, not knowing, half guessing, they dreamed of clouds upon clouds of fat, pink, soft, ardent girls billowing towards them across the horizon of their future. They might just as well have been dreaming of pink porpoises moaning at their feet for love.

In the sweetshop the tall glass jars of coloured sweets shone in the bright lights. The one-armed fruit-machine went zing. Now and again girls from Saint Monica's came in to buy sweets, giggle roguishly and over-pointedly ignore them. Mrs Coffey was young, buxom, fairhaired, blue-eyed and very good-looking. They admired her so much that one night when Georgie Watchman whispered to them that she had fine bubs Dick Franks told him curtly not to be so coarse, and Jimmy Sullivan said in his most toploftical voice, 'Georgie Watchman, you should be jolly well ashamed of yourself, you are no gentleman,' and Tommy Gong Gong said nothing but nodded his head as insistently as a ventriloquist's dummy.

Tommy's real name was Tommy Flynn, but he was younger than any of them so that neither he nor they were ever quite sure that he ought to belong to the gang at all. To show it they called him all sorts of nicknames, like Inch because he was so small; Fatty because he was so puppy-fat; Pigeon because he had a chest like a woman; Gong Gong because after long bouts of silence he had a way of suddenly spraying them with wild bursts of talk like a fire alarm attached to a garden sprinkler.

That night all Georgie Watchman did was to make a rude blubberlip noise at Dick Franks. But he never again said anything about Mrs Coffey. They looked up to Dick. He was the oldest of them. He had long eyelashes like a girl, perfect manners, the sweetest smile and the softest voice. He had been to two English boarding schools, Ampleforth and Downside, and in Ireland to three, Clongowes, Castelknock and Rockwell, and had been expelled from all five of them. After that his mother had made his father retire from the Indian Civil, come back to the old family house in Cork and, as a last hope, send her darling Dicky to the Red Abbey day-school. He smoked a corncob pipe and dressed in droopy plus fours with chequered stockings and red flares, as if he was always just coming from or going to the golf course. He played cricket and tennis, games that no other boy at the Red Abbey could afford to play. They saw him as the typical school captain they read about in English boys' papers like *The Gem* and *The Magnet*, *The Boy's Own Paper*, *The Captain* and *Chums*, which was where they got all those swanky words like Wham, Ouch, Yaroosh, Ooof and Jolly Well. He was their Tom Brown, their Bob Cherry, their Tom Merry, those heroes who were always leading Greyfriars School or Blackfriars School to victory on the cricket field amid the cap-tossing huzzas of the juniors and the admiring smiles of visiting parents. It never occurred to them that *The Magnet* or *The Gem* would have seen all four of them as perfect models for some such story as *The Cads of Greyfriars*, or *The Bounders of Blackfriars*, low types given to secret smoking in the spinneys, drinking in the Dead Woman's Inn, or cheating at examinations, or, worst crime of all, betting on horses with redfaced bookies' touts down from London, while the rest of the school was practising at the nets – a quartet of rotters fated to be caned ceremoniously in the last chapter before the entire awe-struck school, and then whistled off at dead of night back to their heartbroken fathers and mothers.

It could not have occurred to them because these crimes did not exist at the Red Abbey. Smoking? At the Red Abbey any boy who wanted to was free to smoke himself into a galloping consumption so long as he did it off the premises, in the jakes or up the chimney. Betting? Brother Julius was always passing fellows sixpence or even a bob to put on an uncle's or a cousin's horse at Leopardstown or the Curragh. In the memory of man no boy had ever been caned ceremoniously for anything. Fellows were just leathered all day long for not doing their homework, or playing hooky from school, or giving lip, or fighting in class – and they were leathered hard. Two years ago Jimmy Sullivan had been given six swingers on each hand with the sharp edge of a metre-long ruler for pouring the contents of an inkwell over Georgie Watchman's head in the middle of a history lesson about the Trojan Wars, in spite of his wailing explanation that he had only done it because he thought Georgie Watchman was a scut and all Trojans were blacks. Drink? They did not drink only because they were too poor. While, as for what *The Magnet* and *The Gem* really meant by 'betting' – which, they dimly understood, was some sort of depravity that no decent English boy would like to see mentioned in print – hardly a week passed that some brother did not say that a hard problem in algebra, or a leaky pen, or a window that would not open or shut was 'a blooming bugger'.

There was the day when little Brother Angelo gathered half a dozen boys about him at playtime to help him with a crossword puzzle.

'Do any of ye,' he asked, 'know what Notorious Conduct could be in seven letters?'

'Buggery?' Georgie suggested mock-innocently.

'Please be serious!' Angelo said. 'This is about Conduct.'

When the solution turned out to be *Jezebel*, little Angelo threw up his hands, said it must be some queer kind of foreign woman and declared that the whole thing was a blooming bugger. Or there was that other day when old Brother Expeditus started to tell them about the strict lives and simple food of Dominican priests and Trappist monks. When Georgie said, 'No tarts, Brother?' Expeditus had laughed loud and long.

'No, Georgie!' he chuckled. 'No pastries of any kind.'

They might as well have been in school in Arcadia. And every other school about them seemed to be just as hopeless. In fact they might have gone on dreaming of pink porpoises for years if it was not for a small thing that Gong Gong told them one October night in the sweetshop. He sprayed them with the news that his sister Jenny had been thrown out of class that morning in Saint Monica's for turning up with a red ribbon in her hair, a mother-of-pearl brooch at her neck and smelling of scent.

'Ould Sister Eustasia,' he fizzled, 'made her go out in the yard and wash herself under the tap, she said they didn't want any girls.in their school who had notions.'

The three gazed at one another, and began at once to discuss all the possible sexy meanings of notions. Georgie had a pocket dictionary. 'An ingenious contrivance'? 'An imperfect conception (*US*)'? 'Small wares'? It did not make sense. Finally they turned to Mrs Coffey. She laughed, nodded towards two giggling girls in the shop who were eating that gummy kind of block toffee that can gag you for half an hour, and said, 'Why don't you ask *them*?' Georgie approached them most politely.

'Pardon me, ladies, but do you by any chance happen to have notions?'

The two girls stared at one another with cow's eyes, blushed scarlet and fled from the shop shrieking with laughter. Clearly a notion was very sexy.

'Georgie!' Dick pleaded. 'You're the only one who knows anything. What in heaven's name is it?'

When Georgie had to confess himself stumped they knew at last that their situation was desperate. Up to now Georgie had always been able to produce some sort of answer, right or wrong, to all their questions. He was the one who, to their disgust, told them what he called conraception meant. He was the one who had explained to them that all babies are delivered from the navel of the mother. He was the one who had warned them that if a fellow kissed a bad woman he would get covered by leprosy from head to foot. The son of a Head Constable, living in the police barracks, he had collected his facts simply by listening as quietly as a mouse to the other four policemen lolling in the dayroom of the barracks with their collars open, reading the sporting pages of *The Freeman's Journal*, slowly creasing their polls and talking about colts, fillies, cows, calves, bulls and bullocks and 'the mysteerious nachure of all faymale wimmen'. He had also gathered a lot of useful stuff by dutiful attendance since the age of eleven at the meetings and marchings of the Protestant Boys' Brigade, and from a devoted study of the Bible. And here he was, stumped by a nun!

Dick lifted his beautiful eyelashes at the three of them, jerked his head and led them out on the pavement.

'I have a plan,' he said quietly. 'I've been thinking of it for some time. Chaps! Why don't we see everything with our own eyes?' And he threw them into excited discussion by mentioning a name. 'Daisy Bolster?'

Always near every school, there is a Daisy Boister – the fast girl whom everybody has heard about and nobody knows. They had all seen her at a distance. Tall, a bit skinny, long legs, dark eyes, lids heavy as the dimmers of a car lamp, prominent white teeth, and her lower lip always gleaming wet. She could be as old as seventeen. Maybe even eighteen. She wore her hair up. Dick told them that he had met her once at the tennis club with four or five other fellows around her and that she had laughed and winked very boldly all the time. Georgie said that he once heard a fellow in school say, 'She goes with boys.' Gong Gong bubbled that that was true because his sister Jenny told him that a girl named Daisy Bolster had been thrown out of school three years ago for talking to a boy outside the convent gate. At this Georgie flew into a terrible rage.

'You stupid slob!' he roared. 'Don't you know yet that when anybody says a boy and girl are talking to one another it means they're doing you-know-what?'

'I don't know you-know-what,' Gong Gong wailed. 'What what?'

'I heard a fellow say,' Jimmy Sullivan revealed solemnly, 'that she has no father and that her mother is no better than she should be.'

Dick said in approving tones that he had once met another fellow who had heard her telling some very daring stories.

'Do you think she would show us for a quid?'

Before they parted on the pavement that night they were talking not about a girl but about a fable. Once a girl like that gets her name up she always ends up as a myth, and for a generation afterwards, maybe more, it is the myth that persists. 'Do you remember,' some old chap will wheeze, 'that girl Daisy Bolster? She used to live up the Mardyke. We used to say she was fast.' The other old boy will nod knowingly, the two of them will look at one another inquisitively, neither will admit anything, remembering only the long, dark avenue, its dim gaslamps, the stars hooked in its trees.

Within a month Dick had fixed it. Their only trouble after that was to collect the money and to decide whether Gong Gong should be allowed to come with them.

Dick fixed that, too, at a final special meeting in the sweet-shop. Taking his pipe from between his lips, he looked speculatively at Gong Gong, who looked up at him with eyes big as plums, trembling between the terror of being told he could not come with them and the greater terror of being told that he could.

'Tell me, Gong Gong,' Dick said politely, 'what exactly does your father do?'

'He's a tailor,' Tommy said, blushing a bit at having to confess it, knowing that Jimmy's dad was a bank clerk, that Georgie's was a Head Constable, and that Dick's had been a Commissioner in the Punjab.

'Very fine profession,' Dick said kindly. 'Gentleman's Tailor and Outfitter. I see. Flynn and Company? Or is it Flynn and Sons? Have I seen his emporium?'

'Ah, no!' Tommy said, by now as red as a radish. 'He's not that sort of tailor at all, he doesn't build suits, ye know, that's a different trade altogether, he works with me mother at home in Tuckey Street, he tucks things in and he lets things out, he's what they call a mender and turner, me brother Turlough had this suit I have on me now before I got it, you can see he's very good at his job, he's a real dab...'

Dick let him run on, nodding sympathetically – meaning to convey to the others that they really could not expect a fellow to know much about girls if his father spent his life mending and turning old clothes in some side alley called Tuckey Street.

'Do you fully realize, Gong Gong, that we are proposing to behold the ultimate in female beauty?'

'You mean,' Gong Gong smiled fearfully, 'that she'll only be wearing her nightie?'

Georgie Watchman turned from him in disgust to the fruit-machine. Dick smiled on.

'The thought had not occurred to me,' he said. 'I wonder, Gong Gong, where do you get all those absolutely filthy ideas. If we subscribe seventeen and sixpence, do you think you can contribute half-a-crown?'

'I could feck it, I suppose.'

Dick raised his eyelashes.

'Feck?'

Gong Gong looked shamedly at the tiles.

'I mean steal,' he whispered.

'Don't they give you any pocket money?'

'They give me threepence a week.'

'Well, we have only a week to go. If you can, what was your word, feck half-a-crown, you may come.'

The night chosen was a Saturday – her mother always went to town on Saturdays; the time of meeting, five o'clock exactly; the place, the entrance to the Mardyke Walk.

On any other occasion it would have been a gloomy spot for a rendezvous. For adventure, perfect. A long tree-lined avenue, with, on one side, a few scattered houses and high enclosing walls; on the other side the small canal whose deep dyke had given it its name. Secluded, no traffic allowed inside the gates, complete silence. A place where men came every night to stand with their girls behind the elm trees kissing and whispering for hours. Dick and Georgie were there on the dot of five. Then Jimmy Sullivan came swiftly loping. From where they stood, under a tree just beyond the porter's lodge, trembling with anticipation, they could see clearly for only about a hundred yards up the long tunnel of elms lit by the first stars above the boughs, one tawny window streaming across a dank garden, and beyond that a feeble perspective of pendant lamps fading dimly away into the blue November dusk. Within another half-hour the avenue would be pitch black between those meagre pools of light.

Her instructions had been precise. In separate pairs, at exactly half past five, away up there beyond the last lamp, where they would be as invisible as cockroaches, they must gather outside her house.

'You won't be able even to see one another,' she had said gleefully to Dick, who had stared coldly at her, wondering how often she had stood behind a tree with some fellow who would not have been able even to see her face.

Every light in the house would be out except for the fanlight over the door.

'Ooo!' she had giggled. 'It will be terribly oohey. You won't hear a sound but the branches squeaking. You must come along to my door. You must leave the other fellows to watch from behind the trees. You must give two short rings. Once, twice. And then give a long ring, and wait.' She had started to whisper the rest, her hands by her sides clawing her dress in her excitement. 'The fanlight will go out if my mother isn't at home. The door will open slowly. You must step into the dark hall. A hand will take your hand. You won't know whose hand it is. It will be like something out of Sherlock Holmes. You will be simply terrified. You won't know what I'm wearing. For all you'll know I might be wearing nothing at all!'

He must leave the door ajar. The others must follow him one by one. After that...

It was eleven minutes past five and Gong Gong had not yet come. Already three women had passed up the Mardyke carrying parcels, hurrying home to their warm fires, forerunners of the home-for-tea crowd. When they had passed out of sight Georgie growled, 'When that slob comes I'm going to put my boot up his backside.' Dick, calmly puffing his corncob, gazing wearily up at the stars, laughed tolerantly and said, 'Now Georgie, don't be impatient. We shall see all! We shall at last know all!'

Georgie sighed and decided to be weary too.

'I hope,' he drawled, 'this poor frail isn't going to let us down!'

For three more minutes they waited in silence and then Jimmy Sullivan let out a cry of relief. There was the small figure hastening towards them along the Dyke Parade from one lamp-post to another.

'Puffing and panting as usual, I suppose,' Dick chuckled. 'And exactly fourteen minutes late.'

'I hope to God,' Jimmy said, 'he has our pound note. I don't know in hell why you made that slob our treasurer.'

'Because he is poor,' Dick said quietly. 'We would have spent it.'

He came panting up to them, planted a black violin case against the tree and began rummaging in his pockets for the money.

'I'm supposed to be at a music lesson, that's me alibi, me father always wanted to be a musician but he got married instead, he plays the cello, me brother Turlough plays the clarinet, me sister Jenny plays the viola, we have quartets, I sold a Haydn quartet for one and six, I had to borrow sixpence from Jenny, and I fecked the last sixpence from me mother's purse, that's what kept me so late . . .'

They were not listening, staring into the soiled and puckered handkerchief he was unravelling to point out one by one, a crumpled half-note, two half-crowns, two shillings and a sixpenny bit.

'That's all yeers, and here's mine. Six threepenny bits for the quartet. That's one and six. Here's Jenny's five pennies and two ha'pence. That makes two bob. And here's the tanner I just fecked from me mother's purse. That makes my two and sixpence.'

Eagerly he poured the mess into Dick's hands. At the sight of the jumble Dick roared at him.

'I told you, you bloody little fool, to bring a pound note!'

'You told me to bring a pound.'

'I said a pound note. I can't give this dog's breakfast to a girl like Daisy Bolster.'

'You said a pound.'

They all began to squabble. Jimmy Sullivan shoved Gong Gong. Georgie punched him. Dick shoved Georgie. Jimmy defended Georgie with 'We should never have let that slob come with us.' Gong Gong shouted, 'Who's a slob?' and swiped at him. Jimmy shoved him again so that he fell over his violin case, and a man passing home to his tea shouted at them, 'Stop beating that little boy at once!'

Tactfully they cowered. Dick helped Gong Gong to his feet. Georgie dusted him lovingly. Jimmy retrieved his cap, put it back crookedly on his head and patted him kindly. Dick explained in his best Ampleforth accent that they had merely been having 'a trifling discussion', and 'our young friend here tripped over his suitcase'. The man surveyed them dubiously, growled something and went on his way. When he was gone Georgie pulled out his pocketbook, handed a brand-new pound note to Dick, and grabbed the dirty jumble of cash. Dick at once said, 'Quick march! Two by two!' and strode off ahead of the others, side by side with Tommy in his crooked cap, lugging his dusty violin case, into the deepening dark.

They passed nobody. They heard nothing. They saw only the few lights in the sparse houses along the left of the Mardyke. On the other side was the silent, railed-in stream. When they came in silence to the wide expanse of the cricket field the sky dropped a blazing veil of stars behind the outfield nets. When they passed the gates of the railed-in public park, locked for the night, darkness returned between the walls to their left and the overgrown laurels glistening behind the tall railings on their right. Here Tommy stopped dead, hooped fearfully towards the laurels.

'What's up with you?' Dick snapped at him.

'I hear a noise, me father told me once how a man murdered a woman in there for her gold watch, he said men do terrible things like that because of bad women, he said that that man was hanged by the neck in Cork Jail, he said that was the last time the black flag flew on top of the jail. Dick! I don't want to go on!'

Dick peered at the phosphorescent dial of his watch, and strode ahead, staring at the next feeble lamp hanging crookedly from its black iron arch. Tommy had to trot to catch up with him.

'We know,' Dick said, 'that she has long legs. Her breasts will be white and small.'

'I won't look!' Tommy moaned.

'Then don't look!'

Panting, otherwise silently, they hurried past the old corrugated iron building that had once been a roller-skating rink and was now empty and abandoned. After the last lamp the night became impenetrable, then her house rose slowly to their left against the starlight. It was square, tall, solid, brick-fronted, three-storeyed, and jet-black against the stars except for its half-moon fanlight. They walked a few yards past it and halted, panting, behind a tree. The only sound was the squeaking of a branch over their heads. Looking backwards, they saw Georgie and Jimmy approaching under the last lamp. Looking forwards, they saw a brightly lit tram, on its way outward from the city, pass the far end of the tunnel, briefly light its maw and black it out again. Beyond that lay wide fields and the silent river. Dick said, 'Tell them to follow me if the fanlight goes out,' and disappeared.

Alone under the tree, backed still by the park, Tommy looked across to the far heights of Sunday's Well dotted with the lights of a thousand suburban houses. He clasped his fiddle case before him like a shield. He had to force himself not to run away towards where another bright tram would rattle him back to the city. Suddenly he saw the fanlight go out. Strings in the air throbbed and faded. Was somebody playing a cello? His father bowed over his cello, jacket off, shirt-sleeves rolled up, entered the Haydn; beside him Jenny waited, chin sidewards over the viola, bosom lifted, bow poised, the tendons of her frail wrist hollowed by the lamplight, Turlough facing them lipped a thinner reed. His mother sat shawled by the fire, tapping the beat with her toe. Georgie and Jimmy joined him.

'Where's Dick?' Georgie whispered urgently.

'Did I hear music?' he gasped.

Georgie vanished, and again the strings came and faded. Jimmy whispered, 'Has she a gramophone?' Then they could hear nothing but the faint rattle of the vanished tram. When Jimmy slid away from him, he raced madly up into the darkness, and then stopped dead halfway to the tunnel's end. He did not have the penny to pay for the tram. He turned and raced as madly back the way he had come, down past her house, down to where the gleam of the laurels hid the murdered woman, and stopped again. He heard a rustling noise. A rat? He looked back, thought of her long legs and her small white breasts, and found himself walking heavily back to her garden gate, his heart pounding. He entered the path, fumbled for the dark door, pressed against it, felt it slew open under his hand, stepped cautiously into the dark hallway, closed the door, saw nothing, heard nothing, stepped onward, and fell clattering on the tiles over his violin case.

A door opened. He saw firelight on shining shinbones and bare knees. Fearfully, his eyes moved upwards. She was wearing nothing but gym knickers. He saw two small birds, white, soft, rosy-tipped. Transfixed by joy he stared and stared at them. Her black hair hung over her narrow shoulders. She laughed down at him with white teeth and wordlessly gestured him to get up and come in. He faltered after her white back and stood inside the door. The only light was from the fire.

Nobody heeded him. Dick stood by the corner of the mantelpiece, one palm flat on it, his other hand holding his trembling corncob. He was peering coldly at her. His eyelashes almost met. Georgie lay sprawled in a chintzy armchair on the other side of the fire wearily flicking the ash from a black cigarette into the fender. Opposite him Jimmy Sullivan sat on the edge of a chair, his elbows on his knees, his eyeballs sticking out as if he just swallowed something hot, hard and raw. Nobody said a word.

She stood in the centre of the carpet, looking guardedly from one to the other of them out of her hooded eyes, her thumbs inside the elastic of her gym knickers. Slowly she began to press her knickers down over her hips. When Georgie suddenly whispered 'The Seventh veil!' he at once wanted to batter him over the head with his fiddle case, to shout at her to stop, to shout at them that they had seen everything, to shout that they must look no more. Instead, he lowered his head so that he saw nothing but her bare toes. Her last covering slid to the carpet. He heard three long gasps, became aware that Dick's pipe had fallen to the floor, that Georgie had started straight up, one fist lifted as if he was going to strike her, and that Jimmy had covered his face with his two hands.

A coal tinkled from the fire to the fender. With averted eyes he went to it, knelt before it, wet his fingers with his spittle as he had often seen his mother do, deftly laid the coal back on the fire and remained so for a moment watching it light up again. Then he sidled back to his violin case, walked out into the hall, flung open the door on the sky of stars, and straightway started to race the whole length of the Mardyke from pool to pool of light in three gasping spurts.

After the first spurt he stood gasping until his heart had stopped hammering. He heard a girl laughing softly behind a tree. Just before his second halt he saw ahead of him a man and a woman approaching him arm in arm, but when he came up to where they should have been they too had become invisible. Halted, breathing, listening, he heard their murmuring somewhere in the dark. At his third panting rest he heard an invisible girl say, 'Oh, no, oh no!' and a man's urgent voice say, 'But yes, but yes!' He felt that behind every tree there were kissing lovers, and without stopping he ran the gauntlet between them until he emerged from the Mardyke among the bright lights of the city. Then, at last, the sweat cooling on his forehead, he was standing outside the shuttered plumber's shop above which they lived. Slowly he climbed the bare stairs to their floor and their door. He paused for a moment to look up through the windows at the stars, opened the door and went in.

Four heads around the supper table turned to look up inquiringly at him. At one end of the table his mother sat wearing her blue apron. At the other end his father sat, in his rolled-up shirt-sleeves as if he had only just laid down the pressing iron. Turlough gulped his food. Jenny was smiling mockingly at him. She had the red ribbon in her hair and the mother-of-pearl brooch at her neck.

'You're bloody late,' his father said crossly. 'What the hell kept you? I hope you came straight home from your lesson. What way did you come? Did you meet anybody or talk to anybody? You know I don't want any loitering at night. I hope you weren't cadeying with any blackguards? Sit down, sir, and eat your supper. Or did your lordship expect us to wait for you? What did you play tonight? What did Professor Hartmann give you to practise for your next lesson?'

He sat in his place. His mother filled his plate and they all ate in silence.

Always the questions! Always talking at him! They never let him alone for a minute. His hands sank. She was so lovely. So white. So soft. So pink. His mother said gently, 'You're not eating, Tommy. Are you all right?'

He said, 'Yes, yes, I'm fine, Mother.'

Like birds. Like stars. Like music.

His mother said, 'You are very silent tonight, Tommy. You usually have a lot of talk after you've been to Professor Hartmann. What were you thinking of?'

'They were so beautiful!' he blurted.

'What was so bloody beautiful?' his father rasped. 'What are you blathering about?'

'The stars,' he said hastily.

Jenny laughed. His father frowned. Silence returned.

He knew that he would never again go back to the sweetshop. They would only want to talk and talk about her. They would want to bring everything out into the light, boasting and smirking about her, taunting him for having run away. He would be happy forever if only he could walk every night of his life up the dark Mardyke, hearing nothing but a girl's laugh from behind a tree, a branch squeaking, and the far-off rattle of a lost tram; walk on and on, deeper and deeper into the darkness until he could see nothing but one tall house whose fanlight she would never put out again. The doorbell might ring, but she would not hear it. The door might be answered, but not by her. She would be gone. He had known it ever since he heard her laughing softly by his side as they ran away together, for ever and ever, between those talking trees.

The Time of their Lives

Before Miss Gogan finished her fifth lunch in the Grand Hotel Villa Serbelloni she had made a dreadful scene in the dining room – and on a Sunday afternoon at that! It was not that there had been anything wrong with the lunch; not in a hotel honoured by the red print of the *Guide Michelin* for its exquisite situation, gardens, decor, food and unbroken silence. It was simply that as she was finishing her usual excellent *scaloppine*, at her usual table, in the corner of the dining room, with her volume of *The Forsyte Saga* open before her – her fork poised over Soames proposing marriage to the reluctant Irene – seven or eight boys and girls in coloured wraps and sandals came crowding in from the lake, sun-bronzed and wet-haired, to occupy a large table at her elbow, laughing and babbling as noisily as if they were still cavorting on the sunblanched beach.

More annoying still, her old waiter who had hitherto been so attentive to her began to neglect her and cosset them, jocosely called them 'my little daughters' and 'my little sons.' It took her fully ten minutes to persuade him to remove her plate. It took him another ten minutes to bring her the fruit dish. And when she had eaten her peach she found herself beckoning and calling to him in vain for her coffee until she became so cross with him that she could not remember the Italian for waiter and began calling him *garsone, waitore*, and *monsignore*. In the end she got into such a frenzy of irritation that she seized Aunt Rosa's thirty-year-old phrase book and her own new pocket dictionary, composed and rehearsed a speech of protest, got up, slapped her books closed, walked over to the old man, tapped him on the shoulder, and let him have it.

He whirled, wide-eyed, to find the fat little woman with the lovely blue eyes and black eyelashes, the one dressed in red like a robin redbreast, all bosom and bum, announcing (insofar as he could make out at all what she was trying to say) that she had come here from (was it Iceland or Holland?) to search with a skewer (*con fuscellino*) for the peace and the repose, but now, 'Thy fault, O hunter, I go forth alone *abbandonata* to search for a coffeepot in the piazzetta!' Which said, she threw a ferocious, blueblack glare at him – who raised his hands aloft as if to bless her departure – and strode out between the staring diners, most of whom, she observed with chagrin, seemed chiefly interested in her long red cotton dress (bought last week at a sale at Cannocks' in Limerick) that she could feel flapping about her calves at every step like a bloody flag.

The sun in the whirling glass doors blinded her. The heat smote her. Below her lay the piazzetta, shadowless, overexposed, empty. Taking courage from her anger, she decided that she really would have her coffee there and bravely descended to it. To her relief every one of the little round tables outside the cafe was unoccupied. The only person in sight was a beautiful boy in a white apron, shading his eyes to look at a white steamer slowly crossing from Cadenabbia. Looking at him, so young, so lightly poised on one leg, his hand lifted so gracefully to his brow, she felt Italy returning in all its former plenitude. When, with a start, he came hurrying towards her, she knew again that this must be the most simple, innocent, warm and welcoming country in the whole world.

'Signora?' He smiled eagerly.

The word, so clearly implying that she had long ceased to qualify for the younger title, had irked her a little in the mouths of the waiters and chambermaids of the hotel. Coming from this child it accentuated his youth rather than her age.

'Oh, very well!' she laughed. 'As the song says, "Call me Madam," I suppose, anyway, once you turn forty . . .'

'Signora?' he asked again, not understanding a word.

'*Un caffè, per favore.*'

While she waited she stared at the approaching steamer. Why on earth had she made that awful exhibition of herself? It could be nothing to do with the hotel. He was really a very nice poor old waiter. And it could, most certainly, be nothing to do with lovely Bellagio. She looked about her questioningly. Or could it? The quayside was as silent as it was blank. When she heard the hoot of the steamer, she thought for a moment of crossing back on it to pass an hour in Cadenabbia, but a second hollow hoot extended the same sense of blankness up and down the entire lake from north to south. It would be the same story over there. Every shutter closed. A dog stretched panting in the shade.

A boatman asleep beside his boat. She received her answer from a third hollow hoot. 'Pao-o-la,' it said, and she repeated it aloud.

'Who has not rung me since last Friday!'

Unnoticed, her beautiful boy laid her coffee on the table, offered her an unseen smile, retired with an unacknowledged bow. She had snatched up her letter to Aunt Rosa on which she had spent the entire morning, and was lost in the reading of it, very slowly and very carefully, watching now not for the meaning of the words but, as she knew Aunt Rosa would also do, for their tell-tale tone:

> *Bellagio*
> *Lago di Como*
> *Sunday, June 14th*

MY DEAREST AUNT ROSA,

I am sure you got my telegram saying I arrived safely. Now I must tell you all my news. But before I do, I must tell you how wildly grateful I am to you for arranging this wonderful trip for me to your dear, darling Italy. For years and years whenever you spoke of Italy I used to imagine, afterwards, what it must be really like. Now that I have, thanks to you, laid eyes on it I can assure you that it has surpassed my wildest dreams. How right you were! Lake Como is truly a vision of delight. Bellagio is, as you have always said, out of a child's picture book, winding back and up under the bluest sky to the loveliest country walks. Every moment I am enchanted by the magnificent views over the lake, with its dear little white steamers coming and going, offering to transport me to other delights, and its hundreds of darling pink villas dotted like flowers on every hillside. The hotel, the food, the service are beyond description. But I do not need to tell any of this to *you!* I cannot believe that a single thing has changed here since you and poor, dear Sir Julian, may God rest him, came to this very same hotel on your honeymoon thirty-odd years ago. But now I must at once explain to my dear benefactor how it has happened that I am spending the holiday here on Lake Como in this super hotel and not, as you so kindly planned, with Paola Buononcini in the villa at Forte dei Marmi. Well, this is the extraordinary thing that happened, and I can only hope and trust that in the circumstances I have acted just as you would have wished me to act. If I have not done so please write to me at once and I will obey you in every respect.

When I got off the plane at Milan on Tuesday afternoon, there indeed was Paola waiting for me, as you said she would be, as ravishingly elegant and lovely as when she stayed at the Castle last October, wearing pink raw-silk slacks, so tight that I could not imagine either how she got into them or out of them – zipped, do you suppose? – with openwork gold sandals, silver toenails, her fair hair down about her shoulders, looking about seventeen instead of, is it twenty-three? Before she said a word I knew there was something wrong. I could see it in her tragic eyes and the way she kissed me on both cheeks, which she never did in Limerick, and the way she at once began to gesticulate and talk like a machine gun. She told me, half in English, half in Italian, about the terrible *disgrazia* (this, I gather, is the Italians' curious word for an accident) that had happened to their villa in Forte dei Marmi only the night before.

It appears that their villa caught fire in the middle of the night and, though nobody was hurt, her mother had to be taken back at once to Milan suffering badly from shock. So, very apologetically, and sweetly, she really is the sweetest girl, she asked me would I mind if just we two spent the holiday together in this marvellous hotel on Lake Como, where she would be near her mamma in Milan, rather than in some seaside hotel in Forte dei Marmi where she would be very far away from her. Well, I said that I was terribly upset about the loss of the villa, and the shock to her mamma, but that I did not mind the change at all, though I was privately much more worried lest in saying so I might not be acting as you would have wished me to act. Still, looking back at it, I do not really see what else, at that moment, I could have said or done except to take the next plane home, an abrupt action that might well have seemed rather cavalier to the good Buononcinis. Nevertheless, I repeat, if you do not approve of my staying here, please do say so and I will follow your instructions in every particular.

Paola was accompanied by a very tall man, an old friend of the family, one Count Algradi, who had his car waiting outside the airport. In this great, long, white, shining vehicle, called I believe an Alfa-Romeo, like Romeo and Juliet, he at once whirled the pair of us off at a speed which frightened the very life out of me, in through the suburbs of Milan and out and on and up through the lakeside town of Como for my first view of the real Italy. On we drove, over the hills and far away, to this ritzy hotel on the edge of the lake, at the point of a peninsula, surrounded by flowers and gardens, tucked away from all traffic which, Paola told me, can be quite noisy on Sundays and holidays on these narrow roads.

Paola could not, unfortunately stay with me that night as she had to go back to reassure her mother in Milan. On Wednesday night she rang to say her mother was much better though still so shaken that she, Paola, would not be able to join me for another couple of days and would I be alright by myself until then? Of course, I said yes, and of course I am. I mean how could anybody be otherwise in this exquisite place of peace, joy and total relaxation? She could not, apparently, call me on Thursday but on Friday morning she did ring again to explain that her poor mamma was still feeling a little down, but she, Paola, would ring again on Saturday, and join me as soon as possible . . .'

Were those last four words a giveaway? More cold than whatever that Italian phrase was that Paola had used?

It is now Sunday morning and here I am happily sitting in the sun on the hotel terrace awaiting her call. It will, I am sure, come any minute now . . .

The steamer bumped against the pier. She sipped her coffee. It had gone cold. Two motorcars came lumbering on to the quay. A few pedestrians disappeared into the shadows of the village. She wondered again if she ought to cross back on the ferry to Cadenabbia. Those roads behind Bellagio were all the same. Besides, it was really the evenings that got her down. Reading Galsworthy in the hotel lounge, while that chinless, chain-smoking young man doodled at the piano. She glanced over the rest of her letter.

So very, very, very grateful . . . All my love to my dear cousins . . . I do hope the new paying guests are nice, I wish I were there to help . . . I wonder would somebody be so very, very, very kind as to water my white jasmine? Unless there has been more rain? My goodness, it was wet the morning I left . . . Endless love to you all.

Your devoted niece,
MARY ANNE

She folded it and put it into its envelope and looked at the address. *Lady Alleyn, Doon Castle, Castledoon, near Croom, Irlanda.* Limerick's long Sunday afternoons. The black eye of a raincloud glowering over the flat plain. So lush. So level. Damp potholes in the avenue. Tree trunks green on the windy side. Every single one of the battlements along the top of the house a bucket of rain. Water her white jasmine? Nobody's shoes would leave green marks on the grey dew of her lawn these mornings. Her twelve-year-old lawn behind the gate lodge. Where she had lived with old grandaunt Jenny until that Sunday afternoon last March when the poor, silly old soul sat down on a chair that was not there and broke her skull. She sighed, licked a mauve stamp and walloped it on to the envelope so passionately that she toppled her Galsworthy off the table. A cadaverous elderly man who, unobserved, had seated himself at the next table politely restored it, saying in perfect English, with a ghastly lower-lip smile, 'Your book, Miss Gogan.' She turned to stare at him.

'Good gracious!' she cried, enchanted to meet somebody she knew, and who could talk English. 'If it isn't Count Algradi!'

He was dressed in a metallic pink-grey suit, with big gold links in his long white cuffs. He rose above her, a pink flamingo, took her proffered hand by the fingertips and lowered his lips to the back of it. His splendid grey eyes stared frighteningly at her. He was the thinnest man she had ever seen.

'I am so pleased, Miss Gogan,' he said rapidly, precisely and sweetly, 'that you have not forgotten me.'

He resumed his seat, his panama perched on his pointed knee.

'Of course, I remember you,' she smiled, and involuntarily touched her letter to Aunt Rosa. 'But I do not remember your talking English to me at the airport?'

He smiled another lower-teeth smile.

'I did not talk to you at all, Miss Gogan. Paola Buononcini did all the talking. As she always does. Quite a chatterbox, isn't she? I think I should introduce myself again. My name is Federico Algardi. Not Algradi. But everybody calls me Freddy. My father had an enormous admiration for England. He sent me to an English school at Lausanne. They all called me Freddy there too. I went for two years to the University of Nottingham just before the war. Everyone there called me Freddy. Everybody in Milan knows me as Freddy Algardi. But I can talk Scots, too, ye know. I can recite your great poet Shelley in Scots. Shall

I do it for you? *Hael taw thee, bliuthe speerutt! Burrd thaw neverr wurt, With thay baded bobbles winkin' at thay brrum, and thay purple-stained mourth!* Quite good, don't you think? I learned my Scots from the pastor at the Church of Saint James in Cadenabbia. I was there this morning. He is the Reverend Jamie Macandrew, from Aberdeen, an awfully nice fellow, though he does talk an awful lot of rot about hellfire. I am afraid in Nottingham we would have called him a bally ass. Mark you,' he said, and liked the phrase enough to repeat it, 'mark you, he really does believe in hellfire. He almost makes me believe in it.' He laughed another toothy laugh. '"To hell with the Pope!" They taught me how to say that in Nottingham. When I came home and said it to my mamma she was absolutely enchanted. Ye see, my mamma believed strongly in hellfire and she loathed all the popes. They taught me to say it because, like all the English, they think that all Italians are Catholics. It's not true, ye know, I'm not a Catholic. I'm a kind of Protestant. Actually I'm a Waldensian. Ye see, my mamma was not a Milanese. She came from Torino, a great stronghold of the Waldensians. The Scots of Italy, a severe people. Born Manichaeans. The persecuted devoted to persecution. My mamma was a tremendous persecutor. She persecuted me for years and years. Oh, my dear Miss Gogan, I cannot tell you how pleased I am to meet a lady from England. I adore Englishwomen.'

'But, Count Algardi,' she demurred. 'I am Irish!'

His bony fingers flashed gold.

'Same thing! Scots, English, Welsh, Irish. All British.'

He was nut-brown from the sun and, on a second glance, not so bad-looking. In fact, with those greying wings over his ears, he looked quite distinguished, even if he was as thin as a pencil. Aunt Rosa had warned her that all Italian counts are rakes. ('A lot of bad hats,' she had said, remembering Italy under Mussolini. 'Watch out for them, even if you are forty-one. All the more so because you look it.')

'Oh, dear!' he said, and put his bony hand to his mouth, remembering his joke about the pope. 'If Irish, then Catholic? I've made an awful bally bloomer, what, what?'

'Count Algardi,' she said primly, 'all the Irish are not British. And like the Italians, not all the Irish are Catholics. I am a member of the Church of Ireland.'

'Please explain to me Church of Ireland.'

She explained feebly. He waved his wrist again.

'You mean the Church of England in Ireland. I am so relieved. My father greatly admired the Church of England. So do I! In fact, when I was in Nottingham I thought of joining the Church of England, but my mamma put her foot down. She said it was too lax. I have always regretted that I obeyed her. But, I have spent my life regretting that I ever obeyed her in anything. She really *was* an old tyrant.'

He sighed, regretting, and she, feeling also at a loss, stared sidelong at him over imaginary spectacles. Bad counts she could understand. Were there also mad counts? He roused himself from his gloom.

'Mark you, I know a lot about Ireland. The Irish Sweepstakes. Your great patriot De Valera. Your great English writers, Giose, Occasi, Becchetta. How lovely that poem by your great poet Giatsa! *I will rise up and go now far away to Ginnitsfrié*. Miss Gogan, I adore Ireland! The land of ghosts and goblins, of castles and kilts, of murderous queens and murdered kings. Macbeth!'

Miss Gogan decided to take him in hand.

'Count Algardi,' she said. 'What is your news of Paola Buononcini?'

He shifted his chair closer to her table.

'Signorina Gogan, I want very much to talk to you about dear Paola. In fact I badly need your advice about dear Paola. In fact I would like to talk with you about many things. I have a suggestion to make to you. Would you honour me by joining me for dinner tonight? I could collect you at your hotel at six o'clock, we could cross over to Cadenabbia on the ferry, and I would drive you from there to dinner at the Villa d'Este. It is a hotel but it is not a hotel. It is a house that is not a house. It is the most delightful mansion in Europe south of the Alps. I promise to have you back in your hotel by ten o'clock sharp. Please, Miss Gogan, I do so need your help. And your advice. Please join me for dinner.'

She looked into his pleading grey eyes. She thought of those boring hill roads that she had walked and walked. She thought of those empty hours after dinner.

'Thank you, Count,' she said sedately. 'I should be most pleased to join you for dinner.'

'Splendid!' he cried joyfully. 'Until six, then. At your hotel' – and lifted her hand again by the fingertips, bowed over it, and, with long, swift heron steps stooped rapidly away, folded himself into his white car and whirled from the empty quay.

The lake was rippled like a fish by the prow of the steamer. The mountains wavered in the water. She had never met a real count before. Rapidly she changed that. She had never met any sort of count before. Nobody had ever kissed her hand before. Nobody had ever asked her advice about anything, except about such things as whether the paying guests could be fobbed off with liver and bacon. Bad counts? Aunt Rosa must have been joking. Anyway, Aunt Rosa did not have to know every damn thing. She became aware that her beautiful boy was hovering, a bottle in one hand, in the other a tiny glass.

'*Una Strega, signorina?*' (Signorina!) '*Complimenti del Padrone.*'

She glanced where he was glancing, behind him. The portly *padrone* was bowing to her from the door of his café. Bad or mad, the count apparently counted.

'*Grazie,*' she whispered, wondering as she watched him pour out the golden liquor what a Strega was, and was she doing something absolutely awful again? Guardedly she sipped the sweet liqueur. She stayed there quite a while gazing happily around her. Once she slipped her bookmarker under the flap of her letter to add a postcript, paused, and thought better of it. If Limerick only knew! She tossed back her liqueur, and tossed her head. To hell with them! Let them know! She rose, turned and bowed towards the watching *padrone* and the watching boy beside him, and walked back slowly to the Grand Hotel Villa Serbelloni. On the way she deftly consigned her conscience to the red letterbox fixed to the wall of the shuttered tobacconist. To her relief there was no telephone call from Paola.

He came on the first stroke of the angelus, looking, she thought, like a broken thermometer with his white hair, his black dinner jacket, white front, black tie, white socks. She, after two hours of trying on and casting off every rag she possessed, had settled for her shortest frock – black satin, with great, walloping hand-painted roses, a light shawl of pink wool, an evening bag in silvered calf, a trifle cracked, green evening shoes with red Spanish heels. He looked her over, said, 'You look marvellous! I adore English clothes,' and bowed her into his car. There, seated beside her, on the steamer, he at once began to gabble in his rapid way about the vanity of human wishes.

'Today,' he said, 'the air was so dry you could see a golf ball two hundred yards away. The Reverend Macandrew was very good about that this morning. He said, "Life is like a man's breath on a wintry day, appearrring and vonishing. It reminds him of his mortality. Listen," he said to us, "to what the summer says to us. Last week we had a showurr of rain. Now the earth is as dry as snuff. Our life is like the rrain that the earrth cannot hold. It vonishes into the sky. All things tend upwarrds. Here under the great sunlight of Italy we may dream of a life that will last for everrr, but the lakes are more wise. They dream of the sky."'

She agreed that it was a verra, verra beautiful thought. 'But a bit melancholy?' He startled her by saying that all life is melancholy, bumped off the ferry and began to drive so fast past countless other roaring cars, along a road suitable only for cows in single file, that all conversation was out of the question. He tore within inches of pink villa walls whose hanging bougainvillea swayed in their wind at their shoulders and whose plaster had been scored by the axles of generations of previous roaring drivers. She devoutly hoped that they had all long since evaporated into the sky. She looked sideways at him. He was beaming wildly ahead of him. There could be no doubt about it. The man was as mad as a brush. After that she did not dare open her eyes again until she felt the car slowing on the gravel of what she hoped was his Villa d'Este. When she glared at him she found him gazing at her in happy self-admiration and thought of the drive back, through the night, along those awful donkey-roads. The next moment she forgot everything. He had led her, tottering on her fears, through the foyer out to the terrace. Seeing her delight, he pressed her bare arm. This, also, nobody had ever done to her before. She liked it.

'But this,' she cried, 'knocks the Villa Serbelloni into a cocked hat. This must be the most beautiful place in the whole world. This must be Italy at its very, very, very . . .'

'At its verra, verra, verra?' he laughed, and in her relief she laughed back at him.

'At its verra, verra, verra best!'

It was an opinion she was to abandon heartlessly two days later in favour of a smelly hatbox of a place they discovered halfway to Lugano, a fisherman's trattoria where they ate the freshest of sprats and drank horripilous draughts of a nameless wine under an occluded sky whose low clouds sliced the tops of the mountains. A shutter kept banging in the wind. An invisible cat lapped the shore. At its edge there stood the most romantic figure she had ever seen, a young man in black knee gaiters, a black-brimmed hat and a black cloak. While they ate the young man stood there unstirring.

'Do you think he is a poet?' she asked.

He said that he might be a spy for the Swiss customs. It would not have surprised her if the spy had broken out into an aria from *Il Trovatore*.

He released her arm, to her regret. She touched it where he had held it.

'Now for an aperitif! While we watch the shadows creeping over the lake, and the lights coming up across there in Belvio, and the stars envying us from the mountains.'

By her second martini Miss Gogan felt so much at her ease in Zion that she dared to chide him for his driving.

'Count!' she begged. 'Would yeh tell me wan thing and tell me no more, do you always drive as fast as that? Some day you'll break your blooming neck, so ye will! I'm sure it's very bad for yer nerves.'

'*Noi altri Italiani*,' he said proudly, 'have no nerves. It is why we drive like angels, fight like devils, climb like goats, die like heroes and live without a thought for tomorrow. Besides,' he added casually, 'driving is my business. I sell racing cars.'

'Go along with you! Is that really true? A count? Selling motor cars?'

'My dear signorina, counts, as we would have said at Nottingham, are ten a penny these days. We all have to work,' and he nodded towards the affluent-looking gentlemen seated around them under the vines with their low-backed bulbous wives.

'They look very rich,' she said shyly. 'Look at the pearls. They must have paid hundreds of pounds for those evening dresses.'

'Don't let them impress you,' he laughed. 'That is why all these men have to work. And for those,' he added, nodding towards a frieze of golden youth in bottomy bikinis and coloured wraps strolling against the balustrade of the terrace into the hotel. 'But don't let us waste our time talking about these silly people. I want to talk about you. First of all please tell me your first name.'

'Mary Anne.'

'Marianna! How beautiful! The Madonna and Santa Anna all in one. I have a better idea still, let me talk to you about you. I will tell you all about yourself. You are Marianna Gogan. You live with your dear aunt, Lady Rose Alleyn, the widow of the late Sir George Alleyn, in an ancient castle called Doon Castle. Yes?'

She cocked a wary eye at him.

'You mean,' he laughed, 'who told me? Paola. While we were waiting for you at the airport on Tuesday.'

(How much else, she wondered, did that little monkey tell him?)

'But, you see, our dear Paola is such a dreadful liar I never know how much to believe from her. Let me go on. Your ancient castle stands behind high walls and iron gates in the middle of a great, green rolling plain . . .'

'Not so rolling!'

' . . . dark with woods that are full of foxes, stags, hares and boars specially preserved for the hunt. Yes?'

'Did Paola tell you all that too?'

'She did not enlarge, but I have second sight. Like my mother. But I am right about the woods? Yes?'

She saw the rusty gates that were never shut, the gapped walls that were never mended, the big house at the end of the avenue against the wet sunset, old dotty grandaunt Jenny clucking like a hen after her pet tortoise under the bushes, and, for no reason, she wondered who was now carrying the bathwater upstairs in the tall tin containers clad in red padded wickerwork to be poured by astonished American P.G.'s into brown sitbaths.

'Well,' she temporized, 'it is all certainly very green around Doon Castle.'

'You see!' he cried happily. 'I do have second sight! Now! Your castle. It is so very old that it is covered with ivy. It has turrets and battlements. From its highest turret a flag flies in the wind of every Saint George's Day. And it is lighted only by tiny gothic windows, yes?'

She wove her fingers. A flag, my bottom! And what the hell does he want turrets and battlements for? The next thing he will want is a belfry. He ought to go and live there like a bat. She emptied her glass, he clicked his fingers and one of the white-jacketed waiters immediately refilled it. Old? Doon Castle? *Doon* is the Irish for a fort, and wherever that old thing was it must be ancient.

'Doon Castle,' she smiled at him, 'is indubitably very ancient.'

He creaked back in his wickerwork armchair and gazed up at the vine trellis.

'There,' he intoned dreamily, 'I see young Marianna Gogan, in pig's tails, leaning out of a gothic window in the early morning, awakened by the horn of the huntsman. You are wearing a pink peignoir. You are looking out of your wide, blue eyes down at the line of huntsmen in red coats, the hounds baying before them, the red fox streaking ahead of them across the dewy fields. But then,' he raced on, his hand on hers to silence her, 'as you grow older I see you amongst the huntsmen, riding sidesaddle, in your long black skirt, wearing your tall black hat, and at one of the mighty jumps your hat flies off on its string and your black hair floats behind you like a thundercloud. Am I right? Yes?'

She gulped half her third martini. 'Christ!' she moaned to herself (long since infected by all the more colourful vices of Catholicism). 'If he only got one look at the East Limericks! The Master would have a red coat. And I know Corney Costigan the vet has one because he bought all Sir George's old castoffs ten years ago. And I did see Father Binchy one time in a black riding coat with a cravat. And some of the youngsters would have jodhpurs and hunting caps. But if he saw the farmers' sons! Leggings and berets, that's all they'd rise to. And as for the ragtag and bobtail . . .'

But he was galloping on and on again, breathless, to the kill, while she was seeing the old rooky-rawky house in Dublin where she might still be living if her mammy and pappy had not died, and if Sir Julian had not died, and if Aunt Rosa had not had to take in P.G.'s, and get somebody to look after grandaunt Jenny in the gate lodge.

'When I was in Nottingham,' he was sighing, and she was wishing to God he had never left it, 'I once drove over to Melton Mowbray with a fellow named Ranjit Singh to see the hunt. The car broke down. We never saw it. But I have seen it on television, and in the movies. Didn't you love *Tom Jones?*'

She threw back the second half of her martini.

'Count Algardi! *Please* talk to me about Paola Buononcini.'

'Later! At dinner. Let us have a sherry this time. I forgot that in England you always take sherry before dinner. *Xeres*, ye know, is the Italian for sherry, but nobody ever says it. Domenico! *Due* sherry. *Molto secco!* You remember your Homer?' he asked her. 'How Helen threw a drug into the wine and they forgot all their sorrows. As your great Shakespeare says, "Let our joy be unconfined."'

'Count Algardi,' she giggled. 'I think I'm a bit tiddly already. Look't! Leave us be talking about you thish time. Tell me every single bluddy thing about yourself!'

'Everything? I can tell you that in one sentence. I am a poor, half-crazy fellow who sells cars, dreams dreams, and wishes he had a glorious youth like you, and,' he added gloomily, 'remembers his own.'

But to remember is also to forget. Her memories of the rest of that night would be as gapped as her memories of the nights that followed it. She would never remember how she got to the dinner table. She would know only that she found herself under a red and white marquee, crowded with diners, surrounded by boxes of paw-pink begonias, scarlet zinnias, purple lobelias and white geraniums; under great billowing loops of nasturtiums. On every table a small pink lamp gleamed on the silver, the glass, the napery. The shadows had by then climbed to the far tip of Monte Beletto, twilight had become dusk, one vast star sat in a hollow between two peaks, and across the lake a steamer slowly carried past them a cargo of fairy lights and faint music. But she would remember that the ink-blue night and the skin-pale wine so fumed in her head that whenever a white-haired man in a black tie passed their table with a bare-backed lady and nodded and smiled at him she nodded and smiled back boozily at them, and that presently she was calling him Freddy, and he, with equal amiability, was calling her Marianna. Nothing else stayed with her except the moment when he uttered the name Paola. He did it just after he had risen from his chair – for nobody else had he done this – and bowed deeply to a powerfully built lady with blued hair, and to a gentleman of equal size with a tri-coloured button in the lapel of his dinner jacket.

'They,' he whispered to her over his glass of Soave, the lamplight below his nose hollowing his cheeks, 'are the father and mother of Paola Buononcini.'

Startled sober, she stared at him.

'But that is impossible! Her mother is ill in Milan. Freddy! Tell me at once. Where exactly is Paola?'

Feebly he raised his elbows and his eyebrows.

'In Forte dei Marmi.'

'You mean she has been lying to me?'

He laid his lean hand on her chubby hand.

'Marianna! You do not understand Paola. I have known her for years. I have been devoted to her since she was sixteen. And I am not sure that I even still understand her. You see, you British . . .' (She let it pass with an exasperated breath.) '. . . have all the honesty, truthfulness and straightness of your noble race. Your yes means yes, and your no means no. With *la bella* Paola yes means perhaps, and no means maybe.

Paola is young, wilful, selfish, greedy for life. She never decides what she wants until the last minute. At Linate airport, five minutes before your plane arrived, she suddenly left me, telephoned Bellagio, reserved a room for you, came back and told me that I must stay here and look after you for ten days.'

She could hardly speak for rage and shame.

'Are you telling me that the villa was never burned?'

He shook his head sadly.

'Oh! I know. She has always done it. She uses me. She uses everybody. You and I are in the same boat. She has ditched the pair of us. After all, I too was supposed to have gone to Forte dei Marmi. I was to have driven the three of us down there that Tuesday afternoon and stayed for a fortnight. My holidays.'

'I shall take the next plane home,' she said instantly.

His hand tightened on her hand.

'Marianna, please don't be angry with Paola.'

'Angry with her? I could kill the little bitch.'

'No, no! I have as much reason to be cross with her. But I am grateful to her. Because she made me meet you. Besides, she was right about Forte. What is Forte but miles upon miles of coloured *cabane* and umbrellas? Young people shouting, laughing, babbling and flirting all day long, sunbathing or sleeping half the day, dancing or playing canasta half the night. You would have felt out of everything. Paola would not have known what to do with you. Anyway, she probably has a young man there.'

'Then why did she invite me?'

At that he curled.

'Well . . . She didn't really, you know.'

'But Aunt Rosa told me . . .'

'If Paola was telling me the truth, she really invited your cousin, Geraldine. But your cousin could not come. Paola said something about a young American. So, Lady Alleyn suggested you.'

She covered her face in her hands, then slowly parted them and looked at him.

'I see,' she said quietly, 'I was second best – and not wanted. And Aunt Rosa fixed nothing for me. I shall take the plane home tomorrow.'

To her horror, he straightway began to sob like a child who has been struck. He clutched her hands.

'Marianna,' he wailed, while her eyes darted around to see how many people were noticing. 'Please, do not leave me. If you go away, what shall I do without you?'

'You mean I'm to be second best even for that bitch Paola?'

Why, in God's name, had she ever had anything to do with him? With any of them? Filthy Italians! All liars! The whole damned pack of them, all liars. Wops!

'If you go away I'll drink like a fish all day long. I'll do terrible things. I'll drown myself in the lake if you abandon me. I was so happy to meet you again. I came to Bellagio this afternoon solely to meet you. I was looking forward to being your guide, to showing you everything, little villages, little lakes, hidden corners that no foreigner ever sees. Everybody on the Lakes knows me. They are all my dear friends. I owe money to all of them. I owe thousands upon thousands of lire to the old pirate who runs the restaurant on the island of Comacino. We can lunch there every day. I owe millions to the casino at Campione. We will gamble there together and make pots of money. We will visit the Prince Borromeo on Isola Bella – my father was a great business friend of his. He often said it to me, 'I will never, simply *never* forget your father!' We will eat in little *trattorie* around the lakes where I owe nothing and they'll only be delighted to let me run up enormous bills. Marianna! Don't abandon me!'

Her rage sank to the bottom of a sea of pity.

'But if Aunt Rosa finds out that Paola never joined me, what will I do? I'd be disgraced in Limerick if they got one word of the wind of all this.'

'Seal your mouth like a fish. Don't tell anybody. If you knew the things I've done that I never told to anybody. Not even to my own mother.'

They argued and argued, though again about what she would never remember, except only that, there among the pink lights, the scurrying waiters, the elegant diners, the flowers, his eyes as melancholy and his face as long as a wet hake's, she found herself blurting out a terrible thing.

'Freddy! Why are you making yourself out to be a wicked man? Are you a bad man? Aunt Rosa says all Italian counts are bad men.'

He blenched. She curled. Then, for the first time since they had met, he threw himself back and laughed with his whole mouth, and in her relief at his relief she started to weep for the pair of them.

'Your Aunt Rosa!' he laughed, 'she must be just like all the other grownups I've ever known – my mother, my father, the Reverend Macandrew...'

'You mean,' she said, 'she is a bally ass? Oh, Freddy, you are a scream! I always thought that about Aunt Rosa but I never had the courage before to say it' – at which he knew that she would stay. He deftly halted the scurrying wine waiter.

'Sesto! Champagne! The Bollinger. Forty-seven.'

With a single flourishing gesture the young man blessed their happiness and saluted the champagne. 'The first champagne, signorina,' he whispered to her, for there was a table of Germans near them, 'that the Germans did not drink,' and hastened away to serve them.

'He likes us!' she cried.

'He likes you!'

'Me?' eyes wide, looking around her.

'And why not?' he asked haughtily.

'All these elegant women! And fat me?'

'Pfoo! Bought elegance. But you are genuine, you are true, you are the real thing,' and took both her hands. 'Oh! My dear, dear Marianna! We are going to have the time of our lives.'

They were the last to leave the marquee. Over their brandies he spoke with a sad dignity.

'You asked me, Marianna, if I am a bad man. I am.'

'I refuse to believe it,' she cried passionately. 'I think you're a grand fellow.'

'I am bad,' he insisted. 'And growing old in my badness! How old do you think I am?'

'I am thirty-five,' she said. 'If not more!'

'I am a hundred. I go back too far. I must tell you that my grandmamma was a Princess Levashov. One of those mad Russian revolutionaries who fled to Switzerland in the sixties and led such wild lives there that she ran away from them all to live in the Vaud and become a Waldensian. From one craziness to another. She had only one child. My mamma. In Torino my mamma met my papa. She, too, had only one child. I was not born until they had been married for six years, and I swear that she never once slept with my papa before that, and I swear that after I was born she never again let him make love to her. She was a monster! A woman who hated and despised everything to do with the body and with pleasure. Shall I tell you what she did to me when I was fifteen?'

Over the pink lamp he whispered it to her. By its underlight he looked like Mephistopheles.

'It was Easter. She found out through her spies that I was going out every night with the girl who sold cigarettes in the railway station in Milan. She went down into our garden and she cut two of her loveliest madonna lilies. She took her paint box and she daubed black paint all over one of the white chalices, and daubed a hideous red paint all over its golden pistil. She put the two flowers into a vase in my bedroom, and, pointing at them with her bony finger, she said, "That candid lily was you before you met that slut. This horrible thing is what you are now!" She left them in my bedroom for a month. I can still smell their stink.'

She took his hand in both her hands and her eyes filled with pity for him.

'Poor little boy! But, Freddy, you must have had lots of nice girls since then?'

'Only the kind I dare not talk about. Even while I longed only for girls who were pure, and sweet, and innocent and *oneste*. Seven years ago when I first met Paola she was sweet, pure and innocent. Or was she? How do I know? Now she is greedy, thinks only of herself, lies like a trooper and makes a fool of me all the time. Yet, I never once blamed her. I blamed only this corrupt south where we live. Until last Tuesday at the airport when I saw her deceiving you, a trusting, truthful, honourable, straightforward, candid, open woman from the honest north. The scales fell from my eyes. I realized then that all I long for comes only with the years.'

She did the only thing she could do. She closed her eyes and uttered a soft ancestral moan.

'Freddy!' she whispered. 'I'm dhronk! Take me home.'

She woke at ten o'clock to insistent tom-toms, in her head and from the telephone. It was Freddy. She confided about her head.

'I will attend to that. And I have fixed your appointment with Toni for half-past eleven.'

'With Toni? Who is Toni?'

'I told you about him last night. Have you forgotten? You asked me about a hairdresser. He is the best *parruchiere* on the Lakes. You will find him in Bellagio, near the church. He is my second cousin. And you asked me, too, about a boutique, though why I cannot imagine; you dress so beautifully. You will find one two doors away from Toni's, called La Fiorella. She is my uncle's sister. Goodbye, dear Marianna. I will call for you at half-past twelve.'

She fell on her pillow with a groan, dedicating her life to cold water, total abstinence and, even if he was an RC, Father Theobald Mathew, Ireland's apostle of temperance – as her papa used to do long ago in Dublin whenever he woke up after a bad skite. Five minutes later a young waiter knocked and entered. He bore on a silver tray a glass of brown liquid that looked like Mother Siegel's Syrup.

'Compliments of Count Algardi, signorina. Throw it back.'

She did so and he laughed amiably at her face of disgust, assured her with all the sympathy of one who had in his time also paid wages to Bacchus, that she would feel fine within three minutes, and retired with a nod of comradely approval. And, indeed, by the time she had risen, reeled around for a bit, vomited, bathed and vomited again, she did feel better; so much so that when she fared out into the sunshot village in search of his Toni and his Fiorella she was in a state of happy expectation. She saw, blazing in the window of the boutique, a frock so brilliant that it would have seduced a parakeet. Without hesitation she went in, spent half her pocket money on it, and emerged in it feeling half-naked, depraved, a fool, and utterly delighted. Two doors on there was Toni, ready and waiting for her, as hairy, tiny and garrulous as a Yorkshire terrier. He conducted her to a throne, swished pink curtains about her and began to walk around her as if she were a horse, prattling saucily to her about the superiority of all northern Italians to the rest of the entire world in matters of hairdressing and of love.

'We are as hotta as Siciliani. But more *intelligente*. I love plenty. I have five kids. Three masculine, two feminine. Siciliani not *intelligente*. Millions of kids!'

Whereupon he fell into a gloomy silence, clicked his fingers to summon two pink-robed handmaidens, pointed to her and spread his hands in despair. At once the three of them began to argue passionately about her face. As suddenly he switched off their torrent and began to snip and snap. One of the handmaidens stripped her of her stockings, and sat by her feet to manicure her toes and her fingers. The other came and went with trays of powders, creams and golden lipsticks which she matched and rematched to her skin, all the while (or so it sounded) cursing softly under her breath. The rising heat crept through the open door. Drowsing smells invaded her. Far away she heard the drone of a buzzbike. A distant steamer cock-crowed. Voices from the village carried on the thin air. 'Air,' she begged, 'can I have some air?' and they swished back the curtains and there was the wide, metallic light of Italy, powerful, penetrating, pitiless and inviting. Part of her said, 'What am I doing this for?' Part said, 'What can they do for me?' Part said, 'How much is this going to cost?' Part said, 'Are we both out of our minds?' Part said, 'What does he see in me?' Part said, 'Poor Freddy!' And part of her said, 'He may be mad, but I do like him.'

She blew bubbles into the washbasin. As she surfaced, a church bell rang away the half hour. Anaesthetized under the dryer, she was barely aware of fingers touching, drying, dabbing her, and those soft murmuring curses going on all the time. She felt the dryer being lifted and Toni behind her again. Then, just as the church bell was striking the angelus Toni was presenting her with a hand mirror and slowly twirling her throne so that she could see herself from every angle, the girls exclaiming at one another's art, and embracing one another in delight, while she thought, 'Sacred Heart of Jesus! I look like a whore!' She was coffee-brown. Her eyelids were as blue as the lake. Her hair was a blue-black helmet. She had eyelashes a yard long. Her mouth was as big as a letterbox. She beamed at them, clapped her paws, babbled thanks and began to rummage in her handbag, at which Toni gave her the Fascist salute with his right hand and machine-gunned her with a hundred no's.

'The friend of my best friend! *Impossibile*! In the winter I work in Milano. Freddy send me every woman he know.' (Oh, does he?) 'But,' waving his hand royally to the two girls, 'if you wish . . .'

Fishing for two modest notes she gave each girl a thousand lire. They almost palanquined her to the door. There, one of them suspended her stockings above a waste basket, mimicked 'Yes?' with her painted eyebrows, displayed her own pretty, coffee-dyed legs, and smilingly taking her answer for an 'Oh, yes!' discarded her best Cantreces. (Three and sixpence in Cannocks'! And brand new!) More showers of thanks, smiles, wavings, and farewells pursued her as she went scurrying back to her hotel, her handbag to her nose like a yashmak, her other hand feeling her bare thighs, hastening to rub all this stuff off before Freddy saw her. For, in the newfound wisdom of an admired woman, she knew that this could not possibly be what he wanted at all. Unless he really was a bad man? Before her mirror she ruffled her hair, wiped her mouth, and did what she could with the blue eyelids and the coffee face. She hesitated a long time over the beautiful eyelashes. She finally peeled them off, carefully trimmed them with her nail scissors, stuck them back again, and approved. To finish, she started to draw on a fresh pair of stockings and fell back in her chair red with shame. They had painted her *all* the way up. The telephone rang.

'Signorina Gogan? Count Algardi has arrived.'

With a groan she abandoned her stockings and her modesty, slipped on her shoes, covered her naked back with her auntie shawl and went forth to meet him, smilingly holding her hand straight out from her shoulder in the hope that when he bowed over it he would not see her legs. He gave her one quick all-over glance.

'Perfect! As Cicero says, when unadorned the most adorned. But, of course,' he added as he bestowed her into his car, 'it is one of the most extraordinary things about women – I once waited two hours outside a *parruchiere* for Paola and when she came out she was exactly the same as when she went in.'

'Perhaps,' she said tartly, 'you did not see her. You didn't notice my new frock,' she pouted, thinking with annoyance of all the money she had paid for it. 'Freddy, I don't think you see me at all! Or do you?'

'Your frock is wonderful,' he said, giving it a casual look as, with three fingers on the wheel, he halted within inches of the edge of the dock. 'As for seeing you? The Reverend Macandrew said a beautiful thing a few weeks ago. "Love, my dear bretherrn," he said to us, "is a secret that grows within the soul."'

She looked hopelessly over the lake. *More* guff? Her look changed to a quick apprehension as he went on.

'"But, dear bretherrrn, the body is love's open book." Now that we are friends, Marianna, we shall have no secrets from one another.'

From that moment on she never looked forward. A woman without a past can read only the present. A woman with no future must ignore it. Even the sun conspired against foresight. Its heat shrivelled the pages of her calendar. Like a moth under a glazed dome of breathless air, wine-fumy and sticky, she began to move slower and slower. Each morning she woke later, stretched out an arm reluctantly for the telephone, breakfasted in bed, bathed as languidly as an odalisque, had to struggle against the temptation to roll back into bed again. She spent hours over a face that, in Limerick, she would have washed in three minutes out of a basin of rainwater from the barrel outside her door. She never wore stockings again. She left her clothes strewn around the bedroom floor. She lost her *Forsyte Saga*. Only once did she manage to squeeze out five lines to Aunt Rosa (who never wrote) telling her about the sweetness and kindness of Paola Buononcini (who never rang), taking her everywhere, showing her everything.

Every noon she kept Freddy waiting when he called to whirl her off to a long, guffy lunch, after it whirling her back to the Grand Hotel Villa Serbelloni for her siesta, during which he, in his panama hat, would snore in a deckchair directly under her window. They drank afternoon tea on so many different terraces that their names became a jumble in her memory – Stresa, Cannobio, Lugano, Varese, Bellano... Having eaten, between them, as many pastries as six children of fourteen, he would drive on to some other terrace for their aperitif; and on to a third for dinner, which always finished so late – especially if there were dancing; he was like a stork waltzing with a robin – that she was never in bed until long after midnight.

Debauched by pity, corrupted by kindness, demoralized by all the deceits he forced on her, she had no desire but to please him, to be his friend, nurse, slave, handmaiden, ayah, confidante, governess, scheherazade, or – her own words, spoken silently one exasperated night through the wide-open windows of her bedroom to the gigantic stars – whatever in God's name it was that this poor, good, kind, dignified, dotty, deceived man wanted her to be or to do. For him she only wanted one thing: to fatten him – whence those piles of pastries that served only to fatten her. From him she wanted only one small thing: that he might kiss her just once before they parted forever.

As the days and the nights peeled away and she could not do the first and he apparently had no desire to do the second, she became so frustrated, nervous and bewildered – Could he be what they call impotent? – that she led him, one night after dinner, up into the dark gardens behind the Villa d'Este, hoping that the stars, the dark and the view might inspire him to do something else beside talk to her. Whereupon, as they sat on a stone bench among the plumes of the cypresses, under a statue that was more shade than stone, a fountain more whisper than water, the light across the lake quivering in the warm air like the fireflies at their feet, dance music thrumming far below them, she became terrified to recall how, in her teens, in their basement kitchen in Dublin, their old servant Molly Power had told her, screaming with laughter, about the night in her own teens when her fellow took her up into the dark of Killiney Hill, and made her lie among the furze and take off every stitch of her clothes so that he could have a good look at her. ('And the blooming furze sticking into me bottom like needles!') Heart pounding, she waited. At last he touched her hand.

'Look, Marianna, how the stars lie in the laps of the mountains like little babies! See how the night passes. So our life passes. As the Reverend Macandrew says, only truth, like love, lasts forever.'

Then he led her gently back, down to the lakeside, to sit and talk some more on the terrace, while she felt as wicked as if she had been trying to seduce a vicar and as exhausted as if she had succeeded.

So far as she could see he appeared to want nothing at all but to take her life in exchange for his. But what was his life? There were mornings when, breakfasting drowsily, she doubted everything about him. How did she know he was even a count? Paola could have lied about that. But unless everybody else, in the Villa d'Este, the Villa Serbelloni, on the Isola Comacina, in all the other grand places he took her to were also taking part in a conspiracy to deceive her . . . Poor and odd he might be. He *was* Count Algardi. But all this talk about his miserable youth? If she even knew where he lived. If, instead of wandering with her around these lakes he was walking with her around Milan, showing her where he lived, and worked; the house where he grew up as a boy; where he went to school; the garden where his mamma cut the lilies.

She thought of writing to Paola Buononcini. 'Dear Paola, I know that this must sound a curious request that I am about to make to you. Yet, you are a woman of the world who knows the hearts of men, and you will, I am sure, sympathize with the strange predicament of an older woman who . . .' Who what? 'Dear Paola, I feel myself impelled to thank you with all the sincerity of my heart for so generously sharing with me the friendship of your charming friend, Freddy Algardi, who . . .' Who what? Who nothing! 'Yet, I must also confide to you that in my heart I find him . . .' She could see Paola showing the letter around among her gang in Forte dei Marmi. They would crowd over her shoulder. They would roll on the sand laughing themselves sick over her. She thought of calling on Toni. But Toni was related to him, and indebted to him, and there, in terror, she suddenly felt the ultimate isolation of every traveller who, no matter how well he may speak a foreign tongue, can be defeated by the movement of a thumb.

She tried to probe and trap him.

'Freddy, have you written to Paola?'

'Why should I?'

'Have you rung her? Has she rung you?'

He smiled. A shoulder stirred. An eyelid moved.

'Why should she? She has fixed everything the way she wants it. Or so she thinks.'

'Did you always dance as well as this, Freddy?'

'My mamma disapproved of dancing. I had to take lessons secretly. Even when I was thirty I still had to steal out to dancehalls. I never dared go to invitation dances. Her spies would have told her at once.'

'Were they nice dancehalls?'

'Nice? They were rough, gay, noisy places. Nice?' A hand stirred. '*Popolare*. Away out beyond the cemeteries. I used to wear an old trenchcoat and a cap, and go there on the tramway, through the fog. She drove me to such places. It was her own fault. But you? Ah, you! You went to Hunt Balls! Yes?'

'Of course! Every year. Twice a year sometimes.'

'With pipers? And harpers? I can see the whirling kilts. The tartan shawls flying. And other dances? Tell me about them all!'

'You mean Harvest Home dances? And there were Birthday dances, too. And there were the Pony Club dances. And we always had Coming of Age dances, with all the tenantry lighting great bonfires down the avenue. Freddy! Are there brothels in Milan?'

'What a question!'

'But are there?'

'By the score! Or so I would guess.'

She was afraid to pursue the subject.

'Did you ever get drunk, Freddy?'

'That reminds me. What exactly does go into a stirrup cup?'

'Mulled wine. Freddy, you must have enjoyed something! The opera? Used you to take your girl friend to the opera?'

'A girl? To the opera? Alone? In Milan? My dear Marianna, nobody is ever alone in Milan! We went to the opera *en famille*, and only on opening nights, and only to certain operas of which my mamma approved. And while I was doing that, bored to death, think of what you were doing! Wandering with a lantern through your dark fields, spying on elves, goblins, ghosts and fairies. Oh, please tell me all about them, Marianna.'

'Well, it is more in the mornings, you know, that one sees the fairies. Ghosts only at night. Banshees at any time. Elves, very rarely.'

'Tell me!'

Indulgently, she led him by the hand on summer mornings, at sunrise, over the dew-grey grass to pick newborn mushrooms, and watch the leprechauns running away in all directions. She told him every fairy story she had ever read. He listened with her to the dogs at dawn, baying death-warnings, to ghostly whisperings winding down the chimneys on stormy nights. He straightway demanded brigands. She drew the line at that. Instead, she let him see the I.R.A. peeping from behind every tree. Weakly, since he insisted so strongly on it, she allowed them a dirk or two.

'Freddy, there is one thing I'd love to do with you – visit your mamma's grave in Milan.'

'My mamma is buried in Turin.'

'Your father's grave?'

'He was drowned while sailing off Genoa. The body was never recovered.'

She gave it up. She felt, if not happiest, most content, or at least most relieved, when they did not talk at all; seasoned comrades who only needed a glance or a smile to feel the pulse in one another's veins: as when they saw the crescent moon, whose fullness they knew they would not share, look tenderly at itself in the mirror of Orta; or when they stood hand in hand before an orange sun slowly drowning into the mist of Mergozzo; though she did mock him amiably for showing her such expansive lakes and, out of Italian vainglory, calling them small.

'You should see my little loch at Doon Castle! It is hardly big enough for the coots to swim about without bumping one another. I swim there in my pelt every morning.' Just for that, he roused her very early on the morning of their last day, drove her up into the Val Tellina and on and up to the Val del Bitto as far as the village of Gerola Alta. There he left the car and bullied her into panting and puffing, protesting every foot of the way, for another thousand feet to a dammed loch on the northern base of a mountain that he called the Three Men. As they lay there, beside one another, after eating the sandwiches and drinking the white wine that he had brought in an Alitalia carry-all, gazing either into one another's eyes or beyond one another's shoulder at the serrated snow-tipped Alps, her heart burned with happiness that he should have gone to so much trouble to share his lakes with her down even to this last, lost, tiny loch. She became even more happy and more fond of him when he boasted that there was not a pass in Lombardy that he had not climbed on foot when he had been young enough to do it – this at least the poor, unhappy boy had wrested from his miserable youth. They stood up, arms about waists, while he indicated, far and wide, some of the ways that he had gone. Just then a drone in the sky made her lift her swimming eyes to a plane that might be her plane tomorrow, which made him look down at her, say, 'Now your blue lakes tend upwarrrds,' and kissed her parted lips. At once her arms snapped tight about his neck, gripping him close until their mouths had to part for air. 'Again!' she implored, her hand pressing him by his poll into so wild and prolonged a kiss that he became lost to everything until she released him with a gasp. He then saw that she had shaken out her black hair and that her unzipped parakeet frock was shivering to the ground.

'Marianna! What on earth are you doing?'

'The heat! The sun! The wind!' and dragged his hands by the wrists about her bare waist. 'My darling, I want to take off everything for you!'

And even before he had disengaged himself she had unfastened her brassiere, dragged down one strap and exposed one bursting nippled breast.

'Marianna!' he cried, his joined palms jigging in imploration. 'Not now! Not yet! Not here! We must wait until we get Aunt Rosa's permission. When I come to Ireland next month!'

In the silence – even the high drone of the plane had faded – she felt a cold wisp of fog creeping about her thighs. She drew back from him, her arms across her bosom, her eyes staring up at him like a terrified Magdalen.

'What did you say?' she whispered. 'Until you come to *Ireland*? To ask Aunt Rosa *what*?'

Solicitously he knelt to draw up her fallen frock about her hips.

'Aunt Rosa is your guardian, Marianna. I must naturally ask her permission to marry you.'

'To . . . Did you say to marry me?'

'Dress, my darling, there's a sudden fog coming.' And when they both looked about them every hollow was a white lake and the whole plain back to Milan a grey sea. 'You must have known, Marianna! I have been thinking of nothing else since the first moment I saw you!'

'You must be out of your mind, Freddy, I could never marry you. It would be... It would be... It would be most unsuitable, it would be ridiculous, it would be impossible in every way. Me? You? Ireland? I am an old, middle-aged woman. O God, I didn't even tell you the truth about that. I'm forty-one, Freddy. And I have nothing.'

Embarrassed, horrified, ashamed, weeping, she began to dress, and tie up her hair into a knot because she had lost all her hairpins. He lifted his arms to the sky.

'And what have I? I live down there,' throwing one arm back across the plain, 'in three rooms with my mamma's old sister Tanta Giuletta. I am so poor I eat pasta twice a day. I wash my own shirts. I press my own trousers. I go shopping with a little basket. I say to the butcher, "Give me some cheap meat for my little dog", and he knows well that I have no little dog, but because he has known me for years he throws in a good piece of meat for myself and Tanta Giuletta. If you marry me you would live with us. And after all, old Tanta Giuletta can't live forever. I would be happy with you if we lived in a cave. We could make such a lovely world together. We would imagine our world so beautifully that everybody who knew us would think that any other sort of world is a lie.'

She turned her back on him. She looked at the Alps, cold, pure, lofty, remote. She spoke quietly to them.

'I told you lies. I don't live the way I told you I live. I made it all up. I deceived you in everything.'

Behind her back he spoke just as quietly.

'You deceived me in nothing. I know all about you. Paola told me. All mothers are spies. Her mother wrote to her about us. Paola is a bitch in the manger. Even when she doesn't want a thing or a person for herself she hates anybody else to have it. She wrote to me five days ago, a mean, bitchy, jealous letter. About Castle Doon, and the paying guests, and you living in the gate lodge.'

'A penniless retainer?'

'She did not use the word. She wrote in Italian. She said *una stipendiata*.'

She turned on him, blazing.

'Then why did you drag me down like that? Why did you go on making me tell you those stupid, stupid, stupid lies?'

His hands pleaded.

'They were not lies, Marianna. It was just a game we began to play that first night in the Villa d'Este. You were so shy, and so innocent, and so lovely – and all those puffed-up, snobby Milanese about us, bloody Fascisti the whole lot of them – I knew them, my father knew them – and you and I worth a thousand of them. It was my way of telling you what we both really are. Then I went on with it to make our holiday more fun.'

The veined nose, the baggy eyes, the hollow cheeks and stooped back of a defeated old man. His white hair blew across his forehead like dust. She touched his hanging hand. Hopelessly she shook her head.

'Let's go down, Freddy. I must pack. Thank you for everything. You gave me a lovely time. But you made one mistake. You gave me the last thing on earth that I want from anybody. You pitied me.'

And ran through the mist down the path to Gerola farther and farther from his wild, beseeching cries to come back to him, to wait for him, to come back to him, to come back. He must have stumbled as he leaped after her, for it was a long time before he appeared beside his white car, his beginning and his end. His trousers were torn, there was dried blood on his cheek, his right hand was wrapped in his silk handkerchief. In the silence of a fallen tower they drove back to the hotel, where, as he scrambled from the car, he called after her that he would come for her at eight o'clock.

'Our last dinner, Marianna!'

When he came he was handed a note from her saying that she was too upset to join him. All he could do was to leave a note for her saying that he would call for her at eleven in the morning to drive her to the airport. When he did come, the majordomo had to tell him, sympathetically, that she had taken the seven o'clock steamer for Cadenabbia; from there, one presumed, gone by bus to Milan. Freddy glanced at his lean wrist. He could still catch up with her. He descended to the *piazzetta* for a coffee. He had his pride.

For months she expected that he would write, was relieved when he did not, half-hoped for a Christmas card and was again glad that he sent none. She had almost succeeded in putting him out of her mind when, one May morning at the family breakfast table, she heard Aunt Rosa utter an exclamation of surprise and looked up to see her beaming over her half-moon glasses and holding up a big gilt-edged card for them all to see.

'A wedding! And guess who? Our little Paola Buononcini.' (Mary Anne felt her heart go burp.) '*To*,' Aunt Rosa read out, '*il conte Federico Amadeo Emmanuele Levashov-Algardi*.' She turned eagerly to her niece. 'Mary Anne, surely you wrote to me last June that when you met Paola she was with a Count Something-or-other. Could he be the same man? But you said he was an old man. Or did you? What was his name?'

'Count Federico Algardi. I said he was an old friend of the family.'

'What an extraordinary coincidence! Was he, in fact, old? What was he like? Tell us all about him. Is he very rich? If I know anything about Paola Buononcini he must be stinking rich. Or else his pedigree must go back to Romulus and Remus.'

'No, he is not old. Though he is not young, either. He is very handsome, and very dashing. He could be forty-five. I took it that he was very wealthy. He drove an immense white car. An Alfa-Romeo, I think it was. But he did not speak at all. It was at the airport and he just drove us to the Hotel Serbelloni. After that he vanished.'

'Mary Anne, how tiresome of you! You never do notice anybody.' She looked again at the card. 'Well, well, so our little Paola is about to become a countess.'

She glanced at Geraldine, sighed, spread her ringed fingers and, with a long accusatory look, passed the card to her. And this, Mary Anne thought, staring sidewards at his printed name, is the man who once dreamed of innocence, and purity, and honesty and true love. She cradled her teacup in her palms and looked across its rim at the snow-tipped Alps, the sun burning the valleys to dust, the blue lakes dreaming of the sky. He had whispered, 'Now your blue lakes tend upwarrrds,' and kissed her. She closed her eyes and smiled.

'I see,' Aunt Rosa said brightly to Geraldine, 'that she is going to be married next month.'

'Sweating,' Geraldine laughed coarsely, 'like a June bride.'

She opened her eyes wide. Another Paola? Jealous, greedy and envious, and in that second she understood it all. His kiss had been his one, last feeble cry for help. She hesitated. Then, imperceptibly, her head shook. It would not have been honest, and it would not have worked. But nothing he had ever done ever had worked. Nothing ever would work. However! He'd had something. They had both had something. Something precious, brief and almost true that, she felt proudly certain, neither of them would ever forget.

Feed My Lambs

It is about eleven o'clock of a sunny September morning in late September. The unfrequented road that crosses the level bogland from skyline to skyline passes on its way a few beech trees, a white cottage fronted by a small garden still bright with roses and snapdragons, a cobbled path and a small wooden gate bearing, in white celluloid letters, the name *Pic du Jer*. In the vast emptiness of the bog these unexpected and inexplicable beech trees, the pretty cottage, the tiny garden, the cobbled path suggest only a dream in the mind of somebody who, a long time back, thought better of it, or died, or gave up the struggle with the bog.

A young woman in an apron as blue as the sky is sweeping a few fallen beech leaves along the cobbles. She is bosomy, about thirty, with amber hair, and eyelids as big as the two half-domes of an eggshell. Looking idly towards the west she observes, far away, a flash of sunlight. She gives it one thoughtful glance and resumes her sweeping. Whoever the motorist is, he will come and go as slowly as a dot of light emerging from one mirror and as slowly dwindling into another. The bog is as immense as it is flat. It swallows everything.

Pic du Jer? A mountain peak? Asked why, Rita Lamb always says, in her usual saucy, self-mocking way, one quizzical eyebrow cocked: 'Yerrah, it's an old mountain near Lourdes. You go up to it in the funicular. It's where I climbed to the pic of my career. It's where I met Jer.' If she admitted that she really met Jer at the foot of the peak, in the waiting funicular, it would spoil the joke. It would be no joke at all if she said, 'It's where I met Father Tom.'

Under the final whisk of her broom the leaves rustle out through the garden gate. She looks again. The car is half a mile away. Her hands tighten on the broom handle. The cups of her eyelids soar, she runs indoors, tearing off her blue apron, looks at herself in the mirror, punches the cushions of her minute parlour, looks into the sideboard to be sure there is a bottle or two there, and out at the gate again just in time to greet Father Tom with a delighted grin. He has never failed her. He drops in at least three or four times a year, either on his way up to Dublin or on his way back to his parish on the far side of the Shannon. She takes his overcoat, indicates the settee, and begins to make his usual drink, Irish coffee.

'Now!' she says pertly as a parrot. 'What's y'r news? Tell me everything.'

'I'll tell you one thing, Rita,' he laughs. 'You haven't changed one iota since the first day I met you.'

That day, waiting for the funicular to start, the four of them had got talking at once: the two priests, herself and Jer. The older priest – rosy, bony and bald, easygoing and poorly dressed, his waistcoat flecked brown from his scented snuff – simply leaned across and took her paperback from her hand: Franz Werfel's *Song of Bernadette*.

'Not bad,' he conceded, 'For a modern novel. Tell me, my child, did you ever read a novel by Canon Sheehan called *My New Curate?*'

At this, the young priest had pulled down his elegant white cuffs, and all in one breath laughed, groaned, sighed and said, 'Here we go again. Poor old Tom Timlin off to the guillotine once more.'

'Indeed and I did read it,' Rita gushed. 'I think I've read every single thing Canon Sheehan wrote.'

Father Jordan patted her knee.

'Good girl! Most of ye read nothing nowadays but dirty books like the one his reverence here gave me the other day by some young trollop named . . . What was this her name is, Father Timlin?'

'Miss Edna O'Brien,' the young priest said, his natural courtesy qualified by an over-patient smile.

'A fine Irish name! It was the only decent thing about her rotten book. I nearly shoved it behind the fire it made me so mad! Upon my word, Father, I don't know for the life of me what you want to be reading books like that for.'

Father Tom folded the crease of his trousers over his knee and observed urbanely that it is one's duty to know what young people are thinking nowadays.

'After all, one belongs to one's contemporaries, Father Jordan, as Simone de Beauvoir puts it.'

'I read her, too!' Rita exclaimed, and blushed wildly, suddenly remembering the picture of a completely naked woman on the cover of her contraband copy of *The Second Sex*, and how its first chapter was all about the machinery of the inside of a woman and the outside of a man. 'I forget now what book by her it was that I read. I think it was a travel book about France.'

'You probably read *The Second Sex*,' Father Tom said dryly. 'Quite an interesting study. It's a pity she has no sense of humour. Sex can be funny, too.'

The old man threw him a cold look. 'In this excellent novel by the late Canon Sheehan,' he persisted, 'there is a poor old parish priest like myself who has the life plagued out of him by his new curate.'

'I remember the two of them well,' said Rita, patting his knee as approvingly as he had patted hers, 'and, do you know, I felt very sorry for the pair of them.'

'The part I love,' he said with relish, 'is where this poor old P.P. walks in one day into his curate's room and finds him if you please, playing the piano and singing some sloppy German love song about "Roselein, Roselein, Roselein buck – Roselein auf dem heiden"? Wasn't that how the song went, Father?'

Father Tom coughed and said that, yes, it was, indeed, something on those lines.

'Well! Father Timlin here is *my* new curate and he has me plagued out with Italian. Always playing Italian operas on the gramophone. In Italian if you please! Always throwing around words like *Giovannismo*, and *ecumenismo*, and *aggiornamento*, and what's that other word you have, Father, that sounds like an Italian racing car?'

'*La gioventù!*' Father Timlin cried eagerly, and threw his hands out to the two young people seated opposite them. 'And here we have them! Youth at the helm!'

The old priest winked at them.

'He is ancient, you see. He is twenty-six.'

'Ah!' Father Tom said enthusiastically. 'There's nothing like youth. Married or engaged?' he asked.

Rita and the young man beside her looked at one another. He observed that she had eyes as big as a cow, eyelids as sleepy as a cow, soft hair the colour of a Jersey cow, and that she was very well made around the brisket. She liked his grin, his white teeth and his warm voice as he answered. 'We are not even acquainted yet, Father. We just met this minute.'

Father Jordan roared with delight.

'There you are,' he nudged his curate. 'Crashing in as usual.'

'Only anticipating, maybe,' the young priest said, unabashed, and they all introduced themselves. Father Malachy Jordan, P.P., and Father Tom Timlin, C.C., from the parish of Annabwee in the County Galway; Jerry Lamb, farmer and butcher, from Barron in the County Kildare; and Rita Lyons, schoolmistress, from Doon in the County Westmeath; at which point the funicular gave a jolt and they started to climb.

'Talking of marriages,' said Father Tom, paying no attention at all to the descending landscape, 'I suppose ye know that Lourdes is a great place for matchmaking? The best Catholic families in France come here with their children. We have a count, and a prince, and their wives and children in our hotel. The idea is that the best young people in France meet, and if they like one another ... well, you never know your luck.'

Jerry Lamb chuckled.

'It would be one of the unrecorded miracles of Lourdes if I met a princess here and took a shine to her – and she to me!'

Father Tom waved his hand with a man-of-the-world air.

'It would be no miracle at all! We get all kinds in Lourdes. All sorts and sizes come here to see the pilgrimages, Buddhists, Jews, Muslims, Communists, atheists, everybody!'

Rita turned sideways to consider Mr Lamb.

'Wouldn't that be a good joke,' she said, 'if your Catholic princess met a Communist who was a roaring atheist and took a shine to him?'

The old priest's palms applauded silently, but the young priest was unquashable.

'It might be an excellent thing for them both. She might convert him and he might broaden her.'

'Ha!' said his PP sourly. 'She might! And so might a mouse! And supposing they did get married? A mixed marriage! And what about the children? If they had any children!'

Father Tom smiled benevolently.

'Ah, now, Father, you must admit that since the *Concilio* the attitude of the church to mixed marriages has greatly relaxed. And as for the question of having children, that will come too. Do you believe in large families, Mr Lamb?' he asked their butcher.

'I wouldn't be averse to two or three. Or at most four.'

'Two or three?' Father Jordan said sadly. 'I was the youngest of

twelve. Brought up on a scrawny thirty-five-acre farm west of
Ballinasloe. An acre to the cow, they say, and three acres to the child,
we cut it fine.'

'I was the youngest of six myself,' from Father Tom.

'Ai, ai, ai! Father Jordan sighed. 'I suppose this is your *aggiornamento.*' He gazed into a distant valley. 'My mother was one of fifteen.
Twelve of us. Six of you. Mr Lamb here would like three. And if you
have three I suppose they will want one apiece. We progress!'

'What I'd like,' Rita said, looking pensively out over the distant
Pyrenees, 'would be to have a boy and a girl.'

'Two?' Father Tom asked her amiably. 'Four?' he asked Jerry Lamb.
'Why don't ye split the difference and make it three?' – at which Father
Jordan asked him if he was getting a percentage on this, and all four
of them laughed, and the funicular stopped and all the passengers
except Rita looked down.

'Maybe they want us to enjoy the view?' Jer suggested.

'My sister Joanie has seven children,' Rita said to the sky. 'She is
married to a clerk. He gets eleven pounds a week. Seven children. And
they are only married seven years.'

'Fine!' Father Jordan said to the valley. 'Splendid! A proud and happy
mother!'

Rita's mouth tightened. Father Tom was watching her closely.

'Is she happy?' he asked, stressing quietly.

'Tell me, Father,' Rita said to him, 'what's all this about the Pill?'

'It is forbidden,' the old priest said shortly.

'Well, now,' the young priest temporized, 'it is certainly not
authorized. But it is still under discussion. I hope,' he added, looking
around at the crowded carriage, 'we're not stuck forever?'

'Are we stuck?' Father Jordan asked an old Frenchwoman across the
aisle from him, and her husband turned back from where he was
looking up the peak to say that the one coming down was stuck too.
Jer and the old priest crossed over to look out. Father Tom was left with
Rita. She was staring moodily at the sky. He leaned forward, elbows
on thighs.

'You are very silent, Rita.'

She said nothing.

'What is on your mind?'

'Nothing.'

'There is something. What is it?

Struck by the kindness in his voice, she slewed her eyes towards him, and for the first time took stock of him. He had sandy hair; his eyelashes were golden fair; his eyes were as bright blue as a Siamese cat's; he reminded her of her brother who was a sailor. She hesitated. Then she spoke very softly: 'I was remembering why I came to Lourdes.'

'Why did you?'

'Everybody comes to Lourdes to pray for something. I prayed that my sister Joanie won't have any more children. And if I ever get married that I'll only have two.'

He looked at her mischievously. She was to become familiar with that mischievous, mocking way of his – his way of calming her, of calling her to use her commonsense.

'When I was young, Rita, I had a small sister who was mad about a sort of sweet called bull's-eyes. The nuns told her one day to pray to the Blessed Virgin to break her of the habit.'

'And did she?' Rita asked with interest.

'She got a terrible pain in her stomach one day and that cured her. Rita! Which are you? Dying to be married, or afraid to be married?'

'I don't want to have a child every year for the rest of my blooming life.'

He smiled at her. She looked away, annoyed.

'Father, you're like every priest. Ye know all about theology and ye know nothing about feelings. Would you like to have a child every year of your life?'

'Not unless I was a rabbit. Still, nathless, and howbeit, and quid pro quo, and all things being carefully considered, and so on, you would like to get married?'

'I'm human.'

'I should hope so, if that means that you are a normal woman with the normal longings and desires of a woman.'

She faced him crossly, at a disadvantage. If he had been a man she could tell him!

'How do I know what I am?'

'Everybody knows what he is. You've had boy friends, haven't you?'

'Yes.' Then she said coldly, 'Am I going to confession to you?'

'Oh, come off it, girl! This talk about confession that women go on with! Why wouldn't you have boy friends? Anyway, nobody confesses any more to a priest. The priest today is only a kind of spiritual telephone operator. To what part of the otherworld do you want a trunk call today, madam? For all faults, inquiries and difficulties kindly dial Tom Timlin, C.C.'

She laughed.

'But you listen in!' she pointed out.

'And interpret now and again. And add up the charges. Come now, Rita! Face up to yourself.' He chuckled at her. '*Vide, visse, amò*. She saw, she lived, she loved. You embraced. You kissed. And you hated it like poison!'

'I did not!' she said furiously. 'I liked it.'

'As *il buon Dio* intended you to. "So long as things are", Saint Augustine said, and he was a tough man, "they are good". Kissing is like Guinness, Rita. It's good for you. The *osculum* . . .'

'The what?'

'The kiss on the cheek.'

His eyes were mocking her again. She waved an airy hand.

'The *basium*. On the lips.'

Even more jauntily, she waved the other hand.

'The *suavium*?' and he shrugged.

She waved both her hands and was enraged with herself for blushing; and more enraged when he laughed delightedly.

Jer turned back to them and shouted, 'I think it is a life sentence!'

'Anyway,' she protested, 'that's all damn fine,' not quite knowing what was fine, 'but seven kids in seven years? Eight in eight? Nine in nine?'

He glanced across the carriage to where Father Jordan and Jerry Lamb were now trying out their French on the old French lady and her husband.

'You can only do your best, Rita,' he said gently. 'When any man or woman comes to me with your problem all I ever say is, "You can only do your best". If I was speaking as your spiritual telephone operator I'd always say, "He is saying, you can only do your best".'

She glared down at the huddled red roofs of Lourdes until he thought she was going to throw herself out. Then she breathed out a long sigh of exasperation.

'These last three days,' she said, 'I was so happy down there.'

He gave her a melancholy laugh. He looked down at the basketful of roofs.

'Ai! Ai! – as Father Jordan says. Such a mixture! The lovely and the tawdry, sincerity and sentimentality, lies and truth, God and Mammon. It would remind you of life! And here we are now like Mahomet's coffin slung halfway between . . . Where was it slung? I always imagine it was held up between walls of magnetic forces. Impossible?' He paused. 'You mustn't be afraid, Rita.' She kept staring sulkily down at the roofs. 'No woman can do more than her best.' This time he was silent a long while. 'I'd say that to you anytime, anywhere.'

He watched her. She got the point. She smiled at him:

'I have a car. Sometime I might pay you a visit.'

'Do!'

'But you will never know.'

'I will never know. All I will hear will be a voice. It will come and go. Like a bird singing in flight.'

The carriage jolted a little, started to move, and the whole carriage cheered and laughed. Father Jordan and Jer rejoined them.

'*E pur si muove!*' Father Tom cried. 'Galileo. The world does go around the sun. Though I'm not sure Father Jordan entirely believes it. George Bernard Shaw,' he went on, 'once said that in Ireland we still believe that the world, if not exactly flat, is only very slightly removed from the spherical.'

They all chuckled and began to discuss such important things as whether they could get a cool refreshing drink on top of the mountain.

From the peak they gazed far and wide about them, silenced by the gleaming wings of the Hautes Pyrénées, still snow-covered, and the eyes of the lakes in the far valleys, and Father Tom, who knew his Lourdes, pointed out famous peaks like the Pic du Midi de Bigorre that local mountaineers had mastered at the risk of their lives.

'Glory be to God,' said Father Jordan, 'but it's a hard country! Is it good for anything at all?'

'Sheep,' said Jer. 'And I bet you there's fine grazing up there for the cattle in the summertime.'

'I read in the paper this morning,' said Father Tom, 'that the shepherds are complaining that the wolves aren't being shot.'

'Feed my lambs,' said the old priest, and the two of them drifted around, and Rita and Jer went in search of a beer.

Sitting on a rough bench a little apart from the other tourists, she amused him by telling him what it is like to teach in a nun's school, and he entertained her by telling her what it is like to be a farmer-butcher in a small village in the middle of a bog as flat as a slate. When Father Tom and Father Jordan came by, the old man looked as if he were going to join them, but the curate took him firmly by the arm and pointed off into the distance and drew him away around the corner. Presently Mr Lamb was asking Miss Lyons if she had ever been to Biarritz and when she said no, Mr Lamb said he was going by bus the day after tomorrow, and Miss Lyons said she wondered if she ought not to visit it someday.

'Yerrah, why don't you? You earned it. If you like you could come with me. I'm all on my own.'

'But, Mr Lamb,' she said, floating her eggshell eyelids wide open, 'we are hardly acquainted!' – and when his laugh showed his splendid teeth she laughed too, and he went on laughing because she looked so happy, and had such big droopy eyelids and was well made around the brisket.

Father Tom advanced his empty glass of Irish coffee to Rita sideways along the settee, laughed and clinked it with hers.

'So there you have it! That's all my news. Nothing at all since July. I'm the same old three-and-fourpence I always was and always will be.'

She looked at him affectionately.

'We have no news either! Jer goes on with his butchering. I go on with my sweeping. If you are worth three-and fourpence, then between the three of us we're worth exactly ten bob.'

She took up the empty glasses, the bottle, the cream, and the percolator and started to tidy them on the small dining room table by the window. He looked appreciatively at her straight back and her trim legs.

'Rita!'

She turned, observed him and cocked an alert eye.

'You look as if you are about to give birth to a profound thought?'

'Divil a profound thought! It's just that ever since I came within sight of this little cottage of yours this morning I was thinking how you once said to me, five years ago, "I have a car". And you have never once paid me a visit?'

She came back and sat on the settee.

'You are a low scoundrel, Father Tom. You only thought of that just half an hour ago? And in all those five years you never once thought of it before? The truth isn't in you.'

'Well, I admit I did give it a passing thought now and again. I'm not probing, Rita!'

'You are. And I don't mind. Sure we're always probing one another. When we have no news it's all we ever do.'

'Why didn't you?'

'Do you really want to know? I'll tell you. But I think you will be sorry you asked me. One reason I didn't visit you was because I had no need to. I had nothing to tell you. Or to tell any other priest. Now you know!'

Her left hand lay supine on the settee near his. He laid his right hand on her palm. The palm slowly closed on his fingers.

'Poor Rita! I guessed it must be that way. I'm afraid your family hasn't had much luck with Our Lady?'

'Not with three more babies for my sister, and none for me.'

'And poor Jer, too!'

'Oh, he's accepted it now. At first, he minded an awful lot.'

'What was the other reason?'

She looked down at their two hands. She gave him a long silent look – so long that he peered questioningly at her. She leaned over a little and castled her right hand on his.

'Did it ever occur to you, Father,' she said, 'that from the first day we met you called me Rita? Because you're a priest and that made it all right – for you. But I have never once called you Tom. Because I'm a woman, and that mightn't be quite so safe – for me. I love it when you drop in here, Father, and pop off again after an hour or so. I love the chat. I love the way I can say anything I like to you. I love the way you say anything you like to me. I love all the things we argue about. I look forward to it for weeks. I think about it for weeks after you've gone. And that's not just because it's lonely out here on this empty old bog. Now and again friends of Jerry's drop in, and I like them to call too, but I never think of them when they're gone, and if they never came again I wouldn't miss them. I love you to come because you are you. Still, so far, I've always managed to remember that you are a priest and I am a married woman. The other reason I did not visit you is because if I started meeting you outside of here it would be very different. It would be admitting to myself that I am fond of you as a man.'

His golden eyelashes fell. She removed her hand. He laid his on his knee.

'Well?' she asked tartly. 'What's wrong with you? Am I to be the only one to tell the truth today? Or did none of this ever occur to you?'

'You are a wonderful woman, Rita! You are the most honest being I have ever met.'

'Is that all you can say to me?'

'It is all I dare say to you. What the hell is the good of anybody saying anything if he can do nothing about it? What would you want me to say? That I love you? When neither you nor I can ever prove it!'

She shook her amber head at him.

'Well, there's the cat out of the bag at last! Tom! You should never have been a priest. The first day I met you I knew it.'

'Why didn't you say so then?'

'Would it have made any difference?'

He jumped up, walked away from her, whirled and cried, 'I don't know! I was younger then!'

She rose and went over so close to him that he could hear her breathing.

'And now,' she taunted, 'you are a feeble old man?'

He flung his arms around her and kissed her on the mouth. She held his kiss. Then she drew away from him and laid her finger gently but imperatively on his mouth.

'The *basium*?' she mocked. 'You've come a long way in five years, Tom.'

'Do you realize you are the first girl I ever kissed!'

'I do. And I'm the last. You can never come here again.'

He walked away from her and looked angrily at her.

'Is that what you wanted, talking the way you did on that settee?'

'I merely answered your question. I warned you that you might be sorry. You asked for the truth. And you put an end to our story.'

'You didn't have to answer me!'

'I had to. Because immediately you asked me I knew what I'd never let myself know before. And I knew that we both knew it. And I knew something else too. That if it didn't end one day we would explode, and then we'd be torturing one another for the rest of our lives.'

He stared wildly around him.

'There is no sense nor meaning to this. It doesn't hang together. All I ever wanted was a bit of friendship. A bit of companionship. There's nobody else in the world I can talk to but you. That day I first met you I knew that here was somebody at last that I could talk to. Maybe that I could help. That I'd be a better priest if I could . . .'

'Tom! It's long ago that I told you that you knew all about theology and all that stuff, and nothing about feelings. Now you know better! This is what love is like.'

He glared at her in misery and longing. Then, suddenly, he calmed, and then as suddenly broke into a long peal of laughter, at himself, at both of them, at the whole of life.

'Honest to God, Rita! You're worth fifty priests. You're worth a thousand of us. And I that began it all by trying to educate the simple, ignorant schoolteacher! Well, I may have learned slow, but you learned damn fast. Where the hell, Rita, did you learn all you know?'

'Where every woman learns everything. In bed. Am I shocking you? Because if I am, then you really are getting very old.'

He considered her answer bitterly.

'The one classroom no priest ever visits. And I suppose the only one that ever tells anyone anything about the nature of love. So! That's it. I'm never to see you again?'

'Why not? I will go my way. You will go yours. If I live I will become an old woman. If you live you will become an old, old parish priest like poor old Father Malachy Jordan.'

'My God! If Father Jordan was alive today and knew about you and me he'd break his heart laughing at me for a botch of a priest and a fool of a man!'

She flashed out angrily at him. He had never seen her so angry.

'Stop that, Tom! Stop it at once! Never say that again! Never think it! I liked you that day in Lourdes because you were honest with me. I grew fond of you, I fell in love with you if you want the whole bloody truth, because you went on being honest with me. You will always be honest, and you will always be a better priest than old Jordan ever was because you will always remember that, if it was only for one minute of your life, you loved your woman and kissed her. When you run yourself down you are only cheapening yourself and cheapening me. I won't have that! I'm not sorry for anything we've done. I'm proud of it.'

Far away a bell gently, faintly tolled. She listened. 'There's the angelus bell in Barron.' Suddenly she became the bright, capable housewife. 'Jer will be back in an hour. Will you stay and have lunch with us, Tom?'

'No!' he said brusquely, and grabbed his overcoat and dived into it. 'But there's one thing I'll tell you, Rita!' He snatched up his hat and gloves. 'If I met you not five years ago but ten I'd have given up God Himself for you!'

He went out the door and down the cobbled path. She followed slowly after him. At the wicket-gate he paused and looked up and down the long, empty road.

'I'll never pass this road again.' He flipped his gloves against the white celluloid letters on the gate. 'Why did you call it Pic du Jer?'

He watched her great eyelids drooping. He watched the sinking of her amber head. She spoke as softly as if she were whispering to the three foreign words.

'To remind me of you.'

She did not raise her head again until his car started and his wheels spurned the gravel of the road. Then she walked out to the middle of the road to watch him dwindling away, from her into infinity, diminishing like a dot of light until he vanished out of sight.

She looked around the level bog. Miles away the blue smoke of a turfcutter's fire rose out of the flat emptiness straight up into the blue sky. She heard nothing. Then she heard a soft wind and raised her eyes to the blue above her. A host of swallows were flying south. She watched them until they, too, became lost to sight. Soon it would be winter. The rains and the fogs. She turned briskly indoors to prepare a meal for her man.

Only once did she pause in her task, the knife in one fist, the apple in the other, to look out of the window and murmur aloud to herself, 'I know what he'll do. It's what I'd do. Drive past me every time he goes to Dublin.' She added, 'Until it wears off,' and went on with her work.

Our Fearful Innocence

My name is Jerry Doyle. J. T. Doyle, B.E. I am the County Engineer for
W——. I have made this town my home since I first came here as
Assistant C.E. twenty-one years ago. I am a bachelor. Aged forty-six.
I live in this half-comfortable converted flat on the first story of Jack
Jennings's old wreck of a house on Martin's Quay. He lives above me.
Our housekeeper lives above him, although she is beginning to say that
the stairs get longer every year. Below me is Jack's shop. He is a ship
chandler. Or was.

It is such a warm evening that I am sitting in my shirtsleeves by the
open window, with my pipe, and a glass of whiskey in my fist – and
this old red-covered notebook of Jill Jennings's on my lap. I have been
playing golf all day, our own course, above the town, the bay and the
sea, my lungs so full of fresh air that I feel too lazy to do anything but
look out at the seagulls wheeling like ... well, as Jill once said,
wheeling like seagulls. The smoke from Ed Slator's house half a mile
away on Rock Point is as steady as if it was part of the chimney.
Children playing below on the quay. The canon strolling back as usual
to his presbytery, which means that in about fifteen minutes the bell
of Saint Killian's will begin to ring for Benediction. Not that I shall
attend. I do turn up to mass every Sunday, but purely *pro forma*. As the
C.E. I have to keep up appearances. Since what happened to Jill I
believe neither in God nor the Devil. And neither does Jack, whom I
have just heard shuffling about upstairs. The poor old bastard ...

When I first met Jack Jennings he was about forty-two or forty-three;
the grandson of the *Jennings and Son* spelled out in marbled chinaware
lettering on the fascia board over his shop window. He never altered
the form of name on the board. This was stupid of him, and typically
insensitive, because he and Jill had no children. But it was just like him
not to change it – an obstinate, cantankerous old cuss if there ever was
one. After all, when he married Jill Slator he knew he was marrying

into a dynasty famous for long-tailed families. Some of them must often have given that sign a glance that was as good as a process.

I liked Jack from the start, in spite of the seventeen years between us. While he was able to do it we played golf together every weekend. We were never really close to one another, although sometimes we exchanged confidences, mostly about what we chose to call our philosophies. My nickname for him was Zeno because I maintained that he was a born cynic. In revenge he called me Pangloss, the eternal optimist, who 'felt best after meals.' We got on, give and take, kidding, jabbing now and again, never really quarrelling. We got on – the way people always do in small towns. In a big city we might never have bothered about one another. We were an odd pair. We still are. I only gradually realized that Jill was the real bond between us. As she still is.

She was ten years younger than him when she married him. She was about thirty-two when I first met her, and in spite of the fact that she was much older than me I thought her the most attractive woman I had ever met. I must have said so once too often to my secretary May Hennessy because she infuriated me one day by snorting, 'Of course you're in love with Jill Jennings.' I was so mad with her that I nearly ate her. Then, realizing that nobody would ever call her attractive – the poor thing is no oil painting – I had to explain that all I meant was that what I found 'attractive' about Jill was her personality. At which May snorted again. She is a good secretary but she does speak her mind. Which I like now. In this shut-mouthed town everybody else goes around hinting at things they have not the guts to say straight out the way she does. I used to think that it might be because she travelled abroad every summer, and was always full of talk about France or Portugal or Italy and how free life is there compared to Ireland.

Actually, what first attracted me to Jill Jennings was the way she, too, used to burst out with whatever came into her head. She had wide-open eyes, earnest and challenging. Her profile went with that eagerness, face and figure advanced like a ship's figurehead by the slope of her neck, an effect accentuated by the way her beautifully curved upper lip protruded a shade over her lower lip. I loved the way she greeted me whenever we met in the street, the eyelids lifted delighted to see me but abusing the hell out of me for not visiting her more often.

At thirty-two she still had the face of a girl just let out of convent-school, looking everywhere for this wonderful thing called Life that she and her pals had been talking about, and whispering about, and making big eyes about ever since they realized that within a matter of months they would be – heaven help the poor kids – free. How enchanting young girls are at that age, before vanity: unaware of their own looks, their school berets flat as plates on their heads, their pigtails tied with venom, as uninterested in the crowds on the shore as the morning sea. Within a year it is all gone, they have become demons, vulgarians, simpering at every male across the mirrors of their compacts.

Jill never knew vanity. She had glossy hair, the finest and lightest, always untidy, loosely pinned at the nape of her neck in tiny, wandering downy curls that delighted and disturbed me. If she had any fault her skin was too white. On hot days when her arms and shoulders were exposed I used to feel excited to think that all her body was just as white. She dressed in soft, fluffy blouses, light as shadows, or smoke, billowing carelessly. Being so good-looking, she had no need to bother about dress. Her eyes were as grey-green as that sea out there. There was something of the mermaid about her, so free, so fresh, so restless, landlocked, always hearing sounds or voices beyond the town, outside the harbour, this shallow bay.

I loved this old fabric of a house where she and Jim lived. It is now as rundown as Jim's shop but it must have been a fine house and a good business a hundred years ago before the bay became silted up. Now only a couple of coal-tubs and small cargo vessels occasionally moor at the quays, and even they have to wait on the tide to come in. I see one waiting outside the harbour now. High tide will be around ten o'clock. Then it will have to wind carefully through the buoys marking the channels to the quayside.

I loved to visit them on nights when the east wind rattled their windows or blew white spindrift across the water, nights when the three of us would sit before the fire and drink a jorum, and have long wandering arguments about the craziest things, always started off by her. 'What is true happiness?' 'Free Will versus Determinism.' One night after she had been reading some advanced book about religion she suddenly asked, 'Should Faith be based on Life or should Life be based on Faith?' Another night she burst out with 'What is Reality, anyway?' We kept at that one until three o'clock in the morning. Last winter I took down one of her books, *Madame Bovary*, by Flaubert, and when

I came on Emma and her lover talking for hours about Great Art I thought to myself, 'That fellow had us cold!' There was no other house in town where I could have arguments like that. All they talk about is golf, and bridge, and business. But I liked best of all to visit her when she was alone. Otherwise, she tended to take possession of me, ignoring Jack – I do not believe he had read a dozen books in his whole life – lounging on the other side of the fire, puffing his pipe, staring glumly into the fire.

Like that wild March night, in my third year in W———. A force-ten gale howling outside, the rain turning to sleet that threatened any minute to become snow. Jill and I were gabbling away about a performance of *The Three Sisters* that I had driven her up to Dublin to see two months before. Jack, who had obstinately refused to come with us, was saying nothing. Just staring into the fire. From that she went on to talk about the Russian ballet – she had been reading Karsavina's memoirs and she had once been to see a ballet in London. I was not saying much. I was lying back in the old armchair before the fire, between the two of them, enjoying her chat, the fire roaring up the chimney at my feet, and the occasional spat of sleet against the windows, pleasantly aware that every street in the town was empty, when, all of a sudden, Jack jumps up, says, 'I think I'll drop down to the Club,' and walks out on us. We listened to him clumping down the stairs and the front door banging. Then I heard the old Jennings and Son signboard below the window twanging and banging like a drum and I realized that on a night like this there would not be a sinner in the Club – unless it was old Campbell the caretaker sitting by the fire gushing smoke every three minutes into the musty billiard room.

'I'm afraid we've been boring Jack,' I said.

For a few moments it was her turn to stare glumly into the fire. Then as if the wind had hit her into a shiver, she shook herself all over, looked wildly all around the room, and cried, 'Then why does he go on living here? This bloody place is choking the life out of the pair of us. It will choke me like a wood if I don't clear out of it. And clear out of it quick!'

'Aha!' I laughed. 'To Moscow? To Moscow?'

She glared, tossed her head, then leaned forward over the arm of my chair and gripped my hand.

'Did it ever cross your mind, Jerry, that if the three sisters in that play had gone to Moscow they might have been just as unhappy there?'

I barely stopped myself from saying that their brother was not all that unhappy – he at least had the comfort of his child. Instead I said hurriedly that, after all, Jim's business was rooted here, and she could not expect him at the drop of a hat to open up another chandler's store in some place where nobody knew him, and she had all her relations here, and after all, this was not such a bad town, it was lovely in the summer, with the bay, and the sea...

She threw away my hand and said crossly:

'Jerry! There is no such place as Moscow. If I went to Moscow I would hear nothing there but the same stupid, empty chitter-chatter that I hear day after day in this bloody town – and nothing at all going on inside me. That play about the three sisters is marvellous because it is all chatter outside, and all silence inside. The summer! Don't talk to me about the summer! On summer evenings I sit by that window for hour after hour looking at the seagulls wheeling like seagulls, or a yacht manoeuvring in or out, or some little cargo boat with Cardiff or Bristol painted on the stern coming alongside Harry Slator's coalyard, or edging out past the lighthouse, and I watch it until it rounds Rock Point past the chemical factory, out to sea. And what do I think of? Nothing! Unless it is about somebody like you whom I know and like. Like you, or May Hennessy who came here a couple of years before you. Another stranger. People who come and who go before this rotten town knocks the truth and the honesty and the guts out of them.'

'Well, it is a fact that May Hennessy is always coming and going. The most travelled woman in W——!'

She snorted at me.

'Is that all you know? May is a friend of mine. I know a lot about May. And May knows a lot about me. May Hennessy hasn't been out of this town for five years.'

'But she is always telling me about her travels! She knows the Continent like the palm of her hand.'

'All out of books. Five years ago May went to Brittany. I said, "Did you enjoy it?" She said, "All I used to do was to walk along the quay and look at the names at the backs of the ships, and think wouldn't it be nice to be going home." Home! All May Hennessy found in Brittany was this town.'

'Then why are you talking about leaving here? I hope you're not serious about that?'

'I am! I am going somewhere where there are no ships coming and no ships going, where there is nothing except me. No! Not even me! Someplace where I will be born all over again.'

I sat straight up.

'You don't mean by any chance that you are thinking of leaving Jack?'

She nodded, took my hand again and stroked it. Completely misunderstanding her, I felt as if the wind had burst roaring in through every window, door and cranny of the house and that it was sinking like a ship under us both.

'Jerry,' she said. 'You are an ambitious man. Aren't you? You want to be the County Engineer. Don't you? To be king of the castle? If you don't go away from here soon, and very soon, you will get exactly that – and this place will knock the truth and the honesty and the guts out of you too.'

On the instant I knew she was right. Because while one side of me was thinking what an honest, outspoken woman she was, the other part of me was thinking all the mean, petty things they would all be thinking, but not saying openly if she did leave Jack – the behind-the-hand whispering, the consternation of the Slators, and finally that total silence when the town would deliberately forget what it did not dare acknowledge.

She rose. I leaped up, and clipped her in my arms. The little curls on her neck seemed so tender and helpless that I wanted to bury my face in them. The smell of her skin overpowered me. I looked into her eyes and noticed what I had never seen before, the way hard, green little flecks pricked their softness. Before I could say what I wanted to say, her fingers stopped my mouth. Then she kissed me, chastely, not the way a woman kisses a man but the way a mother kisses her child. She held me away from her and shook her head.

'No, Jerry! Don't say it! You are not in love with me. You are only in love with an imaginary me. Somebody you've made up inside in your head. I saw it the first day we met.'

'But,' I cried, 'I have only just discovered the real you!'

'And before that? What real me were you in love with then? I am not real, Jerry. I have no world to be real in. Not yet! Now you had better go, before he comes back.'

I was in such a turmoil I could not have stayed near her. I ran out of the room. I felt that if I stayed there for another minute I would start tearing the blouse off her.

When the hall door banged behind me I could hear it echoing up through the hollow house with that muffled sound that always means snow. The quay was already white with it. The whole town was being smothered in it. It clung to the gaslamps. When I came to the door of the Club I could barely see the light through the snow on its fanlight. Just as I passed it I became aware of a stream of light behind me and, turning, I saw him come out and start to beat his way home, head bowed, the snow flecking his hat and his shoulders. He walked against the wind and snow with the gait of an old man. In a moment he vanished into the darkness, as silently as the snow.

Before April ended she had vanished. I did not need to ask anybody what the Slators thought. One day as I was passing Tom Slator's coalyard he hailed me cheerfully and delivered the agreed formula.

'Hello, Jerry! Did you hear the great news? Jill is after buying a country mansion in County B——.' His laughter pealed. Falsely. 'Ach, it's only an old lockhouse on the canal. A little hideaway for themselves. To get away from the roar and the rumble of W——! Hahaha! Of course between you and me I don't believe she'll ever persuade Jack to go down there. It's just another one of her artistic notions.'

It would work, and she would pay for it. To the 'men's club' side of the town she would henceforth be 'odd,' 'queer,' 'difficult,' 'hard to get on with.' The man who remained would always be defended. What a town!

I did not dare visit her until that July. It was not an easy place to find, a small two-story canal house, of no special distinction apart from its age, in a valley between pinewoods filled with shadows and sunbeams, silence and sloth. The noisy humming of flies or bees. A coot clucking. A heron flapping away. The only real sound was from the water gushing between the timbers of the lock gates. For a mile right and left of her cottage the sky dreaming in the smooth water of the canal. For the dozen or twenty days we get of hot summer it would be as lovely a retreat as it was on that warm day. But in the winter?

She was more beautiful than ever. I knew that she was thirty-five – a middle-aged woman – but she looked about twenty-five. She seemed what I can only call triumphantly lighthearted. Yet our talk was not the old, easy freewheeling talk of three months ago. I felt a distance of reserve in her. There were long silences when we walked, with her little Yorkshire terrier trotting before us along the towpath, or when

I was driving her to the nearest village to do some shopping, or when, once, a Guinness barge passed slowly through the lock and we watched the men lean against the gates to slew them slowly open, and then watched it go slowly dud-dudding away from us along the perspective of the canal until it looked no bigger in the distance than a toy boat. That was the only time I probed her.

'Are you never lonely here?' I asked her.

'Not at all!' she said, in astonishment. 'I have so much to do! Reading about the antiquities around here. I have an old bicycle to visit them. Studying the river flowers. Watching the birds. And it is extraordinary how much time I can spend on the house. It will take me years to get it the way I want it. Dreaming and thinking.'

The only word that held me was *thinking*. Thinking what?

As I was about to leave her she asked me if I would drive her as far as the next lock. (When I said she could drive with me to the end of the world, she laughed and said, 'That *is* the end of my world.') She wanted to buy freshly laid eggs from the wife of the lock-keeper with whom, now and again, if she wanted to hear a voice, she would pass the time of day and, perhaps, glance at the daily newspaper.

'Though it is always,' she smiled, 'yesterday's newspaper!'

This lockhouse was an exact replica of her own. Like the cells of certain monastic orders that are identical the world over, so I suppose is every lockhouse on these decaying canals that slowly creep across Ireland. We sat for a while in its poky kitchen chatting with the woman. Then she did something that I can never forget. She had brought a few sweets for the two small children there, and as she sat, the sweets in her lap, the two little girls standing on either side of her, she put an arm around each, saying, 'One for you' and 'Now one for you,' until the few sweets were evenly shared. The mother fondly watched the group. I went to the door to look out. I could not bear to watch it.

During the three years that she stayed there I never let two months pass without visiting her. I never again spoke to her of my feelings for her. There was no need to. We both knew. Nobody else from W—— visited her. Two or three times I told Jack I had 'dropped in' on her. Each time he asked if she was well – no more. She told me he had written once inviting her to return, and that she had several angry letters from her family telling her it was her duty to return. In the spring of her third year I thought she looked ill and said so to Jack. The next

I heard was from May Hennessy, who told me that she had suddenly been taken to the County Hospital of B——, in an advanced stage of leukaemia.

From that on the family became full of solicitude and pity for her, telling us all that the one wish she and Jack had was that she should leave the hospital and come home. I guessed that she would be too weak to resist them. And that, in fact, was how, in the end, everything was done, all the whispering ended, the scandal smothered and forgotten, if not forgiven.

The last time I saw her was on a June afternoon, just like this one, lying in this front room, her bed near the window so that she could look out over the bay. She was thin and pale, her eyes made wider and brighter by the smallness and pallor of her face. There were half a dozen Slators there, keeping up a cheerful chatter about her. She was not talking, but once she smiled joyfully at the lace curtains blowing in through the open window, and said to me, 'They are like a ballet.' At which I remembered that snowy night three years back when she and I had been talking about *The Three Sisters*, and Jack had suddenly gone off in a sulk to the Club, and she said she was going to go away and be born again, and I began to wonder if she saw all life in the forms or shapes of a ballet that you cannot explain or reason about, but that, somehow, in their own way, say, 'This is right, this is the way it all is really when it is right.' But even as she said it, my eye fell on the black, gold-edged missal by her bed and I wondered if she had, in her weakness, surrendered to all the habits and ways against which she had once decided to rebel. A moment later her face contorted and she said, 'I must ask you all to leave now. I must ask nurse to do something for me.' I never laid eyes on her again. Two mornings later May Hennessy told me she was gone.

It was the right word. Gone she has but I have never felt that she has died. I don't believe it still. All my memories of her are of a vital living woman. I have no other image of her. As I looked out of my office window that morning at the sea, I felt what I still feel – she has gone back into it.

For everybody in the town except Jack and me that was the end of her story. Her death broke him. I never met him that he did not start talking about how lovely and spirited a creature she was, a great-hearted woman. In my misery I began to haunt him, though I was never sure from one day to the next whether it was through friendship or hate. Still there must have been some compassion in it because when he said to me one day, 'Jerry, I can't go on living in that empty house,' I said, 'It's too big for you. Why don't you break it up into two flats and rent one to me? We'd be company for one another.' He jumped at it. He retired to live on the third floor, we put his old housekeeper up under the roof, and he rented me these rooms over the shop, furnished as they stood with all the bits and pieces of antiques she used to buy at auctions, and the shelves full of her books, even the ones she had taken with her to the lockhouse on the canal. He said he didn't want any of them near him. They only kept on reminding him of her.

That is fifteen years ago now, and I never stop thinking of her, coming back and back to all those questions that began to torment me from the morning she left us. Did she win? Or did she lose? What, in God's name, was she thinking during those three years of solitude when she was trying to be born again? What, in God's name, did she think could, should or would happen to her? Did, in fact, anything at all happen to her? Not, of course, that I think of her all day long. I haven't the time – the year after she died I became (as she prophesied) the County Engineer. I am overworked. There are more things I want to do for this town than would keep any man busy for twenty hours a day. And not even a man as madly in love with a woman as I was and as I still am with her can think for every moment of his beloved. But often, on evenings like this and at odd moments, at noon, or late at night, she ambushes me. I see her again gabbling in this room, or walking in that lost valley, under the rain or the sun, and I wonder again what went on inside her, or whether the leaves, or the clouds or the mist ever told her what she wanted to know.

I sometimes now believe they said nothing, because, one night, I found among her books this red-covered notebook – a handwritten journal that she kept during those three years. I stayed awake half the night reading it over and over again hoping to find the answers to whatever it was she wanted to know. Not a clue! She had divided each year into the four seasons, and in each section she had merely written such pointless, passing things as 'I saw a kingfisher today,' followed by the details of the place and the hour and the weather. Or she wrote, 'It is raining, the drops slide down my window, through it the trunks of the pine trees look wavy and puckered and corrugated. The water of the canal is pockmarked. The reeds are bowed down by the wind and rain.' Or she has scribbled down some quotations from whatever book she had been reading, like: '*A little kingdom I possess / Where thoughts and feelings dwell, / And very hard the task I find / Of governing it well. By Louisa May Alcott, when aged 13.*' Or this one: '*The longest journey / Is the journey inward. By D. H.*' whoever he is! Or there are small sums of housekeeping money added up. Or she wrote down some details about some old abbey she had visited on her bicycle. A schoolgirl could have written it all.

The next morning I brought the journal to my office and threw it on May Hennessy's desk.

'I found this last night among Jill Jennings's books. It's apparently her journal. She kept it when she was living by herself in Bunahown.'

I watched her open it at random, reluctantly, almost with distaste. She read a bit. She turned over another thumbful of pages and read another bit.

'I thought,' I said, 'there might be something in it about what she used to be thinking. But there isn't!'

She looked up at me sullenly.

'What would you,' she asked, 'be thinking, if you were her?'

'I might be thinking of God, or Life, or "What is Reality?" or I might be thinking why I could not get on with *him*. Wouldn't you?'

She lowered her head, turned another clutch of pages, and spoke without raising her head.

'She had only one thing against Jack Jennings.'

'What?'

She slapped the book shut and handed it to me with 'This is all about birds.'

'What was the one thing she had against Jack?'

'He is impotent.'

I shouted it at her:

'You have absolutely no right to say a thing like that! It's not true!'

'It is true. I have every right. She told me.'

For a moment we glared at one another.

'But if that was so she could have had an annulment of the marriage in five minutes! Annulments are granted every week of the year for that!'

'And would you,' she said, with contempt, 'expect her to expose him before the whole town? To shame him for the rest of his life?'

I walked from her to the window and looked down into the busy square. How many of them knew?

'So,' she said quietly to my back, 'she went away. It's as simple as that.'

I heard her typewriter clacking away behind me. I snatched up the book and left her. I didn't do a stroke of work that day.

But it is not as simple as that! She never really did go away! She remained. He remained. Both of them remained. She still remains. You cannot just toss aside two lives with 'A man and a woman who married badly,' or 'If she lived anywhere else she could have divorced him and married again.' If! You can do anything, if . . . And if . . . And if . . . There is always that human and immortal If. God's curse on it! Am I one of those damfool Americans who think there is nothing on earth you cannot do? There are things nobody can do! The number of times I have wanted to do something as simple as widen a road, and knew I could only do it if I bulldozed some old woman's cottage that stood in the way, and that she would not give up, not if we gave her a new house a hundred times more comfortable. I once heard that in the middle of Chicago, where real estate is worth millions, there is an old fellow with a farm that he simply will not sell. How often have I wanted to dredge that bay out there, and I could do it in three months if the money was not wanted worse for something else. To build houses, to clear the slums. Why are there slums in America as bad as anything in Singapore? Why are there wars? How many men and women in the world wish to high heaven they had never married and yet they cannot leave one another because of their children, or their compassion, or pity, or their memories of their first happiness that is stronger than the cold years that, God knows why, froze their love to death.

Is that my answer? That she did not marry him for love. Only for pity. Did he tell her before they were married? But that is incredible. The poor bastard probably did not know until he married her. How long did it take her to understand? Years? Of bewilderment, then terror, then misery and pity for them both. But I still do not know what she meant by being born again.

'I bought four eggs today from Mrs Delacey at the lockhouse. Four lovely brown eggs with a feather clinging to one of them.' 'Poor Jerry visited me again today, I wonder what brings him so often.' She knew perfectly well what brought me. 'My wild cherry is a cloud of white blossoms.' What the hell have feathers and cherry blossoms to do with anything?

There's a plane passing over. To London? To Paris? To Rome? If anyone in it looked down at us what would he see? Nothing but an empty harbour, a huddle of roofs, a membrane of blue smoke. He would not see the Slators, or me, or Jack, or the tumbledown backyards, with their rusty sheds, and the valerian growing out of old walls, places I'm going to tear to bits some day if . . . If! And if!

That grey moon up there won't be bright for two more hours. Nor the lighthouse blink. Nor the tide in. The bay looks lovely when the tide is in. A skin of pure water. Moon-tracked. On a moony night like this, when the whole town is sound asleep, what would I not give to see her come floating in, look, and look, and wave one white arm to me before she turns for home again?

Brainsy

The night Tom Kennedy landed off the bus in the long street of Coonlahan to begin his career as a teacher in the Abbatian Brothers' College (popularly known as the A.B.C.) it was raining softly but implacably. He passed no remarks on the rain. He gave one look at Coonlahan and noted the hour: exactly seventy minutes before closing time. The next thing he did was to ask the driver if he could trouble him to show him where the hotel was. The driver laughed. No trouble at all. No hotel. But he might get some class of a room in that tall house down the street that old Mrs Gaston called a Guest House. 'Don't give her more than a quid. She never has any guests.' The old lady showed him by candlelight to a room high up under the roof, large, damp and cold as an aerial vault. That done, he went out at once, shot another despairing look around him and turned into the first pub he met to drown his shame. That telegram from the Brother Superior—'COME AT ONCE BEGIN DUTIES TOMORROW' – could mean only one of two things. Either somebody else had come before him, looked at Coonlahan, and spat on it; or nobody had wanted to come there at all. He drank steadily until the barman put out the oil lamps, clambered up to his room, emptied his pockets on the bed and counted his coins with a shaking finger to see if he had the price of his fare back to Dublin. He found that of the five pounds with which he had started from Dublin all he had left was eleven shillings and two pennies, and stared down through the mist around the street lamp opposite his window at his past and his future . . .

One look at him, a couple of questions, and any stranger would have had it all. He looked about forty-five (he was thirty-six); his hair was grey as a badger; his lower eyelids were as pink as a bloodhound's; his trousers gave him legs like an elephant; he walked like a seal; and he had been on the booze for some fifteen years. As for his qualifications to be a teacher of English: he had, some eight years before, managed to scrape up a B.A. (pass level), by attending night courses at

University College, Dublin, while concurrently (also previously and subsequently) failing at every odd job he had tried – clerk in a travel agency, copywriter for an advertising agency, door-to-door canvasser for the *British Encyclopaedia*, sub-editor for *The Irish Digest*, sub-sub-editor for a comic weekly called *Hullaballoo*, an auctioneer's clerk, a bookie's sidekick, and a collector for a pious organization advocating total abstinence from all spirituous liquors. Only three days ago he had been sacked from that job for arriving on the doorstep of the Parish Priest of Killiney at eleven o'clock at night, speechless and footless. It was then that he decided that there was only one thing left for him to do – take up teaching. Searching the next morning through the small ads in the educational column of *The Irish Independent* he had come on one for the post of English Teacher in the A.B.C. of Coonlahan, in County Kerry. He had written off at once to the Brother Superior saying that he held a first class honours B.A. and had had three years' experience in England, adding, truthfully, that twenty years ago in Cork he had himself been a pupil of the Abbatians. He sent off the letter and prayed that something else except teaching would turn up in the meantime. To his dismay all that turned up was the telegram.

When old Mrs Gaston woke him up in the morning, groaning at her long stairs, he found that although the village consisted of a single Main Street it was a fine, wide street of multi-coloured houses, and the sun shone so warmly on it that roofs exhaled a gentle steam. From his high window he saw a majestic range of mountains, a vast moorland broken here and there by tiny farms, and he could just see a gleaming spit of ocean away off to the west. Better still, when he found the school – grey, square, two-storied, cross-crowned – down a side road, beyond the church that concluded the street at that end, the Superior, one Brother Angelo Harty, turned out to be a kindly, hulking old man who welcomed him warmly, asked him no questions, and, before introducing him to his own pupils, courteously led him around the other seven classrooms to meet his future colleagues – six Abbatian brothers in the old blue-black soutanes with the bony collars, and one lay teacher, Dicky Talbot, a cheerful, skinny little man, wearing pince-nez glasses on a promising prawn-red nose. They all greeted him in the most friendly manner.

'And this,' said Angelo, as he threw open the seventh door, 'is Brother Regis. Our history teacher.'

Tom stared through the ageing mask before him and slowly held out his hand to his oldest schoolboy pal, Brainsy Carty. As slowly, Brother Regis did the same, and then it was a cheerful 'Hello, Tom!' and an astonished 'So it really is you?' and he was back in the Abbatian Brothers' College in Cork, aged thirteen.

For four years – the purest, sweetest, loveliest years of his life – he and Brainsy had sat side by side on the same bench, for every class, every day. They used to meet every afternoon after school. They spent every holiday together. Days of Damon and Pythias. Exchanges of soul years: their diaries, their dreams, their heroes, their poems. Brainsy's 'All hail to Napoleon, dreamer and doer of might,' for Tom's 'O sweetest Virgin, free me of my fetters, / Send my prayer upward to the sky, / That I may suffer among the lonely lepers, / As Father Damien did in far-off Molokai.' Years when Brainsy's ambition was to climb the mountains of India or explore 'the untracked Amazon'; when Tom, if he could not be another Father Damien, wanted to be a Trappist monk, pray all night, work all day, never speak, and dig a foot of his grave every week. Years when, because Tom had no father and Brainsy's mother was also dead, they agreed that it would be marvellous if Tom's mother married Brainsy's father and they would always live together like brothers. They had wept openly when at seventeen Brainsy's father sent him to Dublin to be trained as a teacher, and Tom's mother sent him off to a seminary in County Limerick to become a Capuchin priest. From that moment the pattern of their lives was set. Brainsy got what he wanted, a teacher's job in Dublin, and Tom was fired from the seminary, his Master of Novices dryly intimating to him that his mother (who had died, in the meantime) might have had a vocation for the priesthood, but he . . . Well, he was turned twenty-one now. He had better go up to Dublin and look for a job.

Dublin? Tom's first thought was of Brainsy.

They were soon sharing a small flat, going halves in everything, eating and drinking together, chasing girls together, loyally deceiving them for one another, agreeing that if either of them wanted to bring a girl to the flat the other would walk the streets until he saw the window blind up and an umbrella standing against the light to show that the storm was over; though, in practice, it was always Tom who walked the streets. He liked the company of girls but, as the saying goes, he never 'touched' them. As for their arguments – Brainsy being Brainsy – they were never in short order. For the time was now long gone since Brainsy's hero was Buonaparte at Lodi, or since he wanted to climb great mountains and explore great rivers. His obsessive interest now was in the marvels of modern science. His heroes were men like Bohr, Rutherford, Thomson, Einstein, Planck and Millikin. His villains were every priest, nun, monk, bishop and archbishop on up to the Vatican and the cardinals of the curia. It was a change that bewildered Tom until he remembered those odd questions at school that had won Brainsy his nickname. ('But, Brother, if it is a sin to kill, what about the glories of the religious wars?' Or 'But, Brother, if birds have wings why haven't we?' Or 'But, Brother, if we become dust when we die why can't Catholics be cremated?')

Their dissent only troubled Tom when their roles began to interchange, like a castling in chess; as when Brainsy might yield that if there ever was any truth in religion the last time it was seen was when it was hiding in the catacombs; and Tom would find himself conceding that, yes, it was there alright, but maybe it was really to be found only in our memories of a divine shadow passing along the shores of Galilee? Which would take them on to the analysis of the Gospels until, in agony, Tom began to find his shadow slowly turning to a wisp of smoke. One July night he came tramping home eagerly from his job to have it out, once and for all. He found a note on the table saying, 'Goodbye, we will meet in the great Hereafter.' Since then he had had neither sight nor sound of him until this minute.

Brainsy's smile went back into his mouth. His hair became grey, his back stooped. All that was left of his youth was the broken perpendicular furrow that used to come and go between his eyebrows like wind on water. It seemed now to be dug in there as permanently as the broken line of life in a man's palm. Or, Tom thought, as Angelo led him out of the classroom, like a sentence that starts one way and ends another– Was that an anacoluthon? – like, say, 'If I don't mend my boozy ways what, in God's name, is going to be the end of *me*?' Though, God knows, he thought, following Angelo's broad back down the corridor, anacoluthing like blazes as he went, the truth is isn't it an extraordinary fact, like Brainsy and me, why must everybody in Ireland live like an express train that starts off for heaven full of beautiful dreams, and marvellous ambitions and, halfway, bejasus, you switch off the bloody track down some sideline that brings you back to exactly where you began, with all your machinery falling out of you in bits, and every wagon branded 'What's-the-use-of-doing-anything-at-all?'

Angelo paused with his hand on the doorhandle of Tom's classroom. He turned to say curiously, 'So you know Brother Regis?' A soft babel went on inside. Tom said, cautiously, not knowing what Brainsy might have told him about his own past, that, yes, they had both been at school together in the A.B.C. in Cork.

'But, of course, that was years and years ago. He was a very clever boy at school. Oh, very talented! One of the stars of the A.B.C. And friends in Dublin tell me that he became a marvellous teacher.' He smiled ingratiatingly. 'At school the boys used to call him Brainsy. A nickname, like that, from boys, don't you think, Brother Angelo, is a great compliment?'

Looking steadily at his new teacher, the old man took out his snuffbox, opened it, dabbed in one fat thumb and slowly approached the nicotine to each hairy nostril. Still looking steadily at his man, he slowly replaced the box in his trousers pocket through a slit in his soutane.

'Brainsy? That's not bad, you know. It's extraordinary how penetrating boys can sometimes be. And how cruel!'

'He has been a monk now for how long?'

'Twelve years.'

'Always here?'

'He spent nine years in his old school in Cork.'

Nine years in a big city? And now shunted down to this back-of-beyond? Puzzled as well as worried, Tom ventured a probe.

'I never expected to find him down here.'

There was a sudden silence behind the classroom door. Had the boys heard them talking? In the silence, through the open window of the corridor, he heard the juniors downstairs repeating in unison the voice of a teacher guiding them through a reading lesson, first his deep voice, phrase by phrase, then their piping voices repeating the words after him:

'THE RHINE-O-SAYROS,' the deep voice boomed. 'The rhine-o-sayros,' the children piped. 'IS A WILD BASHTE.' 'Is a wild bashte.' 'HE WOULD ATE YOU.' 'He would ate you.' 'AND DESHTROY YOU.' 'And deshtroy you.'

When Angelo's answer came it was a shade too delicate.

'Well, you see, our Superior General thought he might find it a bit more easy away down here in the quiet of the country.'

It was the word *away* that gave him away. Whenever somebody has what we politely call a nervous breakdown we always say, 'He has been away.'

For several weeks all that Tom saw of his friend was when they passed one another in the corridor between classes, and without halting, Brainsy would lift a hand, smile faintly and say something like 'All going well, I hope?' or 'Bad weather, isn't it?' Tom, deeply hurt, decided finally that if this was the sort of relationship the fellow wanted now he could play that game too – 'Morning, Brother! Nice day, isn't it?' – until, bit by bit, he began to get a hint here and a hint there of the kind of tensions that tauten life in small communities like the A.B.C.

He got his first small shock the day he overheard two boys refer to Regis as Brainsy. It could only mean that Angelo had, unguardedly, mentioned the nickname to one of the brothers who had, at once and maliciously, passed the arrow on to his boys. For a boy to give a nickname like that to another boy was a chummy thing to do. To give it to a teacher was like sticking a firecracker into his tail. He got a more painful hint the day he was trying to persuade his class that when Oliver Goldsmith was writing *The Deserted Village* in his miserable London garret he was all the time sadly remembering the village where he was born, in Ireland.

'Take, for example, the lines...'

At once an ink-fingered hand shot up. It was Micky Brennan, the son of a local publican, a boy he had already come to recognize as one of the smartest boys in the class.

'I know the lines, sir,' Micky said eagerly, and started to quote them fluently and feelingly, from

> In all my wanderings round this world of care,
> In all my griefs – and God has given my share—
> I still had hopes my latest hours to crown,
> Amidst these humble bowers to lay me down...

on down to:

> And, as an hare whom hounds and horns pursue,
> Pants to the place from whence at first she flew,
> I still had hopes, my long vexations past,
> Here to return – and die at home at last.

Immediately Brennan had begun to recite the lines the whole class began to titter. (At what?)

'That's very good, Brennan. But how do you happen to know the lines so well?'

Another boy spoke up, a rough fellow named Harty, the duffer of the class and, Tom suspected, the bully of the school – he had already had to stop him, one day in the yard, from punching a boy half his size and weight.

'He knows them lines, sir,' Harty growled, with an envious look at Brennan, 'only because Brainsy . . .' There was a general titter at this slip of the tongue; if it was a slip. 'I mean Brother Regis, sir, is always quoting them to us at History. He says he's very fond of 'em.'

The whole class laughed openly; Tom understood; and in his fright passed quickly on to something else. If these giggling brats had been smart enough to read Brainsy for Goldsmith he had no need to persuade them to read Lissoy for Auburn. As he looked around at their innocent-wicked-probing eyes he knew that it would not be long before they saw through him too. What nickname had they, maybe already, given him? And did this sort of thing run through the whole school, through the monastery, all through Coonlahan?

Where he now lodged was with a young carpenter and his wife in a tiny pink house rising directly from the pavement that ended with the school and the monks' dwelling place. Beyond that the road became grass-edged and the countryside began; though within a month, merely by facing the window of the small front room of his lodgings as he ate his dinner – at half past three every afternoon – watching the rare cart or the rare pedestrian that passed slowly by, it came to him that Coonlahan was a place where the life of the country had neither beginning nor end. Like any one of the little whitewashed farmhouses on the level bogland that he could see through his window it was just another dot in space and time. That donkey cart trundling slowly by with its roped pyramid of turf to be sold from door to door brought the bogland into the Main Street. The pasturers plodded in every evening with a small herd of black cows, their udders dripping, eager to be milked in somebody's backyard. Coonlahan's one water pump stood on top of three rectangular steps at a fork in the road just beyond the school, its timber casing always wrapped in posters advertising hay or land for sale, so that he occasionally saw the waterman's two barrels, covered with wet sacking, pass his window to the lazy cry of

'Pennyabucketthewa-a-ather!' The carpenter's wife, like many other women in Coonlahan, kept chickens in her backyard – he once saw a hawk swoop down on the hen run to carry off a chicken between its claws; and one hard, wintry morning he found her in floods of tears – a fox had stolen in at night and killed them all. 'I'm beginning to think,' he said to her, 'that the whole village ought to be stockaded!' Yet, one lovely afternoon in the following April he was to see a host of swallows pour in at one end of the Main Street and out at the other as if there were no village there at all. No wonder that old bus driver had laughed at him the night he asked for 'the hotel'! In a place where there was no railway, no cinema, no library, no bookshop, no dancehall, nothing but a handful of shops and pubs? Where, all through the long autumn nights, he soon found that there was nothing whatever to do – after he had corrected his pupils' homework or prepared his own – but to read, or sit with the carpenter and his wife in the back kitchen playing cards, or listening to voices from Dublin fading and returning on the dying batteries of the radio.

At such dead hours he would occasionally wonder what Brainsy was doing at that moment down the road. What did they all do once school was over? One afternoon he had seen two of them playing handball against the gable of the school. Another day he had watched a few of them aimlessly pucking a hurling ball in an empty field, shouting like boys, their soutanes doffed, their bony collars scattered on the grass like crescent moons. On fine afternoons he regularly saw some of them passing his window in pairs to walk, as he sometimes did himself, out some country road until the sun set. Coming on Dicky Talbot one October night in Brennan's pub, he asked him, 'How do ye pass the winter nights here in Coonlahan?' Dicky, married, with eight kids, said he had never needed to consider the problem.

'I mean, the brothers,' Tom said testily. 'Do they play cards? Do they ever read? And if so what?'

'I suppose they read the newspaper. Though it must be a bit of rag by the time it has passed through all their hands? I imagine they read *Our Boys*, or look at the clerical weeklies. They have some sort of a ragtime library of their own but I have no idea what's in it. Textbooks? Lives of the saints? As you know, there's no library here. All the County Librarian can do is dump a couple of cases of books in the back porch of the chapel once a month. A couple of years back he offered them the run of everything he has in his H.Q. in Killarney, but only one of them ever availed of the offer.'

'I bet that was Regis!'

'The very man. But they soon put a stop to his gallop.' Dicky laughed at the happy memory. 'They caught him one night reading a book called *Is There an Afterlife?* by some Calvinist divine named Vaughan. They raised blue hell and bloody murder over it. They complained the poor old County Librarian to the Parish Priest and to the County Committee. A bright boyo, he said he thought the author was Cardinal Vaughan.'

'You're surely not suggesting that Regis was having religious doubts? I mean, did the book deny the existence of immortality?'

'Amn't I after telling you the book was by a Calvinist? And the world knows that no Calvinist could exist for one minute without heaven for himself and hellfire for everyone else. Doubts? Not at all. It was simply the question mark after the title. They weren't going to stand for that! Doubts? Regis have doubts? You obviously don't know our Regis. His trouble is that he's full to the butt of the lugs with certainties. He's the Savonarola of Coonlahan. He's the scourge of the monastery. He thinks they're all a soft, flabby, half-pagan lot, and he's always telling them so. You should hear him saying, "He that is neither hot nor cold I spe-e-ew him out of my mouth." Or you should have been here last year when he made them all agree to give up cigarettes for Lent, and then caught one of them sucking a butt in the jakes. He reported the poor bastard to the Superior, the P.P. and the Bishop. What do they do at night? Sit around and eat one another, I would imagine. Have another pint.'

Tom brooded over that conversation. 'Simply the question mark after the title . . .' That would be right up Brainsy's alley. He decided that he must have a talk with him alone.

It was a frosty afternoon in mid-November before he got his chance. He had finished his dinner and was reading the Dublin paper (it never came in before three o'clock) when his eye was lifted by the lone pencilled shadow of one of the brothers passing swiftly outside the lace curtains. He recognized Nessan, the man who taught the kids Irish, and was just deciding that he was hurrying on some errand down the street when he saw Brainsy slowly passing by, also alone. He seized his umbrella, hat and overcoat and hastened after him. Ahead of him he saw Nessan turning right for the open country, with Brainsy about a hundred yards behind him. He caught up with him.

'Hello, Regis.'

'Hello, Tom.'

'You seem to have lost your companion.'

'He's my non-companion,' Brainsy said gruffly. 'I prefer my own company.'

'Oh? Am I intruding on some great thoughts?'

Brainsy relaxed into a smile as frosty as the grey field beside the road.

'Divil a thought, great or small. Walk along with me and leave us be talking. All that fellow,' nodding his chin towards Nessan's back, 'ever talks about is crossword puzzles. "What is a four-legged domestic animal in three letters beginning with C?" If you say cat he says cow. If you say cow he says cat. Lovely afternoon, isn't it? How's everything with you? Getting along alright?'

Tom let him talk school talk for a bit. Then he drew closer.

'You know that boy Micky Brennan?'

Brainsy's smile became a trifle softer and sadder.

'A bright boy, an inquiring boy, he reminds me sometimes of myself when I was his age.'

'He stood up in class one day and recited a whole chunk of *The Deserted Village* for me. *In all my wanderings round this world of care* . . . You know the lines. He tells me you taught them to him. I never knew you were a Goldsmith fan.'

'As a matter of fact, I am very fond of that poem. Every historian ought to be. It touches on quite a number of modern problems. *Ill fares the land, to hastening ills a prey*. And so on. Poor Oliver knew it all. An exile himself.'

'Who always wanted to go home in the heel of his days? I often wondered whether he had a home to go to. As well I might. Since my mother died I have no home to go to. Is your dad still alive?'

Brainsy said, 'No,' and halted and looked off to where the far mountains rose clear and sharp against the frosty twilight.

'Home?' he said softly. 'The word has various meanings, of course. *Lead, kindly light* . . . *The night is dark and I am far from home*.'

'Newman. The lighthouse in the Strait of Bonifacio. A great stylist.'

'A great teacher. When I read him I feel the next world revolving about me.'

'But you believe in the next world.'

'Meaning?'

'Meaning that I gave up all that sort of thing years ago. Thanks to you, Brainsy.' Brainsy lifted shocked eyes to him. 'You haven't forgotten all our talks in Dublin? Day after day. Night after night. Year in and year out. After you left Dublin I stopped going to church, chapel or meeting. I hope you won't report that to your superior? I don't want to lose my job – just yet.'

They walked on in the frosty silence. After a bit Brainsy spoke.

'I accept no responsibility for your state of mind. You are a grown man. But if that is your state of mind what are you doing here?'

'It's a living.'

Their feet rang on the hard road.

'Well! You are a layman. So I suppose a living is a good enough reason for you to be here. I might do better to ask what am I doing here?' He pointed forward with his umbrella to his lone chaperon. 'Or what is that fellow doing here? Or what are they all doing here?'

'Teaching?'

Brainsy halted again. The line between his eyebrows went red as a scar. His voice became hoarse with fury.

'Teaching what? Isn't that the beginning and end of it? Isn't that what I'm always saying to these fellows? If every single thing we say and do and teach doesn't give the youngsters the feeling that this ball of the world is carrying us inch by inch towards another world where is the sense in any one of us giving up everything to become brothers? But do we do it? Angelo teaches them Latin. Perhaps you can tell me, because he can't, since when did Cicero or Ovid become pillars of Christianity? Oh, laugh away! That's what they do! That man there teaches the Irish language. He thinks he's doing great work for Ireland. He might just as well be teaching them pagan Greek. This year your lads will be reading *Macbeth* or *Julius Caesar*. What's so very Christian about either of them? It may all be a great joke to you. You've just said you have no beliefs. But I have my beliefs. And it's no laughing matter for me.'

He shivered and they resumed their walk.

'Tom! Do you know why I left you that time in Dublin? I'll tell you why. It's not nice. But I'll tell you. It was a Saturday. If you remember?

You were working that day, I wasn't. It was a lovely sunny day. I took a girl down to Brittas Bay. She was eighteen. A sweet, lovely, innocent girl. I sometimes still pray for her. It was a real Irish July day, little showers of rain, great steamy clouds rising up all around us, everything bruised black and blue, the hills, the white fields, the blue sky. We swam and we lay down on the cool sand. Not a soul along the beach for miles and miles. The usual opening gambit. Slipping the strap of her bathing dress off her shoulder. When I did it she looked up at me and I never saw such terror, such contempt, such disgust, such disappointment in any human being's eyes. She looked at me as if I was filth. I put back the strap and I said, "Forget it." I couldn't think what else to say or do. After a while she got up and said, "We'd better go home now, Jerry, you've spoiled everything." The whole way back to Dublin we didn't say one word. When she left me I went back to the flat and I looked at it. Everything ready. The half-bottle of whiskey. The two glasses. The couch in the corner. The sun pouring into the room. It looked exactly what it was. Sordid. That was my moment on the road to Damascus. It came to me like lightning that I was a bad influence on everybody, including you, Tom, and that if I didn't leave the world entirely I was done for. Inside a year I became an Abbatian brother.'

Ahead of them Nessan halted on the brow of a little hill looking at the sky. Hesperus. He could have been one of the Magi. They paused to let him walk on.

'And you have been happy ever since?'

'Within three years I realized that all I'd done was to jump out of the frying pan into the fire. I had thought I had a vocation . . .'

'Like me in the Capuchins!'

' . . . Instead, all I was doing, year after year, was shoving a few score of boys through some examination or other to get some lousy job. Would you give up the whole world just for that? After that it became more and more clear to me every year that if that was all my vocation was good for I was a fool, we were all a lot of fools, and the whole blooming thing was a cod.'

Whom hounds and horns pursue. Until the hare is torn to pieces. They thought he might find it more easy down here in the quiet of the country. Or was it because he was the kind of brainy teacher they couldn't afford, or the expensive makings of one? One small head that, as Goldsmith did not say about the village teacher, could never carry all he thought he knew?

That month ended it. A leak in the roof of the school made Tom's class uninhabitable, and for three weeks, while they were replacing the slates, he had to keep moving his class from room to room. For those three weeks he had a chance to watch them all teaching. None of them interested him except Brainsy, and he was a magician. With him the boys were not in a class at all; they were in a circus, on an ice-hockey rink. His trick, though it was his nature rather than a trick, was to keep them doubling after him all the time, never letting them rest for a minute. He was so good that Tom used to set his class to some written exercise so that he could pretend to be looking out the window while listening, entranced, to the chase going on at the other end of the room.

One such day he was standing like that, looking down into the kitchen-garden of the monastery, with Brainsy behind him luring them on to discuss the suppression of the monasteries. For forty minutes he started argument after argument. 'Sullivan, how would you like it if you saw your father's grazing land being taken away from him?' 'Yes, but supposing it didn't belong to him? Supposing that it originally belonged to the Church?' 'Brennan, what about all those executions of multitudes of poor people wandering all over the country, driven to terrible crimes by hunger? How far was it just, or unjust, to hang them?' Then, at a great leap, he was on to the humanity of John Howard and his plans for Prison Reform. 'Cassidy, what do you make of that idea?' 'Whelan, have you any idea where that humane spirit began in England?' 'Walsh, what about the Church, for example? Was it a humane idea when the Church began to teach that hell is not just fire eating the body but torment eating the soul?' 'Foley, what do you think? Was that a humane idea? Or was it even more inhuman?' 'What do you all think? Which was the more humane in that terrible century, the Pope or the King?' It was then that Tom heard the doorhandle click and, turning, saw old Angelo slide out as softly as he had, apparently, come in.

The very next day Angelo called Tom out of his class and informed him, in the corridor, that after the Christmas holidays he must, in addition to English, teach History.

'But,' Tom cried, 'I never studied History. And Brother Regis is a dab at History. He's marvellous at it. You heard him yourself.'

'I have heard him many times, Mr Kennedy.'

'Then you can see for yourself that I couldn't come within a thousand miles of the way he does it. Compared to him I'm a complete ignoramus! And the boys are mad about his ideas on History!'

Angelo let out an exasperated sigh. He took out his snuffbox, but he was too upset to use it.

'I am very sorry, Mr Kennedy, but you will just have to do what I say. All you need do is to read the set texts and keep a couple of pages ahead of the class. And,' suddenly and uncharacteristically getting excited, 'I want you to know that I don't care two pins whether the boys are interested in Brother Regis's ideas, or your ideas, or anybody else's ideas, or not. My position is quite simple. I want my boys to get through their examinations, and that is all I want. And the plain fact of the matter is that since Brother Regis came here three years ago we have had more failures in History than in any other subject on the entire curriculum. And I'm not one bit surprised. Unless you can explain to me what on earth History has to do with such matters as whether there is real fire in hell or not. Look!' He was trembling in every limb, and his round, soft face had become as purple as a swede turnip. 'This little community of ours was as cosy and happy a little community as you could find in the length and breadth of Ireland until Brother Regis was sent down here on top of us to enjoy the peace and quiet of the country. Peace and quiet? God help us! Since that man joined us there has been neither peace nor quiet in this place. Do you know that last night, in our quiet little library, he and Brother Nessan, two brothers in religion, literally, literally I say, came to blows – I never thought I'd live to see it – before all the brothers. And about what, Mr Kennedy? About the nature of hellfire!' He gripped his soutane across his chest as if he were getting a grip of himself. On the spot he became quiet. 'You will take History in the New Year. Have no fears – you can't be worse than your predecessor. And for the rest of the year I will raise your salary by twenty-five per cent.'

That night Tom decided, over his fourth pint of porter, that Angelo could sack him if he wanted to; but he could not and would not do this to his best friend. In the morning he found he had no option. An ambulance stood outside the monastery door. The sergeant of the Guards and a plainclothesman were talking with Angelo and Nessan inside the gate. Every window in the school was full of white faces. Dicky Talbot whispered to him that Regis had been missing since midnight and that the Guards and the brothers had been out searching for him with lamps until three hours ago, when he was found, unconscious, in a ditch beside the road, presumably knocked down by some yob in a passing motorcar. He was now lying in his bed in the monastery, still unconscious, about to be taken to the County Hospital in Tralee.

He was still unconscious when Tom went to Dublin that Christmas; he was unconscious on his return; he remained unconscious for, in all, sixty-six days. A month later he was discharged from hospital, as well as ever, meaning, as he himself said over a cup of tea in Tom's lodgings, 'Hale and hearty! Except for a bruised liver, a broken leg, two smashed fingers, three ribs that creak whenever I try to touch my toes, and a silver plate in my skull.'

'Well,' Tom joked, in the merry tone we all reserve for such doleful occasions, 'you gave us a nice fright! I expected to hear any day that you were dead.'

From his armchair Brainsy gave him a queer look.

'So I was,' he said quietly.

'Was what?'

'Dead.'

'You look very much alive now, anyway.' Tom laughed uncomfortably.

Brainsy's mouth went tight. The frown between his eyes caved in. This, apparently, was no laughing matter either.

'There is no least doubt about my death, Tom. I have had plenty of time since I came back from the grave to think the whole matter out completely. I have been asking myself a great many interesting questions. And I have arrived at a very simple conclusion. When I was knocked down that night on the highway I was given a blow on the head that plunged me into a state of total oblivion for sixty-six days. I lost all my faculties. I fail to see what more could have happened to me if my heart had stopped beating. I was, in a word, humanly speaking, dead.'

With anybody else Tom would have scoffed or made polite, meaningless noises. He opened his mouth to make one, leaned forward, leaned back; did the same again, did it a third time; and sank back into his armchair. He felt like a lunatic rowing an imaginary boat. You always had to come to the point with Brainsy.

'But your soul was alive!' he said at last.

Brainsy smiled and to enforce the smile adopted, at one and the same moment, a Kerry brogue and what used to be called an Oxford accent

– the common Irish way of being superior without seeming to be lofty.

'Oho! Aren't we a darlint boy! So, now, oo doo believe in the sowl, eh?'

'Well, no! Or, only as a metaphor. Such as, "Brevity is the soul of wit." Shakespeare. Or, "O God, if there is such a thing as a God, please save my soul, if I have such a thing as a soul." Renan. But, I don't believe in the soul in your sense of the word.'

Brainsy sighed.

'After my experience on the road to Tralee I don't believe in anything any longer. How could I? A material man, with no material faculties whatever, but endowed with a soul? That's not a man, that's a vegetable. Are we horseradishes or potatoes? Of course,' he mused, 'there were philosophers who believed, and some may even still believe, that vegetables and animals have souls.'

'God knows,' Tom conceded, 'there are times when I think the one half of me isn't much better than a potato.'

Brainsy waved a languid hand.

'Now you are postulating two souls. One rational, the other irrational. The heresy of Photius. Condemned by the Council of Constantinople in 869.'

'But, surely,' Tom pleaded, 'my soul isn't working all the time? I mean when a pint of porter is flowing down my gullet. Or when my eye looks at you now drinking that cup of tea . . .'

'You are now denying the principle of unity. Condemned by the Council of Vienne in the thirteenth century. Recondemned by Pius the Ninth in 1857. It is the whole man who sees and drinks, not your boozy, bloodshot eyes or your big thirsty mouth. Soul and body drink together. "I drink," said Aristotle, "therefore I am."'

Tom stared goiterously at his friend.

'Brainsy! I'm lost. Would you mind telling me what exactly we are talking about?'

'About a fantasy. Believed in by millions. Real to millions. I sometimes wonder,' he considered, pulling his left ear, 'whether the idea had any existence at all in Western Europe before Aristotle?'

Tom's voice rose to a squeak of desperation.

'Are you saying now that Aristotle invented my soul – if I have such a thing as a soul?'

'The origin of your soul? If you have a soul? That is very difficult.

Saint Augustine suggested that it may have come out of your father's cock. *Incorporeum semen* was his elegant phrase. That was called Generationism. Others thought that God creates the soul and pops it into the embryo in, I can't remember, was it the third or the fourth month? That is Creationism. But that raises an extremely awkward problem. It means that God would have had to stain it deliberately with Original Sin beforehand. No, Tom! It's all a lot of scholastic nonsense. Man was born with a brain. Without a brain he is a beast. Or he is dead as a man. When that fellow left me that night on the road I was no more than a rabbit that somebody took by the hind legs to bash its head against a rock. I died.'

'But your doctor,' Tom cried, 'will tell you that your organs remained alive, your heart, your guts, you were fed intravenously, you breathed, you aged, your tissues went on growing.'

'As your whiskers will keep on growing in the grave. As snakes galvanize after you cut them in two. What is it to be dead? Tom, if anybody knows I should know. I went into black darkness. And there was nothing there.'

The image of Brainsy lying in black nothingness flooded such horror into Tom that he leaped up and, as if he was at a retreat, or a mission, or a revival meeting, or listening to Billy Graham, he shouted out, 'I believe! I believe in the soul! I cannot believe in a man without one!' and he banged the polished round table that the carpenter had made for his wife, with its lace doily under a little silver vase bearing its one artificial rose.

'Anyway!' he cried triumphantly. 'The simple proof of the matter is that you are here now, alive and kicking. If you died, tell me who or what is this sitting there now in front of me talking all this balderdash?'

Brainsy rose on his walking stick and took his black hat.

'I do not know, Tom. I do not know who I am. Or where I came from. Or what I am. That is something I shall have to find out. I'd better go. Whatever I do and wherever I go I seem to have a bad influence on everybody, and upset everybody.'

'Everybody?' Tom asked fearfully, following him to the door. 'Have you been talking like this to anybody else?'

'Why not? I explained it all to Angelo. I explained it all to the Bishop. Oh, yes,' he beamed, seeing Tom's eyes widen, 'they brought the Bishop to me.'

'And what did his Lordship say to you?'

'What could he say? He just kept looking at me. He mentioned Lazarus. "But, my Lord," I said, "Lazarus was not dead. If he was dead when Christ came, you must believe that he was already judged by God and either resting in what your Lordship calls heaven, or suffering in hell. Or can your eternal God upset his own eternal judgments?" That floored him. He left me without another word and I have not seen or heard from him since. Oh, by the way, Tom, I'm forgetting my manners. I never thanked you for that nice cup of tea.'

It was this cheerful mention of the cup of tea that most frightened Tom. The man had no idea at all of what lay ahead of him.

'What are they going to do to you now?' he asked, at the front door.

'Angelo tells me I'm to teach Geography. A safe subject? "What are the chief rivers of France? What's the highest mountain in the world?" Or that's what he thinks. Geography has changed completely since his day. It is everything now – anthropology, sociology, the study of environments, economics, human values, history, religion, science. I'm going to have a lovely time with Geography.'

He waved a hand and limped away back to the monastery.

'I'll pray for you,' Tom called after him, and slowly closed the door.

He did not see him for three weeks. One reason was that since Lent began he had gone completely off the drink, but all this so upset him that every time he neared a pub in the Main Street he had to rush past it and start counting the days to Easter Sunday. The man *was* a bad influence! Nevertheless he could not help wondering how far the story had travelled. On the Sunday before Good Friday he met Dicky Talbot as he came out from mass, and asked him for news of Regis. Dicky stared at him, laughed long and loud, and then fell silent for a full half-minute, staring at him.

'You know,' he said at last, 'Coonlahan must be one of the most extraordinary little places in the whole world. It has one street, one large church, one small convent, one monastery of microscopic proportions, four pubs, it contains about fifteen hundred people, and I'm sure every person here thinks he knows everything about everybody. And he mostly does. But as for what goes on in the convent or the presbytery, or the A.B.C., the three of them might as well all be in Siberia. I swear that at this moment there could be three nuns nailed up by the ears to the back wall of the convent and nobody would know anything about them for six months. Look at you! You are teaching here, and you actually have to ask me where Regis is! For the last week he's been out in the kitchen-garden working as a lay brother.'

'You mean they wouldn't even let him teach Geography?'

'Angelo watched him doing it for a week and whipped him out of it like a shot to go downstairs teaching spelling to the kids. You know the way the kids chant their spelling after the teacher. "C.A.T. Cat. C.A.T. Cat. C.A.T. Cat." Sometimes it's about the only sound you'd hear from one end of Coonlahan to the other. Angelo went into Regis's spelling class one day and he nearly had a fit. Regis had them chanting, "D.O.G. God. D.O.G. God. D.O.G. God."'

Tom wiped his forehead. Dicky looked up and about the sky.

'Grand day, thank God!' he said. 'The first week of April. Nice time for planting spuds. If you go out into the walled garden any afternoon you'll probably find him hard at it.'

It took Tom until Thursday to overcome his dread of the encounter; then, miserably, when he knew the brothers would be out walking, he made his way to the kitchen-garden. It was a warm, sunny day. The remnant white plaster and exposed sandstone of the backs of the houses in the Main Street were islands of red sausage-meat in seas of snow. The gate twanged behind him. The lovely evocative smell of manure. The tops of the new potato ridges already beginning to whiten in the sun. In one corner an old, whitehaired brother digging stolidly. Brainsy sitting on an upturned bucket apparently lost in the passing clouds. His dusty soutane was rucked up by a cincture of twine, his sleeves and his trousers' ends were turned back, heavy boots on his stockingless feet. When he heard the gate he lowered his head to see who his visitor was, waved, got up with the help of his stick and, as graciously as if he were welcoming Tom into his drawing room, indicated a grassy patch where they could lie in the sun and out of the turn of the spring wind.

Tom looked at him apprehensively. He seemed entirely at his ease. Even the furrow between his eyebrows was pale and shallow. They laid down, facing one another, each on his elbow. Tom produced cigarettes, lit for them both, and it was all suddenly as cosy as if they were back in Dublin years ago, talking from bed to bed about the doings of the day, or about girls, or the gossip of the pubs, or the days when they were boys together in Cork.

'How's the old leg?' he asked.

'It works. It will never be up to much. I'll always have to use the stick.'

'And how's the old head?'

'Oh! That never stops. Around and around like a mill horse. Clop. Clop.'

'And how's all the old rest of you?'

'Fine! I get pains now and again. But when they're bad I take pills.'

'At this rate you can't be much use as a gardener, can you?'

'Paul,' nodding to the far corner, 'does all the hard work. I plant, or weed, or anything I can do on my knees. I've got very interested in cooking, too. They used to have a lay brother doing that – he was a ship's cook before he joined the Order – but they've promoted him to teaching the infants. Within a month or two I bet you they will all be eating better than they ever did in their lives. Oho! There's plenty of work in the old horse still.'

It seemed to Tom that he was being much too chipper about it all.

'And how are they treating you?'

'I rarely see them. Lay brothers can, if they want to, sit in the library, but in practice they rarely do. Paul and I live, eat and amuse ourselves in the kitchen. In there at night we are like an old farmer and his son. Reading, or listening to the radio, or playing draughts or chess – he's very good at them both. I read a lot. The County Librarian has promised to keep me well supplied in that quarter.'

'And they don't mind?'

'They don't mind anything I do any longer. I am a man who has lost his faculties. I am off my chump. They are alright. They're a dull bunch. But never forget it, Tom, there is such a thing as Christian charity. I have never in my life experienced such kindness as I have since they shunted me out here.'

Away in his corner Paul's spade rang on a stone. A swallow did a jet dive down and out of the garden. Brainsy was talking of how Paul and himself spent their day. Ten mouths for breakfast, washing up after it, making the beds, sweeping and dusting the whole place, and then off down the Main Street with two big woven shopping bags.

'We're not the most popular customers.' He grinned. 'Probably because they are afraid to cheat us.'

Their shopping done, they might leave the bags behind some counter and go out the road for a stroll, but not before Paul had satisfied his one secret vice.

'He loves his bottle of stout. So, in with us by the back door to Brennan's pub, upstairs to his parlour, and he has his little tipple there like a lord.'

'And you?'

'As you know, I never drink stout. And we can't afford anything else.'

'That's where the ferryboat left you, Brainsy! Guinness and godliness, it's a great combination. You can't whack it.'

'Meaning that you are back on the booze?'

'I wish I was. I'm dying for Easter Sunday to come. Four more days! My stomach thinks my throat is cut. It's very decent of them to give you money for the stout.'

'They give us no money. Poverty, Chastity and Obedience. That's the rule. But we cheat them a bit on the shopping.'

They gossiped about the town. Little gossip. About the tiniest things. Paul knew every hole and corner of the place, every man, woman and child in it. Towards the end Tom said, 'I hope you're not corrupting poor old Paul with all your wild talk. Aren't they afraid you might?'

'I can say anything I like to him. In fact, I say the most outrageous things to him. And they don't mind. He is stone deaf. He's far more likely to corrupt me. He cheats like the devil at chess. There last night when I was waiting for him to make his move I saw a mouse coming out of its hole along the floor under the wainscoting. It had an eye like a robin. I winked at it. It winked at me. I said *Ouutch!* The next thing there was old Paul saying, "Checkmate!" I swear to high heavens he pocketed a pawn while I wasn't looking. We fought all night over it.'

He laughed so heartily that Tom's heart sank. What a way to pass a life! There was a long silence between them. Another swallow swooped in and out of the garden.

'They're coming back,' Brainsy said and Tom, thinking he meant the brothers, got up to go. Brainsy showed him where they were having the peas, and the cauliflowers, and the scarlet runners. Tom looked at them and did not see any of them. When they came, at last, to the gate Brainsy held his hand in a long, hard grip and the furrow between his eyes became intense.

'Look, Brainsy!' Tom cried, holding the holding hand just as tightly. 'If you don't believe in any of this stuff why don't you for God's sake chuck it all up and clear out?'

'And where,' Brainsy asked sadly, 'would I go?'

'Come back with me to Dublin. I'll be quitting here in June. We'll start together all over again.'

'And what would I do? All I'm any good for is teaching. And they've taken that away from me. After all this hullabaloo you know well that I'd never get another job again.'

Their hands parted. He opened the rasping gate. Tom passed through it. They looked at one another through it.

'Don't worry about me, Tom. You know where I live. Come and see me anytime. I'll be alright. All I'll ever miss will be the old chat.'

He raised his hand as if in blessing, and went back to his garden. Tom watched him limping away, turned, went out to the road and shuffled down to the Main Street, where he saw a great host of swallows blowing in through one end of it and out through the other. He went into the first pub he met, and he drank there until he was drunk. It was a habit that would stick to him all his life, always sober as a judge through Lent, always as drunk as an owl on the eve of the Crucifixion. In the dark pool of his pint he saw what the swallows would see: the wide bogland, brown-yellowy, seaweedy green, and the small road driving through it, and the far mountains with their clouds, and a few clustered roofs far below with one or two specks of humans moving between them, and one upturned garden with thickly ivied walls, good for nesting, and a man lying there on his back gazing up at them.

But, O swallow, swallow, swallow! That is the only man I have ever loved. And he is dead.

Thieves

From the beginning it was Fanny Wrenne's idea. The whole gang must go up in a bunch to the cathedral for their Easter Communion. This time a real pilgrimage! It would be like walking to Jerusalem. What was more, they must go up there for first mass. Clamorously the gang danced around her.

'Six o'clock mass! We'll have to get up at four. It'll be pitch-dark. There won't be a soul abroad. We'll be all alone. We'll have all Cork to ourselves. Everybody but us snoring.' Fanny added her masterstroke. 'And after mass, do ye know what we'll do? Buy a bag of broken biscuits and be munching them all the way home.'

It was one stroke too many, as they found when they scattered, racing in all directions to beg pennies from their fathers and mothers, their uncles and their aunts, for the bag of broken biscuits.

Were they gone clean out of their little heads? Were they mad? Kids of nine and ten walking halfway across Cork in the dark of an April morning? To a cathedral that was miles away? Supposing it was raining! And what about if they lost their way? Whose idea was this anyway? Fanny Wrenne's. That kid was ever and always creating trouble.

In the end only two of them met at the bridge that morning. Fanny, because she always got her way, because her mother was dead, and her father away at sea, and she an only child, and her old Aunt Kate was a softie. And Dolly Myles, because her father neither knew nor cared what any one of his eleven children did, and because her mother knew that Fanny Wrenne could be relied on to look after anybody anywhere – a dark, sturdy, bosomy, bottomy boss of a robin who would spend her life bullying every other little bird in the garden away from the crumbs that God meant for all. As for poor Dolly, she was born to be bossed. Eyes as blue and as blank as a doll's, her hair as fair, her cheeks as pink, and her adenoidal lips hanging from her nose in such a sweet little triangle that old gentlemen were always stopping her in the street to pat her curly poll.

They approached one another across the bridge like two dwarf ghosts. Upriver all they could see was the bright window of the waterworks shining down on the smooth curve of its lasher. All they could hear was the faint hum of turbines, and even that came and went on the morning wind. Downriver they saw nothing at all but the daffodil of the first gaslamp, and, far away, one vast cloud reflecting the night glow of the city. Overhead the sky was as black and blue as a mackerel.

Fanny had brought her Aunt Kate's best umbrella. It was red, it bore a red tassel, its handle was a scarlet bird's beak with a glassy eye embedded on each side of its head. She brought it because Dolly had told her the night before that her mother had a good friend named Mrs Levey who lived near the cathedral in a place called Flatfoot Lane. Fanny immediately said they would call on Mrs Levey on the way to mass, and give her the umbrella as an Easter present. In return she would be certain to give them a penny each as an Easter present, and with the two pennies they would buy the broken biscuits on the way home.

The gaslamps were no better than candles. Between their wavering scraps of light they could not so much see the footpath as feel for it with their feet. They walked hand in hand. They did not speak at all. They met nobody. They heard nothing but their own footsteps. Every house was as dark as a prison wall. Then, suddenly in one house they saw a lighted upstairs window. It made them speak. Who could be awake at this hour? Somebody sick? Somebody dying? Staring up at it, Dolly put her arm around Fanny's waist and Fanny clutched the umbrella to her like a baby. Could it be a robber? They hurried on fearfully. Soon they began to dawdle. Once, they looked back towards the west and were glad to see a star floating behind a black cloud. Ahead of them the sky was paling and opening but there was no star to be seen there at all. They sat on a low wall to rest and began to argue about how many broken biscuits you could get for tuppence. They started off again, still arguing, took two wrong turnings, and were only halfway up the long sloping street to the cathedral when Shandon Tower exploded into the three-quarters chime so close to them that Dolly let out a squeak of fright. *Do, So. La. Re ... Re. La ...*

'It's alright,' Fanny soothed. 'We've lots of time. So long as you know where Ma Levey's house is. And,' threateningly, 'I hope to God you do!'

Dolly looked down a dark laneway to their right. 'I know it's up here somewhere.' She looked across the street at the maw of another alley. 'Or could it be that way?' Blankly she looked back down the hill. 'Or did we come too far?' With a wild rush of assurance she chose the first laneway, and in a second, they were swallowed into its black gullet, running around and around in a whale's belly, through dusky gullies and dark guts, thin defiles and narrow, whirling shafts, dead-end lanes and turn-back cross trenches, all nameless and all smelly, only to find themselves ejected exactly where they began just as a soft sprinkle of April rain began to fall. Seeing that Fanny was about to shout, Dolly got her shout in first. 'It must be the other way!' Again they were blown about like two bits of white paper through more revolving lanes, dykes, alleyways and passages, lined with more dwarfs' houses and white-washed cabins, some thatched, some slated, each with its holland blind drawn down tightly, all of them so close together that a woman could, without moving her body, have stretched her hand from her own door to her neighbour's for the loan of a sup of milk or to return yesterday's newspaper. In every one of those cobbled lanes there was a runnel, already trickling with rainwater. There was barely room for it between the lines of cabins. There was no room at all for a footpath. They circled and descended, climbed and came down again, twisted and turned until a vast giant suddenly soared up above them with a great black clock face that silently said five minutes to six. At the sight of Shandon Tower where she least expected to meet it, Dolly burst into tears and Fanny, in a rage, pointed the bayonet of her umbrella at her belly.

'The house!' she screamed. 'Or I'll spit you up against that wall.'

'But,' Dolly wailed, 'I was only up here once. And I was with me mudder. And it was two years ago. And I was only seven.'

'Find that house!'

'If we could only find Flatfoot Lane, I know I'd know the house.'

'How would you know it? This place is maggoty with houses.'

'It have a white card in the window with Mrs Levey's name on it.'

'March!'

Dolly snuffled and pleaded.

'Why can't we keep the umbrella. It's not your umbrella. You stole it. And if it goes on raining we'll be drowned.'

At this sign of grace the sky ceased to weep, but the devil smiled. By magic there appeared, just above their heads, a bright red board that said FLATFOOT LANE. Here there were real houses, small but two-storied, in red brick, with two windows above and one window and a door below. More cobbles, no pavement, another gurgling refuse-runnel, and at the end of it a blank wall. They raced up one side of it and down the other, and, at last, there, between looped lace curtains, was the white card. It said in black print MIRIAM LEVEY. Beneath the name it said LOANS. On its green door there was a brassy knocker shaped like an amputated hand. Fanny seized it, sent a rattle of gunfire echoing up and down the lane, and looked at the upstairs window expectantly. Nobody stirred. She looked across the lane and could just see the tiptop of the clock tower, a tiny green dome carrying a big golden salmon, its weathervane gleaming in the risen sun and stirring faintly in the morning wind. Still, no sound, not a breath, not a thing stirring except when a white cat flowed along the base of the enclosing wall and leaped over it like a wave.

'Maybe,' Dolly said hopefully, 'she's dead?'

Fanny sent another dozen rounds of riflefire up and down the lane. They heard the upper window squeak open, saw ten bony fingers slide over the windowsill and Mrs Levey's tiny witch's face, yawning up at the sky from underneath a cellophane bag full of white hair in blue curlers. She yawned for so long that they thought she would never close her gummy mouth again. When she had finished her yawning she peered sleepily around the lane, said, 'Pusspuss! Pusspuss!' and finally looked down at the two white children. Fanny cheerfully waved the red umbrella at her.

'Good morning, Mrs Levey. Me Aunt Kate sent us up to you with this gorgeous umbrella for a present for Easter.'

'Your Aunt who?' she asked, and the word 'who' turned into another prolonged yawn. She peered down at the pair of them, shook her head, said, 'I'm afraid, child, I don't know no aunts at all. But, anyway, whoever she is . . .' Another yawn. 'Or whatever it is, leave it there on the windowsill and I'll get it when I wake up,' and withdrew, and the window banged.

Fanny gazed reproachfully at Dolly, who, knowing what was coming, lifted her blonde eyebrows, put her hand on her hip, and, self-dissociatingly, began to examine the architecture of every house along the opposite side of the lane.

'So that,' Fanny said scornfully,' 'is your ma's lovely friend?'

'That,' Dolly piped, without as much as a backward glance, 'is your aunt's lovely umbrella.'

'A mangy ould maggoty ould moneylender.'

'Our credit was always good,' Dolly said loftily.

Fanny looked imploringly at the sky. The great gong saved her, booming the full hour, and all over the valley lesser bells softly announcing the angelus.

'We'll be late,' she shouted, threw the scarlet object on the windowsill and they scurried off back to the open street of the hill.

In the valley spires and chimneys were not tipped by the sun. Between these hill-houses the only sign that the night was going was a man who raced before them, lamplighter by night, lampquencher in the morning, plucking the head off every daffodil as he ran.

They hastened into the cathedral, panting. It blazed with lights, candles and white chrysanthemums. Not more than a couple of dozen worshippers. The priest, robed in the violet of Lent, was standing with his back to the altar, reading from a book the gospel story of the woman caught in adultery. ('What does that mean?' Dolly whispered, and Fanny whispered, 'Watering the milk.') Afterwards, Dolly said the bit she liked was where Jesus said to her, 'Run along with you, now, but don't do that any more,' but Fanny said the bit she liked was where Jesus kept stooping to the ground, writing some strange words whose meaning, the priest said, nobody will understand to the end of time. After that the sermon began and it went on so long that their heads began to nod, and they had to nudge and kick at one another to wake up, then making shocked faces and giggling, or, for fun, pretending to yawn like Ma Levey in the window. At last the priest ended his sermon, throwing his white wings open to say, 'Three weeks after He forgave that unfortunate woman they murdered Him, calling Him a criminal, but three weeks from now He will rise again as, in a few minutes, He will appear amongst us in the shape of a white circle, shining and immortal. Leave ye all kneel down now and prepare to welcome Him as He descends from heaven.'

The time for communion came. Side by side, their hands joined like the angels in holy pictures, their eyes modestly cast down, they walked slowly to and from the altar rails, as Sister Angelina at school had taught them to do. Slowly, the mass ended. There were more public prayers after it, and then they were standing in the porch, the city below them, the morning about them, the gaslamps all quenched, the pavements dancing with rain. A postman's black cape shone. A milkman, hooped against the wind and the rain, raced from his cart to pour milk into a saucer-covered jug on a doorstep, leaped back into his chariot and drove off with his whip sailing behind him like a flag.

'What about the umbrella?' Dolly said accusingly, and, because of the rain, longingly.

'Why don't we take it back?' Fanny cried, and hand in hand they galloped down the hill and back into Flatfoot Lane. The trickle of rainwater still ran whispering down the central runnel. In an upstairs window an old man, slowly and dexterously shaving one side of his face before a small square mirror balanced on top of the window sash, suspended his razor to watch them gallop through the rain, halt before the white card, and stare at the empty windowsill. Fanny rattled the hand on the green door and peered upward, the rain pouring down her face. The upper window squeaked open and Mrs Levey looked down.

'Oh, Law!' she said mildly. 'Is it ye again?'

'We made an awful mistake, Mrs Levey, we brought you the wrong umbrella, would yeh ever throw it down to us and we'll bring yeh the right one tomorrow morning at exactly the same time.'

The old face withdrew. After a moment the red object came sailing out through the window over their heads, plonked on the wet cobbles, and the window banged shut.

The umbrella was as old as sin. It bulged like a carrot. It was tied by a bit of string. It had a black bamboo handle. The old man in the opposite window, one half of his face red, the other half white, hailed them.

'Use it, girls,' he shouted. 'That's rain! Oho!' he assured them, waving his frothy razor, 'I seen it all. Ye gave her yeer lovely new umbrella and she throws ye back her leavings. Just like her!' he roared at the top of his voice across the lane. 'The bloody ould Jew' and returned to his tender shaving.

Fanny picked up the carroty umbrella, untied the bit of string, shot the gamp open above her head, and from it there showered scores and scores of pieces of paper that the wind at once sent blowing wildly all over the cobbles. The old man, watching, let out a roar of delight that drowned the last strokes of the seventh hour. Others who must also have been watching from behind their curtains, slammed up their windows, leaned out, cheered and bawled and pointed joyfully to one another.

In astonishment the two children stared around them at what they had done. Up and down the lane, more and more doors opened and more people pointed, laughing and shouting in chorus, 'Levey the thievey, the dirty ould sheeny, rob ye and leave ye!' Overhead the old woman's window opened. She leaned out, screamed like a peacock, vanished, and the next minute shot past them, a man's overcoat over her head and her nightdress like a shawl, racing hither and thither barefooted over the wet cobbles after her dockets. As she raced and stooped and picked, the whole lane kept bawling their horrid chorus at her. Only once did she pause and that was to shake her skinny fist at them. Then, suddenly, there was total silence. She had collapsed on her hunkers in the middle of the lane, her withered arms raised to the pouring sky, her mouth wide open, pleading to it in some strange language. As suddenly she fell silent, her head and her hands sunk into her lap. Slowly, a handsome young man came forward in his bare feet to lift her. After him an old woman came, and then another, and another, began to pick up the bits of paper, until one by one all the watchers were silently gathering up her dockets and pressing them into her crumpled hands. The two children ran.

Not until they halted at the river did Fanny notice that the rotten scarlet thing had accompanied them. She threw it over the quay wall, where, by stretching up on their toes to look, they could see it floating slowly away on the outgoing tide.

'Down the river!' Fanny hooted.

'Under every bridge,' Dolly giggled.

'Out to sea!' Fanny shouted.

Laughing they turned for home, stamping into the puddles of the rain, screaming with delight as they kicked arcs of water at one another. They lifted their wide-open mouths to the trees along the Mall trying to catch the falling drops. When they came to the iron railings opposite their own parish church of Saint Vincent they swung on them like two white wheels to see the rain falling up, and the church spires pointing down, the whole world standing on its head. By the time they came to their own bridge the rain had petered out, the sky was white and blue, the river water was smooth, the fields beyond it were empty and wet.

'Anyway,' Fanny said, 'even if we got the pennies we couldn't have bought broken biscuits. Not a shop open.'

They saw a light in a cottage, and a light in a villa on the side of the hill, and one window in a house beside the river was reflected longingly in the pure water. Dolly cocked her head.

'Listen!' she said.

They listened. Far away, around the bend of the road, from maybe half a mile away they could barely hear it. It would be lighted, and empty. The first tram.

Of Sanctity and Whiskey

As Luke Regan drove down to Saint Killian's for the first sitting he kept shifting around the fading cards of his schoolboy's memories of the place and wishing the press had never got on to this thing. It was a pleasant idea, of course, and he could understand the columnists playing it up – but the stupid things they wrote about it! 'Former pupil returns to his old school to paint his old teacher... This portrait of a distinguished Headmaster by a distinguished Academician is certain to reflect two sensibilities in perfect rapport with one another... This new portrait by Mr Luke Regan, RHA, of Brother Hilary Harty, the retired Head of Saint Killian's College, should record not one journey but two journeys from youth to maturity...' He had already confided to his boozing friends that he found the whole bloody thing extremely embarrassing; not least because he could see that they thought he was just boasting about it. He had only been in that school for three years, between the ages of twelve and fifteen. It was forty years ago. He had not the slightest recollection of this Brother Hilary Harty, and he felt sure that old man could not possibly remember him.

Hilary Harty? He hoped he was not that old snob they used to call Dikey, a fellow with a face like a coffin and eyes like a dead hen. Could he be Flossy, who used to collect jokes in a notebook as fat as a Bible: head and a face like a turnip; purple, orange and green – that would be a nice palette to have to work with! Without affection he remembered Popeyes, always blinking at you like the flicker of a motorcar that the driver had forgotten to turn off. But his name was Hurley. Now, little Regis would be a marvellous subject – a pink-and-white angel face with a fierce furrow between the eyebrows. That would be a challenging puss – if your were lucky enough, and had time enough to get him talking about himself. But Hilary? The name rang no chime, sweet, cracked or otherwise. 'Two sensibilities in perfect rapport with one another...' Had none of these fellows ever been to school themselves? Didn't they know well that no boy ever knows anything human at all about his teachers? Men dressed in black soutanes and bony collars, with names like ships, or stars, or horses – Hyperion, Aquarius, Berengarius, Arkel – floating into your classroom every morning, saying, 'Irregular verbs today!' or 'Did we polish off Queen Anne yet?' and if you didn't know your stuff, giving you three on each hand with the leather strap stuck in their black belts like a policeman's truncheon. All any boy ever wants from any teacher is that he might give you a bit of a chance now and again; understand, or know, or guess that the real reason you did not know your history, or your maths, was not because you lost the book, or had a headache, or broke your pen but because you saw Molly Ryan yesterday with high leather boots halfway up her fat legs and you simply had to dodge out that night to be gassing with her under the gaslamp by the back gate, watching her swinging her pigtails and admiring her toes just to provoke you. Little Regis would have understood; he was the only one of them who understood anything. He would give you a good clout on the ear, look at you hard and say, 'I'll give you this one chance, Master Regan, but if you ever do it again I'll have the hide off you.' And you loved him for it. But the rest of them? Human? The shock he got the day he saw Popeyes laughing with a woman in the Main Street! (Jesus! I must have been a right little prig in those days!) Not to mention the evening he saw Monsieur Joffre, their French teacher, coming out of a pub wiping the froth off his Clemenceau moustache. And by the same token not a drop must pass his lips while he was doing this portrait. Not with two hundred quid from the Past Pupils' Union depending on it. Anyway, he had been off the booze for four months now. 'Drop it, Luke!' – his doctor's last words. 'Or it will drop you into a nice, deep, oblong hole up in Glasnevin. Ninety per cent of your bloodstream is pure alcohol, and you know where that finally lodges?' – and he had tapped his forehead. 'DT's. Epilepsy, Neuritis, Insanity, God knows what!' The memory of it frightened him so much that when he was passing through Kilcrea he halted for one last, one absolutely last quick one before he arrived. And, just for precaution's sake, he packed a bottle of Paddy Flaherty in his hold-all in case he got a cold, or needed a little nightcap to send him to sleep after a day's revving-up at the easel.

The only change he could see, guess, presume or infer in Coonlahan was the rows of cars parked on each side of the Main Street. Surely, in his time, there were only a few horse-drawn carts or donkey-butts?

Chromium everywhere now and neon strips. The street's surface, asphalted, recalled mud and cowdung on market days. With relief he saw a neat-looking hotel called The Shamrock, and booked himself in there.

'How long, Mr Regan?' the freshfaced young woman said with a welcoming smile.

'How did you know my name?'

'Ah, sure the whole town knows about the painting.'

He winced.

'Four nights, please.'

'Only four?'

He winced again. In the Academy his colleagues called him Luca Fa Presto, after a certain Neapolitan painter who could finish any picture in twenty-four hours.

'It's a small portrait. Head and shoulders.'

Did she think he was going to live in the monastery? All the same he felt a bit ashamed that he was not. There were painters who would have done it, toiling to reveal the habits of a lifetime in a face. Degas must have done it before he began his *Uncle and Niece*. Manet must have known every damned thing about those three people he imprisoned behind the green railing of *The Balcony*. Courbet had put a whole countryside into those three men in *Bonjour, Monsieur Courbet*. Still, when he had driven out of the town and come to the big iron gateway, with SAINT KILLIAN'S COLLEGE half-mooned across it in gilded lettering, and saw the half-mile of avenue leading straight as a ruler up to the barrack-bare front of the college, grim as a tombstone against the sinking sun, he wondered whether Degas, or Monet, or Courbet, or Rembrandt, or Holbein or any of them would have wanted to soak himself in so dreary a joint as this either in the name of literal truth or ideal beauty. Wishing that he had had another drink in The Shamrock before facing this Brother Hilary Harty, he rang the bell.

A cheerful little lay brother, spry and bright as a monkey, showed him into the front parlour where, with painful clarity, he remembered the evening his mother had handed him over there to a matron named Miss Wall and with a face like one. The literal truth of the room leaped to the eye: linoleum on the floor, horsehair chairs, a round table glistening with a mock walnut veneer, a gas-fire unlit. As for ideal beauty: pictures in monochrome, *The Agony in the Garden*, the ghostly face of Christ on the pious fraud called *The Veil of Veronica*,

somebody's *Annunciation*, and was that Breughel's *Tower of Babel*
lifting the clouds? The Past Pupils' Union was going to make him earn
every penny of this two hundred quid. The door was hurled open, a
powerful-bodied old brother strode in, jolly-faced and beaming, and on
the spot the setting sun hit face and everything became joyous, and
splendid and okay.

'Luke Regan!' he all but shouted. 'After all these years!'

And the two of them were laughing and shaking one another's hands
as energetically and boisterously as only two men can do who do not
know one another from Adam. But what a head! Ripe for marble! For
marble and porphyry! Nose rubicund, eyes blue as gentians, and an
astonishingly protruding lower lip, the sure sign of a born talker. Hair
white, thin on top but curling like the last of the harpers around his
neck. Manet be blowed! Poor old Rembrandt! It was going to be the
portrait of his life. Green curtain behind, ochre streaks of sunlight,
buckets of carmine, lumps of it laid on with bold hard brushstrokes –
half-inch brushes at that. Energy, strength, tenderness, humour! No
more of that blasted pink toothpaste enamel that he had been floating
all over the gobs of endless company directors for the last ten years. Not,
to be fair, to flatter them but to flatter their stupid wives. 'Oh, Mister
Regan, I think Eddie is much younger than you are making him out to
be!' Or 'D'ye think, Mister Regan, you could make the tie a bit smoother
like? The way you have it makes him look old and careless like.'
Meaning, 'My God, man, do you want people to think *I'm* that old?'

'Brother Hilary, when do you think we can begin?'

He was so excited that when he got back to The Shamrock he had
to go into the bar for a large one to calm his nerves. In its gold pool he
saw the title on the catalogue of the Academy, where the portrait
would be shown publicly for the first time. *The Old Dominie*. By Luke
Regan, RHA. Not for Sale. Or what about *The Good Shepherd*? Or maybe,
Ex Cathedra. Or *Post Multos Annos*? With a neat gold tab at the bottom
of the frame saying, *Gladly wolde he lerne and gladly teche*. Tactile
values? His fingers involuntarily began to mould the face. The man
sitting beside him said, 'Hello, Mister Regan.' He sighed and did not
deny it.

'My name is Halligan, Harry Halligan. We all knew you were
coming. All Ireland knows about the painting. You have a great
character there in old Leatherlip.'

'Leatherlip?'

Far away a bell chimed harshly, curtains parted on a small red light at the end of a mile-long corridor.

'Don't you remember? Or didn't ye call him that in your day?'

'How extraordinary! We did call one fellow that. But surely, not *this* man?'

'*Tempus fugit*. It's twenty-five years since I was at Saint Killian's. He was slim then, bushy black hair, eyes like a razor blade. You knew him in his thirties. And you really can't remember him?'

'He will come back to me. I'll quarry him out. That's how a painter works, working in and in, burrowing, excavating. It's like archaeology, you don't know what you are looking for until you find it. Sooner or later the face speaks.'

Halligan half-turned to the woman on his left: a bosomy, high-coloured little blonde. Horsy type.

'Let me introduce you to my wife. Valerie, this is Luke Regan the famous painter.'

She gave a cool hand and a cooler 'Howdyedo?' in a loud Anglo-Irish voice. No smile. Regan could feel the antagonism in her, and wondered at it. They had two more quick ones together before Mrs Halligan abruptly hauled her husband off with her. Regan took a last one by himself for the road to sleep.

Because of the light he decided to use the front parlour for a studio. It had three tall windows facing north. He could come and go without bother. By two o'clock, when his man would be free and the light good for two hours or so, he had managed to get a throne fixed up, a green curtain hung for background, his easel and work table ready and the inflatable lay figure that he always travelled with (one of his neatest Fa Presto tricks) draped with a black soutane that he would be working on every morning.

'I can't believe, Brother Hilary,' he laughed, as his charcoal lightly and rapidly sketched in the outline, 'that you are really seventy-five. You look about fifty.'

He always talked while he worked to keep his subject from stiffening or sagging.

'Aha!' the old boy laughed triumphantly. 'Mixing with youth all my life, that's what does it. That,' finger magisterially aloft, 'and the regular life. A dull life I suppose, not like you, out in the world, travelling, meeting interesting people, doing interesting things. But I have had my compensations. No worries, no regrets, no tensions. The rut, Luke. The beaten path. The ascetic discipline. Simple food. Good country air. Constant exercise. No excesses of any kind. You wouldn't grow fat on my kind of life, my boy. But that's what turns every monk into a man.'

When he came to the mouth he stared long and hard at the protruding lower lip. Again that far-off bell. Leatherlip? The eyes were curiously small but they gave out sparks when he talked. He would have given anything for an early photograph of the softer eyes of the boy buried behind those sharp orbs. He saw that the nose was red because it was veined all over. If this were a company director he would have said at once, 'Chronic alcoholic.' He knew rosacea when he saw it. Chiefly in elderly women. The wages of virtue. Chronic tea-drinkers. Gastritis. Monastery food. Probably an ulcer. Teeth browning from age and pipe-smoking. There would be black centres on the tip of every one of them. He frowned again at the big lip. A hard mouth in a jolly face. Now, what in hell did that portend? Silence. A good subject – he held the pose patiently.

'The rut?' he murmured, looking up, looking down. 'The beaten path? "The path of the just is as the shining light that shineth more and more unto the perfect day."'

'I'm glad to see that you read your Bible, Luke.'

'Now and again, Brother. A little to the left, Brother. Thank you, Brother.'

The light on the lip threw an interesting shadow. The nose became gory.

'Ah, yes!' concentrating on the jutting lip. 'Now and again... "Return, return O Shulamite. Thy belly is like a heap of wheat set about with lilies... Thy neck is as a tower of ivory... Many waters cannot quench love, neither can the floods drown it."'

He glanced up. The eyes were blazing, the whole expression of the face had changed, the brows gathered down fiercely, the cheeks as scarlet as the nose. His charcoal flew, dragging down the eyebrows. That revealing wet light on the lip, thrust out a whole inch – that, above all, *that* he must keep.

'I think, Mister Regan, I think, Luke, it might have been better if you had concentrated on the New Testament.'

By a forty-year-old reflex he glanced at the black belt around the belly to see if he still carried the strap. No time for that now. Now? Memory was now!

'Now, Brother, I begin painting.'

As he mixed his colours he cooled, a sign that he was in tiptop form. He knew they called him Luca Fa Presto. Bloody fools! You boil at the inspiration. You go cold as ice in the execution.

'You're dead right, Brother,' he said soapily. 'The new Covenant. There is the true wisdom. I learned that here in Saint Killy's.' (Funny how the old slang name came back to him. It was all creeping back to him.) 'I often think, Brother, of those wonderful words of Saint Matthew. "Behold the birds of the air . . . They sow not, neither do they reap . . . Consider the lilies of the fields . . . Even Solomon in all his glory was not arrayed like one of these."'

To his relief the mollified voice quoted back to him.

'"Behold, a greater than Solomon is here."'

He looked up at the veined nose. The tuning fork for a study in *rouge et noir*. He touched the canvas with carmine.

'Oh, a beautiful saying, Brother! A darlint saying, Brother. And so wise, Brother. So very wise.'

Not too red now, for Christ's sake. No wife, but the Past Pupils' Union would have to be pleased. And, after all, two hundred johnny-o'goblins in this job! A long silence.

'And there's another fine phrase. Muscular Christianity. A Jew invented that. Disraeli. A great man in lots of ways.'

'A Jew?' said the voice coldly.

'By the way, Brother,' he said hurriedly. 'Talking of muscle. When I was here in twenty-six, Brother, the Gaelic Football team was going great guns. How is it doing these happy days?'

The old man beamed and told him. The rest of the sitting went as smooth as milk. The only other little lurch came when he looked out at the sky, threw down his brushes, and said that the light was going.

'Can I see what you have done so far, Luke?'

He handled it with expert joviality.

'We never do, Brother, not until we've polished off the victim.'

They parted in laughter and with warm handshakes. He took the key of the parlour with him; he would be working on the lay figure in the morning.

Halligan was waiting for him in the bar; alone this time. Seeing that his glass was at low tide, Regan invited him to freshen it up.

'I won't say no. How's the masterpiece doing?'

A stocky man. Heavy hands, but they could be a craftsman's. A fawn waistcoat with brass buttons. Ruddy cheeks. A gentleman farmer? A fisherman? Not a doctor – no doctor would dare drink at a public bar in a small town like this. The wife had had the smell of money.

'He's coming back to me slowly. Another sitting and I'll have him smoked out.'

'What,' eagerly, 'are you finding?'

Regan eye-cornered him. This fellow might be a member of the Past Pupil's Union.

'A splendid character. I was just wondering did he ever teach me history?'

'Were you a senior?'

'I was only what we used to call a gyb. A Good Young Boy. I came here when I was twelve. Straight from the nuns. Our Ladies of the Holy Bower. You wouldn't think it now to look at me, but I used to be their little angel. Curly hair. They used to make me sing solo at Benediction. In a lacy surplice, purple soutane, red tie. They spoiled me. It was only by the blessing of God I didn't turn into a queer. I may tell you the change from there to here was pretty tough. I only stayed three years.'

'No, you wouldn't have had him. And,' surveying him humorously, 'you may have been a little angel, Mister Regan, but you've put on a bit of weight since then. Thirteen and a half stone? He only taught the seniors, and after he became Headmaster he had no fixed classes at all. Anyway, his particular obsession was English Grammar. He was dotty about it. He was a bit of a megalomaniac, really. Couldn't give it up. Even after he became Head he used to rove around the school from class to class leathering it into us. Of course he's retired now, but I'm told he still does it. Did he never come into your classroom to wallop *I seen* out of you and *I saw* into you?'

Halligan laughed as if in happy memory of the walloping, and, on the spot, Regan had his man whole and entire. The terror of his very first day at Saint Killy's often repeated, seeing the lean black ghost come floating in. Like a starved wolf. One hand waving the leather strap behind his back like a black tail. The rasping voice. 'What is a relative clause? What is an adverbial clause? Decline the verb *see* in the past tense. No, it is not! Hold out your hand. Take that. And that. And that.' And, always, the one thing all boys loathe in teachers, as sarcastic as acid. Oh, a proper bastard!

'Do I take it, Mister Halligan, that you didn't particularly like it at Saint Killy's?'

'I got on there all right. I was good at games. And Leatherlip was mad on games. "The Irish," he was always telling us, "are famous all over the world as sportsmen. Strong men." It was he started boxing at Saint Killy's. He used to knock the hell out of me in the ring. I got so mad at him one day that I deliberately gave him one right under the belt. And I could hit hard that time. When he got his wind back he nearly murdered me. He was the only fly in the ointment.' He leaned over and whispered: 'I often thought afterwards that he was the only wasp in the ointment.' He glanced quickly around the bar and said in a loud voice, 'Mind you, Brother Hilary is a great organizer. He built up a great school here. We are all very proud of Saint Killian's in this town.'

('Fuck *you!*' Regan thought.)

'And most justifiably so, Mister Halligan. By the way, are you a member of the Past Pupils' Union?'

Halligan smiled crookedly. His voice fell.

'I didn't tell you I'm the local vet. I look after the Jersey herd up there.' He beckoned to the barmaid. 'The same again, Miss Noble.'

'Family?' Regan asked.

'Three boys.'

'They at school here?'

Halligan shuffled his glass a bit.

'Not exactly. You see . . . Well, the fact is Valerie is a Protestant. We met at the hunt. Actually, she's a niece of Lord Boyne's.' (A good connection for a vet, Regan thought.) 'Before I married her I knew I'd have to do something to smooth the way for her. For myself, of course, I didn't give a damn. To hell with them. But for poor little Valerie . . . You live up in Dublin, you can do what you like there, you don't understand what it's like in small places like this. But,' he winked, 'there's always ways and means. Two months before I got married, do you know what I did?' He nudged and again winked. 'I joined the local Knights of Columbanus. And, by God, it worked. Though I'll never forget the first time I went to the Club after the wedding. The Grand Knight got up and he says, "Since our last meeting I suppose you all know that one of our brothers got married." Christ Almighty, I thought, here it comes! He's going to give me hell for marrying a Protestant. I'm going to be ruined for life in this place. Far from it! He complimented me most warmly. I drove home that night singing like a bird. I knew I'd done one of the smartest things in my life. After a year I dropped them. But when it came to where we'd send the boys to school, Valerie and myself had one hell of a fight. I said we simply had to send them to Saint Killy's. We started with the oldest boy. The very first day he came home from school with his two hands red as pulp from Leatherlip's strap. After that Valerie put her foot down. We came to a sensible compromise. We sent them all to school in England. One of the finest Catholic schools in the world. Nobody could object to that.'

'Very shrewd. Very wise move. And after that, no opposition? Miss Noble, fill 'em up again.'

'Not half! The day I whipped Tommy out of school Leatherlip wrote me a stinker. He went all around town saying I was a snob, and a lah-di-dah, and an Anglicized Irishman, and a toady, and God knows what else. Just to show you – it wasn't until he retired that I got the job of looking after the college herd.'

Regan laughed.

'Elephants never forget.'

'It's no joke,' Halligan whispered solemnly. 'Don't delude yourself. That man never forgets anything. Or anybody.'

'I wonder,' Regan said uncomfortably.

Just then Valerie Halligan came in. He noted that after one quick one she hauled her husband away. From her manner it was plain that she did not approve of his latest drinking companion. This time Regan did not wonder why.

Not that he had ever been much leathered by anybody at Saint Killy's, and never once by Leatherlip. On the contrary, he had often wished he would leather him after the day he called him out of the class and sat him on his knee, and said to the rest of them after he had leathered them all, 'Look at this clever little boy. He knows what a dependent clause is. And he's only twelve, and straight from the nuns, as small and fresh and rosy as a cherry. Why don't you slobs know it as well as he does?' His nickname became Cherry. They called him Leatherlip's Lapdog or Leatherlip's Pet. They used to corner him and say things like, 'Cherry, if *he* comes in today for more frigging grammar your job is to suck up to him. Get him into a good humour or he'll leather us and we'll puck the hell outa you.' He used to try, but it was always the same, 'See this bright little boy!' And, after school, they would shove him, and taunt him and puck him. Once he deliberately tried to get leathered by failing to write out six sentences that night before on *shall* and *will*. The strap swished, the brows came down, a grey spittle appeared at each corner of the big lip. Terror shook his bones.

'"I *will* go there tomorrow." Is that correct?'

'No, Brother. Plain future statements in the first person must always have *shall*.'

'"We would not win a single match with a team like that." Is that correct?'

'No, Brother. Plain conditional statements in the first person must have *should*.'

'Come here to me, boy. Now, listen to that bright little boy, straight from the nuns . . .'

For three years he had suffered hell from the benign approbation of that accursed old fathead.

'Miss Noble, the same again. No, make it a double this time.'

He went to bed plastered.

'Well, Brother Hilary, I hear nothing all over the town but people singing your praises. You've made a great job of this college. The doyen of Saint Killian's.' The old monk beamed softly.

'Ah, well, Luke, I've done my humble best. But, mind you,' rather less softly. 'I had to fight all the way.' Far from softly: 'Opposition. I had to keep my hand on my dagger every moment of the day.'

'Aha, but you fought well, Brother. You fought the good fight, Brother. "To give and not to count the cost, to fight and not to heed the wounds."'

'Who said that?' – suspiciously.

The lip out again with the lovely wet light on it. Porcine. Sensual. Lickerish. Loose. Deboshed by pride and righteousness. Daringly he slapped on a fleck of viridian. And, by God, it was just right. He kept him waiting for the answer.

'Saint Ignatius Loyola said that. A great body of men, the Jesuits.'

The two eyes cold. Turquoise? No! Pine-needle blue? Hell's bells, snow and ice are the one thing no Irish painter can ever get right. Nor the British. Nor the Italians. You have to live with the stuff like the Dutch and the Scans. The gore of the cheeks would have to bring it out. Cherry? Damn you, I'll give you cherry. No ablation here. Warts and all. Maxillae of an anthropomorph. Ears of a bat. That time he had to sit on his lap in class! The hair stuck out of his ears.

'Have you ever had any Protestants in Saint Killy's, Brother?'

The little finger dug into a hairy ear and wagged there twenty times.

'I don't approve of mixed marriages and I don't approve of mixed schooling. Protestants haven't our morality, Luke. The morality of every Protestant I ever met was written into his cheque-book. They are completely devoid of our mystical sense of the otherworld. Not like you and me. I don't like Protestants. You mentioned some Jew yesterday. I'll be frank with you, Luke. I don't like Jews either.'

'Oh, you're on to something there, Brother. A cunning bloody race. Very able, though. I was talking about Disraeli.' He seized his palette knife for the coarse, oily skin of the cheeks. 'Do you remember what he said the time Dan O'Connell taunted him with being a Jew. "Yes, I *am* a Jew, and when ancestors of the right honourable gentleman were brutal savages in an unknown island, mine were priests in the temple of Solomon."'

The old warhorse out on grass. Teeth bared. Sepia? Burnt sienna?

'For Heaven's sake, Luke! I do wish you'd stop talking about Solomon!'

'All the same, Jesus was a Jew.'

'One of the mysteries of the world!'

'And he chose the Jews.' Laughing delightedly at the furious face on his canvas he quoted. '"How odd/That God/Should choose/ The Jews."'

In laughter the ritual answer pealed from the throne.

'"Oh no, not odd./They hoped to God/Some day/He'd pay."'

They both cackled.

'Ah, Brother, you understand it all!'

'We understand one another, Luke. Two comrades in Christ!'

He worked on. From the distant playing fields young voices cheered. A long silence. When he looked up he saw a profile. The old man was gazing at the moony face of Christ looming through the Veil of Veronica.

'Do you know Greek, Luke? A pity! There is a wonderful Greek word. *Archiropito*. It is the perfect word for that image of Christ. Painted by no human hand. Painted by the angels. The day I became Headmaster I bought three dozen copies of that angelic image. I put one in every classroom. I gave one to every brother to hang over his bed.'

He sighed. Regan looked at the fraud. Then he looked at his portrait.

Never had he felt such a sense of power, energy, truth to life. The light was fading. 'Tomorrow is Sunday. I might do a little work on the background. Then on Monday we'll have the last sitting.'

'And then,' as eagerly as a boy, 'I can see it?'

A laggard nod. As they parted the old man put his arm around his shoulder.

'My dear friend!' He sighed affectionately. 'Take care of yourself, Luke,' who gave one backward glance at his easel; the face was virtually finished, the body half finished, the soul naked. Areas of bare canvas at the edges surrounded it all like a ragged veil.

That evening the Halligans came together, had one quick one and left, promising to call on Sunday afternoon and go out to the college for a secret look at the unfinished masterpiece. He stayed on alone. The Saturday night crowd was dense. He felt he was drinking with half the town. He was the last to leave the bar, pushed out, blind drunk, by the barman and old Noble. He took a bottle of whiskey to bed with him. He woke late. The angelus was slowly tolling and under his window hollow feet were echoing along the pavement to last mass. He drank some more and slept some more. He was wakened by the maid knocking at his door to ask him did he want to eat something. He ordered her to bring him a bottle of whiskey. When she returned she stamped the bottle distastefully on his chest of drawers and banged the door after her. Halligan came up at four, refused to drink with him, said that Valerie was waiting outside in the station wagon, helped him to dress and all but carried him downstairs. He was tolerantly amused by his stumblings and fumblings as he tried to get into the car, but Mrs Halligan was not. 'Oh, for Christ's sake!' she growled at her husband. 'He needs to be pumped!'

When they had pushed open the hall door of the college and crept cautiously across the empty hall to the parlour, she had to take the key from his helpless hand to open the door. They entered twilight. Regan dragged back the window curtains, bade Halligan switch on the light, and with one forensic arm presented them to the easel. For one minute's silence he watched Halligan's mouth fall open and his eyelids soar. Her eyelashes peered.

'God almighty!' Halligan whispered. 'You have him to a T.'

'T for Truth,' he cried triumphantly.

Halligan turned to his wife.

'What d'ye think, Valerie?'

She looked at him, she looked at Regan, she looked at the portrait. Then she edged Halligan aside, stood before the portrait, and, one hand on her hip, extended her silence to two minutes.

'Isn't it stu – PEN – dous, Valerie?'

She walked away to the window, did a tiny drum roll with her nails on the glass, turned to them and spoke, quietly, coldly and brassily.

'Don't be a damn fool, Halligan. Mister Regan! I know nothing about painting, but I know one thing, for certain, about that painting. Nobody will buy it. Not here, anyway. Are you, Halligan, going to get up in the committee of the Past Pupils' Union and say that portrait is stupendous? Vote for it? Pay for it? And hang it? And where? There's only one place in this town where you could hang that picture – in the bar of the Shamrock Hotel, where everybody would laugh their heads off at it and then go out and say it is a public disgrace. And do you think even old Noble would dare hang it? You can vote for that picture, Halligan, over my dead body – we've had trouble enough in this town and I don't want any more of it. And I'll tell you one other little thing about that picture, Mister Regan. If you show it anywhere in this country you might just as well go out and hang yourself because it would be the last portrait you'd be asked to paint as long as you live.'

Regan laughed at her.

'To hell with their money. I'll show it at the Academy. I'll sell it there for twice the price. It'll be reproduced in every paper in Dublin! In every art magazine in the world!'

Halligan looked at him with funky eyes.

'Luke!' (And if Regan had been sober he would have known at once by that use of his first name how grave the issue was.) 'Valerie is right. Listen! Would you do one thing for me, and for yourself and for God's sake. There must be a second key to this room. Anyone might come in here at any moment.' He cocked a frightened ear. 'Any second that door might open. Would you take it back to the hotel for the night, and tomorrow morning look at it calmly and coldly and make up your own mind what you're going to do about it. You know,' he wheedled, 'they might even start pawing it!'

'Pawing? Wise man! Shrewd man! Monkey, monkey,' he approved. 'See all, hear all, say nothing. Let's get it out of here.'

They restored the twilight, the hallway was as empty as before; they drove fast, back to the empty, Sunday afternoon Main Street. Outside

The Shamrock she put her head out through the window of the wagon to say, 'I'll give you one minute, Halligan, no more.' They were lucky. They met nobody on the way to the bedroom. They stood the portrait on the mantelpiece. They sat side by side on the bed and looked at the scarlet, scowling, wet-lipped face of their old master staring down at them. Halligan accepted one slug from the neck of the bottle, slapped his companion on the back, and ran for it. Regan lay back on his pillow, emptying the bottle gulp for gulp, rejoicing strabismally at the face on the mantelpiece that, like a wavering fire, slowly faded into the veils of the gathering dusk.

'*Archiropito!*' he wheezed joyfully as he drained the bottle on its head, let it fall with a crash on the ground and sank into a stupor.

It was dark when he woke. He had no sense of time, of date, of day or night. He thought he heard noises downstairs. He groped for the bell, found it and kept pressing it until the door opened and, against the light, he saw the burly figure of old Noble.

'Mishter Noble, shend me up a bottle of whishkey if you please.'

Silence. Then:

'I will do no such thing, Mister Regan. If I was to do anything I'd send for a doctor. Sleep it off.'

The door closed and he was in darkness again.

'The bitch!' he growled, knowing that she had tipped off the old man. *Must* have a drink! If only . . . Suddenly he remembered. That bottle he had bought on the way down from Dublin. Had he drunk that too? He rolled out of bed, crawled on all fours to the light switch, at last found his hold-all, and there was his golden salvation. The colours of the little map of Ireland on the label swam – purple, and red, and yellow and green. With his teeth he tore off the thin metal covering on the neck, wrested out the cork, twisting its serrated edge, lifted the bottleneck to his mouth, engorged the sweet liquor as if it were water, and sank on the floor in a coma. The maid found him there in the morning, and ran from him down the stairs, screeching.

He recovered his senses only for the few minutes during which he was being put to bed in the monastery. Hilary had him brought there immediately he was informed of his sorry condition by old Noble, then by the community's doctor who had driven him at once to the college door, wrapped in blankets, still in a stupor, his breath coming in gasps, his forehead glistening with cold dots of sweat. It took three brothers to lift him from the car and carry him upstairs to Hilary's bedroom.

Harry Halligan and Valerie Halligan, also alerted by Noble, came after them, carrying his few belongings stuffed into his suitcase and his hold-all. As they packed them, her eye roving about the room saw the portrait on the mantelpiece.

'Halligan,' she ordered. 'Take that thing down and burn it.'

He looked at her, looked at the closed door, told her to lock it, took out his clasp knife and cut the canvas from its frame. But when he approached the empty grate his nerve failed him.

'I can't do it, Valerie. It's like murder.'

She snatched it from him, tore some paper linings from the chest of drawers, crumpled the canvas on top of them in the grate, put her cigarette lighter to the paper and they watched everything burn to ashes. They drove to the college, laid his two cases inside the door, and drove rapidly down the drive for home and a couple of stiff ones. In the middle of her drink, and her abuse of him, she looked at him and laughed, remembering from her schooldays.

'"To be thus is nothing, but to be safely thus,"' jumped up to ring old Noble and warn him never to mention their names to anybody in the college about this affair.

'Rely on me,' the old voice replied. 'We're all in it together,' from which she knew that he, too, had seen the portrait.

Hilary sat by his bed during his few, limp moments of consciousness.

'My poor Luke,' fondling his icy palm. 'What on earth happened to you at all, at all?'

'Brother,' he said faintly. 'Can I have one, last little drink?'

The old man shook his head, sadly but not negatively.

'Of course you can, Luke. I'll leave you a glass of the best here beside your bed for the night. Tomorrow we'll cut it down to half a glass. Then, bit by bit, between us, with God's help,' glancing up piously at the veiled face over the bed, 'we'll wean you back to your old self.'

In the morning a young lay brother stole into the room with a nice hot cup of tea for the patient. He found the glass dry and the body an empty cell. Touched, it was like stuffed leather.

The obituaries were invariably kind. They all stressed the burned portrait, the symbol of every artist's indefatigable pursuit of unattainable perfection. They slyly recalled his convivial nature, his great thirst for friendship, the speed with which he could limn a character in a few lines, the unfailing polish of his work. But as always, it was some wag in a pub who spoke his epitaph.

'Well, poor old Lukey Fa Presto is gone from us. He wasn't much of a painter. And he had no luck. But what a beautiful way to die! In the odour.' His glass raised. All their glasses lifted. 'Of sanctity and whiskey.'

With solemn smiles they drank.

The Kitchen

I was there again last night; not, I need hardly say, deliberately. If I had my own way I would never even think of that house or that city, let alone revisit them. It was the usual pattern. I was in Cork on some family business, and my business required that I should walk past the house and, as usual, although it was the deep middle of the night the kitchen window upstairs was dimly lit, as if by a lamp turned low, the way my mother used always fix it to welcome my father home from night duty. She usually left a covered saucepan of milk beside the lamp. He would put it on the stove to heat while he shook the rain from his cape on the red tiles of the kitchen, hung his uniform on the back of the door, and put on a pair of slippers. He welcomed the hot milk. It rains a lot in Cork and the night rain can be very cold. Then, as happens in dreams, where you can walk through walls like a pure spirit and time gets telescoped, it was suddenly broad daylight, I was standing in the empty kitchen, and that young man was once again saying to me with a kindly chuckle, 'So this is what all that was about?' It was five past three in the morning when I sat up and groped wildly for the bedside light to dispel the misery of those eight dismissive words that I am apparently never going to be allowed to forget, even in my sleep.

It is a graceless lump of a house, three stories high, rhomboidal, cement-faced, built at the meeting point of a quiet side street curving out of an open square and a narrow, noisy, muddy, sunless street leading to one of the busiest parts of the city. Every day for over twenty years I used to look down into this narrow street from the kitchen window – down because of the shop beneath us on the ground floor, occupied in my childhood by a firm of electrical contractors named Cyril and Eaton. Theirs was a quiet profession. Later on, when the shop was occupied by a bootmaker we could hear his machines slapping below us all day long.

My guess is that the house was built around 1870; anyway, it had the solid, ugly, utilitarian look of the period. Not that my father and mother ever thought it ugly. They would not have known what the word meant. To them, born peasants, straight from the fields, all the word 'beautiful' meant was useful or prolific; all 'ugly' meant was useless or barren – a field that grew bad crops, a roof that leaked, a cow that gave poor milk. So, when they told us children, as they often did, that we were now living in a beautiful house all they meant was that it suited our purposes perfectly. They may also have meant something else: because they had been told that the house had originally been put up by a builder for his own use they considered it prime property, as if they had come into possession of land owned by a gentleman farmer for generations. Few things are more dear to the heart of a peasant than a clean pedigree. It keeps history at bay. Not, of course, that they owned the house, although they sometimes talked dreamily about how they would buy it someday. What a dream! Landless people, in other words people of no substance, they had already gone to the limit of daring by renting it for twenty-six pounds a year, a respectable sum in those days for a man like my father – an ordinary policeman, rank of constable, earning about thirty bob a week.

Their purpose in renting so big a place was to eke out his modest income by taking in the steady succession of lodgers who were ultimately to fill the whole house with the sole exception of the red-tiled kitchen where the six of us lived, cooked, idled or worked. I do not count as rooms the warren of attics high up under the roof where we all, including the slavey (half a crown a week and her keep), slept with nothing between us and the moon but the bare slates. Still, we were not really poor. Knowing no better life, we were content with what we had.

During some forty years this was my parents' home; for even after my brothers and I grew up and scattered to the corners of the compass, and my mother grew too old to go on keeping lodgers, and my father retired, they still held on to it. So well they might! I was looking at my father's discharge papers this morning. I find that when he retired at the age of fifty his pension was £48. 10s. 8d. a year. Fortunately he did get a part-time job as caretaker of a garage at night which brought him in another £25. 5s. 5d. a year. Any roof at ten bob a week was nicely within his means. It must also have been a heartbreak to his landlord, who could not legally increase the rent.

One day, however, about a year before I left home – I was the last of us to go – my father got a letter which threatened to end this agreeable state of affairs. When he and my mother had painstakingly digested its legal formalities they found to their horror that the bootmaker downstairs had, as the saying goes, quietly bought the house 'over their heads,' and was therefore their new landlord. Now, forty-odd years in a city, even in so small a city as Cork, can go a long way towards turning a peasant into a citizen. My father, as a lifelong member of the Royal Irish Constabulary, then admiringly called the Force, had over the years imbibed from his training and from the example of his officers, who were mostly Protestants and Gentlemen, not only a strong sense of military, I might even say of imperial, discipline but a considerable degree of urban refinement. My mother had likewise learned her own proper kind of urban ways, house-pride, such skills as cooking and dressmaking, and a great liking for pretty clothes. At times she even affected a citified accent. When they read this letter and stared at one another in fright, all this finery fell from their backs as suddenly as Cinderella's at the stroke of midnight.

They might at that moment have been two peasants from Limerick or Kerry peering timidly through the rain from the door of a thatched hovel at a landlord, or his agent, or some villainous land-grabber driving up their brambled boreen to throw them out on the side of the road to die of cold and starvation. The kitchen suddenly became noisy with words, phrases and names that, I well knew, they could not have heard since their childhood – evictions, bum bailiffs, forcible entry, rights-of-way, actions for trespass, easements, appeals, breaches of covenant, the Land Leaguers, the Whiteboys, Parnell and Captain Boycott, as if the bootmaker downstairs slept with a shotgun by his bed every night and a brace of bloodhounds outside his shop door every day.

Nothing I said to comfort them could persuade them that their bootmaker could not possibly want to evict them; or that, far from being a land-grabber, or even a house-grabber, he was just an ordinary, normal, decent hardworking, citybred businessman, with a large family of his own toiling beside him at his machines, who, if he wanted anything at all, could not conceivably want more than, say, one extra room where he could put another sewing machine or store his leather. And, in fact, as he patiently explained to my father, that was all he did want; or perhaps a little more – two rooms, and access for his girls to our private W.C. on the turn of the stairs. He must have been much

surprised to find himself thrown headlong into the heart of a raging
rural land war.

I left home that year, so I cannot tell if there was or was not litigation
at this first stage of the battle. All I knew for certain is that after about
a year and a half of argufying, both parties settled for one room and
access to the W.C. The rest I was to gather and surmise from their letters
to me. These conveyed that some sort of growling peace descended on
everybody for about three years, towards the end of which my father
died, my mother became the sole occupant, and the bootmaker, seeing
that he now had only one tenant over his head, and that with
expanding business he was even more cramped for space than before,
renewed his request for a second room.

At once, the war broke out again, intensified now by the fact that,
as my mother saw it, a bloody villain of a land-grabber, and a black
Protestant to boot, was trying to throw a lonely, helpless, ailing,
defenceless, solitary poor widow woman out on the side of the road to
die. The bootmaker nevertheless persisted. It took him about two more
years of bitter struggle to get his second room. When he got it he was
in possession of the whole of the second floor of his house with the
exception of the red-tiled kitchen.

Peace returned, grumbling and growling. Patiently he let another
year pass. Then, in the gentlest possible words, he begged that my
mother might be so kind, and so understanding, as to allow one of his
girls, and only one, to enter the kitchen once a day, and only once, for
the sole purpose of filling a kettle of water from the tap of her kitchen
sink. There was, to be sure, he agreed, another tap downstairs in his
backyard – a dank five-foot-square patch of cement – but it stood
outside the male workers' outdoor W.C., and she would not, he hoped
and trusted, wish any girl to be going out there to get water for her poor
little cup of tea? I am sure it was the thought of the girl's poor little cup
of tea that softened my mother's heart. She royally granted the humane
permission, and at once began to regret it.

She realized that she had given the black villain a toehold into her
kitchen and foresaw that the next thing he would want would be to
take it over completely. She was right. I can only infer that as the
bootmaking business went on expanding, so did the bootmaker's sense
of the value of time. At any rate he was soon pointing out to my mother
that it was a dreadful expense to him, and a hardship to his staff, to
have to close his shop for an hour and a half every day while his

workers, including his family, trudged home, in all weathers, some of them quite a long distance, for their midday meal. If he had the kitchen they could eat their lunch, dryshod and in comfort, inside half an hour. He entered a formal request for the kitchen.

Looking back at it now, after the passage of well over a quarter of a century, I can see clearly enough that he thought he was making a wholly reasonable request. After all, in addition to her kitchen my mother still possessed the third floor of the house, containing three fine rooms and a spacious bathroom. One of those rooms could become her kitchen, another remain her bedroom, and the third and largest, which she never used, would make a splendid living room, overlooking the square's pleasant enclosure of grass and shrubs, and commanding an open view up to the main thoroughfare of the city – all in all as desirable an apartment, by any standards, as thousands of home-hungry Corkonians would have given their ears to possess.

Unfortunately, if I did decide to think his request reasonable, what I would have to forget, and what he completely failed to reckon with, was that there is not a peasant widow woman from the mountains of west Cork to the wilds of Calabria who does not feel her kitchen as the pulse and centre of her being as a wife and a mother. That red-tiled kitchen had been my mother's nest and nursery, her fireside where she prayed every morning, her chimney corner where she rested every night, the sanctum sanctorum of all her belongings, a place whose every stain and smell, spiderweb and mousehole, crooked nail and cracked cup made it the ark of the covenant that she had kept through forty years of sweat and struggle for her lost husband and her scattered children.

Besides, if she lost her kitchen what would she do when the Bottle Woman came, to buy empty bottles at a halfpenny apiece? This was where she always brought her to sit and share a pot of tea and argue over the bottles and talk about the secret doings of Cork. Where could she talk with the Dead Man, collecting her funeral insurance at sixpence a week, if she did not have her warm, red-eyed range where he could take off his damp boots and warm his feet in the oven while she picked him dry of all the gossip of the narrow street beneath her window? She had never in her life locked the front door downstairs except at night. Like the door of any country cottage it was always on the latch for any one of her three or four cronies to shove open and call out to her, 'Are ye there, can I come up?' – at which she would hear their footsteps banging on the brass edgings of the stairs while she hastily began to poke the fire in the range, and fill the kettle for the tea, or stir the pot of soup on the range in preparation for a cosy chat. All her life her neighbours had dropped like that into her kitchen. They would be insulted if she did not invite them into her kitchen. She would not have a crony in the world without her kitchen. Knowing nothing of all this, the bootmaker could argue himself hoarse with her, plead and wheedle with her to accept the shiniest, best-equipped, most modern American-style kitchenette, run by electricity, all white and gleaming chromium. Even if it was three stories up from the hall door it seemed to him a marvellous exchange for this battered old cave downstairs where she crouched over a range called the Prince Albert, where the tiles were becoming loose, where he could see nothing to look at but a chipped sink, one chair, a table, one cupboard, a couple of old wooden shelves, and a sofa with the horsehair coming out of it like a moustache. He might just as well have said to a queen, 'Give me your throne and I'll leave you the palace.' While as for proposing as an alternative that she could keep her old kip of a kitchen if she would only let him make a proper kitchen upstairs for himself, his family and his workers . . .

'Aha, nah!' she would cry at me whenever I visited her; and the older and angrier she became the more did her speech revert to the flat accent of her flat West Limerick, with is long vanishing versts of greasy limestone roads, its fields of rusty reeds, its wind-rattling alders, and its low rain clouds endlessly trailing their Atlantic hair across the sodden plain. 'Is it to take me in the rear he wants to now? To lock me up in the loft? To grind me like corn meal between the upstairs and the downstairs? A room? And then another room? And after that another? And then what? When he'd have me surrounded with noise, and shmoke, and shmells, and darkness and a tick-tack-turrorum all day long? Aha. My mother, and my grandmother before her didn't fight the landlords, and the agents, and the helmeted peelers with their grey guns and their black battering rams for me to pull down the flag now! It's a true word, God knows it, them Proteshtants wouldn't give you as much as a dry twig in a rotten wood to light your pipe with it. Well and well do I remember the time ould foxy-whiskers, Mister Woodley the parson, died of the grippe away back in Crawmore, and my uncle Phil stole out the night after his funeral to cut a log in his wood! While he was sawing it didn't the moon come out from behind a cloud, and who do you think was sitting on the end of the log looking at him out of his foxy eyes? Out of my kitchen I will not stir until ye carry me out on a board to lie in the clay beside my poor Dinny. And not one single minit before.'

Which was exactly what happened, six years later.

All in all, from start to finish, my mother's land war must have lasted nearly fourteen years. But what is fourteen years to an old woman whose line and stock clung by their fingernails to their last sour bits of earth for four centuries? I am quite sure the poor bootmaker never understood to the day of his death the nerve of time he had so unwittingly touched.

After the funeral it was my last task to empty the house, to shovel away – there is no other word for it – her life's last lares and penates to a junk dealer for thirty shillings. When it was all done I was standing alone in the empty kitchen, where I used to do my homework every evening as a boy, watching her cooking or baking, making or mending, or my father cobbling a pair of shoes for one of us, or sitting at his ease, smoking his pipe, in his favourite straw-bottomed chair, in his grey constabulary shirt, reading the racing news in the pink *Cork Evening Echo*.

As I stood there I suddenly became aware that a young man was standing in the doorway. He was the bootmaker's son. Oddly enough, I had never spoken to his father, although years ago I had seen him passing busily in and out of his shop, always looking worn and worried, but I had once met this son of his in the mountains of west Cork – fishing? shooting? – and I had found him a most friendly and attractive young fellow. He came forward now, shook hands with me in a warm, manly way and told me how sorry he was for me in my bereavement.

'Your mother was a grand old warrior,' he said, in genuine admiration. 'My father always had the greatest respect for her.'

We chatted about this and that for a while. Then, for a moment, we both fell silent while he looked curiously around the bare walls. He chuckled tolerantly, shook his head several times and said, 'So this is what all that was about?'

At those eight words, so kindly meant, so good-humoured, so tolerant, so uncomprehending, a shock of weakness flowed up through me like defeat until my head began to reel and my eyes were swimming.

It was quite true that there was nothing for either of us to see but a red-tiled floor, a smoke-browned ceiling and four tawny distempered walls bearing some brighter patches where a few pictures had hung and the cupboard and the sofa used to stand. The wall to our right had deposited at its base a scruff of distemper like dandruff. The wall to our left gaped at us with parched mouths. He smiled up at the flyspotted bulb in the ceiling. He touched a loose tile with his toe and sighed deeply. All that! About this? And yet, only a few hours before, when I had looked down at her for the last time, withdrawn like a snail into her shrivelled house, I had suddenly found myself straining, bending, listening as if, I afterwards thought, I had been staring into the perspective of a tunnel of time, much as I stared now at him, at one with him in his bewilderment.

I thought I had completely understood what it was all about that morning years ago when they read that letter and so pathetically, so embarrassingly, even so comically revealed their peasants' terror at the power of time. I had thought the old bootmaker's mistake had been his failure to understand the long fuse he had so unwittingly lighted. But now – staring at this good-humoured young man who, if I had said all this to him, would at once have understood and have at once retorted, 'But even so!' – I realized that they, and that, and this, and he and I were all caught in something beyond reason and time. In a daze I shook hands with him again, thanked him again for his sympathy, and handed him the keys of victory. I was still dazed as I sat in the afternoon train for Dublin, facing the mile-long tunnel that burrows underneath the city out to the light and air of the upper world. As it slowly began to slide into the tunnel I swore that I would never return.

Since then I must have gone back there forty times, sometimes kidnapped by her, sometimes by my father, sometimes by an anonymous rout of shadowy creatures out of a masked ball, and sometimes it is not at all the city I once knew but a fantastically beautiful place of great squares and pinnacled, porphyry buildings with snowy ships drawing up beside marble quays. But, always, whatever the order of my guides, captors or companions, I find myself at the end alone in a narrow street, dark except for its single window and then, suddenly, it is broad daylight and I am in our old kitchen hearing that young man say in his easy way, 'So this is what all that was about?' and I start awake in my own dark, babbling, clawing for the switch. As I sit up in bed I can never remember what it was that I had been babbling, but I do understand all over again what it was all about. It was all about the scratching mole. In her time, when she heard it she refused to listen, just as I do when, in my turn, I hear her velvet burrowing, softer than sand crumbling or snow tapping, and I know well whose whispering I had heard and what she had been saying to me.

She was a grand old warrior. She fought her fight to a finish. She was entirely right in everything she did. I am all for her. Still, when I switch on the bulb over my head I do it only to banish her, to evict her, to push her out of *my* kitchen, and I often lie back to sleep under its bright light lest I should again hear her whispering to me in the dark.

The Faithless Wife

He had now been stalking his beautiful Mlle Morphy, whose real name was Mrs Meehawl O'Sullivan, for some six weeks, and she had appeared to be so amused at every stage of the hunt, so responsive, *entrainante*, even *aguichante*, that he could already foresee the kill over the next horizon. At their first encounter, during the Saint Patrick's Day cocktail party at the Dutch embassy, accompanied by a husband who had not a word to throw to a cat about anything except the scissors and shears that he manufactured somewhere in the West of Ireland, and who was obviously quite ill at ease and drank too much Irish whiskey, what had attracted him to her was not only her splendid Boucher figure (whence his sudden nickname for her, La Morphée), or her copper-coloured hair, her lime-green Irish eyes and her seemingly poreless skin, but her calm, total and subdued elegance: the Balenciaga costume, the peacock-skin gloves, the gleaming crocodile handbag, a glimpse of tiny, lace-edged lawn handkerchief and her dry, delicate scent. He had a grateful eye and nose for such things. It was, after all, part of his job. Their second meeting, two weeks later, at his own embassy, had opened the doors. She came alone.

Now, at last, inside a week, perhaps less, there would be an end to all the probationary encounters that followed – mostly her inventions, at his persistent appeals – those wide-eyed fancy-meeting-you-heres at the zoo, at race-meetings, afternoon cinemas, in art galleries, at more diplomatic parties (once he had said gaily to her, 'The whole diplomacy of Europe seems to circle around our interest in one another'), those long drives over the Dublin mountains in his Renault coupé, those titillating rural lunches, nose to nose, toe to toe (rural because she quickly educated him to see Dublin as a stock exchange for gossip, a casino of scandal), an end, which was rather a pity, to those charming unforeseen-foreseen, that is to say proposed but in the end just snatched, afternoon *promenades champêtres* under the budding leaves and closing skies of the Phoenix Park, with the first lights of the city springing up below them to mark the end of another boring day for him in Ailesbury Road, Dublin's street of embassies, for her another possibly cosier but, he selfishly hoped, not much more exciting day in her swank boutique on Saint Stephen's Green. Little by little those intimate encounters, those murmured confessions had lifted acquaintance to friendship, to self-mocking smiles over some tiny incident during their last meeting, to eager anticipation of the next, an aimless tenderness twanging to appetite like an arrow. Or, at least, that was how he felt about it all. Any day now, even any hour, the slow countdown, slower than the slow movement of Mendelssohn's Concerto in E Minor, or the most swoony sequence from the Siegfried Idyll, or that floating spun-sugar balloon of Mahler's 'Song of the Earth,' to the music of which on his gramophone he would imagine her smiling sidelong at him as she softly disrobed, and his ingenious playing with her, his teasing and warming of her moment by moment for the roaring, blazing takeoff. To the moon!

Only one apprehension remained with him, not a real misgiving, something nearer to a recurring anxiety. It was that at the last moments when her mind and her body ought to take leave of one another she might take to her heels. It was a fear that flooded him whenever, with smiles too diffident to reassure him, she would once again mention that she was a Roman Catholic, or a Cat, a Papist or a Pape, a convent girl, and once she laughed that during her schooldays in the convent she had actually been made an *Enfant de Marie*. The words never ceased to startle him, dragging him back miserably to his first sexual frustration with his very pretty but unexpectedly proper cousin Berthe Ohnet during his lycée years in Nancy; a similar icy snub a few years later in Quebec; repeated still later by that smack on the face in Rio that almost became a public scandal; memories so painful that whenever an attractive woman nowadays mentioned religion, even in so simple a context as, 'Thank God I didn't buy that hat, or frock, or stock, or mare,' a red flag at once began to flutter in his belly.

Obsessed, every time she uttered one of those ominous words he rushed for the reassurance of what he called The Sherbet Test, which meant observing the effect on her of some tentatively sexy joke, like the remark of the young princess on tasting her first sherbet:— 'Oh, how absolutely delicious! But what a pity it isn't a sin!' To his relief she not only always laughed merrily at his stories but always capped them, indeed at times so startling him by her coarseness that it only occurred to him quite late in their day that this might be her way of showing her distaste for his diaphanous indelicacies. He had once or twice observed that priests, peasants and children will roar with laughter at some scavenger joke, and growl at even a veiled reference to a thigh. Was she a child of nature? Still, again and again back would come those disturbing words. He could have understood them from a prude, but what on earth did *she* mean by them? Were they so many herbs to season her desire with pleasure in her naughtiness? Flicks of nasty puritan sensuality to whip her body over some last ditch of indecision? It was only when the final crisis came that he wondered if this might not all along have been her way of warning him that she was neither a light nor a lecherous woman, neither a flirt nor a flibbertigibbet, that in matters of the heart she was *une femme très sérieuse*.

He might have guessed at something like it much earlier. He knew almost from the first day that she was *bien élevée*, her father a judge of the Supreme Court, her uncle a monsignor at the Vatican, a worldly, sport-loving, learned, contriving priest who had persuaded her papa to send her for a finishing year to Rome with the Sisters of the Sacred Heart at the top of the Spanish Steps; chiefly, it later transpired, because the convent was near the *centre hippique* in the Borghese Gardens and it was his right reverend's opinion that no Irish girl could possibly be said to have completed her education until she had learned enough about horses to ride to hounds. She had told him a lot, and most amusingly, about this uncle. She had duly returned from Rome to Dublin, and whenever he came over for the hunting, he always rode beside her. This attention had mightily flattered her until she discovered that she was being used as a cover for his uncontrollable passion for Lady Kinvara and Loughrea, then the master, some said the mistress, of the Clare-Galway hounds.

'How old were you then?' Ferdy asked, fascinated.

'I was at the university. Four blissful, idling years. But I got my degree. I was quick. And,' she smiled, 'good-looking. It helps, even with professors.'

'But riding to hounds as a student?'

'Why not? In Ireland everybody does. Children do. You could ride to hounds on a plough horse if you had nothing else. So long as you keep out of the way of real hunters. I only stopped after my marriage, when

I had a miscarriage. And I swear that was only because I was thrown.'

A monsignor who was sport-loving, worldly and contriving. He understood, and approved, and it explained many things about her.

The only other ways in which her dash, beauty and gaiety puzzled and beguiled him were trivial. Timid she was not, she was game for any risk. But the coolness of her weather eye often surprised him.

'The Leopardstown Races? Oh, what a good idea, Ferdy! Let's meet there . . . The Phoenix Park Races? No, not there. Too many doctors showing off their wives and their cars, trying to be noticed. And taking notice. Remember, a lot of my college friends married doctors . . . No, not *that* cinema. It has become vogueish . . . In fact, no cinema on the south side of the river. What we want is a good old fleabitten picture house on the north side where they show nothing but westerns and horrors, and where the kids get in on Saturday mornings for thruppence . . . Oh, and do please only ring the boutique in an emergency. Girls gossip.'

Could she be calculating? For a second of jealous heat he wondered if she could possibly have another lover. Cooling, he saw that if he had to keep a wary eye in his master's direction she had to think of her bourgeois clientele. Besides, he was a bachelor, and would remain one. She had to manage her inexpressibly dull, if highly successful old scissors and shears manufacturer, well past fifty and probably as suspicious as he was boring; so intensely, so exhaustingly boring that the only subject about which she could herself nearly become boring was in her frequent complaints about his boringness. Once she *was* frightening – when she spat out that she had hated her husband ever since the first night of their marriage when he brought her for their honeymoon – it was odd how long, and how intensely this memory had rankled – not, as he had promised, to Paris, but to his bloody scissors and shears factory in the wet wilds of northern Donegal. ('Just me dear, haha, to let 'em see, haha, t'other half of me scissors.')

Ferdy had of course never asked her why she had married such a cretin; not after sizing up her house, her furniture, her pictures, her clothes, her boutique. Anyway, only another cretin would discourage any pretty woman from grumbling about her husband: (a) because such grumblings give a man a chance to show what a deeply sympathetic nature he has, and (b) because the information incidentally supplied helps one to arrange one's assignations in places and at times suitable to all concerned.

Adding it all up (he was a persistent adder-upper) only one problem had so far defeated him: that he was a foreigner and did not know what sort of women Irish women are. It was not as if he had not done his systematic best to find out, beginning with a course of reading through the novels of her country. A vain exercise. With the exception of the Molly Bloom of James Joyce the Irish Novel had not only failed to present him with any fascinating woman but it had presented him with, in his sense of the word, no woman at all. Irish fiction was a lot of nineteenth-century *connerie* about half-savage Brueghelesque peasants, or urban *petits fonctionnaires* who invariably solved their frustrations by getting drunk on religion, patriotism or undiluted whiskey, or by taking flight to England. Pastoral melodrama. (Giono at his worst.) Or pastoral humbuggery. (Bazin at his most sentimental.) Or, at its best, pastoral lyricism. (Daudet and rosewater.) As for Molly Bloom! He enjoyed the smell of every kissable pore of her voluptuous body without for one moment believing that she had ever existed. James Joyce in drag.

'But,' he had finally implored his best friend in Ailesbury Road, Hamid Bey, the third secretary of the Turkish embassy, whose amorous secrets he willingly purchased with his own, 'if it is too much to expect Ireland to produce a bevy of Manons, Mitsous, Gigis, Claudines, Kareninas, Oteros, Leahs, San Severinas, what about those great-thighed, vast-bottomed creatures dashing around the country on horseback like Diana followed by all her minions? Are they not interested in love? And if so why aren't there novels about them?'

His friend laughed as toughly as Turkish Delight and replied in English in his laziest Noel Coward drawl, all the vowels frontal as if he were talking through bubble gum, all his r's either left out where they should be, as in *deah* or *cleah*, or inserted where they should not be, as in *India-r* or *Iowa-r*.

'My deah Ferdy, did not your deah fatheh or your deah mamma-r eveh tell you that all Irish hohsewomen are in love with their hohses? And anyway it is well known that the favourite pin-up gihl of Ahland is a gelding.'

'Naked?' Ferdinand asked coldly, and refused to believe him, remembering that his beloved had been a hohsewoman, and satisfied that he was not a gelding. Instead, he approached the Italian ambassador at a cocktail party given by the Indonesian embassy to whisper to him about *l'amore irlandese* in his best stage French, and stage French manner, eyebrows lifted above fluttering eyelids, voice as hoarse as, he guessed, His Excellency's mind would be on its creaking way back to memories of Gabin, Jouvet, Brasseur, Fernandel, Yves Montand. It proved to be another futile exercise. His Ex groaned as operatically as every Italian groans over such vital, and lethal, matters as the Mafia, food, taxation and women, threw up his hands, made a face like a more than usually desiccated De Sica and sighed, 'Les femmes d'Irlande? Mon pauvre gars! Elles sont d'une chasteté...' He paused and roared the adjective, '... FORMIDABLE!'

Ferdinand had heard this yarn about feminine chastity in other countries and (with those two or three exceptions already mentioned), found it true only until one had established the precise local variation of the meaning of 'chastity.' But how was he to discover the Irish variation? In the end it was Celia herself who, unwittingly, revealed it to him and in doing so dispelled his last doubts about her susceptibility, inflammability and volatility – despite the very proper Sisters of the Spanish Steps.

The revelation occurred one night in early May – her Meehawl being away in the West, presumably checking what she contemptuously called his Gaelic-squeaking scissors. Ferdy had driven her back to his flat for a nightcap after witnessing the prolonged death of Mimi in *La Bohème*. She happened to quote to him Oscar Wilde's remark about the death of Little Nell that only a man with a heart of stone could fail to laugh at it, and in this clever vein they had continued for a while over the rolling brandy, seated side by side on his settee, his hand on her bare shoulder leading him to hope more and more fondly that this might be his Horizon Night, until, suddenly, she asked him a coldly probing question.

'Ferdy! Tell me exactly why we did not believe in the reality of Mimi's death.'

His palm oscillated gently between her clavicle and her scapula.

'Because, my little cabbage, we were not expected to. Singing away like a lark? With her last breath? And no lungs? I am a Frenchman. I understand the nature of reality and can instruct you about it. Art, my dear Celia, is art because it is not reality. It does not copy or represent nature. It improves upon it. It embellishes it. This is the kernel of the classical French attitude to life. And,' he beamed at her, 'to love. We make of our wildest feelings of passion the gentle art of love.'

He suddenly stopped fondling her shoulder and surveyed her with feelings of chagrin and admiration. The sight of her belied his words. Apart from dressing with taste, and, he felt certain, undressing with even greater taste, she used no art at all. She was as innocent of makeup as a peasant girl of the Vosges. Had he completely misread her? Was she that miracle, a fully ripe peach brought into the centre of the city some twenty years ago from a walled garden in the heart of the country, still warm from the sun, still glowing, downy, pristine, innocent as the dew? He felt her juice dribbling down the corner of his mouth. Was this the missing piece of her jigsaw? An ensealed innocence? If so he had wasted six whole weeks. This siege could last six years.

'No, Ferdy!' she said crossly. 'You have it all wrong. I'm talking about life, not about art. The first and last thought of any real Italian girl on her deathbed would be to ask for a priest. She was facing her God.'

God at once pointed a finger at him through the chandelier, and within seconds they were discussing love among the English, Irish, French, Indians, Moslems, Italians, naturally the Papacy, Alexander the Sixth and incest, Savonarola and dirty pictures, Joan of Arc and martyrdom, death, sin, hellfire, Cesare Borgia who, she insisted, screamed for a priest to pray for him at the end.

'A lie,' he snarled, 'that some beastly priest told you in a sermon when you were a schoolgirl. Pray! I suppose,' he challenged furiously, 'you pray even against me.'

Abashed, she shook her autumn-brown head at him, threw a kipper-eyed glance up to the chandelier, gave him a ravishingly penitential smile, and sighed like an unmasked sinner.

'Ah, Ferdy! Ferdy! If you only knew the real truth about me! Me pray against you? I don't pray at all. You remember Mimi's song at the end of the first act? "I do not always go to Mass, but I pray quite a bit to the good Lord." Now, I hedge my bets in a very different way. I will not pray because I refuse to go on my knees to anybody. Yet, there I go meekly trotting off to Mass every Sunday and holy day. And why? Because I am afraid not to, because it would be a mortal sin not to.' She gripped his tensed hand, trilling her r's over the threshold of her lower lip and tenderly umlauting her vowels. Dürling. Cöward. Li-er. 'Amn't I the weak cöward, dürling? Amn't I the awful li-er? A crook entirrrely?'

Only a thin glint of streetlight peeping between his curtains witnessed the wild embrace of a man illuminated by an avowal so patently bogus as to be the transparent truth.

'You a liar?' he gasped, choking with laughter. 'You a shivering coward? A double-faced hedger of bets? A deceiving crook? A wicked sinner? For the last five minutes you have been every single one of them by pretending to be them. What you really are is a woman full of cool, hard-headed discretion, which you would like to sell to me as a charming weakness. Full of dreams that you would like to disguise as wicked lies. Of common sense that it suits you to pass off as crookedness. Of worldly wisdom still moist from your mother's nipple that, if you thought you would get away with the deception, you would stoop to call a sin. My dearest Celia, your yashmak reveals by pretending to conceal. Your trick is to be innocence masquerading as villainy. I think it is enchanting.'

For the first time he saw her in a rage.

'But it is *all* true. I *am* a liar. I *do* go to Mass every Sunday. I do *not* pray. I *am* afraid of damnation. I . . .'

He silenced her with three fingers laid momentarily on her lips.

'Of course you go to Mass every Sunday. My father, a master tailor of Nancy, used to go to Mass every Sunday not once but three times, and always as conspicuously as possible. Why? Because he was a tailor, just as you run a boutique. You don't pray? Sensible woman. Why should you bother your *bon Dieu*, if there is a *bon Dieu*, with your pretty prattle about things that He knew all about one billion years before you were a wink in your mother's eye? My dearest and perfect love, you have told me everything about Irishwomen that I need to know. None of you says what you think. Every one of you means what you don't say. None of you thinks about what she is going to do. But every one of you knows it to the last dot. You dream like opium eaters and your eyes are as calm as resting snow. You are all of you realists to your bare backsides. Yes, yes, yes, yes, yes, you will say this is true of all women, but it is not. It is not even true of Frenchwomen. They may be realists in lots of things. In love, they are just as stupid as all the rest of us. But not Irishwomen! Or not, I swear it, if they are all like you. I'll prove it to you with a single question. Would you, like Mimi, live for the sake of love in a Paris garret?'

She gravely considered a proposition that sounded delightfully like a proposal.

'How warm would the garret be? Would I have to die of tuberculosis? You remember how the poor Bohemian dramatist had to burn his play to keep them all from being famished with the cold.'

'Yes! Ferdy laughed. 'And as the fire died away he said, "I always knew that last act was too damned short." But you are dodging my question.'

'I suppose, dürling, any woman's answer to your question would depend on how much she was in love with whoever he was. Or wouldn't it?'

Between delight and fury he dragged her into his arms.

'You know perfectly well, you sweet slut, that what I am asking you is, "Do you love me a lot or a little? A garretful or a palaceful?" Which is it?'

Chuckling she slid down low in the settee and smiled up at him between sleepycat eyelashes.

'And you, Ferdy, must know perfectly well that it is pointless to ask any woman silly questions like that. If some man I loved very much were to ask me, "Do you love me, Celia?" I would naturally answer, "No!", in order to make him love me more. And if it was some man I did not like at all I would naturally say, "Yes, I love you so much I think we ought to get married," in order to cool him off. Which, Ferdy, do you want me to say to you?'

'Say,' he whispered adoringly, 'that you hate me beyond the tenth circle of Dante's hell.'

She made a grave face.

'I'm afraid, Ferdy, the fact is I don't like you at all. Not at all! Not one least little bit at all, at all.'

At which lying, laughing, enlacing and unlacing moment they kissed pneumatically and he knew that if all Irishwomen were Celias then the rest of mankind were mad ever to have admired women of any other race.

Their lovemaking was not as he had foredreamed it. She hurled her clothes to the four corners of the room, crying out, 'And about time too! Ferdy, what the hell have you been fooling around for during the last six weeks?' Within five minutes she smashed him into bits. In her passion she was more like a lion than a lioness. There was nothing about her either titillating or erotic, indolent or indulgent, as wild, as animal, as unrestrained, as simple as a forest fire. When, panting beside her, he recovered enough breath to speak he expressed his surprise that one so cool, so ladylike in public could be so different in private. She grunted peacefully and said in her muted brogue, 'Ah, shure, dürling, everything changes in the beddaroom.'

He woke at three twenty-five in the morning with that clear bang so familiar to everybody who drinks too much after the chimes of midnight, rose to drink a pint of cold water, lightly opened his curtains to survey the pre-dawn May sky and, turning towards the bed, saw the pallid streetlamp's light fall across her sleeping face, as calm, as soothed, as innocently sated as a baby filled with its mother's milk. He sat on the side of the bed looking down at her for a long time, overcome by the terrifying knowledge that, for the first time in his life, he had fallen in love.

The eastern clouds were growing as pink as petals while they drank the coffee he had quietly prepared. Over it he arranged in unnecessarily gasping whispers for their next meeting the following afternoon—'*This* afternoon!' he said joyously – at three twenty-five, henceforth his Mystic Hour for Love, but only on the strict proviso that he would not count on her unless she had set three red geraniums in a row on the windowsill of her boutique before three o'clock and that she, for her part, must divine a tragedy if the curtains of his flat were not looped high when she approached at three twenty o'clock. He could, she knew, have more easily checked with her by telephone, but also knowing how romantically, voluptuously, erotically minded he was she accepted with an indulgent amusement what he obviously considered ingenious devices for increasing the voltage of passion by the trappings of conspiracy. To herself she thought, 'Poor boy! He's been reading too many dirty books.'

Between two o'clock and three o'clock that afternoon she was entertained to see him pass her boutique three times in dark glasses. She cruelly made him pass a fourth time before, precisely at three o'clock, she gave him the pleasure of seeing two white hands with pink fingernails – not, wickedly, her own: her assistant's – emerge from under the net curtains of her window to arrange three small scarlet geraniums on the sill. He must have hastened perfervidly to the nearest florist to purchase the pink roses whose petals – when she rang his bell five cruel moments after his Mystic Hour – she found (to her tolerant amusement at his boyish folly) tessellating the silk sheets of his bed. His gramophone, muted by a bath towel, was murmuring Wagner. A joss stick in a brass bowl stank cloyingly. He had cast a pink silk headscarf over the bedside lamp. His dressingtable mirror had been tilted so that from where they lay they could see themselves. Within five minutes he neither saw, heard nor smelled anything, tumbling, falling, hurling headlong to consciousness of her mocking laughter at the image of her bottom mottled all over by his clinging rose petals. It cost him a brutal effort to laugh at himself.

All that afternoon he talked only of flight, divorce and remarriage. To cool him she encouraged him. He talked of it again and again every time they met. Loving him she humoured him. On the Wednesday of their third week as lovers they met briefly and chastely because her Meehawl was throwing a dinner at his house that evening for a few of his business colleagues previous to flying out to Manchester for a two-day convention of cutlers. Ferdy at once promised her to lay in a store of champagne, caviar, *pàté de foie* and brioches so that they need not stir from their bed for the whole of those two days.

'Not even once?' she asked coarsely, and he made a moue of disapproval.

'You do not need to be all that realistic, Celia!'

Already by three fifteen that Thursday afternoon he was shuffling nervously from window to window. By three twenty-five he was muttering, 'I hope she's not going to be late.' He kept feeling the champagne to be sure it was not getting too cold. At three thirty-five he moaned, 'She *is* late!' At three forty he cried out in a jealous fury, glaring up and down the street, 'The slut is betraying me!' At a quarter to four his bell rang, he leaped to the door. She faced him as coldly as a newly carved statue of Carrara marble. She repulsed his arms. She would not stir beyond his doormat. Her eyes were dilated by fear.

'It is Meehawl!' she whispered.

'He has found us out?'

'It's the judgment of God on us both!'

The word smacked his face.

'He is dead?' he cried hopefully, brushing aside fear and despair.

'A stroke.'

She made a violent, downward swish with the side of her open palm.

'*Une attaque? De paralysie?*'

'He called at the boutique on his way to the plane. He said goodbye to me. He walked out to the taxi. I went into my office to prepare my vanity case and do peepee before I met you. The taxi driver ran in shouting that he had fallen in a fit on the pavement. We drove him to 96. That's Saint Vincent's. The hospital near the corner of the Green. He is conscious. But he cannot speak. One side of him is paralysed. He may not live. He has had a massive coronary.'

She turned and went galloping down the stairs.

His immediate rebound was to roar curses on all the gods that never were. Why couldn't the old fool have his attack next week? His second thought was glorious. 'He will die, we will get married.' His third made him weep, 'Poor little cabbage!' His fourth thought was, 'The brioches I throw out, the rest into the fridge.' His fifth, sixth and seventh were three Scotches while he rationally considered all her possible reactions to the brush of the dark angel's wing. Only Time, he decided, would tell.

But when liars become the slaves of Time what can Time do but lie like them? A vat solid-looking enough for old wine, it leaks at every stave. A ship rigged for the wildest seas, it is rustbound to its bollards on the quay. She said firmly that nothing between them could change. He refuted her. Everything had changed, and for the better. He rejoiced when the doctors said their patient was doomed. After two more weeks she reported that the doctors were impressed by her husband's remarkable tenacity. He spoke of Flight. She now spoke of Time. One night as she lay hot in his arms in his bed he shouted triumphantly to the chandelier that when husbands are imprisoned lovers are free. She demurred. She could never spend a night with him in her own bed; not with a resident housekeeper upstairs. He tossed it aside. What matter where they slept! He would be happy sleeping with her in the Phoenix Park. She pointed out snappishly that it was raining. 'Am I a seal?' He proffered her champagne. She confessed the awful truth. This night was the last night they could be together anywhere.

'While he was dying, a few of his business pals used to call on him at the Nursing Home – the place all Dublin knows as 96. Now that the old devil is refusing to die they refuse to call on him anymore. I am his only faithful visitor. He so bores everybody. And with his paralysed mouth they don't know what the hell he is saying. Do you realize, Ferdy, what this means? He is riding me like a nightmare. Soaking me up like blotting paper. He rang me four times the day before yesterday at the boutique. He rang again while I was here with you having a drink. He said whenever I go out I must leave a number where he can call me. The night before last he rang me at three o'clock in the morning. Thank God I was back in my own bed and not here with you. He said he was lonely. Has terrible dreams. That the nights are long. That he is frightened. That if he gets another stroke he will die. Dürling! I can never spend a whole night with you again!'

Ferdy became Napoleon. He took command of the campaign. He accompanied her on her next visit to 96. This, he discovered, was a luxury (i.e., Victorian) nursing home in Lower Leeson Street, where cardinals died, coal fires were in order, and everybody was presented with a menu from which to choose his lunch and dinner. The carpets were an inch thick. The noisiest internal sound heard was the Mass bell tinkling along the corridors early every morning as the priest went from room to room with the Eucharist for the dying faithful. The Irish, he decided, know how to die. Knowing no better, he bore with him copies of *Le Canard Enchaîné*, *La Vie Parisienne*, and *Playboy*. Celia deftly impounded them. 'Do you want him to die of blood pressure? Do you want the nuns to think he's an Irish queer? A fellow who prefers women to drink?' Seated at one side of the bed, facing her seated at the other, he watched her, with her delicate lace-edged handkerchief (so disturbingly reminiscent of her lace-edged panties) wiping the unshaven chin of the dribbling half-idiot on the pillow. In an unconsumed rage he lifted his eyebrows into his hair, surveyed the moving mass of clouds above Georgian Dublin, smoothened his already blackboard-smooth hair, gently touched the white carnation in his lapel, forced himself to listen calmly to the all-but-unintelligible sounds creeping from the dribbling corner of the twisted mouth in the unshaven face of the revolting cretin on the pillow beneath his eyes, and agonizingly asked himself by what unimaginably devious machinery, and for what indivinable purpose the universe had been so arranged since the beginning of Time that this bronze-capped, pastel-eyed, rosy-breasted, round-buttocked, exquisite flower of paradise sitting opposite to him should, in the first place, have matched and mated with this slob between them, and then, or rather *and then*, or rather AND THEN make it so happen that he, Ferdinand Louis Jean-Honoré Clichy, of 9 *bis* rue des Dominicains, Nancy, in the Department of Moselle et Meurthe, population 133,532, altitude 212 metres, should happen to discover her in remote Dublin, and fall so utterly into her power that if he were required at that particular second to choose between becoming Ambassador to the Court of Saint James's for life and one night alone in bed with her he would have at once replied, 'Even for one hour!'

He gathered that the object on the pillow was addressing him.

'Oh, Mosheer! Thacks be to the ever cliving and cloving Gog I khav mosht devote clittle wife in all Khlistendom ... I'd be chlost without her ... Ah, Mosheer! If you ever dehide to marry, marry an Irikh-woman ... Mosht fafeful cleatures in all exhishtench ... Would any Frenchwoman attend shoopid ole man chlike me the way Chelia doesh?'

Ferdy closed his eyes. She was tenderly dabbing the spittled corners of the distorted mouth. What happened next was that a Sister took Celia out to the corridor for a few private words and that Ferdy at once leaned forward and whispered savagely to the apparently immortal O'Sullivan, 'Monsieur O'Sullivan, your wife does not look at all well. I fear she is wilting under the strain of your illness.'

'Chlstrain!' the idiot said in astonishment. 'What chlstrain? I khlsee no khlsignch of kkchlstrain!'

Ferdy whispered with fierceness that when one is gravely ill one may sometimes fail to observe the grave illness of others.

'We have to remember, Monsieur, that if your clittle wife were to collapse under the chlstr ... under the *strain* of your illness it would be very serious, for *you!*'

After that day the only reason he submitted to accompany his love on these painful and piteous visits to 96 was that they always ended with O'Sullivan begging him to take his poor clittle, loving clittle, devoted clittle pet of a wife to a movie for a relaxation and a rest, or for a drink in the Russell, or to the evening races in the park; whereupon they would both hasten, panting, to Ferdy's flat to make love swiftly, wildly and vindictively – swiftly because their time was limited, wildly because her Irish storms had by now become typhoons of rage, and he no longer needed rose petals, Wagner, Mendelssohn, dim lights or pink champagne, and vindictively to declare and to crush their humiliation at being slaves to that idiot a quarter of a mile away in another bed saying endless rosaries to the Virgin.

Inevitably the afternoon came – it was now July – when Ferdy's pride and nerves cracked. He decided that enough was enough. They must escape to freedom. At once.

'Celia! If we have to fly to the end of the world! It won't really ruin my career. My master is most sympathetic. In fact since I hinted to him that I am in love with a *belle mariée* he does nothing but complain about his wife to me. And he can't leave her, his career depends on her, she is the daughter of a Secretary of State for Foreign Affairs – and rich. He tells me that at worst I would be moved off to some place like Los Angeles or Reykjavik. Celia! My beloved flower! We could be as happy as two puppies in a basket in Iceland.'

She permitted a meed of Northern silence to create itself and then wondered reflectively if it is ever warm in Iceland, at which he pounced with a loud 'What do you mean? What are you actually asking? What is really in your mind?' She said, 'Nothing, dürling,' for how could she dare to say that whereas he could carry his silly job with him wherever he went she, to be with him, would have to give up her lovely old, friendly old boutique on the Green where her friends came to chat over morning coffee, where she met every rich tourist who visited Dublin, where she made nice money of her own, where she felt independent and free; just as she could never hope to make him understand why she simply could not just up and out and desert a dying husband.

'But there's nothing to hold you here. In his condition you'd be sure to get custody of the children. Apart from the holidays they could remain in school here the year round.'

So he had been thinking it all out. She stroked his hairy chest.

'I know.'

'The man, even at his best, you've acknowledged it yourself, over and over, is a fool. He is a moujik. He is a bore.'

'I know!' she groaned. 'Who should better know what a crasher he is? He is a child. He hasn't had a new idea in his head for thirty years. There have been times when I've hated the smell of him. He reminds me of an unemptied ashtray. Times when I've wished to God that a thief would break into the house some night and kill him. And,' at which point she began to weep on his tummy, 'I know now that there is only one thief who will come for him and he is so busy elsewhere that it will be years before he catches up with him. And then I think of the poor old bastard wetting his hospital bed, unable to stir, let alone talk, looking up at his ceiling, incontinent, with no scissors, no golf, no friends, no nothing, except me. How *can* I desert him?'

Ferdy clasped his hands behind his head, stared up at heaven's pure ceiling and heard her weeping like the summer rain licking his windowpane. He created a long Irish silence. He heard the city whispering. Far away. Farther away. And then not at all.

'And to think,' he said at last, 'that I once called you a realist!'

She considered this. She too no longer heard the muttering of the city's traffic.

'This is how the world is made,' she decided flatly.

'I presume,' he said briskly, 'that you do realize that all Dublin knows that you are meanwhile betraying your beloved Meehawl with me?'

'I know that there's not one of those bitches who wouldn't give her left breast to be where I am at this moment.'

They got out of bed and began to dress.

'And, also meanwhile, I presume you do *not* know that they have a snotty name for you?'

'What name?' – and she turned her bare back for the knife.

'They call you The Diplomatic Hack.'

For five minutes neither of them spoke.

While he was stuffing his shirt into his trousers and she, dressed fully except for her frock, was patting her penny-brown hair into place before his mirror he said to her, 'Furthermore I suppose you do realize that whether I like it or not I shall one day be shifted to some other city in some other country. What would you do then? For once, just for once in your life tell me the plain truth! Just to bring you to the crunch. What would you really do then?'

She turned, comb in hand, leaned her behind against his dressing table and looked him straight in the fly which he was still buttoning.

'Die,' she said flatly.

'That,' he said coldly, 'is a manner of speech. Even so, would you consider it an adequate conclusion to a love that we have so often said is forever?'

They were now side by side in the mirror, she tending her copper hair, he his black, like any long-married couple. She smiled a little sadly.

'Forever? Dürling, does love know that lovely word? You love me. I know it. I love you. You know it. We will always know it. People die but if you have ever loved them they are never gone. Apples fall from the tree but the tree never forgets its blossoms. Marriage is different. You remember the day he advised you that if you ever marry you should marry an Irishwoman. Don't, Ferdy! If you do she will stick to you forever. And you wouldn't really want that?' She lifted her frock from the back of a chair and stepped into it. 'Zip me up, dürling, will you? Even my awful husband. There must have been a time when I thought him attractive. We used to sail together. Play tennis together. He was very good at it. After all, I gave him two children. What's the date? They'll be home for the holidays soon. All I have left for him now is contempt and compassion. It is our bond.'

Bewildered he went to the window, buttoned his flowered waistcoat. He remembered from his café days as a student a ruffle of aphorisms about love and marriage. Marriage begins only when love ends. Love opens the door to Marriage and quietly steals away. *Il faut toujours s'appuyer sur les principes de l'amour – ils finissent par en céder.* What would she say to that? Lean heavily on the principles of love – they will always conveniently crumple in the end. Marriage bestows on Love the tenderness due to a parting guest. Every *affaire de coeur* ends as a *mariage de convenance.* He turned to her, arranging his jacket, looking for his keys and his hat. She was peeking into her handbag, checking her purse for her keys and her lace handkerchief, gathering her gloves, giving a last glance at her hat. One of the things he liked about her was that she always wore a hat.

'You are not telling me the truth, Celia,' he said, quietly. 'Oh, I don't mean about loving me. I have no doubt about you on that score. But when you persuade yourself that you can't leave him because you feel compassion for him that is just your self-excuse for continuing a marriage that has its evident advantages.'

She smiled lovingly at him.

'Will you ring me tomorrow, dürling?'

'Of course.'

'I love you very much, dürling.'

'And I love you too.'

'Until tomorrow then.'

'Until tomorrow, dürling.'

As usual he let her go first.

That afternoon was some two years ago. Nine months after it he was transferred to Brussels. As often as he could wangle special leave of absence, and she could get a relative to stay for a week with her bedridden husband, now back in his own house, they would fly to Paris or London to be together again. He would always ask solicitously after her husband's health, and she always sigh and say his doctors had assured her that 'he will live forever.' Once, in Paris, passing a church he, for some reason, asked her if she ever went nowadays to confession.

She waved the question away with a laugh, but later that afternoon he returned to it pertinaciously.

'Yes. Once a year.'

'Do you tell your priest about us?'

'I tell him that my husband is bedridden. That I am in love with another man. That we make love. And that I cannot give you up. As I can't, dürling.'

'And what does he say to that?'

'They all say the same. That it is an impasse. Only one dear old Jesuit gave me a grain of hope. He said that if I liked I could pray to God that my husband might die.'

'And have you so prayed?'

'Dürling, why should I?' she asked gaily, as she stroked the curly hair between his two pink buttons. 'As you once pointed out to me yourself all this was foreknown millions of years ago.'

He gazed at the ceiling. In her place, unbeliever though he was, he would, for love's sake, have prayed with passion. Not that she had said directly that she had not. Maybe she had? Two evasions in one sentence! It was all more than flesh and blood could bear. It was the Irish variation all over again: never let your left ass know what your right ass is doing. He decided to give her one more twirl. When she got home he wrote tenderly to her, 'You are the love of my life!' He could foresee her passionate avowal, 'And me too, dürling!' What she actually replied was, 'Don't I know it?' Six months later he had manoeuvred himself into the consular service and out of Europe to Los Angeles. He there consoled his broken heart with a handsome creature named Rosie O'Connor. Quizzed about his partiality for the Irish, he could only flap his hands and say, 'I don't know what they have got. They are awful liars. There isn't a grain of romance in them. And whether as wives or mistresses they are absolutely faithless!'

Something, Everything, Anything, Nothing

1

Somebody once said that a good prime minister is a man who knows something about everything and nothing about anything. I wince – an American foreign correspondent, stationed in Rome, covering Italy, Greece, Turkey, Corsica, Sardinia, Malta, Libya, Egypt and the entire Middle East.

Last year I was sent off to report on pollution around Capri, steel in Taranto, which (as journalists say) 'nestles' under the heel of the peninsula, the Italo-American project for uncovering the buried city of the Sybarites, which is halfway down the coast from Taranto, the political unrest then beginning to simmer in Reggio di Calabria, around the toe of the continent, and, of course, if something else should turn up – some 'extra dimension,' as my foreign editor in Chicago likes to call such unforeseens . . .

Summer was dying in Rome, noisily and malodorously. Down south, sun, silence and sea. It was such a welcome commission that it sounded like a pat on the head for past services. I was very pleased.

I polished off Capri in two hours and Taranto in three days – a well-documented subject. After lunching at Metaponto, now one of Taranto's more scruffy seaside resorts, I was salubriously driving along the highway beside the Ionian when, after about an hour, 'something else' did crop up. It happened in a place too minute to be called a village, or even a hamlet, an Italian would call it a *loguccio* (a rough little place), named Bussano. I doubt if many travellers, not natives of these parts of Calabria – barring Karl Baedeker some sixty years or so ago, or the modern Italian Touring Club guide, or a weary Arab peddler – had ever voluntarily halted in Bussano. The Touring Club guide is eloquent about it. He says, and it is all he says:— 'At this point the road begins to traverse a series of monotonous sand dunes.' Any guide as reticent as that knows what he is not talking about.

Bussano consists of two lots of hovels facing one another across the highway, one backing on that wild stretch of the Calabrian Apennines called La Sila, the other on an always empty ocean; 'always' because there is no harbour south of Taranto for about a hundred and fifty miles, nothing but sand, reeds, a few rocks, the vast Ionian. I presume that during the winter months the Ionian Sea is often shaken by southwesterly gales. In the summer nothing happens behind those monotonous sand dunes except the wavelets moving a foot inward and a foot outward throughout the livelong day, so softly that you don't even hear their seesaw and you have to watch carefully to see their wet marks on sand so hot that it pales again as soon as it is touched. The *loguccio* looked empty.

The only reason I halted there was that I happened to notice among the few hovels on the sea side of the road one two-storied house with a line of brown and yellow sunflowers lining its faded grey-pink walls on which, high up, I could barely decipher the words *Albergo degli Sibariti*. The Sybarites' Hotel. It must have been built originally for travellers by stagecoach, first horse then motor, or by hired coach and horses, or by private carriage, or in later years by the little railroad along the coast that presently starts to worm its slow way up through those fierce mountains that climb seven thousand feet to the Serra Dolcedorme where, I have been told, snow may still be seen in May. It was the same friend who told me about a diminutive railroad in this deep south – could it be this one? – grandiosely calling itself *La Società Italiana per le Strade Ferrate del Mediterraneo-Roma*, five hundred miles from the smell of Rome and barred by the Apennines from the Mediterranean. The *Albergo degli Sibariti* would have flourished in the youth of Garibaldi.

I was about to move on when I glanced between the hotel and its nearest hovel at a segment of sea and horizon, teasingly evoking the wealth of centuries below that level line – Greece, Crete, Byzantium, Alexandria. Once again I was about to drive off, thinking how cruel and how clever of Mussolini, and also how economical, to have silenced his intellectual critics (men like, for instance, Carlo Levi) simply by exiling them to remote spots like this, when an odd-looking young man came through the wide passageway, halted and looked up and down the highway with the air of a man with nowhere to go and nothing to do.

He was dark, bearded and longhaired, handsome if you like mushy

Italian eyes, dark as prunes, eyelashes soft and long, cheeks tenderly browned, under his chin hung a great, scarlet blob of tie like a nineteenth-century Romantic poet, his shirt gleaming (washed and ironed by whom?), his shoes brilliantly polished (by whom?), pants knife-pressed (by whom?), on his head a cracked and tawny straw hat that just might have come many years ago from Panama, and he carried a smooth cane with a brass knob. His unshaven jaws were blackberry blue. His jacket was black velvet. His trousers were purple. All in all more than overdressed for a region where the men may or may not wear a cotton singlet, but a shirt never except on Sundays, apart from the doctor if there is one, or the teacher if there is one, or the local landowner, and there is always one of them.

What on earth could he be? Not a visitor, at this time of the year, and in this non-place. An adolescent poet? More likely an absconding bank clerk in disguise. (Joke. In empty places like this the sand-hoppers for fifty miles around are known by their first names.) The local screwball? I alighted. He saw me. We met in the middle of the road – the roads down here are wide and fine. I asked him if he might be so kind as to tell me where I might, if it were not too much to ask, find the lost city of the Sybarites. At once he straightened his sagging back, replied eagerly, rapidly and excitedly, 'Three kilometres ahead fork left after the gas station then first right along a dirt track can I have a cigarette where are you from may I show you my pictures?'

Well, I thought, this is odd, I am on Forty-second Street, Division, Pigalle, the Cascine, the Veneto, Soho, Pompeii, show me his dirty pictures, what next? His sister? A pretty boy? Cannabis? American cigarettes? I told him I was an insurance salesman from Chicago and bade him lead on. He led me rapidly through the passage to a wooden shack in the untidy yard behind the house, where, as he fumbled with the lock, he explained himself.

'I am a Roman I am a great painter I came down here two years ago to devote my life to my art I have been saving up for years for this a professor of fine arts from New York bought four of my paintings last week for fifty thousand lire apiece.'

I knew this last to be not so immediately he flung open the door on lines of paintings stacked around the earthen floor – there were three or four canvases but he had mostly used chipboard or plywood. His daubs all indicated the same subject, mustard yellow sunflowers against a blue sea, each of them a very long way after van Gogh, each the same greasy blob of brown and yellow, each executed (appropriate word!) in the same three primary colours straight from the tube, chrome yellow, burnt umber, cerulean blue, with, here and there as the fancy had taken him, a mix of the three in a hoarse green like a consumptive's spittle. They were the most supremely splendid, perfect, godawful examples of bad art I had ever seen. As I gazed at them in a Cortes silence I knew that I simply must possess one of them immediately.

Snobbery? A kinky metropolitan taste? I know the feeling too well not to know its source in compassion and terror. To me bad art is one of the most touching and frightening examples of self-delusion in the world. Bad actors, bad musicians, bad writers, bad painters, bad anything, and not just the inbetweeners or the borderliners but the total, desperate, irredeemable failures. Wherever I have come on an utterly bad picture I have wanted to run away from it or possess it as a work of horror. Those 'original' gilt-framed pictures in paper elbow guards displayed for sale in the foyers of big commercial hotels, or in big railroad terminals. A quarter of a mile of even worse 'originals' hanging from the railings of public parks in the summer. Those reproductions that form part of the regular stock of novelty stores that sell china cuckoo clocks, nutcrackers shaped like a woman's thighs, pepper pots shaped like ducks' bottoms. The poor, sad, pathetic little boy with the one, single, perfect teardrop glistening on his cheek. Six camels forever stalking across the desert into a red ink sunset. Three stretched-neck geese flying over a reedy lake into the dawn. That jolly medieval friar holding up his glass of supermarket port to an Elizabethan diamond-paned window as bright as a five-hundred-watt electric bulb.

We know the venal type who markets these *kitsch* objects and we know that they are bought by uneducated people of no taste. But if one accepts that these things are sometimes not utterly devoid of skill, and are on the edge of taste, who paints them? Looking into the earnest, globular eyes of this young man in Bussano (who insofar as he had no least skill and no least taste was the extreme example of the type) I felt once again the surge of compassion and of fear that is always the prelude to the only plausible answer I know: that he was yet another dreaming innocent who believed that he had heard the call to higher things. His type must be legion: young boys and girls who at some unlucky moment of their lives have heard, and alas have heeded that far-off whir of wings and that solitary midnight song once heard, so they have been told, in ancient days by emperor and clown, the same voice that flung magic casements open on the foam of perilous seas and faery lands forlorn. The frightening part of it is that there can be very few human beings who have not heard it in some form or another. If we are wise we either do nothing about it or do the least possible. We send a subscription, join something, vote, are modest.

As I offered him a cigarette I felt like the man in charge of a firing squad; not that I, or anybody else ever can kill such lethal innocence. As he virtually ate the cigarette I saw that his eye sockets were hollowed not by imagination but starvation. He was a living cartoon of the would-be artist as a young man who has begun to fear that he possibly may not be the one and will certainly never again be the other. To comfort him I irresponsibly said, 'You might one day become the van Gogh of Calabria,' to which he said quickly, 'I sell you any one you like cheap.' Should I have said they were all awful? I said I liked the one that, in characteristic burlesque of the real by the fake, he had labelled *Occhio d'oro, Mar' azzurro*. 'Golden Eye, Azure Sea.' Whereupon he said, 'Fifty dollars,' and I beat him down to two. As he pouched the two bills I asked him what he was proposing to do with all that lovely money. He laughed gaily – the Italian poor really are the most gutsy people in the world, as well as the most dream-deluded— 'Tonight I will bring my wife to the hotel for two brandies to celebrate my first sale in two years. It is an omen from heaven for our future.'

All this, and a wife too? I invited him into the hotel for a beer, served by a drowsy slut whom he had imperiously waked from her siesta. I asked him about his wife.

'Roman,' he said proudly. 'And *borghese*. Her father works in a bank. She believes absolutely in my future. When we married she said, "Sesto" – I was a sixth child, my name is Sesto Caro— "I will follow you to the end of the world."' He crossed two fingers. 'We are like that.' He crossed three. 'With our child, like that. The first, alas, was stillborn.'

(The harm innocence can do!)

He said that he, also, was a Roman. And he was! He knew the city as well as I do, and I have spent twenty years living there as a nosy reporter. I found him in every way, his self-delusion apart, an honest young man. He agreed that he had done all sorts of things. Run away from home at fourteen. Done a year in the galleys for stealing scrap.

Returned home, spent two years in a seminary trying to be a monk, a year and a half in a *trattoria* in the Borgo Pio. Was arrested again and held for two years without trial for allegedly selling cannabis. Released, he spent three years in Germany and Switzerland to make money for his present project. Returned home, was apprenticed as an electrician's assistant... He was now twenty-nine. She was now twenty-one. When she was turned off by her father they had come down here to beg the help of her godfather-uncle Emilio Ratti, an engineer living in what I heard him lightly call 'the Cosenza of Pliny and Varro.' I looked out and upward towards the Sila.

'Cosenza? A godfather so far from Rome?'

'He was exiled there by Mussolini and never went back.'

Unfortunately, or by the whim of the pagan gods of Calabria – he contemptuously called it *Il Far Ovest* – his wife, then nineteen, and big with child, got diarrhoea so badly in Naples ('Pollution around Capri?') that they finally tumbled off the train at a mountainy place called Cassano in the hope of quickly finding a doctor there; only to be told as the train pulled away into the twilit valleys that the station of Cassano was hours away from the village of Cassano, whereas their informant, a carter from Bussano, offered to drive them in one hour to his beautiful village by the sea near which (equally untrue) there was a very good doctor. So, with their parcels, their cardboard suitcases, their paper bundles and bulging pillowcases they had come to this *casale* and stayed. Uncle Emilio had visited them once. Still, like her father, he occasionally disbursed small sums of money on condition that they stayed where they were.

2

We shook hands cordially, I gathered my bad painting and drove off fast. I had walked into the middle of a frightening story and I had no idea what its end would be. Murder? Suicide? If I could wait for either that could be a good something else for Chicago. Not now. No lift. No human interest. I looked eagerly ahead of me along the straight highway to my meeting with the skilled Italo-American technicians and archaeologists at Sybaris. About this, at least, van Gogh was accurate. After exactly three kilometres I saw the yellow and black sign of a gas station, whose attendant directed me, without interest, towards a dirt track leading into a marshland of reeds and scrub.

As I bumped along this dusty track I could see no life whatever, nothing but widespread swamp, until I came around a bend in the track and saw ahead of me a solitary figure leaning against a jeep, arms folded, pipe-smoking, well built, idly watching me approach. High boots to his knees, riding breeches, open-necked khaki shirt, peaked cap, sunglasses, grizzled hair. In his sixties? I pulled up beside him, told him who and what I was and asked him where I could see the buried city of Sybaris. Immobile he listened to me, smiled tolerantly, or it might be boredly, then without speaking beckoned me with his pipe to follow his jeep. I did so until he halted near a large pool of clear water surrounded by reeds and mud. Some ten feet underwater I perceived a couple of broken pillars and a wide halfmoon of networked brick.

'Behold Sybaris,' he said and with amusement watched me stare at him, around the level swamp at the immensity of the all-seeing mountains and back to him again.

'You mean that's *all* there is to see of it?'

'All, since, if you believe the common legend, its enemies deflected its great river, the Crathis,' he in turn glanced westward and upward, 'to drown it under water as Pompeii was smothered in volcanic ash. Crathis is now brown with yellow mud. "Crathis the lovely stream that stains dark hair bright gold."'

He smiled apologetically at the quotation.

'But the archaeologists? I was hoping to find them all hard at work.'

He smiled unapologetically. He relit his pipe.

'Where is the hurry? Sybaris has been asleep a long time. They have finished for this year. They have had to work slowly. They have been experimenting with sonic soundings since 1964. They have had to map the entire extent of the city with their magnetometers. It was six miles in circumference. But I am only an engineer. Consultant engineer. Of Cosenza.'

I stared unhappily at the solitary eye of the once largest and most elegant city of the whole empire of Magna Graecia. I recalled and mentioned an odd detail that had stuck in my mind's tooth, out of, I think, Lenormant, supposedly typical of the luxury of the city in its heyday – its bylaw that forbade morning cocks to crow earlier than a stated number of hours after sunrise. He shrugged dubiously. I did know that it was Lenormant who a hundred years ago looked from the foothills of the Sila down at this plain and saw nothing but strayed bulls, long since gone wild, splashing whitely in its marshes. He said he had been much struck by this legendary picture.

'Legendary? You *are* a sceptical man.'

'In this country legend is always posturing as history. We are a wilderness of myths growing out of myths. Along the coast there, at Crotone, my wife, as a girl, walked to the temple of Juno, the Mother of the Gods, in a procession of barefooted girls singing hymns to Mary, the Mother of God. Here Venus can overnight become Saint Venus. *Santa Venera.* A hill once sacred to Cybele becomes sanctified all over again as Monte Vergine. I do not deride any of this. Some myths point to a truth. Some not. I cannot always distinguish. And I have lived in Calabria for thirty years.'

'Not a born Calabrese, then?'

'I am a Roman. I was exiled here by the Fascisti in 1939. Not in this spot! Back up there in a small village called San Giovanni in Fiore. A pretty name, situated beautifully, poor and filthy when you got there. The night they arrested me in Rome they allowed me five minutes and one suitcase. I grabbed the biggest book I could find. It was *Don Quixote.* That winter I reread it by daylight and by candlelight three times. I had nothing else to read, nobody to talk to, nothing to do. Every fine day I tramped over those mountains, sometimes twenty and more miles a day.' He laughed cheerfully. 'Wearing out the Fascist spies detailed to follow me. Today the same men, as old as I am now, joke with me over it. They were bastards every one of them. And would be again if it suited them. They say, "Ah, the good old days, Emilio! You were so good for our bellies. If only we could lead one another that dance all over again!" I came everywhere on old stories written on old stones – myths, charms, omens, hopes, ambitions. The cerecloths of Greece. The marks of Rome. Those bits in that pool are probably Roman. You can tell it by the *opus reticulatum* of the bricks. That was only uncovered in '32. They call this place the *Parco del Cavallo.* What horse? Whose horse? I came on remnants of Byzantium, the Goths, the Saracens, the Normans. Our past. When my spies saw what I was after they stopped following me – I had become a harmless fool – doors opened to me, a landowner's, then a doctor's, even a schoolmaster's, a learned priest's in Rossano. I met and fell in love with a doctor's daughter from Crotone. It was a charming little port in those days.

Good wine of Ciro. Good cigars. Very appealing. One day in September 1943 the British Fifth Army entered Crotone and we were married. Well before then,' he laughed, 'every Fascist of San Giovanni in Fiore had burned his black shirt and started shouting *Viva il Re*. The old woman with whom I had lodged sold me for ten thousand lire to the doctor, who sold me for twenty thousand to the police marshal, who sold me for fifty thousand to a landowner who drove me into Crotone to show the British commanding officer the victim of Fascism whom he had protected for the last four years. I did not give him away. I had fallen in love so much with Calabria that I even liked its ruffians. I settled in Cosenza.'

Why was he unburdening himself like this to a stranger? I said that in September 1943 I was with the American Eighth Army across those mountains.

'My God!' I wailed, throwing a bit of silver wrap from my chewing gum into the pool of the horse. 'Do you realize that all that is over a quarter of a century ago?'

He smiled his tender, stoic's smile.

'I realize it very well. My youngest son is a lieutenant in the Air Force. His brother is studying medicine in Palermo. My eldest child is due to have her first baby at any hour.'

'Why did you not return to Rome?'

He again glanced towards Cosenza. The sun, I observed, sinks early behind those Apennines. For no reason there flashed across my eyes the image of this plain covered by sheets of water made of melting snow.

'I have told you why I never went back to Rome. Because I had fallen in love with a woman and a place, with a woman who was a place. I saw my Claudia as a symbol of the ancientness, the ancestry, the dignity, the unforgettable beauty of Calabria, of its pedigree, its pride, its arrogance, its closeness to the beginning of the beginnings of man and the end of the ends of life. I believed then and believe still that outside Calabria it would be impossible to find such a woman as my Claudia.'

I did not suggest that fifty million Italians might not agree. If a young man in love, and an old man remembering his young love is not entitled to his dreams, who is? I merely suggested that there is also some 'ancientness' in Rome.

'In museums? In Rome the bridge is down. It has no living past. It is just as venal, vulgar, cowardly, cynical and commercial a city as any other in the world.' He jerked his body to a soldierly attention. 'I must get back to Cosenza. We have been warned by the doctor that the birth may be difficult. There may have to be a caesarian. My wife will be praying for an easy birth. When I get back she may have more news.'

No relatives? Ageing both. Alone. I did not say that my own daughter has married far away from me into another continent. All dreams have an ending somewhat different from their beginnings.

'Your daughter is in Cosenza?' I asked hopefully, but he waved his right hand towards the south.

'No. She married a splendid young man in Reggio, an *avvocato*. Bartolomeo Vivarini. It is not very far but it is far too far for my wife and me at a time like this.'

We shook hands warmly. We had in some way lit in those few minutes a small flame to friendship. He waved and went his way. I continued along the coast, deeper into his South, his beloved Past.

I slept in Crotone, badly, woke wondering if I had been as unwise about my food as one so easily can be anywhere south of Rome, or dreamed oppressively, or failed to do something along the road that I ought to have done. It was not until I had dived into the sparkles of the sea and been driving fast for a good hour that the reason for my dejection struck me. I had caught the *mal du pays*. Four days out of Rome and I was already homesick for it. And why not? I am not married to Old Calabria. I am a political animal, a man of reason, interested in the world as it really is. My job is to do with today, occasionally with tomorrow, never with yesterday. I had been seeing far too many memorials to that incorporeal, extramundane, immaterial, miasmic element that is food and drink to men like Emilio Ratti and that Carl Sandburg called a bucket of ashes.

One ancient temple had been exciting, like those fifteen Doric columns at Metaponto deep in weeds and wild flowers. The next, less than a mile away, had been too much. A cartload of stones. Decline, decay, even death is Beauty's due. Never defeat. This South is littered with decay and defeat. Farther on a bare few megaliths recorded another defeated city. A duck pond to call up great Sybaris! Not even a stone had marked another lost city. Juno's great church had been worn by time, weather and robbery to a naked column on the edge of a bleak moor and a bare cliff outside Crotone. All as empty now as the sea, except for ageing women remembering the garlanded girls who once walked there in a line singing hymns in May. At Locri I had paused for gas and found the local museum ill-kept and dusty. *Aranciata Pitagora*. One of Greece's greatest philosophers advertising orange juice over a wayside stall.

I covered my final forty miles in half an hour. I swept into a Reggio bristling with carabinieri, local police, armed troops, riot squad trucks crackling out constant radio reports. The hotel was like a Field H.Q. with pressmen and photographers, cinema crews and TV crews. All because it was widely and furiously feared that Rome intended to pass Reggio over in favour of either Cosenza or Catanzaro as the new provincial capital. Posters all over the walls announced that at four o'clock there would be a Monster Meeting in the Piazza del Popolo. This would leave me just enough time to interview the chief citizens of Reggio: mayor, archbishop, city councillors, parliamentary deputies, labour bosses, leading industrialists if any. For some five hours, lunchless, I patiently gathered from them thousands of flat-footed words, to which at the afternoon meeting a sequence of bellowing orators added their many more.

Weary, hungry and bored I remembered with a click of my fingers the name Vivarini.

3

Twenty minutes later, in a quarter of the city far removed from the noisy piazza, I was admitted by an elderly woman in black – wife? housekeeper? secretary? – to the presence of a very old man in a dusky room cluttered with antiquated furniture, bibelots, statuettes in marble, alabaster and bronze, old paintings, vases, boxes of papers, books, bowls, crystal paperweights, signed photographs in silver frames. It was the kind of room that made me wonder how he ever found anything he might require there. A Balzac would have been delighted to list all its telltale signs, markers or milestones of the fortunes of a business and a family, especially those signed photographs – King Vittorio Emmanuele III, Dr Axel Munthe, one Peter Rothschild, Prime Minister Giolitti (the one who held out against Mussolini until 1921), Facta (who fell to Fascism in 1922), Mussolini's son-in-law Galeazzo Ciano, Marshal Badoglio. As for me, one look and I knew what I was in for. And I was!

'Ah, *signore*, this was once a city of the rarest elegance. My son whom you must meet – he is at the hospital – does not realize this, he is too young. But I myself heard d'Annunzio say that our *lungomare* is one of the most gracious seaside promenades in Europe. What do you think of that?' (I refused to say that if the so-called Prince of Montevenoso ever said so he must have said it before 1908 when this city was flattened by its terrible earthquake, and at that date Signor Vivarini would have been a very small boy indeed.) 'But, now, alas, *signore*, we have been taken over by the vulgar herd, the *popolazzo*. Corruption. Vendettas. Squabbles for gain. Maladministration. And all because our natural leaders, our aristocracy, the landed gentry of Calabria, started to abandon Reggio immediately after the earthquake of 1908 . . .'

In the distance an irritable rattle of rifle fire. He did not seem to hear it. He went on and on. And I should be back there at the rioting.

'Nothing can save us now but a miracle . . . When I was a youth . . .'

I rose at the sound of a distant, dull explosion, ready to run from him without ceremony, when from the doorway I found myself transfixed by the stare of a man whom I took to be his son – a tall, thin, challenging, cadaverous man of about thirty-five, eyes Atlantic grey, peering through eyelashes that hid nothing of his patent awareness of his own merits, his inquisitorial mistrust, his cold arrogance of a pasha. I would have been utterly repelled by him if his clothes were not so much at odds with his manner. His lean body was gloved in a light, metallic, bluish material suggestive of shimmering night and stars, his skintight shirt was salmon pink, his lemon tie disappeared into the V of a flowered waistcoat, the silk handkerchief in his breast pocket lolled as softly as a kitten's tail, or as its eyes, his shoes were sea-suede, and his smoke of hair was blued like a woman's. After all those big mouths in the piazza he looked so promisingly ambiguous that I introduced myself at once, name, profession, nationality. In a courteous and attractively purring voice, and in the unmistakable English of Cambridge (Mass.), i.e., of Harvard, he replied that he had also spent some time in America. In return I told him that I had begun my career as a journalist on *The Crimson*. His laugh was loud, frank, open and delighted. We shook hands amiably. I was on the point of deciding that he was really a most engaging fellow when I recalled his first ice-cold air, his arrogance and his suspicion. I glanced at his clothes and I looked at his face, where now it was the mouth that impressed me: a blend of the soft, the mobile, the vulpine, the voracious, the smiling that made me suddenly think that the essence of his first effect on me had been the predatory and the self-protective nature of a born sensualist. Obviously a man capable of being very attractive to women, but also, I feared, capable in his egoism of being cruel.

'You enjoyed America,' I stated cheerfully.

For a second or two his peering mask returned and he smiled, not unhappily, yet not warmly either, the way I fancied an inquisitor might when watching a heretic slowly gyrating over the flames that would soon deliver his soul to paradise. He said that he had endured the arid rigidities of Harvard University for three years. He laughed gaily at another rattle of gunfire, saying, 'That nonsense will be over in an hour.' He did not so much invite me to dine with him, as insist that I should give him the pleasure.

'And the consolation. I am going through a difficult time.'

The next second he was blazing with fury at his father's tremulous question; 'How is Angelica?' This – I had observed in some embarrassment – had already been iterated four times.

'She has been in labour now for eight hours!' he ground out savagely. 'If she has not given birth within three more hours I insist upon a caesarian.' The old man waved protesting hands. 'My dear father!' he raged at him in a near whisper. 'I have told you twenty times that there is nothing scientifically wrong with a caesarian.'

He turned suavely to me. 'I do wish my dear father would realize that even after three caesarians my wife could still bear him a long line of grandchildren.' He laughed lightly. 'Of course there is no truth in the legend that Julius Caesar was so delivered. I will call for you at your hotel – The Excelsior I presume? – at half past seven. We will dine at the Conti. It is not very much but it is our best.'

I would have preferred to catch the plane for Rome. But I remembered, and shared, some of Emilio Ratti's quiet troublement over his daughter. My own daughter had not had an easy time with her first. There bounced off my mind the thought that a nameless young woman in Bussano had lost her first. Actually it was none of these things decided me but the sound of more shots. I ran from the pair of them.

The rioting was well worth it, water cannon, baton charges, rubber bullets, the lot, women howling Jesu Marias, hair streaming, children bawling, fat men behaving like heroes, the finest fullest crop of De Sica clichés, vintage 1950, and not a cat killed. And all for what? For, at least, more than Hecuba, if for less than Hector. For pride, honour, family, home, ancient tradition, *Rhegium antiquum* so often raped by Messinaians, Syracusans, Romans, Goths, Normans, Saracens, Pisans, Turks, Aragonese, Fascisti, Nazis, and the liberating armies of Great Britain and the USA. Also, no doubt, for something to do with real estate, tourism, air travel, emigration, IRI, Bernie Cornfield's *fonditalia*, Swiss hooks in Chiasso, the Mafia, the *Cassa per il Mezzogiorno*, the Demochristians' majority in parliament... But the journalist's classical symptom is cynicism, the boil of his inward frustration, the knowledge that he will never get at that total truth reserved for historians, novelists and poets who will reduce his tormented futilities to a few drops of wisdom.

By the time Vivarini called for me I was calmed, and if apart from Crotone's morning moonshine coffee still unfed, I was by now not unslaked, braced by two martinis which I insisted that he and I, at the bar, make four; as, in Conti's, he at once ordered not one but two litres of *vino di Ciro* – reminding me of that drunken night, it was in Peking (Oh! Jesus!) years and years ago, that I first became a father.

'No!' he groaned aloud to the totally empty restaurant. (Its usual clients afraid to emerge at night?) 'No baby yet!'

His father ('Don't touch the *scampi!* Even here we have possible pollution!') was a Polonius, a foolish, fond old man whom nobody would mistake for his better, three generations out of date. A sweet, kind man. With fine sensibilities. But, like all Italians, a besotted sentimentalist.

'By comparison I, Bartolomeo...'

'Hi, Bart! Call me Tom!'

'Hi, Tom ... am a cold Cartesian. My wife,' he informed me secretively, evidently making some point, 'is a mortal angel. I have selected her with the greatest care. For I have also had my sorrows. My betrayals. But she is an angel with a Gallic mind. She also loathes all this traditional nonsense of her father's and of my father, all this ridiculous adoration of the Past. Down with Tradition! All it is is confusion! Mythology! Obfuscation!' He hammered the table, a waiter came running and was dismissed. 'I insist on a caesarian! Those two old men with their folksy minds think it bad, wrong, a threat to the long line of children they dream of as their – *their!* – descendants. Excuse me,' he said quietly. 'May I telephone?'

He returned, swaying only a very little, shook his head, looked at his watch, while I thought of my engineer and his wife waiting by the telephone in Cosenza, and that agonized girl hauling on a towel tied to the end of a bedpost, and the old lawyer somewhere up the street moaning to himself among his portraits and his trophies of the dead and I said, 'Look't, for Chrissake, forget me! I know you want to be back in that hospital, or nursing home, or whatever it is. Do please go there!' – to which, intent on behaving as calmly as a Harvard man, that is to say as a Yank, that is to say as an English gentleman (period 1850) would have behaved, he replied that if his papa was irrational his father-in-law Emilio was far more so.

'I can guess how my father explained those riots to you. The decay of the aristocracy? All that shit? But did he once mention the Mafia? With whom, of course, he worked hand in glove all his life? Whereas, on the other hand, Emilio would know all about the Mafia, but he would also tell you that the rioting would have been far worse if it had not been for,' here one could almost hear his liver gurgling bile, 'the "wisely restraining hand of Mother Church." Two complementary types of total unreason.'

At this he bowed his face into his palms and moaned into them.

'If only my love and I could get out of this antiquated, priest-ridden, Mafia-ridden, time-ridden, phony, provincial hole!'

He quickly recovered control of himself sufficiently to beg me, concernedly, to give him the latest news from the States. I did so, keeping it up as long and lightly as I could since the narration seemed to soothe him. But it was only a seeming, because he suddenly cried out, having obviously not heeded one word I had been saying:—

'The Church here is, of course, a master plotter and conspirator. Have you seen their latest miracle?' – as if he were asking me whether I had seen the latest Stock Exchange reports. 'You must. It is a masterpiece. It is only five hundred metres away. A weeping Madonna. Weeping, of course, for Reggio. Like Niobe, from whom the idea most certainly derives. What a gullible people we are! Madonnas who weep, bleed, speak, go pale, blush, sway, for all I know dance. Did you know that before the war Naples possessed two bottles of milk supposed to have been drawn off the breasts of the Virgin which curdled twice a year? Excuse me. May I telephone?'

He disappeared. This made the restaurant twice as empty. The patron asked me solicitiously if all was well. Signor Vivarini seemed upset? I said his wife was expecting a baby.

'A baby!'

Within a minute the restaurant came alive. A fat female cook bustled from the kitchen. After her came a serving woman. The *padrone*'s wife appeared. Two small children peeped. An old man shuffled out in slippers. In a group they babbled about babies. It was nine o'clock. I had lost my plane. I had not yet written my report on Reggio. But he did not come back and he did not come back, and I was cross, bothered, bored and bewildered. The restaurant again emptied – the whole company of family and servitors had gone off in a gabble to regather outside the telephone booth. I had decided to pay the bill and leave when a mini-riot burst into the place, all of them returning, cheering and laughing, to me, as if I was the fertile father, and in their midst Bartolomeo Vivarini, swollen as the sun at noon, beaming, triumphant, bestowing benedictions all around, proclaiming victory as smugly as if he was the fertile mother.

'*Un miracolo gradito!*' he laughed and wept, 'a son! I am the father of a son! I have telephoned my father and my mother, my father-in-law and my mother-in-law. They are all such good people. Are they not?'

The company laughed, clapped, declared that it was indeed a miracle, a splendid miracle, a *miracolo gradito*.

'There will be more children!' the cook assured him.

'And more sons,' the *padrone*'s father assured him.

He sat, sobbed, hiccuped, called for champagne, but this I firmly forbade.

'You haven't yet seen your wife!' I pointed out. 'She must have suffered terrible pain,' at which his sobs spouted like champagne.

'I had forgotten all about her!' he wailed and punished his bony breast. 'I must light a candle for my wife to the Madonna. To the weeping Madonna! Let us go, my dear friend. To the Madonna! She, perhaps, may make them give me one peep at my son. You will drive me? I dare not! It is not far away.'

So, we left, led noisily by all to the door. And nobody asked us to pay the bill.

His car was a Lancia. I drove it furiously to somewhere up the hill, this way, that way, until, above the nightness and lightness of the city, of the straits, of all Calabria and all Sicily, we halted on the edge of a tiny *piazza* crowded with worshippers or sightseers, where there stood an altar, and on the altar a pink and blue commercial statue of the allegedly lachrymose Virgin Mary. A hundred breathless candles adored her, and four steady electric spotlights. Bartolomeo crushed me through the crowds to the altar, bought two candles, one for himself, one for me, refusing to take any change from his thousand-lire bill, lit his candle, fixed it in position and knelt on the bare ground to pray, his hands held wide in total wonder and belief.

As far as I was concerned the miracle was, of course, like every popular Italian miracle preposterous – a word, I had learned at high school, that means in Ciceronian Latin arse-to-front. The object was to me simply an object, bought from some statue vendor in Reggio, with, if even that ever happened, a drop or two of glycerine deposited on its painted cheek by some pious or impious hand. But why should anybody want a miracle so badly, and gradually, as I looked about me and felt the intensity of the human feeling circling the altar like a whirlpool of air, or bees in a swarm, or butterflies over a wave, or fallen leaves whispering in a dry wind, I began to feel awed and even a little frightened. As I moved through the murmuring or silent crowds, conscious of the eloquent adoration of the old, the unexpected fervour of the young, the sudden hysteria of a woman carried away screaming, the quiet insistent stare of two Franciscans fixed on the painted face, I became so affected that at one point I thought that I, too, could, might, perhaps – or did I? – see one single, perfect teardrop gleaming in the spotlights on the face of the mother of their God. I blinked. 'It' vanished.

But had it ever been there? Who had the proof that it had not been an illusion for us all? The night was inflammable, the country explosive, I had too much respect for my skin to ask why even one teardrop had not been looked at through a microscope capable of distinguishing between glycerine, that is to say $C_3H_5(OH)_3$ and the secretions of the lachrymal gland. I might as well have committed instant suicide as suggest that a similar test could be applied to the wine said to change during their Mass into the blood of their God. I found myself beside the two motionless friars. I cautiously asked one of them if he had seen, or knew anybody who had seen, a tear form in the Madonna's eye. He answered skilfully that this was not wholly relevant since if one saw the tear it was so, and if one did not see a tear it was not so, which, he took pleasure in explaining to me courteously, but at some length, marks the difference in Kantian philosophy between the *phenomenon* and the *noumenon*. My mind swam.

Bartolomeo had vanished. I stayed on in that haunted *piazzetta* until well after one in the morning. I collected some opinions, two asserted experiences, stories of miraculous cures. The crowds thinned, but at no time was the statue unattended by at least one worshipping believer. Only when a palsied dumb woman asked me the time by tapping my watch with her finger did I remember that by now the huntsmen might be asleep in Calabria but the foreign editors of America would be wide awake, for who could be drowsy at that hour whose first edition frees us all from everlasting sleep? A few steps away I found a lighted café whose owner must have nourished the same views as Sir Thomas Browne. There, over a couple of Stregas, I disposed in twenty minutes of Reggio's political troubles. Inside another half an hour I evoked the miracle of the Madonna in one of the most brilliant pieces I have written during my whole life. The best part of it was the coda, which I doubted I would ever send – they would only kill it at once. In it I asked Chicago, still daylit, still dining or well dined, rumbling like old thunder, smelling as rank as a blown-out candle, how it is that the Mediterranean never ceases to offer us new lamps for old. I opined that it is because it is in the nature of that restless Mediterranean mind to be divinely discontent with this jail of a world into which we are born. It is always trying to break out, to blow down the walls of its eyes, to extend time to eternity so as to see this world as nobody except the gods has ever seen it before.

No! Not for Chicago. Not that I cared. What is every journalist anyway but an artist *manqué* spancelled to another, who is tethered to a third, and a fourth and a fifth up to the fiftieth and final *manqué* at the top?

I passed slowly back through the little *piazza*. The candles were guttering, the spotlights still shone, it was empty except for one man kneeling in the centre of it before the sleepless statue. I bade her a silent farewell, Juno, Hera, Niobe, Venus, or the Virgin, and went on walking through the sleeping streets downhill to the shore. It was a still night. The sky gleamed with stars like Vivarini's blue coat. I thought of my dauber of Bussano, my van Gogh *manqué*, and I decided that the distinction between Emperor and Clown is irrelevant. Every virtue is woven into its opposite, failure built into ambition, despair into desire, cold reason into hot dreams, delusion into the imagination, death into life, and if a youth does not take the risks of every one of them he will not live long enough to deserve peace.

I paused. In the straits was that a purring motorboat? Not a sound.

Here, at about five twenty o'clock one equally silent morning sixty-one years ago – it was in fact December 28th – people like the father and mother of old Mr Vivarini the lawyer felt their houses sway and shiver for thirty-two seconds, and for twelve miles north and south every house swayed and shook in the same way for two months. At widening intervals the earthquake went on for a year and a half. The entire city vanished. Like Sybaris. Like Pompeii. I looked at my watch. In a few hours another green sheen would creep over the straits. Another pallid premorning lightsomeness would expand behind Aspromonte.

I walked on smiling at the fun the Vivarinis would have disputing over the name of their newborn child.

An Inside Outside Complex

So then, a dusky Sunday afternoon in Bray at a quarter to five o'clock,
lighting up time at five fifteen, November 1st, All Souls' Eve, dedicated
to the suffering souls in Purgatory, Bertie Bolger, bachelor, aged
forty-one or so, tubby, ruddy, greying, well-known as a dealer in
antiques, less well-known as a conflator thereof, walking briskly along
the seafront, head up to the damp breezes, turns smartly into the lounge
of the Imperial Hotel for a hot toddy, singing in a soldierly basso 'my
breast expanding to the ball.'

The room, lofty, widespread, Victorian, gilded, over-furnished, as
empty as the ocean, and not warm. The single fire is small and
smouldering. Bertie presses the bell for service, divests himself of his
bowler, his vicuna overcoat, his lengthy scarf striped in black, red,
green and white, the colours of Trinity College, Dublin (which he has
never attended), sits in a chintzy armchair before the fire, pokes it into
a blaze, leans back, and is at once invaded by a clearcut knowledge of
what month it is, and an uneasy feeling about its date. He might earlier
have adverted to both if he had not, during his perambulation, been
preoccupied with the problem of how to transform a twentieth-century
Buhl cabinet, now in his possession, into an eighteenth-century ditto
that might plausibly be attributed to the original M. Boulle. This
preoccupation had permitted him to glance at, but not to observe,
either the red gasometer by the harbour inflated to its winter zenith,
or the haybarn beside the dairy beyond the gasometer packed with
cubes of hay, or the fuel yard, facing the haybarn, beside the dairy
beyond the gasometer, heavily stocked with mountainettes of coal, or
the many vacancy signs in the lodging houses along the seafront, or the
hoardings on the pagoda below the promenade where his mother, God
rest her, had once told him he had been wheeled as a coiffed baby in
a white pram to hear Mike Nono singing 'I do liuke to be besiude the
seasiude, I do liuke to be besiude the sea,' or, most affectingly of all,
if he had only heeded them, the exquisite, dying leaves of the

hydrangeas in the public gardens, pale green, pale yellow, frost white, spiking the air above once purple petals that now clink greyly in the breeze like tiny seashells.

He suddenly jerks his head upright, sniffing desolation, looks slowly about the lounge, locates in a corner of it some hydrangeas left standing too long in a brass pot of unchanged water, catapults himself from the chair with a 'Jaysus! Five years to the bloody day!', dons his coat, his comforter and his bowler hat, and exits rapidly to make inland towards the R.C. church. For days after she died the house had retained that rank funereal smell. Tomorrow morning a Mass must be said for the repose of his mother's soul, still, maybe – Who knows? Only God knows! – suffering in the flames of Purgatory.

It is the perfect and pitiless testing date, day and hour for any seaside town in these northern islands. A week or two earlier and there might still have been a few lingering visitors, a ghost of summer's luke-warmth, a calmer sea, unheard waves, and, the hands of the Summer Time clocks not yet put backward, another hour of daylight. This expiring Sunday the light is dim, the silence heavy, the town turned in on itself. As he walks through the side avenues between the sea and the Main Street, past rows of squat bungalows, every garden drooping, past grenadiers of red brick, lace curtained, past ancient cement-faced cottages with sagging roofs, he is informed by every fanlight, oblong or halfmoon, blank as night or distantly lit from the recesses behind each front door, that there is some kind of life asleep or snoozing behind number 51, *Saint Anthony's*, *Liljoe's*, *Fatima*, 59 (odd numbers on this side), *The Billows*, *Swan Lake*, 67, *Slievemish*, *Sea View*, names in white paint, numbers in adhesive celluloid. Every one of them gives a chuck to the noose of loneliness about his neck. I live in Dublin. I am a guest in a guest house. I am Mister Bee. I lunch of weekdays at the United Services Club. I dine at the Yacht Club. Good for biz. Bad for Sundays, restaurants shut, homeless. Pray for the soul of Mrs Mary Bolger, of Tureenlahan, County Tipperary, departed this life five years ago. Into thy hands, O Lord.

On these side avenues only an odd front window is lit. Their lights flow searingly across little patches of grass called front gardens, privet-hedged, lonicera-hedged, mass-concrete hedged. Private. Keep Off.

As he passed one such light, in what a real estate agent would have called a picture window, he was so shaken by what he saw inside that after he had passed he halted, looked cautiously about him, turned and walked slowly back to peep in again. What had gripped his attention through the unsuspecting window had been a standing lamp in brass with a large pink shade, and beneath its red glow, seated in an armchair with her knees crossed, a bare-armed woman reading a folded magazine, one hand blindly lifting a teacup from a Moorish side table, holding the cup immobile while she concentrated on something that had detained her interest. By the time he had returned she was sipping from the cup. He watched her lay it down, throw the magazine aside and loop forward on two broad knees to poke the fire. Her arms looked strong. She was full-breasted. She had dark hair. In that instant B.B. became a *voyeur*.

The long avenue suddenly sprang its public lights. Startled he looked up and down the empty perspective. It was too cold for evening strollers. He was aware that he was trembling with fear. He did not know what else he was feeling except that there was nothing sexy to it. To calm himself he drew back behind the pillar of her garden gate whose name plate caught his eye. *Lorelei*. He again peeped around the side of the pillar. She was dusting her lap with her two palms. She was very dark, a western type, a Spanish-Galway type, a bit heavy. He could not discern the details of the room beyond the circle of light from the pink lamp, and he was glad of this: it made everything more mysterious, removed, suggestive, as if he was watching a scene on a stage. His loneliness left him, his desolation, his longing. He wanted only to be inside there, safe, secure, and satisfied.

'Ah, good evening, Bertie!' she cried to the handsome man who entered her room with the calm smile of complete sangfroid. 'I am so glad, Bertie, you dropped in on me. Do tell me your news, darling. How is the antique business? Come and warm your poor, dear hands. It is going to be a shivering night. Won't you take off your coat? Tea? No? What about a drink? I know exactly what you want, my pet. I will fix it for you. I have been waiting and waiting for you to come all the livelong day, melting with longing and love.'

As he gently closed the door of the cosy little room she proffered her hand in a queenly manner, whereupon our hero, as was fitting, leaned over it – because you never really do kiss a lady's hand, you merely breathe over it – and watched her eyes asking him to sit opposite her.

The woman rose, took her tea tray, and the room was suddenly empty. Her toe hooked the door all but a few inches short of shut. He was just as pleased whether she was in the room or out of it. All he wanted was to be inside her room. As he stared, her naked arm came slowly back into the room between the door and the jamb, groping for the light switch. A plain gold bangle hung from the wrist. The jamb dragged back the shoulder of her blouse so that he saw the dark hair of her armpit. The window went black.

He let out a long, whistling breath like a safety valve and resumed his long perambulation until he saw a similar light streaming from the window of an identical bungalow well ahead of him on the opposite side of the roadway. He padded rapidly towards it. As he reached its identical square cement gate-pillars he halted, looked backward and forward and then guardedly advanced a tortoise nose beyond the edge of the pillar to peep into the room. A pale, dawnlike radiance, softly tasselled, hinted at comfortable shapes, a sofa, small occasional chairs, a pouffe, a bookcase, heavy gleams of what could be silver, or could be just electroplated nickel. Here, too, a few tongues of fire. In the centre of the room a tall, thin, elderly man in a yellow cardigan, but not wearing a jacket or tie, stood so close beside a young girl with a blonde waterfall of hair as to form with her a single unanalysable shape. He seemed to be speaking. He stroked her smooth poll. They were like a still image out of a silent film. They were presumably doing something simple, natural and intimate. But what? They drew apart abruptly and the girl, while stooping to pick up some shining object from a low table, looked in the same movement straight out through the window. B.B. was so taken by surprise that he could not stir, even when she came close to the window, looked up at the sky, right and left, as if to see if it was raining, turned back, laughed inaudibly, waved the small silver scissors in her hand.

In that instant, at that gesture, some time after five fifteen on the afternoon of November 1st, the town darkening, the sky lowering, his life passing, a vast illumination broke like a sunrise upon his soul. At the shut-time of the year all small towns become smaller and smaller, dwindle from out-of-doors to in-of-doors; from long beaches, black roads, green fields, wide sun, to kitchens, living rooms, bedrooms, locked doors, drawn blinds, whispers, prayers, muffling blankets, nose-hollowed pillows; from making to mending; to littler and littler things, like this blonde Rapunzel with a scissors and a needle; all ending in daydreaming, and nightdreaming, and dreamless sleeping. How pleasant life could be in that declension to a white arm creeping between a door and a jamb, bare but for a circle of gold about a wrist and a worn wedding ring on one heavy finger. But I am outside. When the town is asleep in one another's arms I will sleep under the walls. No wife. No child. Mister Bee.

The headlamps of a motorcar sent him scurrying down an unlighted lane that may once have led to the mews of tall houses long since levelled to make room for these hundreds of little bungalows. In this abandoned lane the only window-light was one tiny, lofty aperture in the inverted V of a gable rising like a castle out of tall trees. Below it, at eye level the lane was becoming pitch dark. Above it, a sift of tattered light between mourning clouds. Hissing darkness. A sheaving wind. The elms were spiky as if the earth's hair was standing on end. He stiffened. A bird's croak? A sleepless nest? A far-off bark? He stared up at the tiny box of light whose inaccessibility was so much part of its incitement that when it went black like a fallen candle he uttered a 'Ha!' of delight. He would never know who had put a finger on the switch of that floating room. A maidservant about to emerge into the town? To go where? To meet whom? A boy's den? An old woman lumbering down the long stairs?

That Monday morning B.B. was laughing happily at himself. Bertie Bolger, the well-known dealer! The Peeping Tom from Tipperary! That was a queer bloody fit I took! And Jaysus, I forgot all about the mother again: well, she will have to wait until next year now though surely to God they'll let her out before then? Anyway, what harm did she ever do bar that snibby way she treated every girl I ever met; if it wasn't for her I might have been married twenty years ago to that Raven girl I met in 1950 in Arklow. And a hot piece she was, too . . . Mad for it!

The next Sunday evening he was padding softly around the back roads of Bray. He could not locate the old-man-blonde-girl bungalow. He winked up at the little cube of light. But *Lorelei* was dark. The next two Sundays were raining too heavily for prowling. On the fourth Sunday the window of *Lorelei* was brilliantly lighted, and there she was plying a large dressmaker's scissors on some coloured stuff laid across a gate-legged table under the bare electric bulb whose brightness diminished the ideality of the room, increased the attractions of the dressmaker. Broad cheekbones, like a Red Indian; raven hair; the jerky head of a blackbird alert at a drinking pool. He longed to touch one of those fingers, broad at the tip like a little spade. Twice the lights of an oncoming car made him walk swiftly away, bowler hat down on nose, collar up. A third time he fled from light pouring out of the door of the adjacent bungalow and a woman hurrying down its path with her overcoat over her head and shoulders. Loping away fast he turned in fright to the running feet behind him and saw her coat-ends vanish under the suddenly lighted door lamp of *Lorelei*. Damn! A visitor. Spoiling it all. Yet, he came back to his watching post, as mesmerized as a man in a vast portrait gallery who returns again and again to *Portrait of Unknown Woman*, unable to tell why this one unidentified face makes him so happy. The intruder, he found, made no difference to his pleasure.

'Jenny! Isn't that a ring at the door? Who the devil can that be?'

'I bet that will be Mrs Ennis from next door, she promised to give me a hand with these curtains, you don't mind, darling, do you?'

'Mind! I'm glad you have friends, Molly.'

'Hoho! I've lots of friends.'

'Boyfriends, Katey?'

'Go 'long with you, you ruffian, don't you ever think of anything but the one thing?'

'Can you blame me with a lovely creature like you, Peggy, to be there teasin' me all day long, don't stir, I'll let her in.'

In? To what? There might be a husband and a pack of kids, and at once he had to sell his *Portrait of Unknown Woman* for the known model, not being the sort of artist who sees a new face below his window, runs out, drags her in, and without as much as asking her name spends months searching for her inner reality on his canvas.

Every Sunday he kept coming back and back to that appealing, rose-pink window until one afternoon, when he saw her again at her tea, watched her for a while, and then boldly clanged her black gate wide open, boldly strode up her path, leaped up three steps to her door, rang her bell. A soft rain had begun to sink over the town. The day was gone. A far grumble of waves from the shingle. She opened the door. So close, so solid, so near, so real he could barely recognize her. His silence made her lift her head sideways in three slow, interrogatory jerks. She had a slight squint, which he would later consider one of her most enchanting accomplishments – she might have been looking at another man behind his shoulder. He felt the excitement of the hunter at her vulnerable nearness. He suddenly smelled her. Somebody had told him you can always tell a woman's age by her scent. *Chanel* – and Weil's *Antelope* – over sixty. *Tweed* – always a mature woman.

Madame Rochas – the forties. The thirties smell of after-shave lotions: *Eau Sauvage*, *Moustache*. Wisps of man scent. The twenties – nothing. She had a heavy smell. Tartly she demanded, 'Yes?' Unable to speak, he produced his business card, handed it to her spade fingers. *Herbert Bolger/ Antiques/ 2 Hume Street*, *Dublin*. She laughed at him.

'Mister Bolger, if you are trying to buy something from me I have nothing, if you are trying to sell me something I have even less.'

He was on home ground now, they all said that, he expected it, he relied on them to say it. His whole technique of buying depended on knowing that while it is true that the so-called Big Houses of Ireland have been gleaned by the antique dealers, a lot of Big House people have been reduced to small discouraged houses like this one, bringing with them, like wartime refugees, their few remaining heirlooms. Her accent, however, was not a Big House accent. It was the accent of a workaday countrywoman. She would have nothing to sell.

'Come now, Mrs Eh? Benson? Well, now, Mrs Benson, you say you have nothing to sell but in my experience a lot of people don't know what they have. Only last week I paid a lady thirty pounds for a silver Georgian saltcellar that she never knew she possessed. You might have much more than you realize.'

He must get her alone, inside. He had had no chance to see her figure. Her hair shone like jet beads. Her skin was not a flat white. It was a lovely, rich, ivory skin, as fine as lawn or silk. He felt the rain on the back of his neck and turned up his coat collar. He felt so keyed up by her that if she touched him his string would break. She possessed one thing that she did not know about. Herself.

'Well, it is true that my late husband used to attend auctions. But.'

'Mrs Benson, may I have just one quick glance at your living room?' She wavered. They always did. He smiled reassuringly. 'Just one quick glance. It will take me two minutes.'

She looked up at the rain sifting down about her door lamp.

'Well? Alright then . . . But you are wasting your time. I assure you! And I am very busy.'

Walking behind her in the narrow hallway, he took her in from calves to head. She was two women: heavy above, lighter below. He liked her long strong legs, the wide shoulders, the action of her lean haunches, and the way her head rose above her broad shoulders. Inside, the room was rain-dim, and hour-dim, until she switched on a central hundred-and-fifty-watt bulb that drowned the soft pink of the standing lamp, showed the furniture in all its nakedness, exposed all the random marks and signs of a room that had been long lived in.

At once he regretted that he had come. He walked to the window and looked out through its small bay up and down the avenue. How appealing it was out there! All those cosy little, dozing little, rosy little bungalows up and down the avenue, these dark trees comforting the gabled house with its one cube of light, and, her window being slightly raised above the avenue, he could see the scattered windows of other cosy little houses coming awake all over the town. An hour earlier he might have been able to see the bruise-blue line of the Irish Sea. I could live in any one of those little houses out there, and he turned to look at her uncertainly – like a painter turning from easel to model, from model to easel, wondering which was the concoction and which was the truth.

'Well?' she asked impatiently.

His eye helicoptered over her cheap furniture. Ten seconds sufficed. He looked at her coldly. If he were outside there now on the pavement, looking in at her rosy lamp lighting...

'There is,' she said defensively, 'a mirror.'

She opened the leaves of large folding doors in the rear wall, led him into the room beyond them, flooded it with light. An electric sewing machine, patterns askew on the wall, a long deal table strewn with scattered bits of material, a tailoress's wire dummy and, incongruously, over the empty fireplace, a lavish baroque mirror, deeply bevelled, sunk in a swarm of golden fruit and flowers, carved wood and moulded gesso. Spanish? Italian? It could be English. It might, rarest of all, be Irish. Not a year less than two hundred years old. He flung his arms up to it.

'And you said you had nothing! She's a beauty! I'd be delighted to buy this pretty bauble from you.'

She sighed at herself in her mirror.

'I did not say I have nothing, Mr Bolger. I said I have nothing for you. My mirror is not for sale. It was my husband's engagement present to me. He bought it at an auction in an old house in Wexford. It was the only object of any interest in the house, so there were no dealers present. He got it for five pounds.'

He darted to it through an envious groan. He talked at her through it.

'Structurally? Fine. A leaf missing here. A rose gone there. Some scoundrel has dotted it here and there with commercial gold paint. And somebody has done worse. Somebody's been cleaning it. Look here and here and here at the white gesso coming through the gold leaf. It could cost a hundred pounds of gold leaf to do it all over again. Have you,' he said sharply to her in the mirror, 'been cleaning it?'

'I confess I tried. But I stopped when I saw that chalky stuff coming through. I did, honestly.'

He considered her avidly in the frame. So appealing in her contrition, a fallen Eve. He turned to her behind him. How strongly built and bold she was! Bold as brass. Soft as silk. No question – *two* women!

'Mrs Benson, have you any idea what this mirror is worth?'

She hooted at him derisively.

'Three times what you would offer as a buyer, and three times that again for what you would ask as a seller.'

He concealed his delight in her toughness. He made a sad face. He sighed heavily.

'Lady! Nobody trusts poor old B.B. But you don't know how the game goes. I look at that mirror and I say to myself, "How long will I wait to get how much for it?" I say, "Price, one hundred pounds," and I sell it inside a month. I say, "Price, two hundred pounds," and I have to wait six months. Think of my overheads for six months! If I were living in London and I said, "Price, three hundred pounds," I'd sell it inside a week. If I lived in New York, I could say, "Price fifteen hundred dollars," and I'd sell it in a day. If I lived on a coral island it wouldn't be worth two coconuts. That mirror has no absolute value. To you it's priceless because it has memories. I respect you for that, Mrs Benson. What's life without memories? I'll give you ninety pounds for it.'

They were side by side, in her mirror, in her room, in her life. He could see her still smiling at him. Pretending she was sorry she had cleaned it! Putting it on! They do, yeh know, they do! And they change, oho, they change. Catch her being sorry for anything. Smiling now like a girl caught in fragrant delight. Listen to this:—

'It is not for sale, Mr Bolger. My memories are not on the market. That is not a mirror. It is a picture. The day my husband bought it we stood side by side and he said,' she laughed at him in the mirror, '"We're not a bad looking pair."'

He stepped sideward out of her memories, keeping her framed.

'I'll give you a hundred quid for it. I couldn't possibly sell it for more than a hundred and fifty pounds. There aren't that many people in

Dublin who know the value of a mirror like yours. The most I can make is twenty-five percent. You are a dressmaker. Don't you count on making twenty-five percent? Where are you from?' he asked, pointing eagerly.

'I'm a Ryan from Tipperary,' she laughed, taken by his eagerness, laughing the louder when he cried (untruthfully) that he was a Tipp man himself.

'Then you are no true Tipperary woman if you don't make fifty percent! What about it? Tipp to Tipp. A hundred guineas? A hundred and ten guineas? Going, going . . .?'

'It is not for sale,' she said with a clipped finality. 'It is my husband's mirror. It is our mirror. It will always be our mirror,' and he surrendered to the memory she was staring at.

As she closed the door on his departure there passed between them the smiles of equal strangers who, in other circumstances, might have been equal friends. He walked away, exhilarated, completely satisfied. He had got rid of his fancy. She had not come up to his dream. He was cured.

The next Sunday afternoon, bowler hat on nose, collar up, scarfed, standing askew behind her pillar, the red lamp glowing, will now always glow above the dark head of Mrs Benson, widow, hard-pressed dressmaker, born in Tipperary, sipping Indian tea, munching an English biscuit, reading a paperback, her civil respite from tedious labour. How appealing! She has beaten a cosy path of habit that he lusts to have, own, at least to share with her. 'I can make antiques but I can't make age, I could buy the most worn bloody old house in Ireland and I wouldn't own one minute of its walls, trees, stones, moss, slates, gravel, rust, lichen, ageing.' And he remembered the old lady in a stinking dry-rotted house in Westmeath, filled with eighteenth-century stuff honeycombed by wood-worm, who would not sell him as much as a snuffbox because, 'Mister Bulgey, there is not a pebble in my garden but has its story.'

Bray. For sale. Small modern bungalow. Fully furnished. View of sea. Complete with ample widow attached to the front doorknob. Finger-prints alive all over the house.

He pushed the gate open, smartly leaped her steps, rang.

A fleck of biscuit clung childishly to her lower lip. Her grey eye, delicately defective, floated beyond his face as disconcertingly as a thought across surprise.

'Not you again!' she laughed lavishly.

'Mrs Bee! I have a proposition.'

'Mister Bee! I do not intend to sell you my mirror. Ever!'

'Missus Bee! I do not want your mirror. What I have to propose will take exactly two tics. I swear it. And then I fly.'

She sighed, looked far, far away. Out over the night sea?

'For two minutes? Very well. But not *one* second more!'

She showed him into the living room and, weakening – in the name of hospitality? of Tipperary? of old country ways? – she goes into the recesses of her home for an extra cup. In sole possession of her interior he looks out under the vast umbrella of the dusk, out over the punctured encampment of roofs. Could I live here? Why does this bloody room never look the same inside and outside? Live *here*? Always? It would be remote. Morning train to Dublin. In the evenings, this, when I had tarted it up a bit, made it as cosy, lit inside, as it looks from the outside.

'My husband,' she said, pouring, 'always liked China tea. You don't mind?'

'I am very partial to it. It appeals to my aesthetic sense. Jasmine flowers. May I ask what your husband used to do?'

'Ken was an assessor for an English insurance company. He was English.'

He approved mightily, fingers widespread, chin enthusiastically nodding.

'A fine profession! A very fine profession!'

'So fine,' she said wryly, 'that he took out a policy on his own life for a bare one thousand pounds. And I am now a dressmaker.'

'Family?' he asked tenderly.

She smiled softly.

'My daughter, Leslie. She is at a boarding school. I am hoping to send her to the university. What is your proposition?'

Her profile, soft as a seaflower, changed to the obtuseness of a deathmask, until, frontally, its lower lip caught the light, the eyes became alert, the face hard with character.

'It is a simple little proposition. Your mirror, we agree, is a splendid object, but for your business quite unsuitable. Any woman looking into it can only half see herself. What you need is a great, wide, large, gilt-framed mirror, pinned flat against the wall, clear as crystal, a real professional job, where a lady can see herself from top to toe twirling and turning like a ballet dancer.' He smiled mockingly. 'Give your clients status.' He proceeded earnestly. 'Worth another two hundred pounds a year to you. You would be employing two assistants in no time. I happen to have a mirror just like that in my showrooms. I've had it for six years and nobody has wanted it.' He paused, smiling from jawbone to jawbone. 'I would like you to take it. As a gift.'

Shrewdly he watched her turning her teacup between her palms as if she were warming a brandy glass, while she observed him sideward just as shrewdly out of an eye as fully circled as a bird's. At last she smiled, laid down her cup, leaned back and said, 'Go on, Mr B.'

'How do you mean, "go on"?'

'You have only told me half your proposition. You want something in return?'

He laughed with his throat, teeth, tongue and gullet, enjoying her hugely.

'Not really!'

She laughed, enjoying him as hugely.

'Meaning?'

He rose, walked to the window, now one of those black mirrors that painters use to eliminate colour in order to reveal design. The night had blotted out everything except an impression of two or three pale hydrangea leaves wavering outside in the December wind and, inside, himself and a lampshade. He began to feel that he had already taken up residence here. He turned to the woman looking at him coldly under eyebrows as heavy as two dark moustaches and flew into a rage at her resistance.

'Dammit! Can't you give me credit for wanting to give you something for your own sake?' As quickly he calmed. The proud animal was staring timidly, humbly, contritely. Or was she having him on again? She could hide anything behind that lovely squint of hers. He demanded abruptly, 'Do you ever go into Dublin?'

She glanced at the doors of her workroom.

'I must go there tomorrow morning to buy some linings. Why?'

'Tomorrow I have to deliver a small Regency chest to a lady in Greystones. On my way back I could call for you here at ten o'clock, drive you into Dublin and show you that big mirror of mine, and you can take it or leave it, as you like.' He got up to go. 'Okay?'

She gave an unwilling assent but as she opened the front door to let him out added, 'Though I am not at all sure that I entirely understand you, Mister B.'

'Aren't you?' he asked with an impish animation.

'No, I am not!' she said crossly. 'Not at all sure.'

Halfway across her ten feet of garden he turned and laughed derisively, 'Have a look at the surface of your mirror,' and twanged out and was lost in a dusk of sea-fog.

She returned slowly to her workroom. She approached her mirror and peered over its surface. Flawless. Not a breath of dust. With one spittled finger she removed a flyspeck. What did the silly little man mean? Without being aware of what she was doing she looked at herself, patted her hair in place, smoothed her fringe, arranged the shoulder peaks of her blouse, then, her dark eyebrows floating, her bister eyelids sinking, her back straight, her bosom lifted, she drawled, 'I really am afraid, Mister B., that I still do *not* at all understand you,' and chuckled at the effect. Her jaw shot out, she glared furiously at her double, she silently mouthed the word, 'Fathead!' seized her scissors and returned energetically to work. She would fix him! Tomorrow morning she would let the ten o'clock train take her to Dublin.

He took her to Dublin, and to lunch, and to her amused satisfaction admitted that there was a second part to his proposition. He sometimes persuaded the owners of better class country hotels to allow him to leave one or two of his antiques, with his card attached, on view in their public rooms. It could be a Dutch landscape, or a tidy piece of Sheraton or Hepplewhite. Free advertisement for him, free decor for them. Would she like to cooperate? 'Where on earth,' some well-off client would say, 'did you get that lovely thing?' – and she would say, 'Bolger's Antiques.' She was so pleased to have foreseen that there would be some such *quid pro quo* that she swallowed the bait. So, the next Sunday, though he did not bring his big mirror, he brought a charming Boucher fire screen. The following Sunday his van was out of order, but he did bring a handsome pair of twisted Georgian candlesticks for her mantelpiece. Every Sunday, except during the Christmas holidays when he did not care to face her daughter, Leslie, he brought something: a carved, bronze chariot, Empire style, containing a clock, a neat Nelson sideboard, a copper warming pan, so that they always had something to discuss over their afternoon tea. It amused and pleased her until the day came when he produced a pair of (he swore) genuine Tudor curtains for her front window and she could no longer conceal from herself that she was being formally courted, and that her living room had meanwhile been transformed from what it had been four months ago.

The climax came at Easter when, for Leslie's sake, she weakly allowed him to present her with two plane tickets for a Paris holiday. In addition he promised to visit her bungalow every day and sleep there every night while she was away. On her return she found that he had left a comic 'Welcome Home' card on her hall table; that her living room was sweet with mimosa; that he had covered her old-fashioned wallpaper with (he explained) a hand-painted French paper in (she would observe) a pattern of Notre Dame, the Eiffel Tower, the Arc de Triomphe and the Opéra; replaced her old threadworn carpet – she and Ken had bought it nearly twenty years ago in Clery's in O'Connell Street – by (he alleged) a *quali* Persian carpet three hundred years old; and exchanged her central plastic electric shade for (he mentioned) a Waterford cluster. In fact he had got rid of every scrap of her life except her mirror, which now hung over her fireplace, her pink lamp and, she said it to herself, 'Me?'

The next Sunday she let him in, sat opposite him, and was just about to say her rehearsed bit of gallows humour— 'I am sorry to have to tell you, Bertie, that I don't particularly like your life, may I have mine back again please?' – when she saw him looking radiantly at her, realized that by accepting so many disguised gifts she had put herself in a false position, and burst into tears of shame and rage. Bertie, whose many years of servitude with his mother had made all female tears seem as ludicrous as a baby's squealing face, laughed boomingly at her, enchanted to see this powerful woman so completely in his power. The experience filled him with such joy that he sank on his knees beside her, flung his arms about her, and said, 'Maisie, will you marry me?' She drew back her fist, gave him such a clout on the jaw that he fell on his poll, shouted at him, 'Get up, you worm! And get out!'

With hauteur he went.

She held out against him for six months, though still permitting him to visit her every Sunday for afternoon tea and a chat. In November, without warning, her resistance gave out. Worn down by his persistence? Or her own calculations? By her ambitions for Leslie? Perhaps by weariness of the flesh at the prospect of a life of dressmaking? Certainly by none of the hopes, dreams, illusions, fears and needs that might have pressed other hardpressed women into holy wedlock; above all not by the desires of the flesh – these she had never felt for Bertie Bolger.

He made it a lavish wedding, which she did not dislike; he also made it showy, which she did not like; but she was soon to find that he did everything to excess, including eating, always defending himself by the plea that if a man or a woman is any good you cannot have too much of them; a principle that ought to have led him to marry the Fat Lady in the circus, or led her to marry Paddy O'Brien, the Irish giant, who was nine feet high and whose skeleton she had once seen preserved in the College of Surgeons. 'Is he all swank and bluff?' she wondered. Even on their honeymoon she discovered that after a day of boasting about his prowess compared with all his competitors, it was ten to one that he would either be crying on her shoulder long past midnight, or yelping like a puppy in one of his nightmares; both of which performances (her word) she bore with patience until the morning he dared to give her dogs' abuse for being the sole cause of all of them, whereat she ripped him with a kick like a cassowary. She read an article about exhibitionism. That was him! She read a thriller about a manic-depressive strangler, and peeping cautiously across the pillows, felt that she should never go to bed with him without a pair of antique duelling pistols under her side of the mattress.

Within six months they both knew that their error was so plenary, so total, so irreducible that it should have been beyond speech – as it was not. He said that he felt a prisoner in this bloody bungalow of hers. He said that whenever he stood inside her window (and his Tudor curtains) and looked out at those hundreds of lovely, loving, kindly, warm, glowing, little peaked bungalows outside there he knew that he had picked the only goddam one of the whole frigging lot that was totally uninhabitable. She said she had been as free as the wind until he took forcible possession of her property and filled it with his fake junk. He said she was a bully. She told him he was a bluffer. He said, 'I thought you had brains but I've eaten better.' She said, 'You're a dreamer!' He said, 'You're a dressmaker!' She said, 'You don't know from one minute to the next whether you want to be Jesus Christ or Napoleon.' He shouted, 'Outside the four walls of this bungalow you're an ignoramus, apart from what little I've been able to teach you.' She said, 'Outside your business, Bertie Bolger, and that doesn't bear close examination, if I gave you three minutes to tell me all *you* know, it would be six minutes too much.' All of it as meaningless and unjust as every marital quarrel since Adam and Eve began to bawl with one voice, 'But *you* said . . . ,' and 'I know what *I* said, but you said . . .' 'Yes but then *you* said . . .'

His older, her more recent club acquaintances chewed a clearer cud. At the common table I once heard three or four of them mentioning him over lunch. They said next to nothing but their tone was enough. Another of those waxwork effigies that manage somehow or other to get past the little black ball into the most select clubs. Mimes, mimics, fair imitations, plausible impersonations of The Real Thing, a procession of puppets, a march of masks, a covey of cozens, a levee of liars: chaps for whom conversation means anecdotes, altruism alms, discipline suppression, justice calling in the police, pleasure puking in the washroom, pride swank, love lust, honesty guilt, religion fear, patriotism greed and success cash. But if you asked any of those old members to say any of this about Bertie? They would look you straight in the top button of your weskit and say, without humour, 'A white man.' And Maisie? 'A very nice little wife.'

Dear Jesus! Is life in all clubs reduced like this to white men and nice little wives? Sometimes to worse. As well as clubbites there are clubesses to whom the truth is told between the sheets and by whom enlarged, exaggerated, falsified, and spread wide. After all, the men had merely kicked the testicles of his reputation; the wives castrated him. They took Maisie's part. A fine, natural countrywoman, they said; honest as the daylight; warm as toast if you did not cross her, and then she could handle her tongue like the tail end of a whip; a woman who carried her liquor like a man; as agile at Contract as a trout; could have mothered ten and would never give one to Bertie, whom she had let marry her only because she saw he was the sort of weakling who always wants somebody to lean on, and did not find out until too late that he was miles away from what every woman really wants, which is somebody she can rely on. Their judgment made him seem much less than he was, her much more. The result of it was that he was soon feeling the cold wind of Dublin's whispering gallery on his neck and had to do something to assert himself unless he was to fall dead under the sting of its mockery.

Accordingly, one Sunday afternoon in November, a year after his marriage, he packed two suitcases, called a cab, and drove off down the lighted avenue to resume his not unimportant role in life as the Mister

Bee of some lonely guest house. It had not, at the end, been her wish. If she had not grown a little fond of him she had begun to feel a little sorry for him. Besides, next autumn Leslie would be down on her fingers and up on her toes at the starting line for the university, waiting eagerly for the revolver's flat 'Go!'

'This is silly, Bertie!' she had shrugged as they heard and saw the taxi pulling up outside their window. 'Husbands and wives always quarrel.' He picked up his two suitcases and looked around the room at his lost illusions, a Prospero leaving for the mainland. 'It's nothing unusual,' she had said, to comfort him. 'It happens in every house,' she had pleaded, 'but they carry on.'

'You bitch!' he had snarled, making for the door. 'You broke my heart. I thought you were perfect.'

She need not have winced, knowing well that they had both married for reasons the heart knows nothing of. Nevertheless she had gone gloomily into her dining room, which must again become her workroom. The sixty pounds that he had agreed to pay her henceforth every month, though much more than she had had before they met, would not support two people. Looking about it she noted, with annoyance, that she had never got that big mirror out of him.

So then, a dusky Sunday afternoon in Bray, at a quarter to five o'clock, lighting up time five fifteen, All Soul's Eve, dedicated to the souls of the dead suffering in the fires of Purgatory, Bertie Bolger, half Benedict half bachelor, aged forty-four, tubby, ruddy, greying, walking sedately along the seafront, sees ahead of him the Imperial Hotel and stops dead, remembering.

'I wonder!' he wonders, and leaning over the promenade's railings, sky-blue with orange knobs, rusting to death since the nineteenth century, looks down at the damp pebbles of the beach. 'How is she doing these days?' and turns smartly inland towards the town.

At this ambiguous hour few houses in Bray show lighted windows. The season is over, the Sunday silent, landladies once more reckoning their takings, snoozing, thinking of minute repairs, or praying, in *Liljoe's, Fatima, The Billows, Swan Lake, Sea View*. Peering ahead of him Mr B. sees, away down the avenue, a calm glow from a window and feels thereat the first, delicate, subcutaneous tingle that he has so often felt in the presence of some desirable object whose value the owner does not know. Nor does he know why those rare lighted windows are so troubling, suggestive, inviting, rejecting, familiar, foreign, like any childhood's nonesuch, griffin, mermaid, unicorn, hippogriff, dragon, centaur, crested castle in the mountains where there grows the golden rose of the world's end. Not knowing, he ignores that first far-off glow, turns from it as from a temptation to sin, turns right, turns left, walks faster and faster as from pursuing danger, until his head begins to swim and his heart to drumroll at the sight, along the perspective of another avenue, of a lighted roseate window that he knows he knows.

As he comes near to *Lorelei* he looks carefully around him to be sure that he is not observed by some filthy Paul Pry who might remember him from that year of his so-called marriage. He slows his pace. He slowly stalks the pillar of his wife's house. He peeps inside and straightway has to lean against the pillar to steady himself, feeling his old dream begin to swell and swell, his old disturbance mount, fear and joy invade his blood at the sight of her seated before the fire, placid, self-absorbed, her teacup in her hand, her eyes on her book, the pink glow on her threequarter face, more than ever appealing, inciting, sealed, bonded, unattainable.

I *have* neglected her. I owe her restitution. He enters the garden, twangs the gate, mounts the steps, rings the bell, turns to see the dark enfold the town. A scatter of lights. The breathing of the waves. The glow of a bus zooming up Kilruddery Hill a mile away, lighting the low clouds, bare trees, passing the Earl of Meath's broken walls, his gateway's squat Egyptian pillars bearing, in raised lettering, the outdated motto of his line, LABOR VITA MEA.

'Bertie!'

'Maisie!'

'I'm so glad you dropped in, Bertie. Come in. Take your coat off and draw up to the fire. It's going to be a shivering night. Let me fix you a drink. The usual, I suppose?' Her back to him: – 'As a matter of fact I've been expecting you every Sunday. I've been waiting and waiting for you.' She laughed. 'Or do you expect me to say I've been longing and longing for you since you abandoned me last November?'

He looks out, shading his eyes, sees the window opposite light up. They, too, have a pink lampshade.

'That,' he said, 'is the Naughtons' bungalow, isn't it? It looks very cosy. Very nice. I sometimes used to think I'd be happy living there, looking across at you.'

She glances at it, handing him the whiskey, sits facing him, pokes the fire ablaze.

'We're all alike, in our bungalows. Why did you come today, Bertie?'

'It's our marriage anniversary. I didn't know what gift to send you, so I thought I would just ask. Hello! Your mirror is gone!'

'I had to put it back in my workroom. If you want to give me a present give me your mirror.'

'Jesus, I never did give it to you, did I? Next Sunday, I swear! Cross my heart! I'll bring it out without fail. If the van is free.'

In this easy way they chatted of this and that, and he went on his way, and he came back the next Sunday, though not with his mirror, and he came every Sunday month after month for tea or a drink. On his fourth visit she produced, for his greater comfort, an old pair of felt slippers he had left behind him, and on the fifth Sunday a pipe of his that she had discovered at the bottom of a drawer. He did not come around Christmas, feeling that Leslie would prefer to be alone with her mother. Instead he spent it at the Imperial Hotel. In a blue paper hat? She refused to let him send them both to Paris for Easter but she did let him send Leslie. For her own Easter present she asked, 'Could I possibly have that mirror, Bertie?' – and he promised it, and did not keep his promise, saying that someday she would be sure to give up dressmaking and not need it, and anyway he was somehow getting attached to the old thing, it would leave a big pale blank on his wall if he gave it away, and after all she had a mirror of her own, but he promised, nevertheless, that he would sometime give it to her.

The music of the steam carousel played on the front, the town became gay, English tourists strolled up and down the lapis lazuli and orange promenade, voices carried, and now and again he went for a swim before calling on her, until imperceptibly it was autumn again, with the rainy light fading at half past four and her rosy window appealing to him to come inside, and in her mirror he would tidy his windblown hair and his tie, and look in puzzlement around the room, and speculatively back at her behind him pouring his drink, just as if he were her husband and this was really his home, so that it was a full year again, and November, and All Souls' Eve before she saw him drive up outside her gate, accompanied by his man Scofield, in his pale blue-and-pink van, marked along its side in Gothic silver lettering, BOLGER'S ANTIQUES, and, protruding from it his big mirror, wrapped in felt and burlap. She greeted it from her steps with a mock cheer that died when Scofield's eye flitted from the mirror to her door, and from door back to mirror, and Bertie's did the same, and hers did the same, and they all three knew at once that his mirror was too big for her. Still, they tried, until the three of them were standing in a row in her garden looking at themselves in it where it leaned against the tall privet hedge lining the avenue, a cold wind cooling the sweat on their foreheads.

'I suppose,' Bertie said, 'we could cut the bloody thing up! Or down!' – and remembering one of those many elegant, useless, disconnected things he had learned at school from the Benedictines, he quoted from the Psalms the words of Christ about the soldiers on Calvary dicing for his garments: – '*Diviserunt sibi vestimenta mea et super vestem meam miserunt sortem.*'

'Go on!' he interpreted. 'Cut me frigging shirt in bits and play cards for me jacket and me pants,' which was the sign for her to lead him gently indoors and make three boiling hot toddies for their shivering bones.

He was silent as he drank his first dram, and his second. After the third dram he said, okay, this was it, he would never come here again, moving with her and Scofield to the window to look at his bright defeat leaning against the rampant hedge of privet.

And, behold, it was glowing with the rosiness of the window and the three of them out there looking in at themselves from under the falling darkness and the wilderness of stars over town and sea, a vision so unlikely, disturbing, appealing, inviting, promising, demanding, enlisting that he swept her to him and held her so long, so close, so tight that the next he heard was the pink-and-blue van driving away down the avenue. He turned for reassurance to the gleaming testimony in the garden and cried, 'We'll leave it there always! It makes everything more real!' At which, as well she might, she burst into laughter at the sight of him staring out at himself staring in.

'You bloody loon!' she began, and stopped.

She had heard country tales about people who have seen on the still surface of a well, not their own hungry eyes but the staring eyes of love.

'If that *is* what you really want,' she said quietly, and kissed him, and looked out at them both looking in.

Murder at Cobbler's Hulk

It takes about an hour of driving southward out of Dublin to arrive at the small seaside village of Greystones. (For two months in the summer, it calls itself a resort.) Every day, four commuter trains from the city stop here and turn back, as if dismayed by the sight of the desolate beach of shingle that stretches beyond it for twelve unbroken miles. A single line, rarely used, continues the railway beside this beach, on and on, so close to the sea that in bad winters the waves pound in across the track, sometimes blocking it for days on end with heaps of gravel, uprooted sleepers, warped rails. When this happens, the repair gangs have a dreary time of it. No shelter from the wind and spray. Nothing to be seen inland but reedy fields, an occasional farmhouse or abandoned manor, a few leafless trees decaying in the arid soil or fallen sideways. And, always, endless fleets of clouds sailing away towards the zinc-blue horizon.

Once there were three more tiny railway stations along these twelve miles of beach, each approached by a long lane leading from the inland carriage road to the sea. The best preserved of what remains of them is called Cobbler's Hulk. From a distance, one might still mistake it for a real station. Close up, one finds only a boarded waiting room whose tin roof lifts and squeaks in the wind, a lofty signal cabin with every window broken and a still loftier telephone pole whose ten crossbars must once have carried at least twenty lines and now bear only one humming wire. There is a rotting, backless bench. You could scythe the grass on the platform. The liveliest thing here is an advertisement on enamelled sheet metal, high up on the brick wall of the signal cabin. It showed the single white word STEPHEN'S splashed across a crazy blob of black ink. Look where one will, there is not a farmhouse nor cottage within sight.

It was down here that I first met Mr Bodkin one Sunday afternoon last July. He was sitting straight up on the bench, bowler-hatted, clad, in spite of the warmth of the day, in a well-brushed blue chesterfield with concealed buttons and a neatly tailored velvet half collar that was the height of fashion in the Twenties. His grey spats were as tight as gloves across his insteps He was a smallish man. His stiff shirt collar was as high as the Duke of Wellington's, his bow tie was polka-dotted, his white moustaches were brushed up like a Junker's. He could have been seventy-three. His cheeks were as pink as a baby's bottom. His palms lay crossed on the handle of a rolled umbrella, he had a neatly folded newspaper under his arm, his patent-leather shoe tips gleamed like his pince-nez. Normally, I would have given him a polite 'Good day to you' and passed on, wondering. Coming on him suddenly around the corner of the waiting room, his head lowered towards his left shoulder as if he were listening for an approaching train, I was so taken by surprise that I said, 'Are you waiting for a train?'

'Good gracious!' he said, in equal surprise. 'A train has not stopped here since the Bronze Age. Didn't you know?'

I gazed at his shining toes, remembering that when I had halted my Morris Minor beside the level-crossing gates at the end of the lane, there had been no other car parked there. Had he walked here? That brambled lane was a mile long. He peeked at the billycan in my hand, guessed that I was proposing to brew myself a cup of tea after my solitary swim, chirruped in imitation of a parrot, 'Any water?' rose and, in the comic-basso voice of a weary museum guide, said, 'This way, please.' I let him lead me along the platform, past the old brass faucet that I had used on my few previous visits to Cobbler's Hulk, towards a black-tarred railway carriage hidden below the marshy side of the track. He pointed the ferrule of his umbrella.

'My chalet,' he said smugly. 'My *wagon-lit*.'

We descended from the platform by three wooden steps, rounded a microscopic gravel path, and he unlocked the door of his carriage. It was still faintly marked FIRST CLASS, but it also bore a crusted brass plate whose shining rilievo announced THE VILLA ROSE. He bowed me inward, invited me to take a pew (his word for an upholstered carriage seat), filled my billycan from a white enamelled bucket ('Pure spring water!') and, to expedite matters further, insisted on boiling it for me on his Primus stove. As we waited, he sat opposite me. We both looked out the window at the marshes. I heard a Guard's whistle and felt our carriage jolt away to nowhere. We introduced ourselves.

'I trust you find my beach a pleasant spot for a picnic?' he said, as if he owned the entire Irish Sea.

I told him that I had come here about six times over the past thirty years.

'I came here three years ago. When I retired.'

I asked about his three winters. His fingers dismissed them. 'Our glorious summers amply recompense.' At which exact moment I heard sea birds dancing on the roof and Mr Bodkin became distressed. His summer and his beach were misbehaving. He declared that the shower would soon pass. I must have my cup of afternoon tea with him, right there. 'In first-class comfort.' I demurred; he insisted. I protested gratefully; he persisted tetchily. I let him have his way, and that was how I formed Mr Bodkin's acquaintance.

It never became any more. I saw him only once again, for five minutes, six weeks later. But, helped by a hint or two from elsewhere – the man who kept the roadside shop at the end of the lane, a gossipy barmaid in the nearest hamlet – it was enough to let me infer, guess at, induce his life. Its fascination was that he had never had any. By comparison, his beach and its slight sand dunes beside the railway track were crowded with incident, as he presently demonstrated by produc-ing the big album of pressed flowers that he had been collecting over the past three years. His little ear finger stirred them gently on their white pages: milfoil, yarrow, thrift, sea daisies, clover, shepherd's-needle, shepherd's-purse, yellow bedstraw, stone bedstraw, great bedstraw, Our-Lady's-bedstraw, minute sand roses, different types of lousewort. In the pauses between their naming, the leaves were turned as quietly as the wavelets on the beach.

One December day in 1912, when he was fifteen, Mr Bodkin told me, he had entered his lifelong profession by becoming the messenger boy in Tyrrell's Travel Agency, located at 15 Grafton Street, Dublin. He went into Dublin every morning on the Howth tram, halting it outside the small pink house called The Villa Rose, where he lived with his mother, his father, his two young sisters and his two aunts...

The Villa Rose! He made a deprecatory gesture – it had been his mother's idea. The plays and novels of Mr A. E. Mason were popular around 1910. He wrinkled his rosy nose. It was not even what you could call a real house. Just two fishermen's cottages joined front to back, with a dip, or valley, between their adjoining roofs. But what a situation! On fine days, he could see, across the high tide of the bay, gulls blowing about like paper, clouds reflected in the still water, an occasional funnel moving slowly in or out of the city behind the long line of the North Wall; and away beyond it, all the silent drums of the Wicklow Mountains. Except on damp days, of course. The windows of The Villa Rose were always sea-dimmed on damp days. His mother suffered from chronic arthritis. His father's chest was always wheezing. His sisters' noses were always running. His aunts spent half their days in bed.

'I have never in my life had a day's illness! Apart from chilblains. I expect to live to be ninety.'

The great thing, it appeared, about Tyrrell's Travel Agency was that you always knew where you were. The Tyrrell system was of the simplest: Everybody was addressed according to his rank. (Mr Bodkin did not seem to realize that this system was, in his boyhood as in mine, universal in every corner of the British Empire.) Whenever old Mr Bob wanted him, he shouted 'Tommy!' at the top of his voice. After shouting at him like that for about five years, Mr Bob suddenly put him behind the counter, addressed him politely as 'Bodkin' and shouted at him no longer. Five years passed and, again without any preliminaries, Mr Bob presented him with a desk of his own in a corner of the office and addressed him as 'Mr Bodkin.' At which everybody in the place smiled, nodded or winked his congratulations. He had arrived at the top of his genealogical tree. He might fall from it. He would never float beyond it. Very satisfactory. One has to have one's station in life. Yes?

The summer shower stopped, but not Mr Bodkin. (In the past three years, I wondered if he had had a single visitor to talk to.) There were, I must understand, certain seeming contradictions in the system. An eager ear and a bit of experience soon solved them all. For example, there was the case of old Clancy, the ex-Enniskillener Dragoon, who opened the office in the morning and polished the Egyptian floor tiles. Anybody who wanted him always shouted, 'Jimmy!' Clear as daylight. But whenever old Lady Kilfeather came sweeping into the agency from her grey Jaguar, ruffling scent, chiffon, feather boas and Protestant tracts, she clancied the whole bang lot of them.

'Morning, Tyrrell! Hello, Bodkin! I hope Murphy has that nice little jaunt to Cannes all sewn up for myself and Kilfeather? Clancy, kindly read this leaflet on Mariolatry and do, for heaven's sake, stop saying "Mother of God!" every time you see me!'

The aristocratic privilege. The stars to their stations; the planets in their stately cycles about the sun; until the lower orders bitch it all up.

Meaning old Mrs Clancy, swaying into the office like an inebriated camel, to beg a few bob from Clancy for what she genteelly called her shopping. Never once had that woman, as she might reasonably have done, asked for 'Jim.' Never for 'Mr Clancy.' Never even for 'my husband.' Always for 'Clancy.' Mr Bodkin confessed that he sometimes felt so infuriated with her that he would have to slip around the corner to the Three Feathers, to calm his gut with a Guinness and be reassured by the barman's 'The usual, Mr B.?' Not that he had ever been entirely happy about that same B. He always countered it with a stiff, 'Thank you, Mr Buckley.'

It was the only pub he ever visited. And never for more than one glass of plain. Occasionally, he used to go to the theatre. But only for Shakespeare. Or Gilbert and Sullivan. Only for the classics. Opera? Never! For a time, he had been amused by Shaw. But he soon discarded him as a typical Dublin jackeen mocking his betters. Every Sunday, he went to church to pray for the king. He was nineteen when the Rebellion broke out. He refused to believe in it. Or that the dreadful shootings and killings of the subsequent Troubles could possibly produce any change. And did they? Not a damned thing! Oh, some client might give his name in the so-called Irish language. Mr Bodkin simply wrote down, 'Mr Irish.' Queenstown became Cobh. What nonsense! Kingstown became Dun Laoghaire. Pfoo! Pillar boxes were painted green. The police were called Guards. The army's khaki was dyed green. All the whole damned thing boiled down to was that a bit of the House of Commons was moved from London to Dublin.

Until the Second World War broke out. Travel stopped dead. The young fellows in the office joined the army. He remembered how old Mr Bob – they ran the office between them – kept wondering for weeks how the Serbians would behave this time. And what on earth had happened to those gallant little Montenegrins? When the Germans invaded Russia, Mr Bob said that the czar would soon put a stop to that nonsense. Mind you, they had to keep on their toes after 1945. He would never forget the first time a client said he wanted to visit Yugoslavia. He took off his glasses, wiped them carefully, and produced a map. And, by heavens, there it was!

There had been other changes. His mother had died when he was forty-three. His two aunts went when he was in his fifties. To his astonishment, both his sisters married. His father was the last to go, at the age of eighty-one. He went on living, alone, in The Villa Rose, daily mistering thousands of eager travellers around Europe by luxury liners, crowded packet boats, Blue Trains, Orient Expresses, Settebellos, Rheingolds, alphabetical-mathematical planes. He had cars waiting for some, arranged hotels for others, confided to a chosen few the best places (according to 'my old friend Lady Kilfeather') to dine, drink and dance, and he never went anywhere himself.

'You mean you *never* wanted to travel?'

'At first, yes. When I could not afford it. Later, I was saving up for my retirement. Besides, in my last ten years there, the whole business began to bore me.'

He paused, frowned and corrected himself. It had not 'begun' to bore. His interest in it had died suddenly. It happened one morning when he was turning back into the office after conducting Lady Kilfeather out to her grey Jaguar. Observing him, young Mr James had beckoned him into his sanctum.

'A word in your ivory ear, Mr Bodkin? I notice that you have been bestowing quite an amount of attention on Lady Kilfeather.'

'Yes, indeed, Mr James! And I may say that she has just told me that she is most pleased with us.'

'As she might well be! Considering that it takes six letters and eight months to get a penny out of the old bitch. That woman, Mr Bodkin, is known all over Dublin as a first-class scrounger, time waster and bloodsucker. I would be obliged if you would in future bear in mind three rather harsh facts of life that my aged parent seems never to have explained to you. Time is money. Your time is my money. And no client's money is worth more to me than any other client's money. Take it to heart, Mr Bodkin. Thank you. That will be all for now.'

Mr Bodkin took it to heart so well that from that morning on, all those eager travellers came to mean no more to him than a trainload of tourists to a railway porter after he has banged the last door and turned away through the steam of the departing engine for a quick smoke before the next bunch arrived.

Still, duty was duty. And he had his plans. He hung on until he was sixty-five and then he resigned. Mr James, with, I could imagine, an immense sense of relief, handed him a bonus of fifty pounds – a quid for every year of his service, but no pension – shook his hand and told him to go off to Cannes and live there in sin for a week with a cabaret dancer. Mr Bodkin said that for years he had been dreaming of doing exactly that with Mrs Clancy, accepted the fifty quid, said a warm goodbye to everybody in the office, sold The Villa Rose and bought the tarred railway carriage at Cobbler's Hulk. He had had his eye on it for the past five years.

The night he arrived at Cobbler's Hulk, it was dry and cold. He was sweating from lugging two suitcases down the dark lane. The rest of his worldly belongings stood waiting for him in a packing case on the grass-grown platform. For an hour, he sat in his carriage by candlelight, in his blue chesterfield, supping blissfully on the wavelets scraping the shingle every twenty seconds and on certain mysterious noises from the wildlife on the marshes. A snipe? A grebe? A masked badger?

He rose at last, made himself another supper of fried salty bacon and two fried eggs, unwrapped his country bread and butter and boiled himself a brew of tea so strong that his spoon could almost have stood up in it. When he had washed his ware and made his bed, he went out on to his platform to find the sky riveted with stars. Far out to sea, the lights of a fishing smack. Beyond them, he thought he detected a faint blink. Not, surely, a lighthouse on the Welsh coast? Then, up the line, he heard the hum of the approaching train. Two such trains, he had foreknown, would roar past Cobbler's Hulk every twenty-four hours. Its headlamps grew larger and brighter and then, with a roar, its carriage windows went flickering past him. He could see only a half a dozen passengers in it. When it died away down the line, he addressed the stars.

'O Spirits, merciful and good! I know that our inheritance is held in store for us by Time. I know there is a sea of Time to rise one day, before which all who wrong us or oppress us will be swept away like leaves. I see it, on the flow! I know that we must trust and hope, and neither doubt ourselves nor doubt the good in one another... O Spirits, merciful and good, I am grateful!'

'That's rather fine. Where did you get that?'

'Dickens. *The Chimes*. I say that prayer every night after supper and a last stroll up the lane.'

'Say it for me again.'

As he repeated those splendid radical words, he looked about as wild as a grasshopper. 'Thinner than Tithonus before he faded into air.'

Had he really felt oppressed? Or wronged? Could it be that, during his three years of solitude, he had been thinking that this world would be a much nicer place if people did not go around shouting at one another or declaring to other people that time is money? Or wondering why

Mother should have had to suffer shame and pain for years, while dreadful old women like Kilfeather went on scrounging, wheedling, bloodsucking, eating and drinking their way around this travelled world of which all he had ever seen was that dubious wink across the night sea? He may have meant that in his youth, he had dreamed of marriage. He may have meant nothing at all.

He leaned forward.

'Are you sure you won't have another cup of tea? Now that I can have afternoon tea any day I like, I can make a ridiculous confession to you. For fifty years, I used to see Mr Bob or Mr James walk across Grafton Street every day at four-thirty precisely to have afternoon tea in Mitchell's Café. And I cannot tell you how bitterly I used to envy them. Wasn't that silly of me?'

'But, surely, one of the girls on the staff could have brewed you all a cup of tea in the office?'

He stared at me.

'But that's not the same thing as afternoon tea in Mitchell's! White tablecloths? Carpets? Silverware? Waitresses in blue and white?'

We looked at each other silently. I looked at my watch and said that I must get going.

He laughed happily.

'The day I came here, do you know what I did with *my* watch? I pawned it for the sum of two pounds. I have never retrieved it. And I never will. I live by the sun and stars.'

'You are never lonely?'

'I am used to living alone.'

'You sleep well?'

'Like a dog. And dream like one. Mostly of the old Villa Rose. And my poor, dear mamma. How could I be lonely? I have my beautiful memories, my happy dreams and my good friends.'

'I envy you profoundly,' I said.

On which pleasant lying coda we parted. For is it possible never to be lonely? Do beautiful memories encourage us to withdraw from the world? Not even youth can live on dreams.

He had, however, one friend.

One Saturday evening in September, on returning from the wayside shop on the carriage road, he was arrested by a freshly painted sign on a gate about two hundred yards from the railway track. It said FRESH

EGGS FOR SALE. He knew that there was not a house nor a human being in sight. Who on earth would want to walk a mile down this tunnelled lane to buy eggs? Behind the wooden gate, there was a grassy track, leading, he now presumed, to some distant cottage invisible from the lane. He entered the field and was surprised to see, behind the high hedge, an open shed sheltering a red van bearing, in large white letters:

FLANNERY'S

HEAVENLY BREAD

After a winding quarter of a mile, he came on a small, sunken freshly whitewashed cottage and knocked. The door was opened by a woman of about thirty-five or forty, midway between plain and good-looking, red-cheeked, buxom, blue-eyed, eagerly welcoming. She spoke with a slight English accent that at once reminded him of his mother's voice. Yes! She had lovely fresh eggs. How many did he want? A dozen? With pleasure! Behind her, a dark, heavily built man, of about the same age, rose from his chair beside the open turf fire of the kitchen and silently offered him a seat while 'Mary' was getting the eggs.

Mr Bodkin expected to stay three minutes. He stayed an hour. They were the Condors: Mary, her brother Colm – the dark, silent man – and their bedridden mother lying in the room off the kitchen, her door always open, so that she could not only converse through it but hear all the comforting little noises and movements of her familiar kitchen. Their father, a herdsman, had died three months before. Mary had come back from service in London to look after her mother, and poor Colm (her adjective) had come home with her to support them both. He had just got a job as a roundsman for a bakery in Wicklow, driving all day around the countryside in the red van.

Mr Bodkin felt so much at ease with Mary Condor that he was soon calling on her every evening after supper, to sit by the old woman's bed, to gossip or to read her the day's news from his *Irish Times* or to give her a quiet game of draughts. That Christmas Day, on Mary's insistence, he joined them for supper. He brought a box of chocolates for Mary and her mother, one hundred cigarettes for Colm and a bottle of grocer's sherry for them all. He recited one of his favourite party pieces from Dickens. Colm so far unbent as to tell him about the bitter

Christmas he had spent in Italy with the Eighth Army near a place called Castel di Sangro. Mary talked with big eyes of the awful traffic of London. The old woman, made tipsy by the sherry, shouted from her room about the wicked sea crossing her husband had made during 'the other war,' in December of 1915, with a herd of cattle for the port of Liverpool.

'All travelled people!' Mr Bodkin laughed, and was delighted when Mary said that, thanks be to God, their travelling days were done.

As he walked away from their farewells, the channel of light from their open door showed that the grass was laced with snow. It clung to the edges of his carriage windows as he lay in bed. It gagged the wavelets. He could imagine it falling and melting into the sea. As he clutched the blue hot water bottle that Mary had given him for a Christmas present, he realized that she was the only woman friend he had made in his whole life. He felt so choked with gratitude that he fell asleep without thanking his spirits, the merciful and the good, for their latest gift.

What follows is four fifths inference and one fifth imagination; both, as the event showed, essentially true.

On the Monday of the last week in July, on returning from the roadside shop with a net bag containing *The Irish Times*, tea, onions and a bar of yellow soap, Mr Bodkin was startled to see a white Jaguar parked beside the level crossing. It was what they would have called in the travel agency a posh car. It bore three plaques, a GB, a CD and a blue-and-white silver RAC. Great Britain. *Corps Diplomatique*. Royal Automobile Club. He walked on to his platform to scan the beach for its owner. He found her seated on his bench, in a miniskirt, knees crossed, wearing a loose suede jacket, smoking a cigarette from a long ivory holder, glaring at the grey sea, tiny, blonde (or was she bleached?), exquisitely made up, still handsome. Her tide on the turn. Say, fifty? He approached her as guardedly as if she were a rabbit. A woven gold bangle hung heavily from the corrugated white glove on her wrist. Or was it her bare wrist? Say, fifty-five? Her cigarette was scented.

'Fog coming up,' he murmured politely when he came abreast of her and gave her his little bobbing bow. 'I do hope you are not waiting for a train.'

She slowly raised her tinted eyelids.

'I was waiting for you, Mr Bodkin,' she smiled. (One of the sharp ones?)

Her teeth were the tiniest and whitest he had ever seen. She could have worn them around her neck. Last month, he saw a field mouse with teeth as tiny as hers, bared in death.

'Won't you sit down? I know all about you from Molly Condor.'

'What a splendid woman she is!' he said and warily sat beside her, placing his net bag on the bench beside her scarlet beach bag. He touched it. 'You have been swimming?'

'I swim,' she laughed, 'like a stone. While I waited for you, I was sun-bathing.' She smiled for him. 'In the nude.'

Hastily, he said, 'Your car is *corps diplomatique!*'

'It is my husband's car. Sir Hilary Dobson. I stole it!' She gurgled what ruder chaps in the agency used to call the Gorgon Gurgle. 'You mustn't take me seriously, Mr Bodkin. I'm Scottish. Hilary says I am fey. He is in the F. O. He's gone off on some hush-hush business to Athens for a fortnight, so I borrowed the Jag. Now, if it had been Turkey! But perhaps you don't like Turkey, either? Or do you? Athens is such a crumby dump, don't you agree?'

'I have never travelled, Lady Dobson.'

'But Molly says you once owned a travel agency!'

'She exaggerates my abilities. I was a humble clerk.'

'Eoh?' Her tone changed, her voice became brisk. 'Look, Bodkin, I wanted to ask you something very important. How well do you know Molly Condor?'

He increased his politeness.

'I have had the great pleasure of knowing Miss Mary Condor since last September.'

'I have known her since she was twenty-two. I trained her. She was in my service for twelve years. But I have never looked at Molly as just a lady's maid. Molly is my best friend in the whole world. She is a great loss to me. Of course, as we grow older, the fewer, and the more precious, our friends become.'

He considered the name, Molly. He felt it was patronizing. He had never lost a friend – never, before Mary, having had one to lose. He said as much.

'Too bad! Well! I want Molly to come back to us. My nerves have not been the same since she left.'

He looked silently out to sea. He was aware that she was slowly

turning her head to look at him. Like a field mouse? He felt a creeping
sensation of fear. Her nerves seemed all right to him. He watched her
eject her cigarette, produce another from a silver case, insert it, light
it smartly with a gold lighter and blow out a narrow jet of smoke.

'And then there is her brother. Condor was our chauffeur for five
years. It would be simply wonderful if they both came back to us! I
know poor old Hilary is as lost without his Condor as I am without my
Molly. It would be a great act of kindness if you could say a word in
our favour in that quarter. Hilary would appreciate it no end. Oh, I
know, of course, about the mother. But that old girl can't need the two
of them, can she? Besides, when I saw her this morning, I had the feeling
she won't last long. Arthritis? *And* bronchitis? *And* this climate? I had
an old aunt just like her in Bexhill-on-Sea. One day, she was in splendid
health. The next day, her tubes were wheezing like bagpipes. For six
months, I watched her, fading like a sunset. In the seventh
month . . .'

As she wheedled on and on, her voice reminded him of a spoon inside
a saucepan. He listened to her coldly, with his eyes, rather than his
ears, as for so many years he used to listen to old ladies who did not
know where exactly they wanted to go nor what they wanted to do,
alert only to their shifting lids, their mousy fingers, their bewildered
shoulders, their jerking lips. Crepe on her neck. French cigarettes.
Sun-bathing nude. Bodkin. Condor. Molly. 'Poor old Hilary.' What did
this old girl really want? Coming all this way for a lady's maid? My
foot!

'And you know, Bodkin, Molly has a great regard for you. She thinks
you are the most marvellous thing she ever met. I can see why.' She
laid her hand on his sleeve. 'You have a kind heart. You will help me,
if you can, won't you?' She jumped up. 'That is all I wanted to say. Now
you must show me your wonderful *wagon-lit*. Molly says it is
absolutely fab.'

'I shall be delighted, Lady Dobson,' he said and, unwillingly, led her
to it.

When she saw the brass plate of THE VILLA ROSE she guffawed and
hastened to admire everything else. Her eyes trotted all over his
possessions like two hunting mice. She gushed over his 'clever little
arrangements.' She lifted potlids, felt the springiness of the bed,
penetrated to his water closet, which she flushed, greatly to his
annoyance because he never used it except when the marshes were very

wet or very cold, and then he had to refill the cistern with a bucket every time he flushed it.

'I find it all most amusing, Bodkin,' she assured him as she powdered her face before his shaving mirror. 'If you were a young man, it would make a wonderful weekend love nest, wouldn't it? I must fly. It's nearly lunchtime. And you want to make whatever it is you propose to make with your soap, tea and onions. Won't you see me to my car? And do say a word for me to Molly! If you ever want to find me, I'm staying in the little old hotel down the road. For a week.' She laughed naughtily. 'Laying siege! Do drop in there any afternoon at six o'clock for an aperitif,' and she showed half her white thigh as she looped into her car, started the engine, meshed the gears, beamed at him with all her teeth, cried, '*A bientôt*, Bodkin,' and shot recklessly up the lane, defoliating the hedges into a wake of leaves like a speedboat.

Watching her cloud of dust, he remembered something. A chap in the office showing him a postcard of *Mona Lisa*. 'Ever seen her before? Not half! And never one of them under fifty-five!' Indeed! *And* indeed! 'I am afraid, Lady Dobson, we must make up our minds. A cool fortnight in Brittany? Or five lovely hot days in Monte Carlo? Of course, you *might* win a pot of money in Monte Carlo . . .' How greedily their alligator eyelids used to blink at that one! He returned slowly to his *wagon-lit*, slammed down the windows to let out the smell of her cigarette, washed the dust of yellow powder from his washbasin, refilled his cistern and sat for an hour on the edge of his bed, pondering. By nightfall, he was so bewildered that he had to call on Mary.

She was alone. The old lady was asleep in her room. They sat on either side of the kitchen table, whispering about the hens, the up train that had been three minutes late, the down train last night that was right on the dot, the fog that morning, both of them at their usual friendly ease until he spoke about his visitor. When he finished, she glanced at the open door of the bedroom.

'I must say, she was always very generous to me. Sir Hilary was very kind. He went hard on me to stay. He said, "You are good for her." She had her moods and tenses. I felt awfully sorry for him. He spoiled her.'

'Well, of course, Mary, those titled people,' Mr Bodkin fished cunningly and was filled with admiration for her when she refused to bite.

All she said was, 'Sir Hilary was a real gentleman.'

'They are married a long time?'

'Fifteen years. She is his second wife. She nursed his first wife. But I *had* to come back, Mr Bodkin!'

'You did quite right. And your brother did the right thing, too. I mean, two women in a remote cottage. Your brother is never lonely?'

She covered her face with her hands and he knew that she was crying into them.

'He is dying of the lonesome.'

From the room, the old woman suddenly hammered the floor with her stick.

'Is he back?' she called out fretfully.

Mary went to the bedroom door and leaned against the jamb. It was like listening to a telephone call.

'It's Mr Bodkin . . . He went up to the shop for cigarettes . . . I suppose he forgot them . . . About an hour ago . . . He may be gone for a stroll. It's such a fine night . . . Och, he must be sick of that old van . . .' She turned her head. 'Was the van in the shed, Mr Bodkin?' He shook his head. 'He took the van . . . For God's sake, Mother, stop worrying and go to sleep. He maybe took the notion to drive over to Ashford for a drink and a chat. It's dull for him here . . . I'll give you a game of draughts.'

Mr Bodkin left her.

A nurse? It was dark in the lane, but above the tunnel of the hedges, there was still a flavour of salvaged daylight. He started to walk towards the road, hoping to meet Condor on his way back. The air was heavy with heliotrope and meadowsweet. A rustle in the ditch beside him. Far away, a horse whinnied. He must be turned forty by now. Behind him, Africa, Italy, London. Before him, nothing but the road and fields of his boyhood. Every night, that solitary cottage. The swell of the night express made him look back until its last lights had flickered past the end of the lane and its humming died down the line.

But I have lived. An old man, now, twice a child.

By the last of the afterlight above the trees of the carriage road, he saw the red nose of the van protruding from the halfmoon entrance to the abandoned manor house. He walked to it, peered into its empty cabin, heard a pigeon throating from a clump of trees behind the chained gates. He walked past it to the shop. It was closed and dark. He guessed at a lighted window at the rear of it, shining out over the stumps of decapitated cabbages. Condor was probably in there, gossiping. He was about to turn back when he saw about one hundred yards farther on, the red taillights of a parked car. Any other night, he might have given it no more than an incurious glance. The darkness, the silence, the turmoil of his thoughts finally drew him warily towards it along the grassy verge. Within fifteen yards of it, he recognized the white Jaguar, saw the rear door open, the inner light fall on the two figures clambering out of it. Standing on the road, they embraced in a seething kiss. When he released her, she got into the driver's seat, the two doors banged and everything was silent and dark again. She started her engine, floodlit the road and drove swiftly away around the curve. Crushed back into the hedge, he heard Condor's footsteps approach, pass and recede. In a few moments, the van's door banged tinnily, its headlamps flowered, whirled into the maw of the lane, waddled drunkenly behind the hedges, down towards the sea.

Before he fell asleep that night, Mr Bodkin heard a thousand wavelets scrape the shingles, as, during his long life, other countless waves had scraped elsewhere unheard – sounds, moments, places, people to whose lives he had never given a thought. *The Irish Times* rarely recorded such storms of passion and, when it did, they broke and died far away, like the fables that Shakespeare concocted for his entertainment in the theatre. But he knew the Condors. This adulterous woman could shatter their lives as surely as he knew, when he opened his eyes to the sea sun shimmering on his ceiling, she had already shattered his.

It was his custom, on such summer mornings, to rise, strip off his pyjamas, pull on a bathing slip and walk across the track in his slippers, his towel around his neck, down to the edge of the sea for what he called a dip: which meant that since he, too, swam like a stone, he would advance into the sea up to his knees, sprinkle his shoulders, and then, burring happily at the cold sting of it, race back to the prickly gravel to towel his shivering bones. He did it this morning with the eyes of a saint wakened from dreams of sin.

On Tuesday night, he snooped virtuously up the lane and along the carriage road. The red van was not in its shed. But neither was it on the road. Lascivious imaginings kept him awake for hours. He longed for the thunderbolt of God.

On Wednesday night, it was, at first, the same story; but on arriving back at the foot of the lane, there were the empty van and the empty Jaguar before him, flank to flank at the level crossing. He retired at once to his bench, peering up and down the beach, listening for the sound of their crunching feet, determined to wait for them all night, if necessary. Somewhere, that woman was lying locked in his arms. The bared thigh. The wrinkled arms. The crepey neck.

Daylight had waned around nine o'clock, but it was still bright enough for him to have seen shadows against the glister of the water, if there had been shadows to see. He saw nothing. He heard nothing but the waves. It must have been nearly two hours later when he heard their cars starting. By the time he had flitted down to the end of the platform, her lights were already rolling up the lane and his were turning in through his gateway. Mr Bodkin was at the gate barely in time to see his outline dark against the bars of the western sky. As he looked at the van, empty in its shed, it occurred to him that this was one way in which he could frighten him – a warning message left on the seat of the van. But it was also a way in which they could communicate with each other. Her message for him. His answer left early in the morning at her hotel.

On Thursday night, the van lay in its shed. But where was Condor? He walked up the grass track to the cottage and laid his ear to the door. He heard Mary's voice, his angry voice, the mother's shouting. He breathed happily and returned to his bed.

On Friday morning, the Jaguar stood outside Mary's wooden gate. Laying siege? That night, the scarlet van again lay idle in its pen. Wearied by so much walking and watching, he fell asleep over his supper. He was awakened around eleven o'clock by the sound of a car. Scrambling to his door, he was in time to see her wheeling lights hit the sky. He went up the lane to the van, looked around, heard nothing, shone his torch into the cabin and saw the blue envelope lying on the seat. He ripped it open and read it by torchlight. 'Oh, My Darling, for God's sake, where are you? Last night and tonight, I waited and waited. What has happened? You promised! I have only one more night. You are coming back with me, aren't you? If I do not see you tomorrow night, I will throw myself into the sea. I adore you. Connie.' Mr Bodkin took the letter down to the sea, tore it into tiny pieces and, with his arms wide, scattered them over the receding waves.

That Saturday afternoon, on returning from the shop with his weekend purchases in his net bag, there was the Jaguar beside the level crossing, mud-spattered and dusty, its white flanks scarred by the whipping brambles. Rounding the corner of the waiting room, he saw her on his bench, smoking, glaring at the sparkling sea. She barely lifted her eyes to him. She looked every year of sixty. He bowed and sat on the bench. She smelled of whiskey.

'What an exquisite afternoon we are having, Lady Dobson. May I rest my poor bones for a moment? That lane of mine gets longer and longer every day. Has everything been well with you?'

'Quite well, Bodkin, thank you.'

'And, if I may ask, I should be interested to know, you have, I trust, made some progress in your quest?'

'I could hardly expect to with that old woman around everybody's neck. I have laid the seeds of the idea. Molly now knows that she will always be welcome in my house.'

'Wait and see? My favourite motto. Never say die. Colours nailed to the mast. No surrender. It means, I hope, that you are not going to leave us soon.'

'I leave tonight.'

'I do hope the hotel has not been uncomfortable.'

'It is entirely comfortable. It is full of spinsters. They give me the creeps.'

He beamed at the sea and waited.

'Bodkin! There is one person I have not yet seen. For Hilary's sake, I ought to have a word with Condor. Have you seen him around?'

Her voice had begun to crumble. Eyes like grease under hot water. Cigarette trembling.

'Let me think,' he pondered. 'On Thursday? Yes. And again last night. We both played draughts with his mother. He seemed his usual cheerful self.'

She ejected her cigarette and ground it into the dust under her foot.

'Bodkin! Will you, for Christ's sake, tell me what do young people do with their lives in Godforsaken places like this? That lane must be pitch dark by four o'clock in the winter!'

He looked at his toes, drew his handkerchief from his breast pocket and flicked away their dust.

'I am afraid, Lady Dobson, I no longer meet any young people. And, after all, Condor is not a young man. I suppose you could call him a middle-aged man. Or would you?'

She hooted hoarsely.

'And what does that leave me? An old hag?'

'Or me? As the Good Book says, "The days of our years are threescore years and ten; and if by reason of strength they be fourscore years, yet is their strength labour and sorrow; for it is soon cut off, and we fly away."'

She spat it at him:

'You make me sick.'

From under her blue eyelids, she looked at the clouds crimped along the knife of the horizon. He remembered Mary's twisted face when she said, 'He is dying of the lonesome.' She turned and faced him. Harp strings under her chin. Hands mottled. The creature was as old as sin.

'Do you happen to know, Bodkin, if Condor has a girl in these parts? It concerns me, of course, only insofar as, if he has, I need not ask him to come back to us. Has he?'

Mr Bodkin searched the sea as if looking for a small boat in which to escape his conscience.

'I believe he has,' he said firmly.

'Believe? Do you know? Or do you not know?'

'I saw them twice in the lane. Kissing. I presume that means that they are in love.'

'Thank you, Bodkin,' she said brightly. 'In that case, Hilary must get another chauffeur and I must get another lady's maid.' She jumped up. He rose politely. 'I hope you all have a very pleasant winter.' She stared at him hatefully. 'In love! Have you ever in your life been in love? Do you know what it means to be in love?'

'Life has denied me many things, Lady Dobson.'

'Do you have such a thing as a drink in that black coffin of yours?'

'Alas! Only tea. I am a poor man, Lady Dobson. I read in the paper recently that whiskey is now as much as six shillings a glass.'

Her closed eyes riveted her to her age like a worn face on an old coin.

'No love. No drink. No friends. No wife. No children. Happy man! Nothing to betray you.'

She turned and left him.

The events of that Saturday night and Sunday morning became public property at the inquest.

Sergeant Delahunty gave formal evidence of the finding of the body on the rocks at Greystones. Guard Sinnott corroborated. Mr T. J. Bodkin was then called. He stated that he was a retired businessman residing in a chalet beside the disused station of Cobbler's Hulk. He deposed that, as usual, he went to bed on the night in question around ten o'clock and fell asleep. Being subject to arthritis, he slept badly. Around one o'clock, something woke him.

CORONER: What woke you? Did you hear a noise?

WITNESS: I am often awakened by arthritic pains in my legs.

CORONER: Are you quite sure it was not earlier than one o'clock? The reason I ask is because we know that the deceased's watch stopped at a quarter to twelve.

WITNESS: I looked at my watch. It was five minutes past one.

Continuing his evidence, the witness said that the night being warm and dry, he rose, put on his dressing gown and his slippers and walked up and down on the platform to ease his pains. From where he stood, he observed a white car parked in the lane. He went towards it. He recognized it as the property of Lady Constance Dobson, whom he had met earlier in the week. There was nobody in the car. Asked by a juror if he had seen the car earlier in the night, before he went to bed, the witness said that it was never his practice to emerge from his chalet after his supper. Asked by another juror if he was not surprised to find an empty car there at one o'clock at night, he said he was but thought that it might have run out of petrol and been abandoned by Lady Dobson until the morning. It did not arouse his curiosity. He was not a curious man by nature. The witness deposed that he then returned to his chalet and slept until six o'clock, when he rose, rather earlier than usual, and went for his usual morning swim. On the way to the beach, he again examined the car.

CORONER: It was daylight by then?

WITNESS: Yes, sir.

CORONER: Did you look inside the car?

WITNESS: Yes, sir. I discovered that the door was unlocked and I opened it. I saw a lady's handbag on the front seat and a leather suitcase on the rear seat. I saw that the ignition key was in position. I turned it, found the starter and the engine responded at once. At that stage, I became seriously worried.

CORONER: What did you do?

WITNESS: I went for my swim. It was too early to do anything else.

Mr Bodkin further stated that he then returned to his chalet, dressed, shaved, prepared his breakfast and ate it. At seven o'clock, he walked to the house of his nearest neighbours, the Condors, and aroused them. Mr Colm Condor at once accompanied him back to the car. They examined it and, on Mr Condor's suggestion, they both drove in Mr Condor's van to report the incident to the Guards at Ashford.

CORONER: We have had the Guards' evidence. And that is all you know about the matter?

WITNESS: Yes, sir.

CORONER: You mean, of course, until the body was found fully clothed, on the rocks at Greystones a week later; that is to say, yesterday morning, when, with Sir Hilary Dobson and Miss Mary Condor, you helped identify the remains?

WITNESS: Yes, sir.

CORONER: Did you have any difficulty in doing so?

WITNESS: I had some difficulty.

CORONER: But you were satisfied that it was the body of Lady Constance Dobson and no other.

WITNESS: I was satisfied. I also recognized the woven gold bangle she had worn the day I saw her. The teeth were unmistakable.

Dr Edward Halpin of the sanatorium at Newcastle having given his opinion that death was caused by asphyxiation through drowning, the jury, in accordance with the medical evidence, returned a verdict of suicide while of unsound mind. The coroner said it was a most distressing case, extended his sympathy to Sir Hilary Dobson and said no blame attached to anybody.

It was September before I again met Mr Bodkin. A day of infinite whiteness. The waves falling heavily. Chilly. It would probably be my last swim of the year. Seeing him on his bench – chesterfield, bowler hat, grey spats, rolled umbrella (he would need it from now on), his bulging net bag between his feet, his head bent to one side as if he were listening for a train – I again wondered at a couple of odd things he had said at the inquest; such as his reply to a juror that he never emerged from his railway carriage after supper; his answer to the coroner that he was often awakened at night by his arthritis ('I sleep like a dog,' he had told me. 'I have never in my life had a day's illness, apart from chilblains'); and he had observed by his watch that it was five past one in the morning ('I live by the sun and the stars'). Also, he had said that from the platform, he had noticed the white car parked at the end of the lane. I had parked my Morris a few moments before at the end of the lane and, as I looked back towards it now, it was masked by the signal box.

He did not invite me to sit down and I did not. We spoke of the sunless day. He smiled when I looked at the sky and said, 'Your watch is clouded over.' I sympathized with him over his recent painful experience.

'Ah, yes!' he agreed. 'It was most distressing. Even if she *was* a foolish poor soul. Flighty, too. Not quite out of the top drawer. That may have had something to do with it. A bit spoiled, I mean. The sort of woman, as my dear mother used to say, who would upset a barrack of soldiers.'

'Why on earth do you suppose she did it? But I shouldn't ask; I am sure you want to forget the whole thing.'

'It is all over now. The wheel turns. All things return to the sea. She was crossed in love.'

I stared at him.

'Some man in London?'

He hesitated, looked at me shiftily, slowly shook his head and turned his eyes along his shoulder towards the fields.

'But nothing was said about this at the inquest! Did other people know about it? Did the Condors know about it?'

His hands moved on his umbrella handle.

'In quiet places like this, they would notice a leaf falling. But where so little happens, every secret becomes a buried treasure that nobody mentions. Even though every daisy on the dunes knows all about it. This very morning, when I called on Mary Condor, a hen passed her door. She said, "That hen is laying out. Its feet are clean. It has been walking through grass." They know everything. I sometimes think,' he said peevishly, 'that they know what I ate for breakfast.'

(Was he becoming disillusioned about his quiet beach?)

'How did you know about it? Or are you just guessing?'

He frowned. He shuffled for the second time. His shoulders straightened. He almost preened himself.

'I have my own powers of observation! I can keep my eyes open, too, you know! Sometimes I see things nobody else sees. I can show you something nobody else has ever seen.'

Watching me watch him, he slowly drew out his pocketbook and let it fall open on a large visiting card. I stooped forward to read the name. LADY CONSTANCE DOBSON. His little finger turned it on to its back. There, scrawled apparently in red lipstick, was the word *Judas*. When I looked at him, he was smiling triumphantly.

'Where on earth did you find it?'

'That morning at six o'clock, it was daylight. I saw it stuck inside the wind-screen wipers' – he hesitated for the last time – 'of the Jaguar.'

My mind became as tumbled as a jigsaw. He was lying. How many other pieces of the jigsaw were missing? Who was it said the last missing bit of every jigsaw is God?

'You did not mention this at the inquest.'

'Should I have? The thought occurred to me. I decided that it would be more merciful not to. There were other people to think of. Sir Hilary, for one. And others.' He replaced his pocketbook and rose dismissively. 'I perceive that you are going for a swim. Be careful. There are currents. The beach shelves rapidly. Three yards out and the gravel slides from under your feet. And nobody to hear you if you shout for help. I had my usual little dip this morning. Such calm. Such utter silence. The water was very cold.'

He bobbed and walked away. I walked very slowly down to the edge of the beach. I tested the water with my hand. He was right. I looked around me. I might have been marooned on some Baltic reef hung between an infinity of clouds and a lustre of sea gleaming with their iceberg reflections. Not a fishing smack. Not even a cormorant. Not a soul for miles, north and south. Nobody along the railway track. Or was somebody, as he had suggested, always watching?

If he were concealing something, why had he admitted that he had come out from his railway carriage at all? Why did he choose to mention one o'clock in the morning? Did he know that she had died around midnight? Was he afraid that somebody besides himself might have seen her lights turn down the lane? A timid liar, offering a half-truth to conceal the whole truth?

Above the dunes, I could just see the black roof of his railway carriage. I measured the distance from where I stood and let out a loud 'Help!' For ten seconds, nothing happened. Then his small, dark figure rose furtively behind the dunes. When he saw me, he disappeared.

Foreign Affairs

1

Georgie Freddy Ernie Bertie Atkinson's mature speech style when holding forth at the bar of the Hibernian United Services Club went something like this – though he would doubtless dismiss it complacently as a vulgar parody of an inimitable original; a pastiche, or, if he were in his Italian vein *un pasticcio*, or in his French mood *un pastichage*, or in his Old French humour a *pasté* ('As the Old French used to say'), or if in a Latin frame of mind a *pasta* ('As Cicero might have said'), or if in his Greek role a παστή.

'Hear *my* case!' he might orotundate to the bar. 'When I, at the tender age of approximately twenty minutes and an unspecified number of seconds, at or around ten in the morning on November 11th, 1918, was tenderly deposited in my father's outstretched and trembling arms by the woman who had for so long borne me, none other, I am relieved to be able to say, than his dear wife Eliza, it is not surprising, in view of the day and the hour, forever after to be remembered as Armistice Day, that the bloody old fool should have instantaneously decided to christen me George Frederick Ernest Albert, to express his fervent gratitude, not to the Lord God, in which case he might prophetically have christened me Lord Atkinson, but to King George the Fifth, Reigning Majesty of the United Kingdom of Great Britain and Ireland, head of the once more triumphant Empire, as well as of a whole lot of other institutions ranging from titular admiral of the Royal Fleet to Colonel of the Canadian Mounties, titles and subtitles all, as anyone may absorb in a twenty-five minutes' perusal of any half-decent British almanack spelled with a K.

'Now, when I say that my dear fathead of a father decided thus to label me for life I do not wish to suggest that he calmly made up his mind to do so, and that having made it up he did so. In my experience my father was as nearly mindless as it is possible for any man to be while engaged in selling insurance policies with, it would appear, unusual success, to the normally improvident Irish. I merely wish to convey that he did what he did as absently as one winds one's watch at midnight after heaving one's beloved to the other side of the bed to unwind herself as best she can. Yet, I do assure you gentlemen that, even after I discovered to my cost what exactly he had done to me, I could not find it in my heart to blame him for his folly, nor – and here I do raise my index finger in solemn oath – can I fault him for it even now.

'After all, in that far-off Dublin of 1918 how much common sense could one reasonably expect from a man of his class, origins, upbringing and religious beliefs? Royalist to his rappers, bourgeois to his boots, primitive Methodist Connexion, spelled if you please with an X. Open-air revivalist meetings. Second cousins to the Salvation Army. Hymns in the street under black bowler hats. Belting the Bible like a drum. Come to Jesus! Total certainty of one's own salvation and an even more serene certainty of the damnation of everybody else. How could any such man have foreseen all the political upheavals that within two brief years would turn this British Isle of his fathers' adoption into a free, roaring Irish Republic? Nevertheless, though I forgive the old boy for not having been able to foresee all this political faldirara when he tied "Georgie Freddy Ernie Bertie" to my tail like a firecracker I do blame him, and most severely blame him for having been so unobservant of the meaning and trend of everything happening under his eyes in the years after as to have gone on bestowing on his next four unfortunate children, all distaff, the names of four further members of the English Royal Family. The result is that my eldest sister is now Alexandra Caroline Marie Charlotte Louise Julie. We used to call the second, in my boyhood, Amelia Adelaide and All That Stuff. The third we knew as C.A.I., meaning Caroline Amelia Inc. He christened his fourth and last after that unfortunate bitch Queen Marie Charlotte Sophia of Mecklenburg-Strelitz who was obliged to present her husband King George III with fifteen brats before, as we all know, his imperial Anglo-Teutonic Majesty went completely off his chump.

'I do not know what agonies my sisters may have had to endure at the hands, or tongues, of their school friends because of those outrageous prefixes. I vividly recall the taunting tones in which, even at school, my more nationalistic fellow Mountjoyians used to hail me as loudly as possible with a "Hello, Georgie Freddy Ernie Bertie," accompanied, when affected by the current xenophobia, by a blaze of homicidal scorn in their green Irish eyes or, if a little less categorically patriotic, the clearest flicker on their lips of what I can only describe as *l'équivoque sympathique . . .*'

A monologuist? That was his form, all right! So infectious that one wants to describe it as port winy, portentous, pompous, pomaded. Any other P's? Patchouli? Well, it is, he was, he *is* an Edwardian hangover. Nevertheless, give the man his due. If he had not had an unfortunate knack of delivering his monologues with such a hang-jawed pelican smile, an archness perilously close to the music hall leer, wink, nudge, lifted eyebrow, he might have ranked with the best of Dublin's legendary monologuists. He lacked their professional self-assurance. However carefully guffers like Wilde, Shaw, Stephens, Yeats or Gogarty prepared their *dits* they always threw them away, assured that there would be an infielder to catch them, an audience to applaud. With Georgie Freddy you were aware of a touch of insecure self-mockery, as if he were always trying to kick his own backside before somebody else did it for him.

  'Basta!'

It was his common finale when he wished to indicate that he had made a good point with unusual felicity. Enough on this theme, anyway, to establish that his father was not only a fool but an insuppressible outsider, unusually lucky to have escaped a tarring and feathering, if not assassination, during the revolutionary troubles of the Twenties. And he went on inviting slaughter for years after by bragging every single working day of the year about Georgie Freddy to his eyes-up-to-the-ceiling colleagues during their regular lunch in the crowded basement of Bewley's Oriental Café in Grafton Street. The location is relevant: that it was a café, not a club or restaurant, gives the modest measure of the old chap's commercial standing. Still, though paternal boasting can be boring it can also be touching – one man's daydream is another man's despair. His bored colleagues, remembering their own sons, could sadly shrug. Unfortunately the most aggravating side of the old man's bragging was that Georgie Freddy's career really was outstandingly brilliant from the day he entered Trinity College, Dublin, as a poor sizar to the day he left it with a first class degree in classics, a gold medal in Greek, a sound command of modern Italian and French language and literature, and a good reading knowledge of German. Even more aggravatingly, his career went on being brilliant after he exchanged the university for the British Army in 1942, starting as a lieutenant, promoted to staff-captain in the desert, finally elevated to major in Italy.

With Italy old Bob Atkinson elevated himself to the rank of God the Father. He was now able, thanks to Georgie's dispatches, to gas the whole lunch table of insurance men with prolonged, detailed, hour by hour, beach by beach, blow by blow accounts of how Georgie landed in Sicily at the head of the Eighth Army, advanced to Catania and Messina and crossed between Scylla and Charybdis to the Italian mainland. There, surpassing all, an event occurred that sent the old man into a blazing, vertical takeoff from Bewley's perfumed basement up through every floor and out through the slates of the roof into Dublin's sea-gulled September air.

This event was Georgie's personal encounter with General Alexander, the commander of the Eighth Army, in a war-battered Calabrian hamlet called Galiana at one o'clock of a warm, sticky morning in September shortly after the capture of the city of Reggio di Calabria.

'Think of it, gentlemen!' the old buffer embraces the coffee table with a gleeful laugh. 'There is our brave bucko, Captain George Frederick Ernest Albert Atkinson, my son, my very own son, lying flat on his ass on the upstairs floor of a fleabitten hut in the volcanic mountains of Calabria, dead to God and the world, sound asleep, white as a statue from the dust, and the dirt and the brunt of the battle, shagged from fighting the Eyties the whole bloody sweating day, when he is suddenly shaken awake by one of his fellow officers and a blaze of light blinding his eyes through the windows. He thinks it's the rising sun. It is the headlamps of a military jeep.

'"What in the hell's blazes," says he, "is up now?"

'"Up," sez the officer. "Did you say *up*? You'll soon know what's up," sez he, "if you're not down in five seconds," sez he, "because it's the general that's up," sez he, "that is to say down them ladders thirsting for your blue Oirish blud."

'"What flaming general, for God's sake?" sez our young hero, still lost in the arms of Murphy.

'His comrade stands to attention and sings out the answer as if he was on a barrack square.

'"I refer to General Harold Rupert Leofric George Alexander Irish Guards Military Cross Companion of the Order of the Star of Indiar

ADC to His Majesty whom God preserve since 1936 born in Tyrone in good ould Oireland . . .'

'Well, I needn't tell ye, gentlemen, that at the mention of the general's name it didn't take Georgie boy a week of Sundays to get down that ladder, buttoning his uniform. He clatters into the kitchen, salutes to attention, wondering what in God's name Alexander can have let go wrong with the campaign while he was catching a wink of sleep, and gets the usual polite lift of the finger in return.

'"Captain Atkinson," says Alex very quietly, for he is on all occasions most polite and courteous, one of nature's gentlemen, one of the real old Irish stock. "I regret to have to tell you, Captain, that to my nostrils this village stinks. From the point of view of the health and morale of my troops, such dirt is not a good thing. Can you, as the officer in charge of the area, explain to me why it is so?"

'Gentlemen! Does Georgie tremble? Does Georgie blench? Is Georgie rattled? No, gentlemen. Georgie stares Alex straight in the eye, as cool as that cucumber sandwich there on me plate. "Dirty?" sez he, and now don't let us forget that Georgie was a gold medallist in Ancient Greek when he was at Trinity College, Dublin. "I entirely agree with you, sir. This village stinks to high heaven. It is an absolutely filthy hole. But, sir, if you would care to recall from your days at Eton your Herodotus, book three, chapter four, paragraph one, I think you will remember, sir, that this village has been dirty, evil-smelling and nauseating since the year 434 B.C." Well, gentlemen, do you know what Alex did, at three minutes past one o'clock in the morning in that battered ould canteen in Calabria? He laffed. And he laffed. And he laffed! "I perceive, Captain," he decides at last, "that you are a linguist and a scholar. What other languages do you command besides Greek?" Georgie replies that as well as being a gold medallist in Ancient Greek he speaks fluent Italian, fluent French and has a useful knowledge of German. The general raises the one finger. "The very man for me! Consider yourself promoted from this moment to the rank of major. Report to me at Field H.Q. this morning at seven, ready to assume the post of Military Commander of the City of Reggio di Calabria until further orders." And with that he turns on the leather heel of his brown, polished high boots, climbs into his jeep, leaving Major Atkinson stunned – stunned, gentlemen – as he watches its lights vanishing like a kangaroo into the blackness of the Eyetalian night. And that is how my boy became a major, in command of the first city in Italy taken by Allied troops. Is that, gentlemen, or is that not an astonishing ringside view of contemporary history?'

Undeniably! The coffee cups toast him. If true! The cups are sipped silently. But...

Now, we Irish, like certain other peoples honed hard by history – some of them our best friends – are a double helix of softness and hardness, of passion and calculation, which is why one of the men at that table, an envious, nosy, aquiline character named Cooney got so fed up to his zinc-filled molars (insurance salesmen cannot afford gold) with this oft-repeated yarn about Alex and Georgie that he snuck off to consult a professorial friend in the clerical College of Maynooth, who in turn snuck off to an Irish Catholic archaeologist friend in the Dublin Institute for Advanced Studies, about this Methodist yarn about a Calabrian village called Galiana said to have been unflatteringly mentioned by the great Herodotus in the fifth century B.C. After prolonged searching through the entire corpus of the historian's works none of the three of them could find any mention whatever of any such settlement in any known part of Magna Graecia.

Cooney – for even the most cooneyish Cooney in the world has a heart – was far too kind to mention this fact to old Bob Atkinson. Instead, he waited for four years, and for the appropriate jovial company, to tax the then retired major with his lie. The answer he got made him blush slowly from his neck to his chin, to his eyes, to the peak of the rampant cupola of his bald skull.

'There is, of course,' Georgie declaimed, *ore rotundo* as always, 'no mention of any such place in Herodotus. Indeed, only an illiterate would expect to find it there. I simply embellished a trivial but actual encounter to give a little harmless pleasure to an old man, who, by the way, if, sir, the matter is of any interest to you, we moved late last night into Sir Patrick Dun's Hospital, situated beside the canal once justifiably acclaimed as The Grand Canal. It now barely moves. Weedy. Muddy. Tin cans. Dead cats. He moves not at all. His doctor tells me he has not the strength left to die. He will probably float away, like Joyce's last Liffey leaf, to join his cold, old, dreary fathers tonight.'

'You told a lie,' Cooney insisted coldly.

'Mr Cooney, I did speak to General Alexander. I was promoted major. I was O.C. in Reggio di Calabria. And that is not a world away from the ruins of Thurii, on the Italian Ionian, which Herodotus helped to found, and from which, by then a great and famous city, as famous at least as Dublin, he is believed to have finally floated into his own history. May I, Mister Cooney, give my father your kind wishes, whether false or true, before he in his turn returns to his proper sea?'

'Having told one lie,' Cooney said, 'I am sure you can manage another.'

'I admit,' Georgie replied ever so gently, 'that I did allow my imagination a little latitude. It is a national failing. You, unfortunately, do not appear to suffer from it.'

2

Ex-major. Home to roost. Portly. Savile Row suit, blue and grey pinstripe, blue weskit, mother-of-pearl buttons, T.C.D. tie, rolled gamp, *Times*, of London not Dublin, flat folded under right oxter, pallid blue Peep O'Day handkerchief in breast pocket, Italian shoes. At thirty a man with a past, to be taken seriously, for the moment, another wandering fighter returned reluctantly to stay-at-home Dublin. War-scarred by a bullet that grazed his inside right thigh at Potenza. ('Another inch and I'd be a *castrato*.') Far travelled, through France as a beggarly student, through Greece as a frayed-at-the-cuffs classicist, sweating under North Africa's steely sun, Sicily baked him, Magna Graecia rained on him, England demobbed him, Ireland reopened her arms to him. Pensionless.

'My *epikedeion*,' he liked to sigh and to translate. 'My threnody. My graveside oration.'

He was already inventing his own legend to fortify himself, an alien in a city that had been his ever since he burst upon it on that historic morning thirty years ago via Saint Assam's Nursing Home off Hatch Row, in Ballsbridge.

The place is relevant: the prelude to his myth, his *domus omnium venerum*, to be flourished with bravura on all suitable occasions as Dublin's most famous house of pleasure, patronized by procreative jockeys, trainers, handicappers, bloodstock exporters, breeders (also of horses), dignitaries of the Turf Club, pouring in at all hours of the day and night to view the offspring of their loins, as laden with flowers as if Ireland were Hawaii; wine merchants' messenger boys constantly bearing cases of champagne in and out of the wrong bedrooms; lean, goitre-eyed greyhounds lolloping up and down deeply upholstered, much urinated on stairs; a home less given to displaying umbrellas in its hall stands than bridles, hunting crops, horse blinkers as rigid as leather bras. The city of his pimpled and impoverished schoolboy years under the switch of Parson Magee in Mountjoy Square. He recalls the ribald smiles of his bare-kneed fellows whenever they mentioned the double-meaning name of a square whose latter-day decline from Georgian *piazza* to Joyceian slum both betrayed and confirmed (pure and total legend this) his ruttish teens. His personal city, his *dolce domum* from the day it flowered superbly, generously, ubertosely (he invented the word) as a metropolis of the mind during his student days in its major university, founded by Elizabeth the First. The scene and source of his proudest achievements, his *alma noverca* whose knighting queen had transformed (first battering break) this poorborn Methody into newborn gentleman, man of the world, soldier of the Empire, inheritor of all the ages of the world . . .

'Behold me now!' he loved to groan. 'Back in Ithaca, fatherless, motherless, wifeless, loveless, homeless. Our old family home in Mount Pleasant Square sold! O God!' At this his voice would break. 'With the military barracks to the west of us, bugle-calling at dawn, and the monastery to our east, hymning hymns, and the road through Windy Arbour, Dundrum, Sandyford, Golden Ball, to the lovely, lonely moors beyond the Scalp; and the canal floating seaward silently past its Dickensian tenements on Charlemont Place, every bum painter's delight; and Harcourt Terrace around the corner, odorous of Saint John's Wood, frankincense, classic grace and decadent nineteenth-century vice!

'And now? Not a relative left. My four sad sisters scattered through the British Isles, nursing, typing, clerking, married or otherwise gone to the bitches. As witness my dearest, youngest sister Charlie, she homonymously of Mecklenburg-Strelitz, obliged to marry at seventeen, when apparently – the adverb sounds aerie but is accurate – pregnant by a hot theological student at Trinity. Thereafter obliged, like her famous eponym, to bear his reverence one infant per annum, a fair excome on a poor investment, exiled in a sea-sprayed parsonage on the coast of West Cork, facetiously called "a living," endlessly fertile because, again apparently, neither of them can think of anything better to do when the paraffin ebbs in the pink glass bowl of the lamp, and the hearth goes grey and the Atlantic waves claw at the naked shingles of the western world.'

Such groans were masochist – apart from that sincere reference to Mount Pleasant Square. Names like that fell on the ears of his generation like far-off music, the horns of elfland; especially so for every boy come up from the provinces to a Dublin that had been a promise and a legend. For these, now grown men, Dundrum, Windy Arbour, Sandyford, Golden Ball would always happily evoke days of idleness and pleasure in the mountains with their lost girls and their faded youth. They fell like a knell on the memory of the ex-major; he had been too poor, pressed, and pimply for girl-play. Those nostalgic place-names suggested to him the youth he had never had.

Nevertheless! No regrets! Chin up! He was a man! He had campaigned! He had travelled and proved himself! He dismissed his non-youth without an audible sigh, and smartly unpacked his *elegantissimi* bags, purchased in vanquished Rome, in the bedroom of a modest Leeson Street guest house, called *The Anchor*, directly opposite the nuns' hospital, and from this base began thoughtlessly, blissfully, improvidently to live the life of a clubman. The United Services, five minutes across the Green, ten if he dawdled to watch the geese, ducks, seagulls. Its paths were, in the summer, lined with deck chairs, female legs to glance at covertly, an extra paper to buy, a sixpence for the old woman with the flowers outside the Saint Stephen's Green Club who always flattered him with her, 'Ah! God be good to you, *Colonel!*'

At lunch, at the Round Table, there was always somebody to talk to. He could easily kill time after it in the reading room, if lucky in the billiard room, then over afternoon tea in town. He lived extravagantly – his well-earned due – even slipped in a couple of expensive visits to Paris and Cannes. Before the year was out he had the beginnings of a duck's belly. For ten months he flourished. Then, suddenly, always an ominous word, while still abed one damp March morning he found on his breakfast tray, beside his London *Times*, three envelopes that caused his pleasant life to stammer, hiccough, wobble, shake and halt like a car out of petrol. His monthly bank sheet drew his eye swiftly to a total in red.

'Aha!' he laughed. '*Enfin, je suis dans le rouge.*'

The secretary of his Club also politely requested £50 in renewal of his annual subscription, plus £75. 6. 10 for drink and food consumed on the premises during the previous quarter. ('And well worth it!') His London tailor's bill brought him to the ground.

He steadily perused his *Times*, lit a cigarette and gazed calculatingly across the street at the nuns' hospital. Long before he was halfway through his cigarette he agreed that he possessed only one solid asset. His scholarship was unsaleable. Nobody except headmasters of schools would want his gift of languages. Majors were as little in demand in the Dublin of 1949 as Jesuits in the Geneva of 1549. His one solid asset was Moll Wall. He sent her an invitation to dinner at his Club. She agreed happily. With her usual shrewdness she had been expecting it for months.

3

Moll Wall was an Irish-speaking, Dublin-born Jewess whose father was known all over the world to every serious collector of Irish glass and silver. He ran a small antique business on one of the Dublin quays, a widower, the doyen of his profession, respected as a man of knowledge and probity. Alas for his only child, he took so much delight in his craft that he never had time to make money out of it. Accordingly Moll had had to work her way into college by winning scholarships, and knew that when she finished she would always, like her father, be comparatively poor. She worked now in the Department of External Affairs.

At Trinity she had been Georgie Atkinson's only female friend. He had been happy to spend months of hours with her over morning coffees or cups of afternoon tea in cheap cafés – he could never afford to take her to lunch – exchanging carefully prepolished student repartees and epigrams, solemnly discussing politics and languages, especially ancient tongues. They used to talk most warmly about loyalties, which at that time chiefly meant family loyalties and college personalities; spreading out later to international personalities; which in turn gradually hardened into political principles. They talked of religion, especially of its history. Here she had the edge on him, a Jewish mind ranging aeons behind Christianity into the vast Asiatic desert between the world-mothering rivers, finding everything he associated with the nineteenth century already matured four thousand years before in the thoughts of Ur and Babylon. He never dared to discuss love with her—

How could he? He so poor, she so proper – though she did attract him: lean, hard, lank, black, bony, muscular – they first met at the Foils Club. She was his senior, due to leave college before him, stern of character, good humoured, but also unpredictably puritanical, a woman whose moral force he frankly feared, whose Jewish sense of what is righteous and just he burningly admired, whose chosen vocation he wished he had dared to imitate. But even at college he was already (that English Connexion) hearing not the far-off echoes of Babylon but the imminent bellowings of Hitler, reading Houston Stewart Chamberlain, wondering how 'his' Empire and 'her' race would fare in the years before them.

Her real name was not Moll. It was Miriam, but since in her excessive efforts to nationalize herself she always signed her name not only in Gaelic but in an outmoded script, Máire de ball, her fellow students called her Moira, or Maurya, or Maureen, until she ended up by being universally known as Moll Wall. Whenever she lapsed into one of her more solemn moods they called her The Wailing Wall. He always respectfully called her Miriam. She always kindly called him George.

As he watched her sip her abstemious aperitif ('A small dry sherry, please') he guessed at her age. Thirty-five? Halfway to three score and ten. Perhaps more? Why had she never married? Took love too solemnly? Warned chaps off? She had always warned him off. Or was it he who warned her off? No beauty, yet she did unarguably have her fine points, even if each of them suffered a 'but' from the poor company it kept. Her skin was delicate, but tinged like a quarter gypsy's; her black hair was rich, oily and luxuriant, but it hung straight as threads beside her fine eyes; which were as lightly blue as two morning glories but set in eyelids as misshapen as scalene triangles recumbent against the bridge of her Hebraic nose; her teeth were as healthy and white as the teeth of a hound, but the canines and incisors crossed voraciously; her lips, if set in a gentler face, might have been prettily described as bee-stung, but in her strong countenance their pouting suggested not an insatiable kisser but an insuppressible talker. He liked her best when she laughed with a zany triumph that lit up her whole being. He had seen it often behind the flashing foils. She was at her best there – breastless, black from masked face to hissing foot, strong-calved, aggressively competitive, swift as her mind that was as sharp as a pitiless diamond in the hand of a glasscutter. How often had he not seen her at a public debate in college slash through some speaker's clever sophistry with one clean, arrogant stroke and casually chuck his bits into the rubbish bin beside her. He feared her – she was female. She envied him – he was male.

'You look very well,' he quizzed, raising his glass to her. 'How is life in your wicked Quai d'Orsay?'

'In order,' she smiled.

'Meaning in your order. I do congratulate you, Miriam. You always have ordered your life. Unlike those of us who have lived not wisely but too well, you have lived most wisely if not too well.'

'Where did *you* steal that piece of wit?'

'Othello. But he said "loved." He, too, admired a dark skin.'

'He too?' She smiled crookedly – it was as far as he would ever go. Timid? Shy? Unsexy? Androgynous? Selfish, like all bachelors? Frightened of women, like all Irishmen. But with her racial humility, her Jewish submissiveness – a female Job, *I have said to the worm Thou art my mother and my sister* – she had long since accepted that for him a wife would always be a poor substitute for the cosy filial relationship that always seemed sufficient for so many Irish *goyim* and so many Jewish Jews. And what if I *have* ordered my life? Had I any alternative? And how well I did it! His useless Greek, my useful Semitic languages, Arabic, Hebrew, even that spot of Aramaic, and then modern Irish, and that second degree in political science.

She could read his mind as if she were sitting inside it.

'George! What is the English for *cul-de-sac*?'

'Blind alley?' he suggested.

Years before he went marching off down his blind alley to the sound of guns and drums, and drums and guns, in defence of an Empire that even one of his father's actuaries could have told him would be stone dead within ten years, I was within steps of the top in External Affairs. I'd be an ambassador now if I were a man. Some woman once said of penis-envy, 'Who wants the stupid thing anyway?' O God! It must be worth five thousand pounds a year at least. Certainly worth an ambassadorship.

As if he could read her thoughts he told her sympathetically that with her Talmudic mind, so regulative, so legalistic, she was far too honest for foreign service, and, of course, far too idealistic, too romantic, much too sentimental. She hooted with laughter, well used to male romantics boasting of their realism. Ireland is full of them. She calmly declared her role – the *Eminence rose* of Ireland, guiding it knowledgeably through all its conflicts with the wicked world; at which they laughed so merrily that they ended by casting flickering glances of mistrust at one another. It was how they always sparred, advancing, receding to and from some sort of understanding, affinity, or intimacy that seemed to be regarded as best left undefined. One of their comrades once summed it up with, 'They are completely different and they are two of a kind.' And had she not once told him, with the air of somebody passing on a clue in a game, the sad story of the Egyptologist who, on finding a tiny flower in a freshly opened tomb, scooped it out of the dusk, into the sun, where it straightway died.

'I see you have settled back into Dublin all right,' she stated so firmly that he frowned. Had the witch been bugging him for the last ten months?

'I am back,' he shivered at her, 'in the cold bosom of Mother Ireland. Surrogate paps.'

She raised an eyebrow, observed that he had been drinking a lot of wine. On top of three martinis. Lacking courage? To pop his question? Whose nature she foresaw from his joke, disconnected, about owing a debt to his tailor and to society. Through the smoke of his cigar, over his port, her brandy, he finally posed the problem with a blend of bluster and nonchalance, so transparent that her heart was touched. Poor kid! Up against it?

'Miriam, I've come to the end of this bloody city. If you were me what would you do to keep boredom profitably at bay?'

'Join the army.'

'They sacked me a year ago!'

'The Irish army.'

'My God!' he cried rudely. 'A joke army! They are about as martial as the Pope's Swiss Guards. They haven't fought since 1922.'

'Snob! And ignoramus! It is for its size as good an army as any in the world. It also happens that the Swiss Guards have in their time fought skilfully and died bravely. Anyway,' glancing at his midriff, 'most of your fighting was conducted in an office. I must fix you up with some fencing soon. Think about it, George. Good quarters, a good mess – those we have inherited from your British Army – good pay, no expenses, all your financial troubles solved. Okay?'

'Well,' he mumbled, abashed by her penetration, 'I know my merits. I am quite sure I could teach those chaps a thing or two. But what about my deplorable genealogy? Even my name marks me as what your race would call "a gentile."'

'If you have the luck to be even so much as considered by them at all it will be solely because of your deplorably Saxon background. Consider! Our army is aggressively patriotic, ninety-five percent Roman Catholic, one hundred percent proletarian. Can't you see the kick we would get out of introducing you with deadpan faces to some visiting foreign brass? "Our Captain Atkinson." The brass looks at you superciliously. You turn out to be a first class Greek scholar, from a sixteenth-century university, a practising Methodist, ex-British Army, widely travelled, an Oxford accent, commanding five languages. You would be our prize exhibit. Our Uncle Tom.'

His cheeks blazed. She raised two palms and pouted at him with her shoulders, chin, eyebrows, lower lip, even with that shrugging of the bottom known as the *cul de poule*.

'It's what I am, George. Their Auntie Tom. It does not prevent me from doing my job as well as anybody in the department, indeed a hell of a sight better.'

For a while he was too aghast to speak. Finally:—

'I am *not*,' he insisted, 'a practising Methodist. And I do *not* speak five languages. I speak only Greek, French, Italian and English.'

She laid her hand on his wrist. His throat gobbled. He looked in astonishment at her radiant eyes and triumphant mouth. She could be damned attractive sometimes.

'The fifth language is the quintessence of our plot. It will be our master stroke. You must also be able to talk Gaelic to visiting brass. In fact I wonder could we put you into kilts?'

'Me?' he railed in his most haughtily offensive tone – excusable, she felt, in a man whom she had been deliberately kicking in the balls. 'I don't know a word of your bloody lingo.'

'My lingo,' she yielded gently, 'is Hebrew. You are a good linguist, George. Almost as good as I am. In six weeks I can teach you enough Irish to get you through the interview. With the strings I can pull for you they will see that you are on a plate for them. After that, the more you behave like a bally ass the more they will love you. But I am afraid you simply must also be some sort of a Protestant because it so happens that by pure luck we just now badly need one to represent the President and the army on such sad occasions as the funerals of such alien sects as Jews, Methodists, Jehovah's Witnesses, Baptists, Orangemen, Free

Masons, Buddhists, members of the Church of Ireland and all that pagan lot.'

He gazed at her lean and yellow abstinence. Sardonic bitch! A victim of genes. Also sexual frustration. And a countervailing lust for power. He said grandly that he would 'look them over.' Her sable eyelids drooped. She did not say it but he heard it. 'Good doggy!' Was this the beginning of his servitude or his success?

4

Those army years proved to be the best years of his life. Financed, fed, clothed, housed, flattered, fathered and, he was right, he *could* teach them a thing or two. They asked his views about lots of things – about cigars, wines, cricket, social protocol, Methodism, French letters, the English public school system, cocktails, gloves, ties, polo, English whores, John Wesley, The Royal Family, London clubs. Splendid fellows. Most intelligent. Some of my best friends.

If only, he sighed sincerely to her – and she smoothly agreed – they had some cultural interests. To remedy this, being unmarried and with no more than a peripheral interest in Woman and none in Marriage he was able to afford a secret, tiny, pink-papered bedsitter in the city where he could store his L.P. records, his beloved Loeb Classics, his French novels, relax in his Hong Kong pyjamas, sip a *pastis*, or a *Punt e Mes*, or a *retsina*, or a *Chambéry vermouth*, or a *cassis vin blanc*, unfold his *Times*, smoke a ten-shilling cigar, even entertain a rare female acquaintance. Naturally he never told Moll about this hideaway. She would have closed her bistre eyelids and laughed with her blue serpentine tongue at his rosy refuge. She would have known at once that he would have lost more battles there with Dublin's virgins than would bankrupt the honour of an entire army in any other part of the globe except Uganda, Israel and Maoist China. She was pleased that he did, now and again, take her to dinner at his Club. There he always had the grace to thank her for what she had done for him. Secretly he wished she had less moral character and more immoral flesh.

Those lovely fat years ended the day he heard her, to his bewilderment, abruptly telling him on the telephone that he was wasting his talents in the army and that he must stop it at once. He invited her to dinner in the Club. There she repeated her extraordinary opinion. He bluntly told her to mind her own damned business, he was hunkydory where he was, he had every intention of going on being hunkydory, and thank her VERY much! He saw her lower lip curl. He saw her slanted canines. He also noted, with an ingenuous satisfaction, that she seemed to have no ready reply – she merely changed the subject. That, he decided, was the way to do it. Treat them rough. A month later he discovered from a chummy note slipped under his door that he was about to be transferred to a civilian post in the Department of Defence. He at once sent her a dispatch, by motor cyclist, marked *Supremely Urgent*, informing her that as soon as he had put his affairs in order he would resign. The final haughty sentence of this dispatch recalled Alfred de Musset. *On ne badine pas avec moi!* Unfortunately a month of frantic search showed him that Fate *could* trifle with him. She had rightly assumed penury, hoped for boredom, was satisfied that he would not succeed in locating any alternative income. She had experienced it all herself.

He suffered in the Department of Defence. Why had he ever been so foolish as to return home to this mist-shotten island? If only, he groaned, there were another war, another lovely, bloody, muddy, dusty, murderous war to free him from this womb! Nevertheless, as a man of courage, an Odysseus, he must suffer Ithaca! And Penelope! He gave up his London *Times*. He had to surrender his pink-papered hideaway, sell his Loebs, wear cotton pyjamas, even have his suits off the rack. But he clung, by God, he clung to his Club. *On ne badine pas* . . . It should be the motto of the arms of the Atkinsons. He endured his lot until, perceptibly, some secret powers realized his true worth. He gradually found himself being used as a liaison between External Affairs and Defence, involving certain (not always intelligible, but nonetheless always welcome) explorations of the continent of Europe, for four weeks at a time and not less than four times a year. Bit by bit his bitter blood became sweeter, until, on a day no different to any other, he decided now that he had taught the foolish woman a lesson – namely that his worth would always be appreciated by somebody – he could afford to be generous. He took her back into his favour. He invited her to dinner at his Club.

5

Before the night was out she realized sadly that the Civil Service had taught him only a little. She knew his age to the hour, as who did not, forty-two on November 11th. He was as portentous as if he were still twenty-seven, a trifle less supercilious, capable at last of an occasional two minutes' silence. He found her as alert as always, regrettably one of those women who bear the lineaments of unsatisfied desire, as garrulous as ever but, now that he had learned what a desk and a dictaphone can do to the human spirit, he had to admire the way she had preserved her identity over the years *senza rancor*. It was the foils, he presumed, that preserved her sanity. No swordsman can feel rancour against an opponent who slips a blade under his defence.

All in all it was a most pleasant evening. Warmed by the wine he was so daring as to say to her as they parted on the pavement outside her flat, 'As Mr Churchill once said to Mr Roosevelt, *Amantium irae amoris integratio est.*' He cautiously spoiled it by adding, 'The maxim is also found in Publilius Cyrus, Maxim twenty-five. Speaking also of the quarrels of lovers as a renewal of friendship's bond.' She was to recall the moment as a missed opportunity. If only she had said – even with so shy a man, so conditioned a Methody, so late in the game – 'Aren't you going to kiss me good night?' she might have saved him some shame and herself some misery. Her excuse could only have been that at that moment she was gazing past him at the lamps of the square like a painter before his landscape, a sculptor before his model, a writer before his theme, wondering what the hell to do next to, with or for so intractable a subject. She merely said, 'Thanks for a delightful dinner, George! Good night!'

Sin loomed. Pride, vainglory, hubris, even some of that very bumptiousness that she held against him. It was natural, to be sure, that she should want not only to have his apple on her tree but to pluck it, feel it in the palm of her hand, under her eye, shining on her own desk, in her own department – she managed it easily even though she was well aware that it is the one department whose men are supposed to be mobile, even nomadic. 'But not our George!' George was no pilot; he was ground staff, a born adjutant, no more. She was amusedly confident of it – until, against her vehement, fervent, pleading, even irascible advice her superiors insisted on posting him as Second Secretary to the Paris embassy. When, in a drawling voice, he told her that, after careful consideration, he had agreed to accept this minor post, she foresaw with satisfaction that within a month Paris would return him to her lap.

To her rage he succeeded brilliantly there. A year later the powers beyond her control (and understanding) decided to send the boy to Oslo. He succeeded there as impeccably. Two years later she shudderingly saw him depart as First Secretary in the embassy to the Quirinal. Within a month he was the toast of Rome's diplomatic corps. (*Questi Irlandesi! Argutissimi! Spiritosi! Un gros gaillard. Ces Irlandais! Jolly able chap, take him for an Englishman any day. Ein so witziger Kerl.*) She gave in. Anyway she knew that the whispering gallery of the department had long since marked him down as their *Eminence rose's* personal creation. She had no option left but to pilot him to greater and greater achievements. An embassy? But not too far away! Canberra was mentioned. She cursed the Corona Australis in Irish. Africa offered. She Hebrewed it into a fog. Canada produced an obscenity in Arabic. The hand of chance crept forward on two fingers towards the E.E.C. The United States of Europe? *Chef de cabinet* in the Commission for Culture and Civilization? That would be worthy of her. But there was one danger. The U.S.E. is supranational. Its officers serve Europe, not their own country. She could have him sent on a string – seconded. Even so, to recall him might not be easy. Threatened by Australia, Canada and Africa, she yielded.

Brussels. 1972. *And Belgium's capital had gathered then her beauty and her chivalry.* A few miles north of Waterloo. *To arms! And there was mounting in hot haste . . . Or whispering with white lips, 'The foe! They come! They come!'*

6

She came one sunny November morning. Her cold camera's eye smilingly interrupts and startingly arrests one of his slow and stately steps as, bearing his fawn gloves, rolled gamp, bowler hat, he strolls from and now proudly leads her back to his modest but elegant three-roomed apartment on the Avenue des Arts.

'I chose it myself as befitting my not inconsiderable rank in the bureaucratic hierarchy of the new supranational Europe.'

His housekeeper, a lean, dark, sallow Flamande of middle age, makes them some excellent fresh French coffee, and Moll settles back to consider her protégé.

To her knowledge, she informs him, he is now fifty-four.

'Matured and wise?' she hopes.

She is, he flatters her, by his reckoning fifty. 'Would I wish any contemporary older?'

His living room she finds most untidy: letters, newspapers, books, magazines, reports on this and that all strewn about.

'My fingers itch.'

He is, she mocks, bloated from vanity and luxury. She is, he quips, lean from unsatisfied desire. She retorts with the fat weed that roots itself in ease on Lethe's wharf. He pulls in his gut.

'An elegant suit, it flatters your figure, George.'

'A charming frock. Do I perceive one teeny grey hair? The vanity of that necklet must have set you back at least a hundred pounds.'

Husband and wife could not have sparred more equivocally, each with reason. He would have preferred an ambassadorship and is sure she has denied it to him. He is behaving arrogantly just to show that he has slipped out of my power. He owes her more than his pride approves. She could do so much, oh, so very much more for him if only he would be a tiny bit more accommodating. At which point they both suddenly experienced a painful revelation of shared loss. In small countries like the green island to which they both belonged – as in all small cities, towns, houses, offices, institutions, workshops throught-out the world – familiarity breeds envy, and that conspiracy, and that skulduggery – it is their greatest disadvantage. However, just because they are so close, so small, so familiar, so personal, so intimate, one understands their skulduggery – it is one of their greatest advantages. Here? One can never keep track of the conspiracies of impersonal, ever-shifting Babels like the League of Nations, The United Nations, The Council of Europe, the E.E.C. They both suddenly begin to talk about Dublin, its gossip, its personalities, its plotters and planners, its news, its . . . It was she who, in the end, had to rise, and sadly send him about his business. Still, as she went her way she was humming, *He might have been a Rooshian,/ A French or Turk or Prooshian/ Or perhaps Itali-AN,/ But in spite of all temptations/ To belong to other nations,/ He still remains an Irishman.*

In high good humour she fished among her own informants around the city – the U.S.E. had already brought some four hundred Irish to

Brussels – took stock, weighed up, relaxed, expanded and returned to Dublin satisfied at long last with her offspring, her everything, husband, uncle, aunt, father, mother, sister, brother, fat, folly, power, freedom, fame. She began to boast of My Man in Bruxelles. She paced the corridors of power, moved across the chessboard of mirrored Europe, equipped with almost a dozen western and eastern languages, dropping amiably into this office and that, thriving on all those old Dublin yarns, legends, memories, characters, another Irish wit. From that on she flowered in the sun of his delightfully regular, secret dispatches from the front, intimate vignettes, witty, salted by a touch of the malicious, the flirtatious, even the salacious. He revelled in hers, so full of naughty local gossip. For them both it was like being back in T.C.D. all over again, except that she began to dress more and more carefully, had her straight hair waved every week, favoured restaurants where the headwaiter called her Madame, flaunted costume jewellery, wore Chamade scent and, the department groaned, talked like a bloody minister. During the next nine months she visited him there four times and he returned four times to Dublin. It was his heyday, her green period, his mature style period, the time when from Dublin she possessed Europe. A year passed. Never the tiniest spray of yew.

It was around the second quarter of his second year that the dry palmetta leaves of gossip began to clack. Long accustomed to such mutterings she made nothing of them. A woman? She laughed sardonically. The palm leaves still rattled their loose skin in the wind. What woman? She laughed in hysterical relief. She had met the poor creature five times. His hard-working, middle-aged, plain, surly, dark, unprepossessing, skinny housekeeper! Her assurance persisted until the September afternoon when:

Dear Miriam,

I have last week been here for exactly a year and a half, and I can say in all modesty that we have left our mark on Europe. I have now decided to show the flag. Accordingly I have taken a roomy apartment at 132 *bis*, two blocks farther along the avenue where I can suitably house a visitor or entertain a colleague. There are three bedrooms, one for me, one for a guest, one for my housekeeper, Miss Virginie Nieders. You may remember Ginnie. Or did you ever notice her at all? She is a splendid cook and, as I have just discovered, a superb if expensive shirtmaker, a marvellous find. She is Flemish and in many ways a remarkable creature. Lean as a greyhound, blackhaired, sallow as tallow, a coiled spring of energy, eyes shadowed as if by a gauze of libidinous soot, filled with a proud, Aristophanic scorn of all mankind, most entertainingly outspoken about my international colleagues, and especially about their wives. Where *does* she collect all this scandal? Moody if reproved, even thunderous, but absolutely devoted to me. And what a vocabulary! You would enjoy it. Yesterday evening I said that it was a charming sunset. She cried, '*C'est transcendant.*' Last week when she was fitting one of her splendid shirts on me I mentioned to her that it was rather tight under the armpits. What did this child of nature reply? She cried out in agony, in Walloon – though she can speak French too – that her soul was lacerated. Can you imagine any woman of any other race relating souls and shirts? Except perhaps an Italian? '*Mi straccia l'animal!*' But these Flemish women can be highly tempestuous creatures. If I did not accept this as a fact of nature I do not think I could, or even should have put up with some of her more outspoken remarks about our visitors. Anyway, it is a charming apartment and the next time you come to Brussels you must bring a chaperon and stay with us.

Ever, G.

Another woman reading this letter might have merely raised a speculative eyebrow, wonderingly turned down the corners of the mouth. Moll, who knew her man to the backbone, not so much turned the pages as whirled them. At the imprecise word 'our' in 'our visitors' she stopped breathing. At the final sentence she became taut, at the final word 'us' her spring snapped. 'Our' visitors? Her finger accused him. Rage blinded her. The fool wondered where the woman got her amusing scandals? She saw one of those inevitable international *kaffeeklatschen* of valets, hall porters, cooks, maids, chauffeurs, housekeepers, remembered her first glance about his earlier apartment, the untidy desk, the letters and papers strewn about it, covered her face in fury at the thought of her letters to him being eagerly deciphered over so many full-breasted and elbowed kitchen tables. She pulled herself up, and back. The essential word was not 'our.' It was the final word 'us.' When he wrote that word he convicted himself.

She must make certain. But could anybody ever know for certain what exactly, if anything, had happened between these two idiots? Not even he, perhaps he least of all, for when men of his age compromise themselves they lose all touch with reality. Her brain went cold and her heart went hard for one concentrated hour by which time she had established five points.

1. Though nothing is impossible in this area, it was unlikely that he had slept with her.

2. Even if he had she was not affected by the slightest feeling of jealousy – on this she had to be clear, and was.

3. Something either had happened, was happening, or was about to happen, well-known to Brussels, as the gossip at home showed, implying enough laughter in the *coulisses*, the *couloirs*, the cafés to show her that he was letting down the side.

4. The crunchy bit. An international U.S.E. aide is beyond the direct control of his home country: unless, *a.*, he has made such a fool of himself as to embarrass his resident Minister or, *b.*, deeply offended his own resident racial community (in this case the proper, puritanical, R.C., inferiority-complexed and supersensitive Irish), or, best/worst of all, *c.*, created gross scandal or ribald laughter at home.

5. There was one way in which he just might be persuaded to do Number 4, *c.*

She sat to her typewriter and wrote to him, in French, her thanks for his invitation, and of her joy and delight at all the dear letters he had been sending to her over the last year or so. She had at last broken their secret code, she had lifted the curtain of their timid and, for that very reason, all the more delightful intimations. She understood, at last, all that his dear, fond heart had so tremulously been trying to say. 'How blind I have been! How my heart burns to think of all the days and nights we shall have together!' She would be in his arms in Brussels by next Friday night, happy that they need no longer conceal their passion from the world. Of course, she would be charmed to stay with him, *sans chaperon*. In fact he must send that silly old housekeeper on a holiday for the weekend. *Je me prends a pleurer de joie. Je t'embrasse*. M.

It was Wednesday. She posted her letter, to his new flat, before noon. She left the flap open. He (they) should be reading it by Friday morning. She had left him no time to reply by letter. He would not risk telephoning. The answer must be a telegram, and everything would now depend on its tone. It would be a blisterer if he was completely innocent; a blusterer if he was half innocent; evasive if he were guiltily unsure about whatever the hell he had or had not been up to. If he was guilty he would rush across to Dublin at once to find out what precisely he had been guilty of in his sleep.

His telegram came on Friday afternoon. AM FLYING TO DUBLIN FRIDAY SOONEST WILL TELEPHONE FROM CLUB SATURDAY MORNING SOONEST. EVER, GEORGE.

She no sooner read it than she found herself unable to swallow. Could the idiot – she was prepared to swear in open court that the possibility had not occurred to her before – could he, whether innocent or guilty, have taken her declaration *au pied de la lettre?* She suffered a night of sleeplessness, nightmare and nervous indigestion while pondering on all the uncomfortable as well as on some of the pleasing if also tormenting implications of the idea. He did not telephone on Saturday morning. Instead, the hall porter at his Club did, to tell Miss Miriam Wall that The Major had arrived, after a bad crossing, had a cold and neuralgia, was confined to his room, but would ring her in the afternoon. An hour later a great heap of red roses arrived from the florist near the Club. She extra-mured them in her hall. What was this all about? Oozing courage? For what? Up to some trickery? She waited indoors all day. He did not telephone.

He had decided to let her wait, which is to say that – like his old father long ago who could never make up his mind about anything – he was cowering in his room, not with a bad cold and neuralgia but with a bad conscience and nerves. He had already had a scene with one woman in Brussels; he could not bring himself to face another scene in Dublin. Let her be the one to telephone! Dammit! Was he a man or a mouse? (His honest insides whispered, 'Mouse!') Around five o'clock, being just about to descend to the bar for a bracer, a knock at his door and the page boy outside informed him that a lady of the name of Wall was inquiring for him downstairs.

He had always said it! Treat them rough! He tremblingly brushed back the greying wings of his green fifties, checked the lie of his tie, plucked the dark red handkerchief in his breast pocket an inch higher and then with stately tread slowly descended the winding stairs to meet the wench. There below him, foreshortened in the middle of the tesselated hall, stood Virginia Nieders, black-clothed, blackhaired, her black spring wound tight, the aureoles about her eyes as brown as thunder. Cornered, even a mouse will bare its tiny teeth. Reverting instantly to type Major Atkinson strode past her to the porter's glass box, whipped out his wallet, slipped a fiver into the man's hand, said, 'Get rid of her at once,' emerged, howled at her in Walloon, French, Flemish, English and Italian, 'Go away!', while bounding in long leaps like an obese giraffe for the stairs. Behind him the porter's brass-buttoned tails did such an effective flying tackle about her whirling waist that two arriving diners, both rugby threequarters, cheered his grappling speed. A lifted telephone, a Guard opportunely passing, peacock screams in Walloon, French and Flemish diminuendoed into the street. Calm returned to the Hibernian United Services Club. The porter stood staring at her through the barred glass door. The Guard stood warily watching her from the balcony of the double steps. Georgie leaned from the tiptop bedroom of the club peering at her glistening poll until God sent the miracle of a cloudburst whose downpour washed her ark away.

The Major galloped downstairs, rang for a taxi, drove to his old Guest House on Leeson Street. They were delighted to see him. But there was no room in the inn. Oh! A foreign lady, they slyly said, had been asking after him only an hour ago. Phew! Being without his address book he drove on to External Affairs, on Saint Stephen's Green, to collect a few friendly telephone numbers from the usual solitary Casabianca holding the Saturday fort. He had barely time to shout 'Full speed ahead' to the cabby before she bounded like a dripping mermaid from the portico down to the pavement to shriek in Walloon after him. He remembered an old Irish army friend who had a base on Earlsfort Terrace, around the corner from the Green. Terror poured its adrenaline all over his kidneys at the sight of her black, spearlike figure under the spotlight of that portico too. 'Down the Hatch!' he roared, and with whistling tyres down the Hatch they went. Were there ten of her? He must think. He must have a drink. He must eat. Round the Green to the Unicorn. Or had he by chance spoken to her of that estimable restaurant as a haunt of his legendary student days? He evidently had. Peeping from his knees on the floor of the taxi, he saw her against the restaurant's lighted, curtained window. He surrendered. Back to the Club! There for the first time in his life he was relieved to find the bar empty. It took him half an hour and three brandies to clarify the situation.

What were the simple facts? He shook his head wildly. Damnation! What WERE the simple facts? He had been lonely. Right? She had been lonely. Right? What more natural than that he should want to comfort her, be kind to her? Right? And if he ever had gone beyond that whose business was it but his own? Anyway everybody knew that half the international population of Brussels was living in sin – except the cagy Irish. It would all have been hunkydory if the cow hadn't pulled the teat out of the baby's bottle. Chasing him over here in broad daylight! And God knows what she had been saying to whatever junior she had found across the Green in External Affairs! And, no doubt, she would be back there on Monday morning screaming fit for a French farce. Right? No! Yes!!!

He was a ruined man.

A third brandy was needed to give him the courage to ring for the firing squad.

'Miriam! It is me. I'm simply dying to see you.'

'George!'

She sounded sad. Could she be shy? How dicey was this going to be? He tried to make his own voice sound neither soft nor hard. It came out as hoarse as an old hinge.

'I needn't tell you, Miriam, that I'd have rung you at once if it hadn't been for this wretched cold.'

'Your poor cold! Caught, I presume, racing around Dublin from that woman.'

His stomach fell a foot.

'How soon can I see you, Miriam?'

'I am afraid not tonight, George. Nor tomorrow. Ever since your housekeeper arrived in Dublin she has been telephoning me every half hour. You must have confided greatly in her, she is so accurately informed about this city. Have you been telling her all about your golden youth? Also you left your address book behind you. For all I know she may have rung the Secretary. Even the Minister. Perhaps the entire Cabinet? Some little while ago she took up her position on the pavement opposite my flat, parading up and down under the rain between two lampposts like an unemployed whore. After watching her through my curtains for half an hour I brought her in. Soaked to the skin, poor slut! I gave her a stiff drink, let her pour some of her European despair over me, gave her some dry clothes and sent her to soak in a hot bath where she is wallowing at this moment. When she emerges I suppose I shall have to listen to a few more lurid revelations about our man in Bruxelles before I park her in some modest guest house where she can prepare herself for her interview with the Secretary on Monday morning.'

'But the woman is daft, Miriam! You can't, nobody can believe a word she says!'

'It is not only what she says, it is what she sees. She says you have a mole in the small of your back. Have you, George?'

'She makes shirts for me!'

'How intimate! And that you have a scar on the inside of your right thigh.'

'I must have mentioned it to her.'

'She has a letter you wrote to her from Paris two months ago. It almost made me blush.' Her voice became soft and sad again. 'I am sorry, George. You ought to have stayed in Trinity and become a tutor in Ancient Greek. I realize now that what you are is a man so afraid of the lonely, little Irish boy in you that you have grown fold after fold of foreign fat to keep him in. Just as this poor woman may well have had an exuberant Peter Paul Rubens goddess bursting to get out of her skinny body ever since the day she was born. O dear! I sometimes wonder how many Ariels were imprisoned in Caliban. And how many Calibans were imprisoned in Ariel? It is a thought that makes one feel sorry for the whole human race.'

'Well!' he blustered, 'since you are so damned sorry for the whole human race would you kindly tell me what I had best do now?'

'That is quite simple. You have only two alternatives. The first is to resign and return. You would have to accept a spot of demotion. But, never fear, we will find a cosy berth for you somewhere. A consulate in South America? In Africa? Say in Uganda? We won't let you starve. The other possibility you must surely have gathered from my letter. If you should still wish me to announce that we have been privately engaged for the past six months you can blow the whole business out like a candle. But you must decide at once so that I may ring up the Secretary, or the Minister, and a gossipy friend or two, and have it published in Monday's *Irish Times*, and break it gently to the poor slut upstairs, and drive her to the airport tomorrow. You could then break off our engagement at your convenience. Only, in that case, George, please do, I beg you, return my letter. It puts me so completely in your power as a woman.'

She knew that the flattery of that last bit would be irresistible.

'You mean ... I mean ... You mean you meant all that in your letter?'

'George! Do you not realize how attractive you are to women?'

He answered her without hesitation in the voice of a small boy saying, 'Mummy! May I go to the pictures?':—

'Miriam! Let us be married at once.'

'I hear her bath water running out. At once cannot be too soon, George. I must hurry. Get on a plane for Brussels *il più presto*. If you don't she will strip our flat naked and then set fire to it. Goodnight, darling. Ring me from Brussels.'

For a long time he looked with a dazed smile into the mouth of the receiver. He carried the same smile to his mirror. Attractive to women? Well! He brushed his greying wings, chucked his lapels, arranged his lolling peony handkerchief, smilingly went downstairs to dinner. What a woman! Such tact, ability, foresight! He would have ample time for dinner before catching the last plane for London. His concierge in Brussels would do the rest. Touching his empty *boutonnière* at the turn of the stairs his descent was halted by a memory: her story of the rash Egyptologist whose frail flower wilted at the sight of day.

She, hit at that precise moment by a memory of a different sort, hastily concluded a swift goodnight to her most gossipy gossip –

'Happy? I remember what happened to poor Pygmalion. He worked for years on a statue of the perfect woman and found himself left with a chatterbox of a wife. I think of all the years I have devoted to my chatterbox.' She laughed philosophically. 'Never mind. I am really very fond of poor old George. I always have been. And he needs me. I must fly. Tell the world!'

As she replaced the receiver she turned in her chair to watch the china handle of the door slowly turning. When it was thrown wide open her eyes stared at her dark visitor staring at her, wearing the long, soft, white, woollen shawl, interwoven with gold thread, always kept in tissue in her tallboy, the gold torque that had so diverted George, three bracelets from her dressing table on each scraggy arm, and a red rose in the black mat of her hair. For one statuesque second the door became a bevelled mirror asking, 'And who is who, now?' Then, resolutely conquering her weakness, she rose and advanced with her arms wide open.

'Virginia!'

They sat side by side on the cosy sofa beside the fire. There, speaking ever so gently, but firmly, she tenderly, gradually, almost absentmindedly, woman to woman, stripped her guest of her dreams and her plumes. From both a few tears, a shrug, a hug and, in three or four languages, 'Men!'

Falling Rocks, Narrowing Road, Cul-de-Sac, Stop

The day Morgan Myles arrived in L—— as the new county librarian he got a painful boil under his tongue. All that week he was too busy settling into his new quarters to do anything about it beyond dribbling over his mother's hand mirror into a mouth as pink and black as a hotel bathroom. Otherwise he kept working off the pain and discomfort of it in outbursts of temper with his assistant, Marianne Simcox, a frail, long-legged, neurotically efficient, gushingly idealistic, ladylike (that is to say, Protestant) young woman whom he hated and bullied from the first moment he met her. This, however, could have been because of his cautious fear of her virginal attractiveness.

On his fourth day in the job he was so rude to her that she turned on him, called him a Catholic cad, and fled sobbing behind the stacks. For fifteen minutes he went about his work humming with satisfaction at having broken her ladylike ways; but when she failed to come trotting to his next roar of command, he went tearing around the stacks in a fury looking for her. He was horrified to find her sitting on the floor of the Arts Section still crying into her mouse-sized handkerchief. With a groan of self-disgust he sat on the floor beside her, put his arm around her shoulder, rocked her as gently as if she was a kid of twelve, told her he was a bastard out of hell, that she was the most efficient assistant he had ever had in his life and that from this time on they would be doing marvellous things together with 'our library.' When she had calmed, she apologized for being so rude, and thanked him so formally, and so courteously, and in such a ladylike accent that he decided that she was a born bitch and went off home in a towering temper to his mother who, seeing the state her dear boy was in, said, 'Wisha, Morgan love, why don't you take that gumboil of yours to a doctor and show it to him. You're not your natural nice self at all. You're as cranky as a bag of cats with it.'

At the word 'doctor' Morgan went pale with fear, bared his teeth like a five-barred gate and snarled that he had no intention of going next nor nigh any doctor in this one-horse town. 'Anyway,' he roared, 'I hate all doctors. Without exception of age or sex. Cods and bluffers they are, the whole lot of them. And you know well that all any doctor ever wants to do with any patient is to take X-rays of his insides, order him into hospital, take the clothes down off of him, stick a syringe into his backside and before the poor fathead knows where he is there'll be half a dozen fellows in white nightshirts sawing away at him like a dead pig. It's just a gumboil. It doesn't bother me one bit. I've had dozens of them in my time. It's merely an Act of God. Like an earthquake, or a crick in the neck. It will pass.'

But it did not pass. It went on burning and smarting until one windy sunstruck afternoon in his second week when he was streeling miserably along the Dublin Road, about a mile beyond the town's last untidy lot, beside its last unfinished suburban terrace. About every ten minutes or so, the clouds opened and the sun flicked and vanished. He held the collar of his baggy, tweed overcoat humped about his neck. His tongue was trying to double back acrobatically to his uvula. Feeling as lost and forlorn as the grey heron he saw across the road standing by the edge of a wrinkled loch, he halted to compose. '*O long-legged bird by your ruffled lake/ Alone as I, as bleak of eye, opaque . . .*' As what? He unguardedly rubbed his under-tongue on a sharp tooth, cursed, the sun winked, and he was confronted by one of destiny's infinite options. It was his moment of strength, of romance, of glamour, of youth, of sunshine on a strange shore. A blink of sunlight fell on a brass plate fastened to the red-brick gate pillar beside him, DR FRANCIS BREEN.

The gate was lined with sheet metal. Right and left of it there was a high cutstone wall backing on a coppice of rain-black macrocarpa that extended over the grassgrown border of the road. The house was not visible. He squeaked the gate open, peered timidly up a short curved avenue at it, all in red brick, tall, turreted and baywindowed. An empty-looking conservatory hooped against one side of it (intended, presumably, for the cultivation of rare orchids). Along the other side, a long veranda (intended, doubtless, to shelter Doctor Francis Breen from Ireland's burning tropical sun). He opened his mouth wide as he gazed, probed with his finger for the sore spot, and found it.

It did not look like a house where anybody would start cutting anybody up. It did not look like a doctor's house at all. It looked more like a gentleman's residence. Although he did remember the American visitor to Dublin who said to him that every Irish surgery looked as if it had been furnished by Dr Watson for Sherlock Holmes. As he cautiously entered the avenue he observed that the gate bore a perpendicular column of five warning signs in blue lettering on white enamel. NO DOGS. NO CANVASSERS. NO HAWKERS. NO CIRCULARS. SHUT THE GATE. He advanced on the house, his fists clenched inside his overcoat pockets, his eyebrows lifted to indicate his contempt for all doctors. Twice on the way to the front door he paused, as if to admire the grounds, really to assure himself that no dog had failed to read the NO DOGS sign: a born cityman, he feared all living animals. He was very fond of them in poetry. He took the final step upward to the stained glass door, stretched out his index finger, to tip, to tempt, to test, to press the brass bellknob. (An enamel sign beneath it said, TRADESMEN TO THE REAR.) His mother had spoken of a deficiency. She had also mentioned pills. He would ask this sawbones for a pill, or for a soothing bottle. He would not remove his shirt for him. And he would positively refuse to let down his pants. 'Where,' he foresaw himself roaring, 'do you think I have this boil?'

A shadow appeared behind the door. He looked speculatively over his glasses at the servant who partly opened it. She was grey and settled, but not old, dressed in black bombazine, wearing a white starched apron with shoulder frills. When he asked for the doctor she immediately flung the door wide open as if she had been eagerly expecting him for years and years; then, limping eagerly ahead of him, dot and carry one down a softly upholstered corridor, she showed him into what she called 'the dachtar's sargery,' quacking all about 'what an ahful co-eld dayeh it iss Gad bliss itt' in what he had already scornfully come to recognize as the ducks' dialect of this sodden, mist-shotten dung-heap of the Shannon's delta.

Left to himself he had time only to be disturbed by the sight of one, two, three barometers side by side on the wall, and one, two, three, four clocks side by side on the mantelpiece; relieved by an opposite wall lined with books; and enchanted by a dozen daintily tinted lithographs of flying moths and half a dozen hanging glass cases displaying wide-winged butterflies pinned against blue skies, when the door was slammed open by a tall, straight, white-haired, handsome, military-looking man, his temper at boiling point, his voice of the barrack-square, the knuckles of his fist white on the doorknob as if he were as eager to throw out his visitor as his Bombazine had been to welcome him in. Morgan noted that his eyes were quiet as a novice of nuns, and that his words were as polite, and remembered hearing somewhere that when the Duke of Wellington gave his order for the final charge at Waterloo his words to his equerry had been, 'The Duke of Wellington presents his compliments to Field Marshal von Blücher and begs him to be so kind as to charge like blazes.'

'Well, sir?' the doctor was saying. 'Would you be so kind as to tell me what you mean by entering my house in this cavalier fashion? Are you an insurance salesman? Are you distributing circulars? Are you promoting the Encyclopaedia Britannica? Are you a hawker? A huckster? A Jehovah's Witness?'

At these words Morgan's eyes spread to the rims of his lake-size glasses. He felt a heavenly sunlight flooding the entire room. He raised two palms of exultant joy. More than any other gift of life, more than drink, food, girls, books, nicotine, coffee, music, more even than poetry and his old mother (whom he thought of, and saw through, as if she were a stained glass image of the Mother of God), he adored all cranks, fanatics, eccentrics and near-lunatics, always provided that they did not impinge on his personal comfort, in which case he would draw a line across them as fast as a butcher cuts off a chicken's head. More than any other human type he despised all men of good character, all solid citizens, all well-behaved social men, all mixers, joiners, hearty fellows and jolly good chaps, always provided that he did not require their assistance in his profession as librarian, in which case he would cajole them and lard them and lick them like a pander, while utterly despising himself, and his job, for having to tolerate such bores for one moment. But, here, before his eyes was a figure of purest gold. If there were any other such splendid crackpots in L—— then this was heaven, nor was he ever to be out of it.

'But,' he protested gaily, 'you are a doctor! I have a gumboil! We are the perfect match.'

The old man moaned as if he had been shot through by an arrow of pain.

'It is true that I am, by letters patent, a man licensed to practise the crude invention called medicine. But I have never practised, I have never desired to practise and I never do intend to practise medicine. I know very well, sir, what you want me to do. You want me to look down your throat with an electric torch and make some such solemn, stupid and meaningless remark as "You have a streptococcal infection." Well,' he protested, 'I will do nothing of the kind for you. Why should I? It might be only a symptom. Next week you might turn up with rheumatic heart disease, or a latent kidney disease, as people with strep throats have been known to do. You talk airily of a gumboil. You may well be living in a fool's paradise, sir. Even supposing I were to swab strep out of your throat and grow it on a culture medium, what would that tell me about the terrible, manifold, creeping, subtle, lethal disease-processes that may be going on at this moment in the recesses of your body as part of that strep infection, or set off by it? The only thing I, or any other doctor – bluffers and liars that we all are – could honestly say to you would be the usual evasion. "Gargle with this bottle three times a day and come back in a week." By which time Nature or God would have in any case cured you without our alleged assistance. I know the whole bag of tricks from the Hippocratic collection, the treatises of Galen and the Canon of Avicenna down. I suppose you imagine that I spent all my years in Dublin and Vienna studying medicine. I spent them studying medicos. I am a neurologist. Or I was a neurologist until I found that what true medicine means is true magic. Do you know how to remove a wart? You must wait on the roadway to the cemetery until a funeral passes, and say, "Corpse, corpse, take away my wart." And your wart will go, sir! That is true medicine. I believe in miracles because I have seen them happen. I believe in God, prayer, the imagination, the destiny of the Irish, our bottomless racial memory – and in nothing else.'

Morgan's left hand was circling his belly in search of manifold, creeping, secret diseases.

'But, surely to God, doctor,' he whined, 'medical science can do *something* for a gumboil?'

'Aha! I know what you're up to now. X-rays! That's the mumbo-jumbo every patient wants. And neither will I suggest, as you would probably like me to suggest, that you should go to hospital. All you would do there would be either to pass your infection to some other patient or pick up his infection from him. I will have nothing to do with you, sir. And please keep your distance. I don't want your beastly infection. If you want to mess about with your gumboil you will have to go to a doctor. If you wish me to pray for your gumboil I will pray for it. But I refuse to let you or anybody else turn me into the sort of mountebank who pretends he can cure any tradesman's sore toe or any clerk's carbuncle in one second with a stroke of his pen and a nostrum from the chemist's shop. Good afternoon to you, sir. You are now in the hands of God!'

Morgan, stung by arrogance and enraged by fear, roared back a line fit for his memoirs.

'And good afternoon to you, sir! From one who is neither clerk nor tradesman, higgler nor hawker, huckster nor hounddog but, by God's grace, a poet whose poems will live long after,' hand waving, 'your butterflies have been devoured by the jaws of your moths.'

The old man's rage vanished like a ghost at cockcrow. He closed the door gently behind him.

'A poet?' he asked quietly. 'Now, this is most interesting.' Courteously he indicated a chair. 'Won't you sit down? Your name is?'

'Morgan Myles,' Morgan Myles boomed as if he were a majordomo announcing Lord Byron.

'Mine is Francis Breen. Yours is more euphonious. I can see it already on your first book of verses. But a poet should have three names. Like American politicians. Percy Bysshe Shelley. George Gordon Byron. Thomas Stearns Eliot. William Butler Yeats. Ella Wheeler Wilcox. Richard Milhous Nixon. You have a second name? Taken at your Confirmation? Arthur? There we have it! *First Poems*. By Morgan Arthur Myles!'

Morgan, like most men who are adept at flattering others, could never resist flattery himself. He waggled his bottom like a dog. His grin was coy but cocksure. Three minutes later the doctor was tenderly parting his lips and illuminating the inside of his mouth. He extinguished the torch. He lifted his eyes and smiled into Morgan's.

'Well, Doc?' Morgan asked fearfully. 'What did you see there?'

'You are not even,' his new-found friend smiled, 'about to give birth to a couplet. Just a blister.' He sat to his desk. 'I will give you a prescription for a gargle. Rinse your mouth with this three times a day. And come back to me in a week. But if you wish to get better sooner come sooner, any evening for a drink and a chat. I have no friends in L——.'

'Nor have I!'

Within a week they were bosom cronies.

From start to finish it was a ridiculous friendship. Indeed, from that day onward, to the many of us who saw them every day after lunch walking along O'Connell Street arm in arm like father and son, or nose to nose like an ageing ward boss with a young disciple, it seemed an unnatural business. Can the east wind, we asked one another in wonder, lie down with the west wind? A cormorant mate with a herring? A heron with a hare? An end with a beginning? We gave their beautiful friendship three months. As a matter of fact we were only two years and eleven months out.

Even to look at they were a mismatch: the doctor straight and spare as a spear, radiating propriety from every spiky bone of his body, as short of step as a woman, and as carefully dressed from his wide-brimmed bowler hat to the rubber tip of his mottled, gold-headed malacca cane; the poet striding beside him, halting only to swirl his flabby tweeds; his splendid hydrocephalic head stretched behind his neck like a balloon; his myopic eyes glaring at the clouds over the roofs through the thick lenses of his glasses; a waterfall of black hair permanently frozen over his left eye; his big teeth laughing, his big voice booming, he looked for all the world like a peasant Yeats in a poor state of health. The only one of us who managed to produce any sort of explanation was our amateur psychiatrist, Father Tim Buckley, and we never took him seriously anyway. He said, with an episcopal *sprinkle me O Lord with hyssop* wave of his hand, 'They have invented one another.'

Now, we knew from experience that there was only one way to handle Tim Buckley. If he said some fellow was a homosexual because he had fallen in love with his hobbyhorse when he was five you had to say at once, 'But, Tim, why did he fall in love with his hobbyhorse when he was five?' If he said that it was because the poor chap hated his mother and loved his father you had to say, at once, 'But, Tim, why did he hate his ma and love his da?' If he then said that it was natural for every child to prefer one parent to another, you had to say at once, 'But, Tim, why . . .' And so on until he lost his temper and shut up. This time, however, he was ready for our counterattack.

'They have invented one another,' he said, 'for mutual support because they are both silently screaming for freedom. Now what is the form of slavery from which all human beings most want to be free?'

'Sex,' we conceded, to save time, knowing our man.

'Passion!' he amended. 'For this agony there are only three solutions. The first is sin, which,' he grinned, 'I am informed on the best authority is highly agreeable but involves an awful waste of time. I mean if you could hang a girl up in the closet every time you were finished with her that would be very convenient, but. Then there is marriage, which as

Shaw said is the perfect combination of maximum temptation and maximum opportunity. And there is celibacy of which, I can say with authority, as the only member of the present company who knows anything at all about it, that it bestows on man the qualified freedom of a besieged city where one sometimes has to eat rats. Of our two friendly friends the older man needs approval for his lifelong celibacy. The younger man needs encouragement to sustain his own. Or so they have chosen to imagine. In fact neither of them really believes in celibacy at all. Each has not only invented the other. He has invented himself.'

Our silence was prolonged.

'Very well,' he surrendered. 'In that case thicken your own plot!'

Of course, we who had known Frank Breen closely ever since we were kids together in L——, knew that there was nothing mysterious about him: he had simply always been a bit balmy, even as a four-eyed kid. When his parents sent him to school in England we saw much less of him; still less when he went to Dublin for his MB, and from there on to Austria for his MD. After he came back to L—— to settle down for life in the old Breen house on the Dublin Road on the death of his father, old Doctor Frank, and of his mother, we hardly saw him at all. We knew about him only by hearsay, chiefly through the gossip of his housekeeper, Dolly Lynch, passed on to Claire Coogan, Father Tim Buckley's housekeeper, and gleefully passed on by him to the whole town.

That was how the town first heard that the brass plate on his gate pillar – his father's, well polished by chamois and dulled by weather – would never again mean that there was a doctor behind it; about his four clocks and his three barometers; about his collection of moths and butterflies; about the rope ladder he had coiled in a red metal box under every bedroom window; about his bed always set two feet from the wall lest a bit of cornice should fall on his head during the night; about the way he looked under the stairs for hidden thieves every night before going to bed; that his gold-knobbed malacca cane contained a sword; that he never arrived at the railway station less than half an hour before his train left; that he hung his pyjamas on a clothes hanger; had handmade wooden trees for every pair of his handmade boots; that he liked to have his bootlaces washed and ironed; that his vest-pocket watch told the time, the date, the day, the year, the points of the

compass, and contained an alarm buzzer that he was always setting to
remind him of something important he wanted to do later on, but
whose nature he could never remember when the buzzer hummed over
his left gut – very much the way a wife will leave her wedding ring at
night on her dressing table to remind her in the morning of something
that by then she has incontinently forgotten.

So! A bit odd. Every club in the world must have elderly members like
him – intelligent and successful men of whose oddities the secretary
will know one, the headwaiter another, the bartender a third, their
fellow members smile at a fourth. It is only their families, or if they live
for a long time in a small town their townsfolk who will, between
them, know the lot. Frank Breen might have gone on in his harmless,
bumbling way to the end of his life if that brass plate of his had not
winked at Morgan Myles, and if Father Tim Buckley – was he jealous?
– had not decided to play God.

Not that we ever called him 'Father Tim Buckley.' He was too close to
us, too like one of ourselves for that. We called him Tim Buckley, or
Tim, or even if the whiskey was fluming, Bucky. He was not at all like
the usual Irish priest who is as warm as toast and as friendly and
understanding as a brother until you come to the sixth commandment,
and there is an end to him. Tim was like a man who had dropped off
an international plane at Shannon; not a Spencer Tracy priest from
downtown Manhattan, all cigar and white cuffs, parish computer and
portable typewriter, fists and feet, and there is the end to him; perhaps
more like an unfrocked priest from Bolivia or Brazil, so ungentlemanly
in his manners as to have given acute pain to an Evelyn Waugh and
so cheerful in spite of his scars as to have shocked a Graham Greene;
or still more like, among all other alternatives, a French workers' priest
from Liège; or in other words, as far as we were concerned, the right
man in the right place and as far as the bishop was concerned, a total
disaster. He was handsome, ruddy and full-blooded in a sensual way,
already so heavy in his middle thirties that he had the belly, the chins
and (when he lost his temper) something of the voracity of Rodin's
ferocious statue of Balzac in his dressing gown; but he was most himself
when his leaden-lidded eyes glistened with laughter, and his tiny
mouth, crushed between the peonies of his cheeks, reminded you of a
small boy whistling after his dog, or of some young fellow saucily

making a kiss-mouth across the street to his girl. His hobby was psychoanalysis.

His analysis of the doctor was characteristic. He first pointed out to us, over a glass of malt, the sexual significance of pocket watches, so often fondled and rubbed between the fingers. He merely shrugged at the idea of ladders unfolding from red containers, and said that swords being in sword sticks needed no comment. Clocks and barometers were merely extensions of pocket watches. (The wristwatch, he assured us, was one of the great sexual revolutions of our age – it brought everything out in the open.) But, above all, he begged us to give due attention to Frank Breen's mother complex – evident in his love of seclusion behind womblike walls, dark trees, a masked gate; and any man must have a terrible hate for his father who mockingly leaves his father's brass plate on a pillar outside his home while publicly refusing to follow his father's profession inside it. ('By the way, can we ignore that NO DOGS sign?') The looking for thieves under the stairs at night, he confessed, puzzled him for the moment. Early arrival for trains was an obvious sign of mental insecurity. 'Though, God knows,' laughing in his fat, 'any man who doesn't feel mentally insecure in the modern world must be out of his mind.' As for this beautiful friendship, that was a classical case of Narcissism: the older man in love with an image of his own lost and lonely youth.

'Any questions?'

No wonder he was the favourite confessor of all the nubile girls in town, not (or not only) because they thought him handsome but because he was always happy to give them the most disturbing explanations for their simplest misdemeanours. 'I kissed a boy at a dance, Father,' they would say to some other priest and, as he boredly bade them say three Hail Marys for their penance, they would hear the dark slide of the confessional move dismissively across their faces. Not so with Father Tim! He would lean his cheek against the grille and whisper, 'Now, my dear child, in itself a kiss is an innocent and beautiful act. Therefore the only reason prompting you to confess it as a sin must refer to the manner in which the kiss was given and the spirit in which it was received, and in this you may be very wise. Because, of course, when we say *kiss*, or *lips*, we may – one never knows for certain – be thinking of something quite different...' His penitents would leave his box with their faces glowing, and their eyes dazed. One said that he made her feel like a Magdalen with long floating hair.

Another said he made her want to go round L—— wearing a dark veil.
A third (who was certain to come to a bad end) said he had revealed
to her the *splendeurs et misères de l'amour*. And a fourth, clasping her
palms with delight, giggled that he was her Saint Rasputin.

We who met him in our homes, with a glass in his fist and his Roman
collar thrown aside, did not worry about what he told our daughters.
We had long since accepted him as an honest, innocent, unworldly
man who seemed to know a lot about sex-in-the-head – and was always
very entertaining about it – but who knew sweet damn all about
love-in-the-bed, not to mention love at about eleven o'clock at night
when your five kids are asleep and the two of you are so edgy from
adding up the household accounts that by the time you have decided
once again that the case is hopeless all 'to go to bed' means is to go
sound asleep. But we did worry about him. He was so outspoken, so
trustful of every stranger, had as little guard over his tongue as a sailor
ashore, that we could foresee the day when his bishop would become
so sick of getting anonymous letters about him that he would shanghai
him to some remote punishment-curacy on the backside of Slievenamuck.

We would try to frighten him into caution by telling him that he
would end up there, exiled to some spot so insignificant that it would
not be marked even on one of those nostalgic one-inch-to-the-mile
British Ordnance maps of 1899 that still – indifferent to the effects of
time and history, of gunshot and revolution – record every burned out
constabulary barracks, destroyed mansion, abandoned branch-rail-
way, eighteenth century 'inn,' disused blacksmith's hovel, silenced
windmill, rook-echoing granary or 'R.C. Chapel,' where, we would tell
him, is where our brave Bucky would then be, in a baldface presbytery,
altitude 1750 feet, serving a cement-faced chapel, beside an anonymous
crossroads, without a tree in sight for ten miles, stuck for life as curator,
nurse and slave of some senile parish priest. He would just raise his
voice to spit scorn at us; like the night he gobbled us up in a rage:—

'And,' he roared, 'if I can't say what I think how the hell am I going
to live? Am I free or am I not free? Am I to lie down in the dust and
be gagged and handcuffed like a slave? Do ye want me to spend my
whole life watching out for traffic signs? Falling rocks! Narrowing Road!
Cul-de-sac! Stop! My God, are ye men or are ye mice?'

'Mice!' we roared back with one jovial voice and dispelled the tension
in laughter so loud that my wife looked up in fright at the ceiling and

said, 'Sssh! Ye bastards! If ye wake the kids I'll make every one of ye walk the floor with them in yeer arms till three in the morning. Or do ye think ye're starting another revolution in yeer old age?'

'We could do worse,' Tim smiled into his double chin.

Whenever he smiled like that you could see the traffic signs lying right and left of him like idols overthrown.

It was a Sunday afternoon in May. The little island was deserted. He was lying on the sunwarmed grass between the other two, all three on their backs, in a row, their hats on their faces. They were neither asleep nor awake. They were breathing as softly as the lake at their feet. They had driven at their ease that morning to the east side of the lake past the small village of Mountshannon, now looking even smaller across the level water, rowed to the island (Tim Buckley at the oars), delighted to find every hillocky green horizon slowly bubbling with cumulus clouds. They had inspected the island's three ruined churches, knee-deep in nettles and fern, and its tenth-century Round Tower that had stood against the morning sun as dark as a factory chimney. They had photographed the ruins, and one another, and then sat near the lake and the boat to discuss the excellent lunch that Dolly Lynch always prepared for 'the young maaaster' on these Sunday outings: her cold chicken and salad, her handmade mayonnaise, her own brown bread and butter, the bottle of Liebfraumilch that Frank had hung by a string in the lake to cool while they explored the island, her double roasted French coffee, flavoured, the way the maaaster always liked it, with chicory and a suspicion of cognac. It was half an hour since they had lain back to sleep. So far everything about the outing had been perfect. No wonder Morgan had jackknifed out of bed that morning at eight o'clock, and Frank Breen wakened with a smile of special satisfaction.

Before Morgan came, exactly two years and eleven months ago, it had been the doctor's custom, at the first call of the cuckoo, to take off now and again (though never too often to establish a precedent), on especially fine Sundays like this, with Father Timothy Buckley in Father Timothy's roomy secondhand Peugeot – Frank did not drive – in search of moths and butterflies, or to inspect the last four walls, perhaps the last three walls, of some eighth-century Hiberno-Romanesque churchlet, or the rotting molar of some Norman castle smelling of cow dung, purple mallow, meadowsweet and the wood-

smoke of the last tinkers who had camped there. After Morgan came
he had begun to drive off every fine Sunday with Morgan in Morgan's
little Ford Prefect. Still, *noblesse oblige*, and also if the journey
promised to be a rather long one, he had about twice a year suggested
to Morgan that they might invite Father Timothy to join them; and
Tim had always come, observing with amusement that they indulgently allowed him to bring his own car, and that they would, after
loud protestations, allow him to do all the driving, and that he also had
to persuade them forcibly to allow him to pack the luggage on the seat
beside him, so as to leave plenty of room – at this point they would all
three laugh with the frankest irony – for their lordships' bottoms in the
soft and roomy rear of the Peugeot. This luggage consisted of Frank's
two butterfly nets, in case one broke, three binoculars and three
cameras, one for each, two umbrellas for himself and Morgan, the
bulging lunch basket for them all, two foam-rubber cushions, one for
his poor old back, one for Morgan's poor young back, and a
leather-backed carriage rug so that the dear boy should not feel the cold
of the grass going up through him while he was eating his lunch and
enjoying – as he was now enjoying – his afternoon siesta.

Retired, each one, into his own secret shell of sleep, they all three
looked as dead as they would look in fifteen years' time in one of the
photographs they had just taken of themselves. The day had stopped.
The film of the climbing towers of clouds had stopped. The lake was
silent. The few birds and the three cows they had seen on the island
were dozing. Thinking had stopped. Their three egos had stopped. Folk
tales say that when a man is asleep on the grass like that, a tiny lizard
may creep into his mouth, devour his tongue and usurp its power. After
about an hour of silence and dozing some such lizard spoke from the
priest's mouth. Afterwards he said that he had been dreaming of the
island's hermits, and of what he called the shortitude and latitude of
life, and of how soon it stops, and that those two selfish bastards beside
him were egotistical sinners, too concerned with their comfort as
adolescents to assert their dignity as men. 'And I?' he thought with a
start, and woke.

'In Dublin last month,' his lizard said hollowly into his hat, 'I saw
a girl on a horse on a concrete street.'

'What?' Morgan asked drowsily, without stirring.

'A girl on a horse,' Tim said, removing his hat, and beholding the
glorious blue sky. 'It was the most pathetic sight I ever saw.'

'Why pathetic?' Morgan asked, removing his hat and seeing the blue Pacific sweep into his ken.

'She was riding on a concrete street, dressed as if she was riding to hounds. The fantasy of it was pathetic. Miles away from green fields. But all the girls are gone mad on horses nowadays. I wish somebody would tell them that all they're doing is giving the world a beautiful example of sexual transference. They have simply transferred their natural desire for a man to a four-legged brute.'

'Balderdash,' said Morgan, and put back his hat as Frank patiently lifted his to ask the blueness what all the poor girls who haven't got horses do to inform the public of their adolescent desires.

'They have cars,' Tim said, and sat up slowly, the better to do battle. Morgan sat up abruptly.

'So,' he demanded, 'every time I drive a car I become a homosexual?'

Tim considered the matter judicially.

'Possibly,' he agreed. 'But not necessarily. There are male cars for women, and female cars for men. For women? Clubman, Escort, Rover, Consort, Jaguar, Triumph. Fill 'em up and drive them at seventy miles an hour! What fun! For men? Giulietta. Whose Romeo? Morris Minor. The word means moor – symbolical desire for a small negress. Mercedes? Actually that is Mrs Benz's name. Also means Our Lady of Mercy. Symbolical desire for a large virgin. Ford Consul? Consuela, Our Lady of Consolations. Volvo? Vulva. Volkswagen. Double V. Symbolical...'

'Well of all the filthy minds!' Morgan roared.

The doctor sat up with a sigh. His siesta was ruined. His anger was hot upon his humour and his honour.

'I do think, Father Timothy, that you, as a priest of God...'

Tim scrambled to his feet, high above him, black as a winetun against the pale sheen of the lake.

'A priest, a presbyter, an elder, a sheikh, an old man, a minister, a pastor of sheep? What does that mean? Something superior, elegant, stainless and remote from life like yourself and Master Poet here? An angel, a seraph, a saint, a mystic, a eunuch, a cherubim, a morning star? Do I look like it? Or like a man fat from eating too much, wheezy from smoking too much, sick and tired from trying to do the job he was called on to do? A priest of God is a man with a bum and a belly, and everything that hangs out of a belly or cleaves it, with the same appetites and desires, thirsts and hungers as the men and women, the boys and the girls he lives and works with. It may be very nice for you to look at us before the altar in Saint Jude's all dressed up in our golden robes, swinging a censer, and to think, "There is heavenly power, there is magic." But I have no power. I'm nothing alone. I merely pretend to a power that is an eternity beyond me. When I was in Rome, as a student, a priest in Southern Italy went mad, ran down to the bakery to turn the whole night's baking into the body of God, and from there to the wine factory to turn every flask and vat of flowing wine into the blood of the Lord. But did he? Of course not. Alone he hadn't the power to make a leaf of basil grow. But I will pretend to any boy or girl who is troubled or in misery that I have all the power in heaven to cure them, do mumbo-jumbo, wave hands, say hocus pocus, anything if it will only give them peace. And if that doesn't work I tell them the truth.'

'You are shouting, Father,' Doctor Frank said coldly.

Tim controlled himself. He sat down again. He laughed.

'Ye don't want to hear the truth. Too busy romanticizing, repressing, rationalizing, running away, when everybody knows the pair of ye think of nothing but women from morning to night! Your moths, Frank, that come out in the twilight, your easy girls, your lights o' love, fluttering against your windowpanes? Do you want me to believe that you never wish you could open the window to let one in? I saw you, Morgan, the other day in the library fawning over that unfortunate virgin Simcox, and a child could see what was in the minds of the pair of ye. And what do you think she thinks she's doing every time she goes out to the yard to wash the backside of your car with suds and water? Why don't you be a man, Morgan, and face up to it – one day you'll have to be spliced. It's the common fate of all mankind.'

'It hasn't been yours, Father,' Frank snapped.

'Because I took a vow and kept to it, logically.'

'Pfoo!' Morgan snarled at him. 'You know damned well that logic has as much to do with marriage as it has with music.'

Tim looked at him with the air of a small boy who is thinking what fun it would be to shove his Auntie Kitty down the farmyard well.

'You know,' he said slyly, 'you should ask Fräulein Keel about that the next time she is playing the Appassionata for you,' and was delighted to observe the slow blush that climbed up Morgan's face and the black frown that drew down the doctor's eyebrows. The silence of his companions hummed. He leaned back.

It was about two months ago since Frau Keel had come to L—— with her daughter Imogen and her husband Georg, an electrical engineer in charge of a new German factory at the Shannon Free Airport complex. He was about fifty and a Roman Catholic, which was presumably why he had been chosen for this Irish job. His wife was much younger; blonde, handsome, curlyheaded, well-corseted, with long-lashed eyes like a cow. Hera-eyed, Morgan said; dopey, Frank said; false lashes, Tim Buckley said. She was broad of bosom and bottom, strong-legged as a peasant and as heavy-shouldered, one of those abundant, self-indulgent, flesh-folding bodies that Rubens so loved to paint in their pink skin. Imogen was quite different; small, black-avised, black-haired, her skin like a bit of burned cork. She was a *belle laide* of such intensity, so packed and powerful with femininity that you felt that if you were to touch her with one finger she would hoop her back and spring her arms around you like a trap. Morgan had met her in the library, let her talk about music, found himself invited by her mother to hear her play, and unwisely boasted about it to Tim Buckley.

In the sullen silence he heard the lake sucking the stones of the beach. The clouds were less bright. The doctor said primly that he wanted to try his hand with his butterfly net. Morgan said gruffly that he wanted to take some more pictures before the sun went down. Together they walked away across the island. Tim reached for his breviary and began to read the office of the day. 'Let us then be like newborn children hungry for the fresh milk...'

The delicate India paper of his breviary whispered each time he turned a page. Presently a drop of rain splashed on his knuckles. He looked about him. The sun still touched the island but nowhere else. The lake hissed at the shore. He stood on a rock but could see no sign of his companions. Were they colloguing with the seventh century? He packed the lunch basket, rolled up the rugs, loaded the cargo, sat in the stern of the boat, opened an umbrella, lit his pipe and waited. He was sick of them. No doubt when slaves fall in love they feel more free...

They returned slowly and silently. Little was said as he rowed them to the mainland, and less on the way back to L—— because the rain became a cloudburst, and he was alone peering into it. On previous excursions he had always been invited to dine with them. He knew he would not be this evening: a snub that Morgan aggravated by assuring

him that they must all meet soon again 'on a more propitious occasion.'
He gave them a cheerful goodbye and drove off along the rain-dancing
asphalt. To the devil with their four-course dinner. His freedom was
more important to him. Anyway there were a dozen houses in town
where the wife would be delighted to give him a plate of bacon and
eggs.

Frank said nothing until he had poured their usual aperitif – a stout
dollop of malt.

'That,' he said as he handed the glass of whiskey to Morgan deep in
the best armchair on the side of the turf fire, 'is probably the last time
we shall meet his reverence socially.'

Morgan looked portentously over his glasses at the fire.

'A terrible feeling sometimes assails me,' he said, smacking each
sibilant, 'that Timothy John Buckley has a coarse streak in him.'

Frank took the opposite armchair.

'I would call it a grave lack of tact. Even presuming that La Keel has
not already told him that she is a patient of mine.'

'Imogen?' said Morgan, sitting straight up. 'Good God! Is there
something wrong with her?'

'Imogen? Oh, you mean the child? I was referring to the mother.'

Morgan sat back.

'Oh, and what's wrong with that old battle-axe? Are you beginning
to take patients?'

Frank frowned.

'I have done my best to avoid it. The lady, and her husband, ever
since they heard that I studied neurology in Vienna, have been very
persistent. As for what is wrong, I should not, ethically speaking as a
doctor, discuss the affairs of any patient but, in this case, I think I may
safely speak to you about the matter. Aye. Because I can trust you. And
Bee. Because there is nothing whatsoever wrong with the lady.'

'Then why did she come to consult you?'

Frank answered this one even more stiffly.

'She speaks of her cycles.'

Morgan, like an old lady crossing a muddy road, ventured between
the pools of his inborn prudishness, his poetic fastidiousness and his
natural curiosity:—

'Do you by any chance mean she has some sort of what they call
woman trouble?'

'If you mean the menopause, Madame Keel is much too young for that. She means emotional cycles. Elation-depression. Vitality-debility. Exultation-despair. The usual manic-depressive syndrome. She says that ever since she came to Ireland she has been melancholy.'

'Jaysus! Sure, aren't we all melancholy in Ireland? What I'd say that one needs is a few good balls of malt every day or a dose or two of cod liver oil. If I were you, Frank, I'd pack her off about her business.'

The doctor's body stirred restively.

'I have made several efforts to detach myself. She insists that I give her comfort.'

Morgan looked over his glasses at his friend.

'And what kind of comfort would that be?' he asked cautiously.

'That,' his friend said, a trifle smugly, 'is scarcely for me to say.'

Morgan glared into his glass. For a moment he wished Bucky was there to crash through the ROAD NARROWS sign, the CUL-DE-SAC, the FALLING ROCKS.

'It is a compliment to you,' he said soapily.

'I take small pride in it, Morgan. Especially since she tells me that she also gets great comfort from her pastor.'

Morgan rose to his feet, dark as a thundercloud, or as a Jove who had not shaved for a week.

'What pastor?' he demanded in his deepest basso.

'You have guessed it. Our companion of today. The Reverend Timothy Buckley. He also gives great comfort to Herr Keel. And to the girl. He holds sessions.'

Jehovah's thunder-rumble rolled.

'Sessions?'

'It is apparently the latest American-Dutch ecumenical idea. Group confessions.'

'The man,' Morgan boomed, 'must be mad! He is worse than mad. Who was it called him Rasputin? He was born to be hanged! Or shot! Or poisoned! That man is e-e-e-evil. Frank! You must stop this monstrous folly at once. Think of the effect on that innocent poor child.'

'I have no intention whatsoever of interfering,' Frank fluttered. 'It's a family affair. I have no least right to interfere. And I suspect she is not in the least innocent. And she is not a child. She is eighteen.'

'Frank!' Morgan roared. 'Have you NO principles?'

A mistake. It is not a nice question to be asked by anybody. Suppose

Morgan had been asked by somebody if he had any principles himself! How does any of us know what his principles are? Nobody wants to have to start outlining his principles at a word of command.

'I begin to fear,' Frank said huffily, 'that in all this you are not thinking of me, nor of Frau Keel, nor of Herr Keel, nor of my principles, nor of any principles whatever but solely of the sexual attractions of Fräulein Keel. She has hairy legs. A well-known sign of potency.'

At which moment of dead silence Dolly Lynch opened the door, put in her flushed face and in her slow, flat, obsequious Shannon voice, said, 'Dinner is i-now-eh sarvedeh, Dachtar.' Her employer glared at her. Why was she looking so flushed? The foul creature had probably been outside the door for the last three minutes listening to the rising voices. By tomorrow the thing would be all over the town.

They entered the dining room in silence. She served them in silence. When she went out they maintained silence, or said small polite things like, 'This spring lamb is very tender,' or 'Forced rhubarb?' The silences were so heavy that Morgan felt obliged to retail the entire life of Monteverdi. Immediately after the coffee, in the drawing room, he said he had better go home to his mother, and, with fulsome thanks for a splendid lunch and a marvellous dinner, he left his friend to his pipe and, if he had any, his principles.

Morgan did not drive directly to his cottage on the Ennis Road. He drove to the library, extracted from the music section a biography of Monteverdi and drove to the Keels' flat in O'Connell Square. It was Frau Keel, majestic as Brünnhilde, who opened the door, received the book as if it were a ticket of admission and invited him to come in. To his annoyance he found Buckley half-filling a settee, winking cheerfully at him, smoking a cigar, a coffee in his paw, a large brandy on a small table beside him. Herr Keel sat beside him, enjoying the same pleasures. Through the dining room door he caught a glimpse of Imogen with her back to him, clearing the dinner table, her oily black hair coiled as usual on either side of her cheeks. As she leaned over the table he saw the dimpled backs of her knees. She was not wearing stockings. The dark down on her legs suggested the untamed forests of the north.

'Aha!' Herr Keel cried, in (for so ponderous a man) his always surprising countertenor. 'It is Mister Myles. You are most welcome.

May I offer you a coffee and a good German cigar? We had just begun a most interesting session.'

Morgan beamed and bowed ingratiatingly. He almost clicked his heels in his desire to show his pleasure and to conceal the frightening thought: – 'Is this one of Bucky's sessions?' He beamed as he received the cigar and a brandy from Herr Keel, who bowed in return. He bowed as he accepted a coffee from Frau Keel who beamed in return before she went back to her own place on a small sofa of the sort that the French – so he found out next day from a History of Furniture – call a *canapé*, where she was presently joined by Imogen. Thereafter he found that whenever he glanced (shyly) at Frau Keel she was staring anxiously and intently at Buckley, and whenever he glanced (shyly) at Imogen she was looking at himself with a tiny smile of what, crestfallen, he took to be amusement until she raised her hairy eyebrows and slowly shook her midnight head, and he heard a beautiful noise like a bomb exploding inside his chest at the thought that this black sprite was either giving him sympathy or asking sympathy from him. Either would be delightful. But, then, her eyebrows suddenly plunged, she shook her head threateningly, her smile curled, anger and disapproval sullied her already dark eyes.

'As I was saying,' Father Tim was saying, magisterially waving his cigar, 'if adultery is both a positive fact and a relative term, so is marriage. After all, marriage is much more than what The Master of the Sentences called a *conjunctio viri et mulieris*. It is also a union of sympathy and interest, heart and soul. Without these marriage becomes licensed adultery.'

'I agree,' Frau Keel sighed. 'But no woman ever got a divorce for that reason.'

Buckley pursed his little mouth into a provocative smile. 'In fact people do divorce for that very reason. Only they call it mental cruelty.'

'Alas,' said Brünnhilde, 'according to our church, there is no such sin as mental cruelty and therefore there is no divorce.'

'There are papal annulments,' Herr Keel said to her coldly, 'if you are interested in such things.'

'I am very interested,' she said to him as frigidly, which was not the kind of warm domestic conversation that Morgan had read about in books.

'You were about to tell us, Father Tim,' Imogen said, 'what you consider unarguable grounds for the annulment of a marriage.'

Sickeningly Buckley beamed at the girl; fawningly she beamed back. *She!* The Hyrcanian tigress! Had this obese sensualist mesmerized the whole lot of them? But he could not, as Buckley calmly began to enumerate the impediments to true wedlock, centre his mind on what was being said, so dumbfounded was he to find that nobody but himself seemed to be forming images of the hideous realities of what he now heard. All he could do was to gulp his brandy, as any man of the world might in such circumstances, and struggle to keep his eyes from Imogen's hirsute legs. (Where had he read that Charles XII had a woman in his army whose beard was two feet long?)

'It is not,' Buckley said, 'a true marriage if it has been preceded by rape. It is not a true marriage if either or both parties are certifiable lunatics. It is not,' here he glanced at Keel, 'a genuine marriage if the father marries the daughter,' smiling at Imogen, 'or if the sister marries the brother. It is not marriage if by error either party marries the wrong person, which can happen when a number of people are being married simultaneously. If either party has previously murdered the wife or husband of the other party it is not really a very good marriage. Nor if either party persuades the other party into adultery beforehand by a promise of marriage afterwards. It is not marriage if the male party is impotent both antecedently and perpetually. Nor if a Christian marries a Jew or other heathen . . .'

At which point they all started talking together, Imogen declaring passionately, 'I would marry a Jew if I damn well wanted to,' and Georg Keel demanding, 'How can you prove impotency?', and Frau Keel protesting with ringed fingers, 'Kein Juden! Kein Juden!', Buckley laughingly crying out, 'I agree, I agree,' and Morgan wailing that it was all bureaucratic balderdash, all quashed suddenly into silence by the prolonged ringing of the doorbell. Keel glanced at his watch and said testily, 'Who on earth . . .?' Imogen, unwilling to lose a fraction of the fight, rushed to the door and led in the latecomer. It was the doctor.

Morgan had to admire his comportment. Though he must have been much taken aback to see all his problems personified before him, the old boy did not falter for a moment in his poise and manners. He formally apologized for his late call to Frau Keel, who revealed her delight in his visit by swiftly patting her hair as she passed a mirror, making him sit beside her, fluttering to Imogen to sit beside Morgan, and yielding him a brandy glass between her palms as if it were a chalice. He accepted it graciously, he did not allow it to pass over him, he bowed like a cardinal, he relaxed into the company, legs crossed, as easily as if he were the host and they his guests. Morgan observed that the cuffs of his trousers were wet. He had walked here in the rain. He must be feeling greatly upset.

'Are you a friend of this dirty old doctor?' Imogen whispered rapidly to Morgan.

'I know him slightly. I like you very much, Imogen.'

'He is a vurm!' she whispered balefully. 'You are another vurm. You both turned Father Tim from the door without a meal.'

'Neither,' said Tim, resuming control, 'is it a marriage if it is clandestine, that is, performed secretly.'

'I would marry in secret if I wanted to,' like a shot from Imogen.

'It wasn't my house,' Morgan whispered. 'I wanted him to stay.'

'What does "secret" mean?' Keel asked petulantly.

'I know you lie,' she whispered.

'It means failing to inform your parish priest.'

'That's more bureaucratic fiddlesticks!' Morgan said, and an electric shock ran up his thigh when Imogen patted it approvingly.

'So,' Tim said dryly to him, 'the Empress Josephine thought; but her failure to obey the regulation meant that the Pope was able to allow the Emperor to eject her from his bed and marry again.'

'Then,' Keel agreed, 'it is a wise precaution.'

'It's bosh!' Morgan declared. 'And cruel bosh.'

'Good man!' said Imogen, and gave him another shock, while Frau Keel turned inquiringly to her pastor who said that the rule might be useful to prevent bigamy but was really no reason for dissolving a marriage, whereat she said, 'Then it is bosh!' and her husband, outraged, proclaimed, 'In my house I will allow nobody to say I am defending bosh!'

She waved him aside, clasped her paws, beamed at Father Timothy and cried, 'And now, for adultery!'

'Alas, Madame, adultery by either party is not sufficient cause to annul a marriage.'

'So we women are trapped!'

'While you men,' charged Imogen, glaring around her, 'can freely go your adulterous ways.'

The doctor intervened mildly.

'Happily none of this concerns anybody in this room.'

'How do you know what concerns me?' she challenged, jumping to her feet, her gripped fists by her lean flanks, her prowlike nose pointing about her like a setter. 'I, Imogen Keel, now, at this moment, vant to commit adultery with somebody in this room.'

Morgan covered his face in his hands. O God! The confessions! She means me. What shall I say? That I want to kiss her knees?

'Imogen!' Keel blazed at her. 'I will not permit this. In delicacy! Not to say, in politeness!'

'Please, Georg!' his wife screamed. 'Not again!' She turned to the company. 'Always I hear this appeal to politeness and delicacy. It is an excuse. It is an evasion. It is an alibi.'

'Aha!' Imogen proclaimed, one hand throwing towards her father's throat an imaginary flag or dagger. 'But he has always been excellent at alibis.'

Keel slammed his empty brandy glass on the coffee table so hard that its stem snapped. 'How fiery she is!' Morgan thought. What a heroic way she has of rearing her head back to the left and lifting her opposite eyebrow to the right. A girl like that would fight for her man to her death – or, if he betrayed her, to his. Has she, he wondered, hair on her back? Father Tim, amused by the whole scene, was saying tactfully but teasingly, 'Imogen, there is one other injustice to women that you must hear about. It is that you will in most countries not be permitted to marry, no matter how much you protest, until you have arrived at the age of twelve and your beloved at the age of fourteen.'

She burst into laughter. They all laughed with relief.

'Finally,' he said tristfully, 'priests may not marry at all.'

'They are nevertheless doing so,' the girl commented pertly.

He looked at her, seemed to consider saying something, drank the last drop of his coffee, and did not say it. Frau Keel said it for him, compassionately.

'Only by giving up their priesthood.'

'Or more,' he agreed in a subdued voice.

'The whole caboodle,' Imogen mocked.

They talked a little about current examples of priests who had given up everything. The subject trailed away. Keel looked at the window. 'Rain,' he sighed, in so weary a voice that the doctor at once rose, and all the others with him. As the group dissolved towards the entrance hall of the apartment Morgan found himself trailing behind with Imogen.

'What have you against the doctor?' he asked her.

'He is just like my father. And I hate my father. The only good thing I say about your doctor is that he helps my mother to put up with my father.'

He must drive old Frank home – he must go on helping Frau Keel; they must talk about the best way to handle Buckley in future; they must have Georg Keel on one of their excursions; if the girl was lonely perhaps Keel would like to bring her with them. She was a superb, a wonderful, a marvellous girl, so heroic, so wild, so passionate. The very first thing they must do was to have Buckley to dinner, and maybe Buckley would bring the girl with him . . . Just then he heard Frank ask Keel if it was too late for them to have a brief word together before he left. If this meant the old fool was falling back on some ridiculous, bloody point of principle about treating Frau Keel . . . As he was making his way towards his friend to offer him a lift home Frau Keel absently shook his hand, handed him his hat, opened the door, bade him good night and the door closed on her voice suggesting to Imogen to drive the good Father to his presbytery in her little car. A minute later he was in the street cursing.

There was not a soul in sight. The rain hung like vests around the lamplights of O'Connell Street. When his car refused to start his rage boiled against that stupid cow Marianne Simcox who must have let water (or something) get into the petrol. After many fruitless zizzings from the starter he saw Imogen's little blue car with the priest aboard shoot past in a wake of spray. More zizzings, more pulling at the choke, a long rest to deflood the carburettor and the engine roared into life, just as Keel's Mercedes, with the doc aboard, vanished through the rain towards the bridge and the Dublin road. He circled wildly, followed their taillights, halted twenty yards behind them outside Frank's house, dowsed his lights, saw him get out and Keel drive away. He ran forward to where Frank was unlocking his iron gate, and clutched his arm beseechingly.

'Frank! I simply must talk to you about Buckley. What is he doing to all those people? What is he doing to that Imogen girl? For God's sake what's going on in that Keel family? I won't sleep a wink unless you tell me all you know about them.'

The doctor marvelled at him for a moment and then returned to his unlocking.

'I do not feel disposed,' he said in his haughtiest voice, holding the gate six inches ajar for the length of his reply, 'to discuss such matters at twelve o'clock at night, on an open road, under a downpour of rain, and all the less so since, so far as I can see, nothing is, as you so peculiarly put it, "going on" that is of any interest to me. Everything seems perfectly normal and in order in the Keel family, except that Herr Keel is a total idiot who seems unable to control his wife, that she seems to me to have developed a most unseemly sexual interest in Father Timothy Buckley, that she is intent on divorcing her husband, that their daughter, who is both impertinent and feckless, is a nympho-maniac, who has quite obviously decided to seduce you, and that I am very glad to say that I need never again lay eyes on them for the rest of my natural life. And, now, sir, goodnight to you.'

With which he entered his drive, banged the metalled gate behind him, and his wet footsteps died into a voice from his front door wailing, 'Oh, dachtar, dachtar! Wait for me! I have the umberella here for you. You'll be dhrowneded all together with that aaahful rain . . .'

Morgan spat on the gate, turned and raced for his car, which resolutely refused to start. He implored it until its exhausted starter died into the silence of a final click. He got out, kicked its door soundly, and then overwhelmed by all the revelations he had just heard, especially the one about Imogen and himself, he walked home through the empty streets of L——, singing love songs from the *Barber* and *Don Giovanni* at the top of his voice to the summer rain.

One of the more pleasantly disconcerting things about wilful man is that his most table-thumping decisions rarely conclude the matter in hand. There is always time for a further option. Every score is no better than half-time. *Viz:*—

1. That July our poor, dear friend Tim Buckley left us for a chin-pimple of a village called Four Noughts (the vulgarization of a Gaelic word meaning Stark Naked) on the backside of Slievenamuck. We loyally cursed His Lordship the bishop, while feeling that he had had no option. For weeks the dogs in the streets had been barking, 'Im-o-gen Keel.' At the farewell party Tim assured us that the bish had neither hand, act nor part in it. He had himself asked His Lordship for a transfer. He asked us to pray for him. He said sadly that he believed

he was gone beyond it. The die was cast, the Rubicon crossed, it was the Ides of March, and so forth and so on.

One effect of this event (Dolly Lynch reporting, after her usual survey of her master's wastepaper basket) was that Mister Myles had been invited to dinner with the dachtar at his earliest convenience.

2. That August we heard that Frau Keel was claiming a separation from her husband *a mensa et a thoro;* that she was also applying for a papal annulment of her marriage on the ground of his impotence, which meant that she was ready to swear that Imogen was not his child. Herr Keel, we gathered, had knocked her down, broken one of her ribs with a kick and left for Stuttgart swearing that he would foil her if it cost him his last deutschmark.

Mister Myles was by now dining every week with the doctor, who was also (Dolly Lynch's knuckle suspended outside the dining room door) seeing Frau Keel regularly, who (Dolly Lynch's hand on the doorknob) was also in constant consultation, through Imogen, with Father Tim Buckley in his exile on Slievenamuck.

3. That September Tim Buckley disappeared from Four Noughts, Imogen Keel disappeared from the Keel flat, and both were reported to have been seen at Shannon Airport boarding a plane for Stockholm. This blow brought us down. Tim's way of living life had been to tell us how to live it. Now that he was starting to live it himself he was no better than any of us. He was the only one of us who had both faced and been free of the world of men, of women, of children, of the flesh. Now we knew that it cannot be done. You must not put your toe into the sea if you do not want to swim in it.

Myles was by now dining with Frank Breen three times a week, friendship glued by gossip.

4. October. Dreadful news from Stuttgart. Herr Keel had accidentally killed himself while cleaning a shotgun. When the news came Morgan was having tea with Frau Keel. She collapsed, calling for the doctor. Morgan drove at once to Frank's house and brought him back to her. For the rest of that month Myles was dining every night with the doctor.

5. By November Dolly Lynch reported that Mister Myles had stopped dining with the doctor, but Mrs Keel, she spat, was coming as often as 'tree taimes every bluddy wee-uk.' When we heard this we looked at one another. Our eyes said, 'Could it be possible?' We asked Morgan. He was in no doubt about it.

'Buckley was right!' he stormed. 'The man is a sexual maniac! A libertine! A corrupter of women! A traitor and a liar. As that foolish woman will discover before the year is out.'

It was a spring wedding, and the reception was one of the gayest, most crowded, most lavish the town had ever seen. The metal sheeting was gone from the gate, the cypresses cut down, the warning signs inside the gate removed, the brass plate removed, the conservatory packed with flowers, the only drink served was champagne. The doctor became Frank to every Tom and Harry. For the first time we found out that his wife's name was Victorine. With his hair tinted he looked ten years younger. Long before the reception ended he was going around whispering to everybody, as a dead secret, that Victorine was expecting.

6. Morgan, naturally, did not attend the wedding. He took off for the day with Marianne Simcox, and they have since been taking off every fine Sunday in her red Mustang, together with Morgan's mother, in search of faceless churchlets in fallow fields where the only sound is the munching of cattle. His mother prepares the lunch. Marianne reads out his own poems to him. They both feed him like a child with titbits from their fingers. But who knows the outcome of any mortal thing? Buckley – there is no denying it – had a point when he insisted that man's most ingenious invention is man, that to create others we must first imagine ourselves, and that to keep us from wandering, or wondering, in some other direction where a greater truth may lie, we set up all sorts of roadblocks and traffic signals. Morgan has told his Marianne that he has always admired the virginal type. It is enough to put any girl off her stroke. A wink of a brass plate in a country road set him off on one tack. A wink from her might set him off on another. What should she do? Obey his traffic signs, or acknowledge the truth – that he is a born liar – and start showing him a glimpse of thigh?

Heaven help the women of the world, always wondering what the blazes their men's next graven image will be.

How to Write a Short Story

One wet January night, some six months after they had met, young Morgan Myles, our country librarian, was seated in the doctor's pet armchair, on one side of the doctor's fire, digesting the pleasant memory of a lavish dinner, while leafing the pages of a heavy photographic album and savouring a warm brandy. From across the hearth the doctor was looking admiringly at his long, ballooning Gaelic head when, suddenly, Morgan let out a cry of delight.

'Good Lord, Frank! There's a beautiful boy! One of Raphael's little angels.' He held up the open book for Frank to see. 'Who was he?'

The doctor looked across at it and smiled.

'Me. Aged twelve. At school in Mount Saint Bernard.'

'That's in England. I didn't know you went to school in England.'

'Alas!'

Morgan glanced down at twelve, and up at sixty.

'It's not possible, Frank!'

The doctor raised one palm six inches from the arm of his chair and let it fall again.

'It so happened that I was a ridiculously beautiful child.'

'Your mother must have been gone about you. And,' with a smile, 'the girls too.'

'I had no interest in girls. Nor in boys either, though by your smile you seem to say so. But there was one boy who took a considerable interest in me.'

Morgan at once lifted his nose like a pointer. At this period of his life he had rested from writing poetry and was trying to write short stories. For weeks he had read nothing but Maupassant. He was going to out-Maupassant Maupassant. He was going to write stories that would make poor old Maupassant turn as green as the grass on his grave.

'Tell me about it,' he ordered. 'Tell me every single detail.'

'There is nothing to it. Or at any rate, as I now know, nothing abnormal. But, at that age!' – pointing with his pipestem. 'I was as innocent as . . . Well, as innocent as a child of twelve! Funny that you should say that about Raphael's angels. At my preparatory school here – it was a French order – Sister Angélique used to call me her *petit ange*, because, she said, I had "*une tête d'ange et une voix d'ange.*" She used to make me sing solo for them at Benediction, dressed in a red soutane, a white lacy surplice and a purple bow tie.

'After that heavenly place Mount Saint Bernard was ghastly. Mobs of howling boys. Having to play games; rain, hail or snow. I was a funk at games. When I'd see a fellow charging me at rugger I'd at once pass the ball or kick for touch. I remember the coach cursing me. "Breen, you're a bloody little coward, there are boys half your weight on this field who wouldn't do a thing like that." And the constant discipline. The constant priestly distrust. Watching us like jail warders.'

'Can you give me an example of that?' Morgan begged. 'Mind you, you could have had that, too, in Ireland. Think of Clongowes. It turns up in Joyce. And he admired the Jesuits!'

'Yes, I can give you an example. It will show you how innocent I was. A month after I entered Mount Saint Bernard I was so miserable that I decided to write to my mother to take me away. I knew that every letter had to pass under the eyes of the Prefect of Discipline, so I wrote instead to Sister Angélique asking her to pass on the word to my mother. The next day old Father George Lee – he's long since dead – summoned me to his study. "Breen!" he said darkly, holding up my unfortunate letter, "you have tried to do a very underhand thing, something for which I could punish you severely. Why did you write this letter *in French?*"' The doctor sighed. 'I was a very truthful little boy. My mother had brought me up to be truthful simply by never punishing me for anything I honestly owned up to. I said, "I wrote it in French, sir, because I hoped you wouldn't be able to understand it." He turned his face away from me but I could tell from his shoulders that he was laughing. He did not cane me, he just tore up the letter, told me never to try to deceive him again, and sent me packing with my tail between my legs.'

'The old bastard!' Morgan said sympathetically, thinking of the lonely little boy.

'No, no! He was a nice old man. And a good classical scholar, I later discovered. But that day as I walked down the long corridor, with all its photographs of old boys who had made good, I felt the chill of the prison walls!'

'But this other boy?' Morgan insinuated. 'Didn't his friendship help at all?'

The doctor rose and stood with his back to the fire staring fixedly in front of him.

(He rises, Morgan thought, his noble eyes shadowed. No! God damn it, no! Not noble. Shadowed? Literary word. Pensive? Blast it, that's worse. "Pensive eve!" Romantic fudge. His eyes are dark as a rabbit's droppings. That's got it! In his soul . . . Oh, Jase!)

'Since I was so lonely I suppose he *must* have helped. But he was away beyond me. Miles above me. He was a senior. He was the captain of the school.'

'His name,' Morgan suggested, 'was, perhaps, Cyril?'

'We called him Bruiser. I would rather not tell you his real name.'

'Because he is still alive,' Morgan explained, 'and remembers you vividly to this day.'

'He was killed at the age of twenty.'

'In the war! In the heat of battle.'

'By a truck in Oxford. Two years after he went up there from Mount Saint Bernard. I wish I knew what happened to him in those two years. I can only hope that before he died he found a girl.'

'A girl? I don't follow. Oh yes! Of course, yes, I take your point.'

(He remembers with tenderness? No. With loving kindness! No! With benevolence? Dammit, no! With his wonted chivalry to women? But he remembered irritably that the old man sitting opposite to him was a bachelor. And a virgin?)

'What happened between the pair of ye? "Brothers and companions in tribulation on the isle that is called Patmos"?'

The doctor snorted.

'Brothers? I have told you I was twelve. Bruiser was eighteen. The captain of the school. Captain of the rugby team. Captain of the tennis team. First in every exam. Tops. Almost a man. I looked up to him as a shining hero. I never understood what he saw in me. I have often thought since that he may have been amused by my innocence. Like the day he said to me, "I suppose, Rosy," that was my nickname, I had such rosy cheeks, "suppose you think you are the best-looking fellow in the school?" I said, "No, I don't, Bruiser. I think there's one fellow better-looking than me, Jimmy Simcox."'

'Which he, of course, loyally refused to believe!'

The old doctor laughed heartily.

'He laughed heartily.'

'A queer sense of humour!'

'I must confess I did not at the time see the joke. Another day he said, "Would you like, Rosy, to sleep with me?"'

Morgan's eyes opened wide. Now they were getting down to it.

'I said, "Oh, Bruiser, I don't think you would like that at all. I'm an awful chatterbox in bed. Whenever I sleep with my Uncle Tom he's always saying to me, 'Will you for God's sake, stop your bloody gabble and let me sleep.'" He laughed for five minutes at that.'

'I don't see much to laugh at. He should have sighed. I will make him sigh. Your way makes him sound a queer hawk. And nothing else happened between ye but this sort of innocent gabble? Or are you keeping something back? Hang it, Frank, there's no story at all in this!'

'Oh, he used sometimes to take me on his lap. Stroke my bare knee. Ruffle my hair. Kiss me.'

'How did you like that?'

'I made nothing of it. I was used to being kissed by my elders – my mother, my bachelor uncles, Sister Angélique, heaps of people.' The doctor laughed. 'I laugh at it now. But his first kiss! A few days before, a fellow named Calvert said to me, "Hello, pretty boy, would you give me a smuck?" I didn't know what a smuck was. I said, "I'm sorry, Calvert, but I haven't got one." The story must have gone around the whole school. The next time I was alone with Bruiser he taunted me. I can hear his angry, toploftical English voice. "You are an innocent mug, Rosy! A smuck is a kiss. Would you let *me* kiss you?" I said, "Why not?" He put his arm around my neck in a vice and squashed his mouth to my mouth, hard, sticky. I thought I'd choke. "O Lord," I thought, "this is what he gets from playing rugger. This is a rugger kiss." And, I was thinking, "His poor mother! Having to put up with this from him every morning and every night." When he let me go, he said, "Did you like that?" Not wanting to hurt his feelings I said, imitating his English voice, "It was all right, Bruiser! A bit like ruggah, isn't it?" He laughed again and said, "All right? Well, never mind. I shan't rush you."'

Morgan waved impatiently.

'Look here, Frank! I want to get the background to all this. The telling detail, you know. "The little actual facts" as Stendhal called them. You said the priests watched you all like hawks. The constant discipline, you said. The constant priestly distrust. How did ye ever manage to meet alone?'

'It was very simple. He was the captain of the school. The apple of their eye. He could fool them. He knew the ropes. After all, he had been there for five years. I remember old Father Lee saying to me once, "You are a very lucky boy, Breen, it's not every junior that the captain of the school would take an interest in. You ought to feel very proud of his friendship." We used to have a secret sign about our meetings. Every Wednesday morning when he would be walking out of chapel, leading the procession, if that day was all right for us he used to put his right hand in his pocket. If for any reason it was not all right he would put his left hand in his pocket. I was always on the aisle of the very last row. Less than the dust. Watching for the sign like a hawk. We had a double check. I'd then find a note in my overcoat in the cloakroom. All it ever said was, "The same place." He was very careful. He only took calculated risks. If he had lived he would have made a marvellous politician, soldier or diplomat.'

'And where would ye meet? I know! By the river. Or in the woods? "Enter these enchanted woods ye who dare!"'

'No river. No woods. There was a sort of dirty old trunk room upstairs, under the roof, never used. A rather dark place with only one dormer window. It had double doors. He used to lock the outside one. There was a big cupboard there – for cricket bats or something. "If anyone comes," he told me, "you will have time to pop in there." He had it all worked out. Cautious man! I had to be even more cautious, stealing up there alone. One thing that made it easier for us was that I was so much of a junior and he was so very much of a senior, because, you see, those innocent guardians of ours had the idea that the real danger lay between the seniors and the middles, or the middles and the juniors, but never between the seniors and the juniors. They kept the seniors and the middles separated by iron bars and stone walls. Any doctor could have told them that in cold climates like ours the really dangerous years are not from fifteen up but from eighteen to anything, up or down. It simply never occurred to them that any senior could possibly be interested in any way in a junior. I, of course, had no idea of what he was up to. I had not even reached the age of puberty. In fact I honestly don't believe he quite knew himself what he was up to.'

'But, dammit, you must have had some idea! The secrecy, the kissing, alone, up there in that dim, dusty box room, not a sound but the wind in the slates.'

'Straight from the nuns? *Un petit ange?* I thought it was all just pally fun.'

Morgan clapped his hands.

'I've got it! An idyll! Looking out dreamily over the fields from that dusty dormer window? That's it, that's the ticket. Did you ever read that wonderful story by Maupassant – it's called *An Idyll* – about two young peasants meeting in a train, a poor, hungry young fellow who has just left home, and a girl with her first baby. He looked so famished that she took pity on him like a mother, opened her blouse and gave him her breast. When he finished he said, "That was my first meal in three days." Frank! You are telling me the most beautiful story I ever heard in my whole life.'

'You think so?' the doctor said morosely. 'I think he was going through hell all that year. At eighteen? On the threshold of manhood? In love with a child of twelve? That is, if you will allow that a youth of eighteen may suffer as much from love as a man twenty years older. To me the astonishing thing is that he did so well all that year at his studies and at sports. Killing the pain of it, I suppose? Or trying to? But the in between? What went on in the poor devil in between?'

Morgan sank back dejectedly.

'I'm afraid this view of the course doesn't appeal to me at all. All I can see is the idyll idea. After all, I mean, nothing happened!'

Chafing, he watched his friend return to his armchair, take another pipe from the rack, fill it slowly and ceremoniously from a black tobacco jar and light it with care. Peering through the nascent smoke, Morgan leaned slowly forward.

'Or did something happen?'

'Yes,' the doctor resumed quietly. 'Every year, at the end of the last term, the departing captain was given a farewell dinner. I felt sad that morning because we had not met for a whole week. And now, in a couple of days we would be scattered and I would never see him again.'

'Ha, ha! You see, you too were in love!'

'Of course I was, I was hooked,' the doctor said with more than a flicker of impatience. 'However... That Wednesday as he passed me in the chapel aisle he put his right hand in his pocket. I belted off at once to my coat hanging in the cloakroom and found his note. It said,

"At five behind the senior tennis court." I used always chew up his *billet doux* immediately I read it. He had ordered me to. When I read this one my mouth went so dry with fear that I could hardly swallow it. He had put me in an awful fix. To meet alone in the box room was risky enough, but for anybody to climb over the wall into the seniors' grounds was unheard of. If I was caught I would certainly be flogged. I might very well be expelled. And what would my mother and father think of me then? On top of all I was in duty bound to be with all the other juniors at prep at five o'clock, and to be absent from studies without permission was another crime of the first order. After lunch I went to the Prefect of Studies and asked him to excuse me from prep because I had an awful headache. He wasn't taken in one bit. He just ordered me to be at my place in prep as usual. The law! Orders! Tyranny! There was only one thing for it, to dodge prep, knowing well that whatever else happened later I would pay dearly for it.'

'And what about him? He knew all this. And he knew that if *he* was caught they couldn't do anything to him. The captain of the school? Leaving in a few days? It was very unmanly of him to put you to such a risk. His character begins to emerge, and not very pleasantly. Go on!'

The doctor did not need the encouragement. He looked like a small boy sucking a man's pipe.

'I waited until the whole school was at study and then I crept out into the empty grounds. At that hour the school, the grounds, everywhere, was as silent as the grave. Games over. The priests at their afternoon tea. Their charges safely under control. I don't know how I managed to get over that high wall, but when I fell scrambling down on the other side, there he was. "You're bloody late," he said crossly. "How did you get out of prep? What excuse did you give?" When I told him he flew into a rage. "You little fool!" he growled. "You've balloxed it all up. They'll know you dodged. They'll give you at least ten on the backside for this." He was carrying a cane. Seniors at Saint Bernard's did carry walking sticks. I'd risked so much for him, and now he was so angry with me that I burst into tears. He put his arms around me – I thought, to comfort me – but after that all I remember from that side of the wall was him pulling down my short pants, holding me tight, I felt something hard, like his cane, and the next thing I knew I was wet. I thought I was bleeding. I thought he was gone mad. When I smelled whiskey I thought, "He is trying to kill me." "Now run," he ordered me, "and get back to prep as fast as you can."'

Morgan covered his eyes with his hand.

'He shoved me up to the top of the wall. As I peered around I heard his footsteps running away. I fell down into the shrubs on the other side and I immediately began to vomit and vomit. There was a path beside the shrubs. As I lay there puking I saw a black-soutaned priest approaching slowly along the path. He was an old, old priest named Constable. I did not stir. Now, I felt, I'm for it. This is the end. I am certain he saw me but he passed by as if he had not seen me. I got back to the study hall, walked up to the Prefect's desk and told him I was late because I had been sick. I must have looked it because he at once sent me to the matron in the infirmary. She took my temperature and put me to bed. It was summer. I was the only inmate of the ward. One of those evenings of prolonged daylight.'

'You poor little bugger!' Morgan groaned in sympathy.

'A detail comes back to me. It was the privilege of seniors attending the captain's dinner to send down gifts to the juniors' table – sweets, fruit, a cake, for a younger brother or some special protégé. Bruiser ordered a whole white blancmange with a rosy cherry on top of it to be sent to me. He did not know I was not in the dining hall so the blacmange was brought up to me in the infirmary. I vomited again when I saw it. The matron, with my more than ready permission, took some of it for herself and sent the rest back to the juniors' table, "with Master Breen's compliments." I am sure it was gobbled greedily. In the morning the doctor saw me and had me sent home to Ireland immediately.'

'Passing the buck,' said Morgan sourly, and they both looked at a coal that tinkled from the fire into the fender.

The doctor peered quizzically at the hissing coal.

'Well?' he slurred around his pipestem. 'There is your lovely idyll.'

Morgan did not lift his eyes from the fire. Under a downdraft from the chimney a few specks of grey ashes moved clockwise on the worn hearth. He heard a car hissing past the house on the wet macadam. His eyebrows had gone up over his spectacles in two Gothic arches.

'I am afraid,' he said at last, 'it is no go. Not even a Maupassant could have made a story out of it. And Chekhov wouldn't have wanted to try. Unless the two boys lived on, and on, and met years afterwards in Moscow or Yalta or somewhere, each with a wife and a squad of kids, and talked of everything except their schooldays. You are sure you never did hear of him, or from him, again?'

'Never! Apart from the letter he sent with the blancmange and the cherry.'

Morgan at once leaped alive.

'A letter? Now we are on to something! What did he say to you in it? Recite every word of it to me! Every syllable. I'm sure you have not forgotten one word of it. No!' he cried excitedly. 'You have kept it. Hidden away somewhere all these years. Friendship surviving everything. Fond memories of . . .'

The doctor sniffed.

'I tore it into bits unread and flushed it down the W.C.'

'Oh, God blast you, Frank!' Morgan roared. 'That was the climax of the whole thing. The last testament. The final revelation. The summing up. The *document humain*. And you "just tore it up!" Let's reconstruct it. "Dearest Rosy, As long as I live I will never forget your innocence, your sweetness, your . . ."'

'My dear boy!' the doctor protested mildly. 'I am sure he wrote nothing of the sort. He was much too cautious, and even the captain was not immune from censorship. Besides, sitting in public glory at the head of the table? It was probably a place-card with something on the lines of, "All my sympathy, sorry, better luck next term." A few words, discreet, that I could translate any way I liked.'

Morgan raised two despairing arms.

'If that was all the damned fellow could say to you after that appalling experience, he was a character of no human significance whatever, a shallow creature, a mere agent, a catalyst, a cad. The story becomes your story.'

'I must admit I have always looked on it in that way. After all it did happen to me . . . Especially in view of the sequel.'

'Sequel? What sequel? I can't have sequels. In a story you always have to observe unity of time, place and action. Everything happening at the one time, in the same place, between the same people. *The Necklace*. *Boule de Suif. The Maison Tellier*. The examples are endless. What was this bloody sequel?'

The doctor puffed thoughtfully.

'In fact there were two sequels. Even three sequels. And all of them equally important.'

'In what way were they important?'

'It was rather important to me that after I was sent home I was in the hospital for four months. I could not sleep. I had constant nightmares, always the same one – me running through a wood and him running after me with his cane. I could not keep down my food. Sweating hot. Shivering cold. The vomiting was recurrent. I lost weight. My mother was beside herself with worry. She brought doctor after doctor to me, and only one of them spotted it, an old, blind man from Dublin named Whiteside. He said, "That boy has had some kind of shock," and in private he asked me if some boy, or man, had interfered with me. Of course, I denied it hotly.'

'I wish I was a doctor,' Morgan grumbled. 'So many writers were doctors. Chekhov. William Carlos Williams. Somerset Maugham. A. J. Cronin.'

The doctor ignored the interruption.

'The second sequel was that when I at last went back to Mount Saint Bernard my whole nature changed. Before that I had been dreamy and idle. During my last four years at school I became their top student. I suppose psychologists would say nowadays that I compensated by becoming extroverted. I became a crack cricket player. In my final year I was the college champion at billiards. I never became much good at rugger but I no longer minded playing it and I wasn't all that bad. If I'd been really tops at it, or at boxing, or swimming I might very well have ended up as captain of the school. Like him.'

He paused for so long that Morgan became alerted again.

'And the third sequel?' he prompted.

'I really don't know why I am telling you all this. I have never told a soul about it before. Even still I find it embarrassing to think about, let alone to talk about. When I left Mount Saint Bernard and had taken my final at the College of Surgeons I went on to Austria to continue my medical studies. In Vienna I fell in with a young woman. The typical blonde fräulein, handsome, full of life, outgoing, wonderful physique, what you might call an outdoor girl, free as the wind, frank as the daylight. She taught me skiing. We used to go mountain climbing together. I don't believe she knew the meaning of the word fear. She was great fun and the best of company. Her name was Brigitte. At twenty-six she was already a woman of the world. I was twenty-four, and as innocent of women as . . . as . . .'

To put him at his ease Morgan conceded his own embarrassing confession.

'As I am, at twenty-four.'

'You might think that what I am going to mention could not happen to a doctor, however young, but on our first night in bed, immediately she touched my body I vomited. I pretended to her that I had eaten something that upset me. You can imagine how nervous I felt all through the next day wondering what was going to happen that night. Exactly the same thing happened that night. I was left with no option. I told her the whole miserable story of myself and Bruiser twelve years before. As I started to tell her I had no idea how she was going to take it. Would she leave me in disgust? Be coldly sympathetic? Make a mock of me? Instead, she became wild with what I can only call gleeful curiosity. "Tell me more, *mein Schätzerl*,' she begged. "Tell me everything! What exactly did he do to you? I want to know it all. This is *wunderbar*. Tell me! Oh do tell me!' I did tell her, and on the spot everything became perfect between us. We made love like Trojans. That girl saved my sanity.'

In a silence Morgan gazed at him. Then coldly:—

'Well, of course, this is another story altogether. I mean I don't see how I can possibly blend these two themes together. I mean no writer worth his salt can say things like, "Twelve long years passed over his head. Now read on." I'd have to leave her out of it. She is obviously irrelevant to the main theme. Whatever the hell the main theme is.' Checked by an ironical glance he poured the balm. 'Poor Frank! I foresee it all. You adored her. You wanted madly to marry her. Her parents objected. You were star-crossed lovers. You had to part.'

'I never thought of marrying the bitch. She had the devil's temper. We had terrible rows. Once we threw plates at one another. We would have parted anyway. She was a lovely girl but quite impossible. Anyway, towards the end of that year my father fell seriously ill. Then my mother fell ill. Chamberlain was in Munich that year. Everybody knew the war was coming. I came back to Ireland that autumn. For keeps.

'But you tried again and again to find out what happened to her. And failed. She was swallowed up in the fire and smoke of war. I don't care what you say, Frank, you *must* have been heartbroken.'

The doctor lifted a disinterested shoulder.

'A student's love affair? Of thirty and more years ago?'

No! He had never enquired. Anyway if she was alive now what would she be but a fat, blowsy old baggage of sixty-three? Morgan, though shocked, guffawed dutifully. There was the real Maupassant touch. In his next story a touch like that! The clock on the mantelpiece whirred and began to tinkle the hour. Morgan opened the album for a last look at the beautiful child. Dejectedly he slammed it shut, and rose.

'There is too much in it,' he declared. 'Too many strands. Your innocence. His ignorance. Her worldliness. Your forgetting her. Remembering him. Confusion and bewilderment. The ache of loss? Loss? *Lost Innocence?* Would that be a theme? But nothing rounds itself off. You are absolutely certain you never heard of him again after that day behind the tennis courts?'

They were both standing now. The rain brightly spotted the midnight window.

'In my first year in Surgeons, about three years after Bruiser was killed, I lunched one day with his mother and my mother at the Shelbourne Hotel in Dublin. By chance they had been educated at the same convent in England. They talked about him. My mother said, "Frank here knew him in Mount Saint Bernard." His mother smiled condescendingly at me. "No, Frank. You were too young to have met him." "Well," I said, "I did actually speak to him a couple of times, and he was always very kind to me." She said sadly, "He was kind to everybody. Even to perfect strangers."'

Morgan thrust out an arm and a wildly wagging finger.

'Now, *there* is a possible shape! Strangers to begin. Strangers to end! What a title! *Perfect Strangers.*' He blew out a long, impatient breath and shook his head. 'But that is a fourth sequel! I'll think about it,' as if he were bestowing a great favour. 'But it isn't a story as it stands. I would have to fake it up a lot. Leave out things. Simplify. Mind you, I could still see it as an idyll. Or I could if only you hadn't torn up his last, farewell letter, which I still don't believe at all said what you said it said. If only we had that letter I bet you any money we could haul in the line and land our fish.'

The doctor knocked out the dottle of his pipe against the fireguard, and throating a yawn looked at the fading fire.

'I am afraid I have been boring you with my reminiscences.'

'Not at all, Frank! By no means! I was most interested in your story. And I do honestly mean what I said. I really will think about it. I promise. Who was it,' he asked in the hall as he shuffled into his overcoat and his muffler and moved out to the wet porch, the tail of his raincoat rattling in the wind, 'said that the two barbs of childhood are its innocence and its ignorance?' He failed to remember. He threw up his hand. 'Ach, to hell with it for a story! It's all too bloody convoluted for me. And to hell with Maupassant, too! That vulgarian oversimplified everything. And he's full of melodrama. A besotted Romantic at heart! Like all the bloody French.'

The doctor peeped out at him through three inches of door. Morgan, standing with his back to the arrowy night, suddenly lit up as if a spotlight had shone on his face.

'I know what I'll do with it!' he cried. 'I'll turn it into a poem about a seashell!'

'About a seashell!'

'Don't you remember?' In his splendid voice Morgan chanted above the rain and wind: – "*A curious child holding to his ear/ The convolutions of a smoothlipped seashell/ To which, in silence hushed...*" How the hell does it go? " *...his very soul listened to the murmurings of his native sea.*" It's as clear as daylight, man! You! Me! Everyone! Always wanting to launch a boat in search of some far-off golden sands. And something or somebody always holding us back. "The Curious Child". *There's* a title!'

'Ah, well!' the doctor said, peering at him blankly. 'There it is! As your friend Maupassant might have said, "*C'est la vie!*"'

'*La vie!*' Morgan roared, now on the gravel beyond the porch, indifferent to the rain pelting on his bare head. 'That trollop? She's the one who always bitches up everything. No, Frank! For me there is only one fountain of truth, one beauty, one perfection. Art, Frank! Art! and bugger *la vie!*'

At the untimely verb the doctor's drooping eyelids shot wide open.

'It is a view,' he said courteously and let his hand be shaken fervently a dozen times.

'I can never repay you, Frank. A splendid dinner. A wonderful story. Marvellous inspiration. I must fly. I'll be writing it all night!' – and vanished head down through the lamplit rain, one arm uplifted triumphantly behind him.

The doctor slowly closed his door, carefully locked it, bolted it, tested it, and prudently put its chain in place. He returned to his sitting room, picked up the cinder that had fallen into the hearth and tossed it back into the remains of his fire, then stood, hand on mantelpiece, looking down at it. What a marvellous young fellow! He would be tumbling and tossing all night over that story. Then he would be around in the morning apologizing, and sympathizing, saying, 'Of course, Frank, I do realize that it was a terribly sad experience for both of you.'

Gazing at the ashes his whole being filled with memory after memory like that empty vase in his garden being slowly filled by drops of rain.

Liberty

Three men are seated on a low grassy wall opposite the high, white, wide, double, wooden, open gates and porter's lodge of a mental institution a mile from the modest town of B—— in the province of D——. Once it was frankly called The Madhouse, later more delicately The Asylum, still later, more accurately, The Mental Hospital, finally, less candidly, Saint Senan's Home. Two of the three men are fat and wear peaked-cap uniforms. The third, thin and tall, wears another kind of uniform, the usual, grey, hirsute, tweed suit, hairy grey cap, woollen shirt and the boots without laces worn by all housebound patients. A few, so-called 'good' patients, who are encouraged to walk freely about the neighbouring town and countryside, dress like you and me. This man is privileged to sit just outside the gates of the Home.

The three men are looking at the ground under their feet, considering whether, without spoiling this favoured spot, it would be feasible to have some gravel spread there as an insurance against the fog, damps and miasmas rising under their boots when the ground tends to become soft and muddy. The patient, answering to the name Mister Cornfield, has just suggested that the low wall would be a more comfortable seat if paved with flagstones. This suggestion meets with a majority disapproval.

'Cold flags,' says the fatter of the attendants, slowly and paternally circling his belly with his open palm, 'could give you piles.'

Mr Cornfield argues quietly that damp grass and damp earth are 'just as conducive to haemorrhoids.'

At this the two attendants begin to discuss the meaning of the words *piles* and *haemorrhoids*. Mr Cornfield, for whose knowledgeability and cleverality they entertain a very proper respect (he was once a journalist) informs them that the word *piles* comes from Old English and etymologizes from the same source as the word *pellets*, or as the Spanish form of tennis known as pelota. 'By God!' says the fatter attendant whose paw is still comfortably navigating his belly. 'You

could get tennis balls from piles all right!' Soon after this an obese
woman from the lodge inside the gates appears on her doorstep with
her right index finger placed horizontally on her left index finger to
symbolize Tea. The attendants at once abandon their patient who
hangs his hands, clasped, between his thighs and contemplates the
earth they have been discussing until a refined Saxon female voice says,
'Good awfternoon, Mister Cornfield.'

He rises and bows.

'Good afternoon, Miss Huggard.'

The lady and the lunatic sit side by side. Some three miles farther on,
she teaches in a tiny rural Protestant school a few remnant children of
the Reformation. He sees her almost every day, in fine weather, at this
hour, appearing underneath the tunnel of trees that mark the
penultimate stage of her daily three-mile trudge out to the school and
back to the old family home of the Huggards, a tall weather-slated
house that has stood in its own grounds outside the town for four
generations, and of which she is now the only occupant. She stretches
out her feet and surveys her brogues. He knows what she is about to
say: she says it every time.

'Those skates won't lawst me another month. Every yeah I weah out
three paihs of boots going east and west. So you are back?' she adds in
astonishment and admiration. 'I missed you, you know. Back from
London!' she annotates, as if he were Marco Polo. 'It was naughty of
you, I gathah, to have run away?'

'The caged bird always flies away,' he laughs.

'And how is good old London?' she asks as breezily as a games mistress
– if games mistresses ever reach fifty.

'Not much different really since I saw it last. Which was eleven years
ago. Too many people. More coloureds. Noisier. When did you see
London last, Miss Huggard?'

'I was there only once, Mister Cornfield. When I was fifteen. Just
before the war. Daddy met me at Victoria Station, and took me by
Underground down to the docks. The next place I set foot on was the
Barbados. As a rule, women, it appears, are not very popular aboard
ships, but I had great fun. But of course I was not a woman. I was just
Captain Huggard's little girl.'

The word 'Barbados' had visibly excited him.

'Are they wonderful, the Barbados?'

'Rather Britishish. Of course in a long, long ago way. A bit ungainly. I suppose they are all changed now.'

She grimaced and spread her hands in a long, long ago way. Rather ungainly, with her sand-grey hair, her humble spinster's eyes, her stooped back. He wished she did not have to feel that the one adventurous image of her life had altered.

'My father was drowned in 1943. I had just got my teacher's diploma. It was very fortunate. I was free to look after Mummy.'

The walls had closed early on her. She smiled, looked towards the distant outline of her home.

'There was a First World War song called "The Last Long Mile." I've got to face it. Tell me! Does your recent escapade mean that now that you have shown that you can travel you may at last be allowed to visit the town? Walk the roads? You might even visit my school? Wouldn't that be jolly!'

'It may work the other way around. They may now feel confirmed in their notion that I am irresponsible.'

'Oh, dear! I do hope not, Mr Cornfield.'

She rose. He rose.

'I have stolen some begonia bulbs for you,' he said in a naughty-boy voice. 'If you come up to the corner by the land steward's house this evening before the supper bell I'll have them for you.'

'I will come. I do hope you may continue to help the gardener, Mr Cornfield. Your trouble is you do not occupy your mind enough. Work is good for the soul. It is always pleasant talking with you, Mr Cornfield.'

She smiled again, he lifted his cap as she walked away from him. How Protestant!

His two caretakers presently returned and sat on either side of him. Over their tea they had decided that flags underneath their bottoms and flags underneath their feet would be best of all, about which they became so excited that they had barely time to salute Doctor Reynolds in her scarlet sports Triumph, her black curls leaping in the wind as she whirled through the gateway so sharply that her front fender barely missed its left pillar.

Her eyebrows soared with pleasure. He was back! She had a snapshot of him in her side mirror rising to bow after her the way he always used to do. As she sped up the avenue she was still chuckling at his cap lifting sedately from his head inclining baronially, as if he owned the whole

blooming madhouse. Odd how that those old-fashioned ways of his got
on the nerves of every doctor in the place except herself. 'Cornfield's
folie de grandeur!' – until she gave them their answer one night at
dinner.

'So far as I can see the only unusual thing about his manners is that
they are so good: the one man in the place who knows how to treat a
lady properly.'

They had guffawed of course, but she knew she had drawn a spot of
blood: also from herself, who had taken a whole year to pick him out
from among the hopeless herds brought in here from the moors, the
mountains and the dying islands, mooing as softly and ceaselessly as
a village pound. Yet all he had done that morning four years ago had
been to waist-bow to a nurse who had responded with a wink and
provocative cock of the ankle. A nurse had known how to handle him.
She had never known whether to treat him as a patient or as a man.

She braked in the doctors' parking space at the top of the avenue, got
out, banged the door and stood glaring across the river valley ridges of
Magharamore. She conjured up from behind it the narrow glen of the
Owenaheensha. She had fished both rivers many times but there was
really no good fishing that way until you came to the lakes at Laoura.
She slewed her head eastward to a round hill, ten miles away, horned
like Moses by two beams of upthrown sun. Every horizon shouldered
white clouds that shouldered more white clouds, that shouldered still
more clouds up and up into the deepening blue. Below her the daffodils
scattered about the grounds did not sway. The air smelled freshly of the
Easter rains. In exasperation she ruffled her poll. She would give it to
him straight this time.

'Jack, you damned fool! You've balloxed it for keeps. For years you've
been telling us that all you want is to be allowed to stroll around the
roads and into the town for an hour a day. Solid John C. Reliable John
C. To prove it he runs away from us to London. And then, after six
months of AWOL here he comes crawling back like the Prodigal Son.'
She knew that what she would actually say would be, 'Welcome home,
Mister Cornfield. I trust you know that you were mad to have left this
madhouse. In your five years among us nothing became you less than
your leaving us, and nothing more than your return to the village
pound.' He would laugh politely. He always saw through her defensive
jokes. The one thing she would not dare to say would be, 'I missed
you.'

She started to empty her car, furiously throwing the stuff on the cement – rod, waders, basket, suitcase. She became aware of a familiar smell. That would be Mac, pipe smoking, delivered through the revolving glass doors, his lean cheeks insucked, his heavy eyelids lowering at her legs. He would not speak until she deigned to turn. She finally did. He lifted his pipe silently. She noted that he was not coming forward to help her with her gear. If she had been a pretty nurse . . .

'Nice holiday, Doctor Reynolds?' he asked circumspectly.

'Yes, if you don't mind lashing rain, and a force ten gale. If I'd been a flying fish I might have caught a flying fisherman. I played poker, drank Irish, chain smoked and read six whodunits.'

'And won every game hand down I bet? And drank them all under the table? And had the villain spotted by page fifteen?'

'One has to shine at something.'

'You shine! Your boyfriend is back.'

She stared him down.

'So London didn't work?'

'We warned them, didn't we? Six months to the day. I'd have given him six weeks. He stayed with his daughter, that fat, rich American Jewess who kidnapped him from us in October. Four days ago he bombed her. Two black eyes, a crushed rib and a broken septum.'

'Good for him! She is a right bitch.'

'On that, doctor, if on little else we are of one mind. There were occasions when even I felt my toe itching. However, you and I, not being mental patients – so far – can afford to dream violently. With him, an itch today, a black eye tomorrow, a knife the day after.'

She faced him full and crossly, her yellow sou'wester in one fist, her gaff in another.

'I have repeatedly pointed out to you, Doctor MacGowan, that Cornfield is as sane as I am. Even if you think that's not saying very much.'

Furiously she turned her back on him, threw down gaff and sou'wester, rummaged for her bookbag. He would be looking at her bottom now. He spoke pleadingly.

'Judy!'

She turned.

'I missed you.'

'Lookit, Mac. Are you by chance jealous of Cornfield?' He scoffed defensively. 'Then why can't you lay off me? The place is full of passionate nurses mad for it.' She switched herself off. 'How did he get back?'

'His American son-in-law threw him on a plane at London airport last Sunday morning. With a fiver stuffed into his vest pocket. At a quarter to one this Tuesday morning I was awakened by somebody at my doorbell. An old hand, he knows all the ways in. I hauled up the window. There was your ladyship's lordship below on my doorstep shouting against the wind and rain for God's sake to let him in. He was like a water rat with his big, effluent knob of a nose. We had quite an interesting chat, roaring up and down to one another at the tops of our voices. I've never seen such a night. I wouldn't have left a milk bottle out on such a night. No hat. No overcoat. He'd eaten nothing since he left the plane. Hiked the whole way. He was carrying a cardboard suitcase containing dirty linen, a large photograph of his daughter and two small pictures of her that he had been painting. I let him in, poked up the fire, gave him a hot toddy and watched him steam larger than life. That man has a superb constitution. You saw him just now, fresh as a daisy after being storm-battered for nearly forty hours.' One side of his knife-edged mouth smiled. 'While I am deciding what to do with him next I have sent him up to Ward Three.'

Her voice soared.

'Now why the hell should I have the silly bugger under my care?'

He looked paternally at her over his glasses.

'We all have our special babies, Judy. Admit you are pleased to have him back.'

'Not particularly,' she said, sulkily lowering her owl-lidded eyes. 'I have lost interest in his case. He is simply a sound, healthy, ordinary, bad-tempered man whom we have ruined by domesticating, nationalizing, habituating, acclimatizing or, in the neologistic gobbledygook of our bombastic profession, institutionalizing so thoroughly that he is now afraid to live a normal life. We have turned him into that well-established male Irish type, the baa-ram bleating for his mummy's teats. Which we provide. Self-absorbed? Self-pitying? Egocentric? Chip on the shoulder? Truculent? Timid? Incurably self-referential? All that, but even if he really did give his blond cow of a daughter a couple of shiners does that make him insane? Any more than it would if you were to marry me as you say you would like to, but would not, and gave me two pandas when you discovered the sort of bitch you would sooner or later decide I am? That would not be you walloping me. It would be your dear little ego revenging itself on the whole monstrous regiment of women from Old Mother Hubbard, and Old Mother Goose, and Holy Mum the Church, down to Mother Ireland and your own dear departed and long-suffering Mother Machree. Doctor MacGowan!' She said it sweetly and gently. 'Why have I to explain these elementary things to you so often? Did you never, when younger perhaps, think of taking up plumbing, or dentistry, or some other study a bit more obvious than psychiatry?'

'Some day, Judy,' he said quietly, 'I will black your fucking eye without the blessing of either Father Freud or Mother Church and it might do you a power of good. Meanwhile . . .'

She barely felt the trap snap on her neck.

'. . . I have been rereading your dossier on Cornfield. This afternoon, in fact. You stress that he should be allowed a limited freedom. I think you are on the right track. If this man can travel once to London why should he not travel twice? Turn the matter over again in your mind, Doctor Reynolds. If we are in accord I propose to tell Mrs Reuther that she must henceforth accept full custody and responsibility for her father. In London. Or in New York. Or wherever else she damned well likes.'

He turned to go. The shrillness of her voice halted and turned him.

'Mac! You can't do this! You can't encourage this poor devil to get attached to us -- and then boot him out into the streets of London.'

'Isn't it what you have always been asking for on his behalf? Freedom of the city?'

'Not of London! What is he going to do in the purlieus of Sloane Square, Lowndes Street, Kinnerton Street, Eaton Square, Belgravia? A man who has been accustomed for five years to sitting on the side of a country road watching that evening sun go down, chatting with passers-by, looking at a spider in the grass, the drops of dew hung out to dry on a cobweb, able to sit in the gate-lodge by the fireside in the winter with Patrice's fat wife, poke the coals, lift the curtains, look at the flooded river, look . . .'

With a sob, incoherently, she waved around to the grey-stemmed daffodils and the climbing clouds.

His voice became precise and hateful.

'This may be pointed out to his daughter. We have done our bit. See you at dinner,' and the glass valves of the door whirled the blues and whites of the sky behind his back.

'Damn you!' she said bitterly at the slowing doors. Then, luggage-laden, she bumped up the stairs to her rooms.

At the window she took up her old bird-watching binoculars. He was there still, a blurred figure sitting on the low wall, alone. She focused him to sharpness. His back to the fields, his hands hanging between his knees, he was looking at the earth. Suddenly he rose, straightened, braced his aching back, lifted his Atlas arms to grasp the sky. A fine figure of a man, six foot one, red nose like a sailor, brisk black hair. Aged fifty? Not much in his head. Soft-cored. Too gentle. A bit of a coward? She hungered to eat him. She had never seen him stripped but Mac, who had checked his condition several times, reported that he had the physique of a man of thirty. My soul thirsts for him in this wet and rainy land where there is no sun. I want him where every woman longs for the leap of a child. What do I see in him? Myself.

She laid down her field glasses, drew a hot bath, stripped, and filled herself a glass of Irish. She glanced at her mirrored face, her bulldog nostrils, pocked skin, big mouth, prognathous jaw, laid herself in her hot bath and slowly sipped her liquor. She glanced along her full fish-length in the bath, calmly aware that the gods had never created a more preeminently beautiful body, as far as the neck. She cheerfully informed her wriggling toes, 'If I had been dug up in marble two hundred years ago as a headless Venus I'd be in the Louvre now under spotlights.'

Her eyes wandered out of her bathroom to her bookbag squatting like a black cat in the middle of the carpet of her living room. *Jessica's Daughter*. According to his publisher, 'John Cornfield's magnificent 100,000 words cry for Freedom.' He should have been dug up as a brainless gladiator. Four months it had taken her to wheedle it out of his besotted daughter, and then only under a solemn promise that nobody else, not even he, must know that a copy of the novel still existed.

Now, it may be agreed that every visible and celestial achievement is, in the nature of nature, flawed. That thing was an embarrassment. Autobiographical as she had expected, which was why she wanted it; and almost straight autobiography at that, which was why it was a failure. When she was a student at Westminster Hospital she had had a lover who was a real writer who had made her see that the truth is always much too complicated to be told straight out. Here everything was as implacably grim as grime. The hero, like the author, a lone child. Named Shawn. Scene, a grey English mining town. Father and mother Irish-born, Roman Cats, elementary school teachers. At twenty Shawn flies from insensitive and brutal England to warmhearted, kindly Ireland. She snorted. What John-Shawn had fled from was the War, the blackout, roving searchlights, ack-ack, austerity. End of Book One. Dublin. Our hero is found working in Dublin. On an R.C. magazine. That word had always amused her: a storehouse for explosives, the part of a rifle where you put bullets, French for a shop. This shop provokes his last wild cry for freedom when he meets a Jewish girl, named Jessica, visiting Ireland from New York, loses his virginity to her, marries her, gets booted out by his warm-hearted and kindly employers, disowned by his father and mother and angrily returns to cruel, cloddish England. End of Book Two. Fleet Street. Updating obituaries and checking sports results. Lives in a flat in a semi-detached in Crouch End. Constant quarrels with wife. Conscience in flitthers. Drinks. A chaste and tender friendship with an Irish prostitute whose conscience is also in flitthers. And then, casually, simultaneously and without warning he fathers a beautiful daughter and a highly successful novel. Peace? Achievement? Freedom?

In real life *Jessica's Daughter* had been a flop.

To his credit, by the time she was compiling his original dossier, he was able to refer to this fiasco with a bitter humour. But he could not remember even the titles of his four subsequent, unpublished novels.

'Four? What persistence, Mr Cornfield! Still, I hope you enjoyed writing them?'

'I hated every moment of them. Every one of those bloody things,' his cassette recorded, 'was written under the whip of the most characteristically bossy conceited insensitive ambitious misanthropic egomaniacal woman who ever issued out of the loins of Abraham.'

A pity he did not wait another few years before writing these failures. He would have had at least a splendid ending for one of them.

The cassette again:

'We came back to Ireland on holidays eleven years ago she started nagging at me to write a sixth novel one morning I saw red for ten seconds I've often timed it I went for her with a loose brick we had to keep the door of the kitchen open a cottage we hired a small pink Georgian brick six inches by three it didn't do her any harm only for all that blood streaming down her face and she running around in a circle like a dog with the distemper and poor little Beryl staring.'

His wife was probably right to commit him to a private clinic and go back to New York with the kid. Five years later she died, the cash stopped, they had to take him in.

She sucked down the last drops of her whiskey, deposited the glass on the bath mat, sat up and slowly and softly began to soap her armpits and her lavish breasts. Eleven years behind walls and, in her view, only one symptom of abnormality: the pathetic smallness of his protest against his life of a castaway – his plea to be granted sixty minutes a day alone. Crusoe would probably have got that way in the end, with no more than an occasional dreamy wish to walk on Tower Hill or Cheapside. Still, Crusoe had coped, made a new world. There was nothing wrong with Jack Cornfield except that at some time his wish to cope had got a knockout blow. In what part of him, why, where, nobody would ever know, unless some psychiatrist had him every week for five years, breaking him down and down until he was a little naked man at the bottom of a deep, dark cone begging for the last cruel drop of truth to be squeezed from him – the price of his release to the upper air.

Am I his female Orpheus?

She clambered out of her bath, grumbling 'Cure thyself,' towelled herself with energy, began to dress. She leaned to her mirror to test her upper lip. 'The passing shadow on her upper lip . . . Blown hair about her mouth . . . Thy shadow, Cynara . . . Swan's neck and dark abundant hair . . .' She stiffened. Her watch said six thirty. She rang the head nurse of Ward Three. If it was convenient could Mr Cornfield be sent to her surgery at eight o'clock for ten minutes. No, nothing special.

'But we may have to have a conference about him tomorrow morning.'

He was waiting in her office. She lifted down the overcoat hanging on the back of the door.

'I think, Mr Cornfield, we might stroll. It is still bright. I shan't keep you ten minutes.'

They strolled to the highest and quietest corner of the grounds, just below the farm and the land steward, Billy Victory's, house. He recognized the clatter from the kitchens after the usual tasteless meal. If he could only have a glass of beer sometimes with his supper. The country slowly expanded. Soon it would be veiled. She talked about her fishing. He asked if it was very far away and she waved towards the horizon. He asked in which direction, and when she pointed he paused and stared. She waited and watched.

They came to the white seat, cast iron, where he had sat an hour ago with Elsie Huggard, giving her six corms of gladioli in a cardboard box marked *Saint Senan's Confectionery*. The name was a common eponym in the town – Saint Senan's Maternity Home, School, Church, Bridge, Furnishing, Insurance, Credit Union, Hospital, Cemetery. The old Huggard home had the Saint's name carved on the pillars of its entrance gate.

'I'm glad to see you back, Mr Cornfield. I hope you realize how mad you were to have left this madhouse.' (Like her to call it that. Honest. No palaver.) 'In all your years nothing became you less than your leaving us and nothing more than your return to the fold.' He laughed obligingly. Who did she think she was fooling? 'Why did you let Mrs Reuther kidnap you away from us?'

He smiled his crooked smile, replied circumspectly:—

'Beryl is half-Irish, half-American. And a hundred per cent Jewish. Married to a Jew. Eat your spinach. Drink your chicken soup. One obeys.'

A plane hummed over. Its wingtips blinked. Escaping to London, New York, Amsterdam, or Paris, Brussels?

'I missed you,' she said to the grass.

'I thought of you many times,' he said to the sky, and accepted one of her cigarettes. Her lighter ran a line down the shinbones of her legs. It incised the aquiline face of a revolutionary sucked dry by years of jail. At the sense of so much helplessness in so strong a body a surge of power hit her like a contraction of the womb, a four-beat stoppage of the heart. Her cigarette flew in an arc of anger against the deepening sky. She spoke out of the corner of her mouth like a gangster's moll.

'What are you going to do, Mr Cornfield, when we send you back to your daughter in London?'

'Could you?' he demanded so fiercely that she slewed her head a full hundred and eighty degrees the better to relish his smell of fear, sweat, tobacco.

'If you can travel once you can travel again.' She sweetened her voice. 'You have a very pretty daughter. A lovely girl.'

'Isn't she though?' Eagerly.

'You must be very proud of her.'

'She's all I have in the world.'

'Then why did you go for her, break her nose, crack her ribs, black her pretty eyes?'

He patted her knee. She dribbled for him.

'Me go for Beryl? I just said I did that in order to get back to my featherbed.'

'In that case you should not be here. Perhaps you never even attacked your wife?'

'Now her I did do! With a hammer.'

'You said with a brick, six by three, pink, Georgian.'

'I can't remember. Do you think I'm lying?'

'If you can't remember it's probably true.'

'But little Beryl! For God's sake, not Beryl! It wasn't she pushed me out of that flat in Sloane Square, it was her husband, not that I blame him, he got me four jobs, I couldn't keep any of them, he was quite nice about it, really. One day he even called me "chum." He has his own life to lead, and Beryl is expecting. He had a drink with me at the airport, he stuffed two fivers into my pocket, I drank them in Dublin. I tell you this because you are the only person I can trust in this bin. Will I be chucked out?'

She looked around her. All she could see clearly was a row of lighted windows.

'Mr Cornfield, you did attack your wife with intent to kill. Please let us be clear about that, and no nonsense. You did attack your daughter. And let us have no shilly-shallying about that either. You put them both in mortal danger. You gave your Beryl two shiners, broke her septum, cracked two of her ribs, in a word went off your chump again. Do you understand?'

'I am not,' he said furiously, 'I repeat *not*, off my chump.'

She lifted her eyes imploringly to the one great planet in the sky.

'In that case you wish me to report that you are as gentle as a mouse? That you never really went berserk? That you never will, that you are fit to pack your bag, leave this featherbed and earn your living out there in that dark, wide, windy world? Do you understand all that, you great, big stupid slob?'

He became as gentle as a mouse.

'I am not insane and I will never say otherwise. It simply happens that I do not like this horrible world. And that is your own word. Or, you said it, quoting Bertrand Russell, "This world," you said he said, "is horrible! Horrible! Horrible! Once we admit that we can enjoy the beauty of it.'"

'I ought not to have repeated the witticism to somebody only too eager to take my every lightest word seriously. After all, His Lordship might just as well have said, "This world is lovely! Lovely! Lovely! Once we admit that we are ready to suffer the horrors of it." I find plenty of pleasant things sandwiched between the horrors of life. Good fishing. Good drink. Good friends.'

'I do not fish. I do not drink. I have no friends.'

She considered the bizarre angle of his hairy cap against the stars. She wished only that she could strip him, scrub him in a hot, hot bath, and dress him like a free man.

'So be it, Mr Cornfield. You must make your own miserable decisions. And if you still do not like this horrible ship we are sailing in there is a very simple way to solve your tiny problem.'

She drew her index finger across his bristly throat, shivered at the nutmeg-grater feel of it, jumped up and abruptly walked away. 'Damn you!' he shouted after her and sulkily watched her stately figure sink from sight down the hill.

She felt her pulse banging in her right ear. Her calves were groggy. Mac's black house rose against the ash of the Easter moon. Their passionate widower. Twice married. Father of seven. If I became his third they certainly would not become fourteen. She halted to reconnoitre. Doctors were entitled to receive friends in their rooms provided they were not patients or nurses, whether M or F, but in this fortified village everybody saw, suspected, invented, scoffed, hinted. Even as she looked around she saw a white edge of skirt, a shoe, a stocking, a black cloak slide through young Carty's door. In such matters Mac was neither a Puritan nor a Paul Pry, but if he suspected her of trying to saddle him with Cornfield he would not give her a grass blade of leeway.

There was no corner inside these walls where they could meet after dark. No corner where some eye, some fly, some spy would not sooner or later surprise them. But would either of us dare to? Can a bird fly with a broken wing? A man who had not had a woman for eleven years? That story he told about himself when he was a kid and the fledgling jackdaw that their yard-cat in Stockport struck down with a crooked claw. How he capped it under a cardboard box, and then put this box into a larger box, and then covered that larger box with wire netting, and found a

worm for the bird, and gave it a saucer of water, hoping it would
recover from the shock, and its wing would mend and it would be able
to fly away again.

'But in the morning it was on its side, its eyes glazed, half-closed, its
claws and feet extended. Even my worm was dead. The nights in the
North can be bitter.'

Well, Judy? And how is our precious cornfed baby? You have become
a cat who walks by night. You never drop in for a drink with me these
nights. If I may make so bold, Dr Reynolds, am I wrong in imagining
that you have, so to speak, been avoiding me lately? Damn you, Jack
Cornfield, you know the form just as well as I do. No, Mac! For the
hundredth time. No! And if I did let you that night after Easter it was
not, I assure you, because I was madly in love with you but simply that
I felt randy as hell and sorry for all poor, bloody mankind. Oh, yes
indeed, Dr MacGowan, I cannot tell you how happy I am here, safe
from all temptations and troubles, all of us together in this cosy little
world of our own. Oh, you just reminded me, Mr Cornfield, I have a
book about the South Pacific that you might like to collect from my
office this evening...

A week later she applied for a post in Dublin. On the night she told
him so eleven years of celibacy fell from his back. Hand in hand, like
children, they ran for their lives. Three weeks later they were married.
To establish his pride his Beryl settled a generous income on him. Elsie
Huggard said to him, 'While you are looking for a house why don't you
rent my ground floor? "Saint Senan's" is big enough the Lord knows,
built to house ten children at least. I shan't butt in on you.' He accepted
without even examining the house, but when the two of them first
entered it he was as boastful and triumphant as if he had inspected it
as carefully as a real estate broker.

'I couldn't have chosen better. See! A ship's bell, with the name
engraved on it. PYLADES. A Turkish hookah. A sailing ship inside a
Barbados rum bottle. An Indian coffee table, brass inlaid. A Moroccan
tapestry. Junk from all over the globe. I bet you we'll come on a
fifty-year-old album of photographs. The place smells of the seven
seas.'

She laughed at his zany laughter, told him he was like a lark in the
air, whereupon, without embarrassment, he recited, and at the end slid
into song: – *'Dear thoughts are in my mind/ And my soul soars
enchanted/ When I hear the dear lark sing/ In the clear air of the day./*

For a tender, beaming smile/ To my hopes has been granted/ And I know my love tonight will come/ And will not say me nay.'

'You entertain strong feelings, Mr Cornfield.'

'And what other feelings would you expect your husband to entertain for his wife, Dr Reynolds?'

Every day he wandered the streets of the town, or along the tunnelled, bud-bright roads of Spring. Every evening, over dinner, her first question was always, 'What sage did you meet today? What wisdom did you collect?' and he would empty a pocketful into her lap, a word, a leaf, a stone, a broken eggshell, a sound, a chestnut, a colour, an acorn, a feather. For a long time she puzzled over the inordinate amount of satisfaction he could get out of the slightest bit of chat on a road, in a field, a side street. She decided in the end that he was extending, expanding, marrying everybody and everything, giving birth by communion with other selves. For eleven years he had been imprisoned on a barren island. At last, she smiled proudly, her odd man was out, coupling like an unspancelled goat.

She watched him intently. She knew her man better than he her. She observed that his strolls changed from walks to expeditions, extending farther and farther. He bought a bicycle to go farther still. She noted that he would not come salmon fishing with her, hating, so he said, that prolonged playing of the hooked fish in from the wide ocean; but she noticed that when she took down her trout rod he came, she teased, illogically, although he insisted that he came then only because he liked the long drive across the parallel ridges of Magharamore, and the Owenaheensha on to Lough Laoura. She noted further that on their return he would always ask her to pull up on some ridge where he would alight and look back.

One day he asked the question outright. 'What's out there behind those Laoura mountains?' and was patently astonished when she just said, 'Another county. No fishing. Shallow streams.'

The testing time came with the winter, cold, wet and seemingly endless. Work and fishing sufficed to distract her. He felt bottled up. The town offered few distractions. She suggested a trip to London but the look he gave her silenced her. The wintry roads discouraged him although he was abashed every morning to see Elsie Huggard start off on her three-mile trudge, head bowed into the weather, cowled under a shining black mackintosh down to her ankles. He watched television all day, or sat reading by the fire, mostly historical biographies, histories of exploration, travel books. He developed a taste for astronomy, had a brief craze for books on mountaineering. She hated to think of him sitting there in silence, his book sinking to his lap, his eyes facing an unseen fire, and for the first time a truth about him that she had always known in an abstract way became visually real – he had been beaten into subjectivity by years of loneliness. They had not killed his spirit, but he would always be at risk.

Driving home one dank, dusky, February afternoon, the hood of her red Triumph closed tight, she was startled to see him standing beside the gate-lodge greeting her with his old polite bow and raised hat. He sat in beside her; for one second, perhaps for as long as two, he smiled at her dilated eyes and then burst into a laugh.

'It's all right, darling. I am not suffering what is known as a regression to a chronologically earlier pattern of feeling. I just came up to have a chat with old Dawson the cook.'

'About what?' Suspiciously.

'He used to be a ship's cook. He sailed the seven seas in his heyday. I've been reading a book about Gauguin in Tahiti. Are you going fishing this weekend?'

'Come?'

'Yes. I could leave you at the lake and drive on. I want to see what's beyond those Laoura hills.'

'But you don't drive!'

'I've been taking lessons secretly,' he said with his naughty-boy grin. 'I got my licence yesterday.'

She said nothing for a long minute. Then she said that that was a fine idea. All the same he really might have mentioned it to her? He asked her if she would not, in that case, have wanted to teach him herself; at which she admitted that it is apparently, all too easy for a wife to begin behaving like a wife.

He duly drove her to her chosen corner of the lake, promised to meet her in the afternoon at the local pub, drove away. Twilight came. He did not. She had a drink while waiting. He did not come. She had another drink. She kept glancing at her watch. Her hands were tight. He came. When he did not say he was sorry for being late she found it hard not to behave like a wife; wondered was he finding it hard to behave like a husband. He asked her easily as they drove away how she had fared.

'Nothing worth talking about. A couple of brown trout. Under a pound each. You?'

'In the distance between two clefts of hills like breasts I saw a V of sea.'

'That,' she said sourly, 'means you were only ten thousand miles away from Tahiti.'

He comforted her knee.

'When Gauguin was a child he went to Peru, came home, sailed with the merchant marine and the French navy, chucked it, got a job, married, chucked it when he was thirty-six, tried Brittany, sailed for Martinique, chucked it, tried Paris again, chucked it, tried Brittany again, sailed to Tahiti, lived and painted there, chucked it, sailed for the Marquesas, and died. Let's fry our brown trout.'

For some fifteen miles the windscreen wipers hissed. Then the mist stopped, the sky cleared, and for the rest of the drive they were aware of a vast tumescence of moon in command of all wintry life. Immediately they got into their dusty old living room in 'Saint Senan's' he lit the laid fire. When it was blazing they sat before it with two whiskeys, exchanging trifles about their day. Presently he got up and went into the kitchen – old, flagged, vast, that nobody had refurbished for forty years. He came back wearing her butcher's blue-and-white apron, and went to her fishing basket for the two fish. She got up to help, but he waved her back commandingly.

'You stay there. I'm going to gut'em and cook'em. *Meunière?* Fresh butter just turning brown. A touch of lemon? A spot of parsley? Plates straight from oven to table.' He winked at her over his disappearing shoulder. 'This I *can* do.'

'But I'd like to help!'

'I need no help,' he said arrogantly and left her.

She sank back into her armchair and, without relish, finished her drink. Presently she heard him humming over his chopping block. To command her feelings she inhaled slowly and slowly exhaled, aware that something far less than a chorus ending from Euripides or a sunset touch would be more than enough to make her burst into tears at her Grand Perhaps singing over her two fish. Suddenly he reappeared in the door of the kitchen with a look of farcical helplessness, advanced, turned his shoulders to her and asked her to tighten those damned strings, so she knotted the cords more tightly and with an approving pat on the bottom sent him on his way.

When he was gone she covered her face with her palms and began blowing into them like waves dying in caves. This was, no doubt, since it had so happened, and, after all, Saint Augustine once said that whatever is is right, exactly what was to be expected, but it was not at all what she had wanted. She blew one last mighty wave of discontent into her hands, rose and listened to him tra-la-la-laing merrily through the Blue Danube waltz. Then, with a philosophic smile she dutifully began to lay the table. For what, as Aeschylus says, can be more pleasing than the ties of host and guest? To drown his tra-la-la-laing she murmured to herself certain famous lines by another prisoner that had always entertained her:—

> If I have freedom in my love,
>   And in my soul am free,
> Angels alone that soar above
>   Enjoy such libertee.

Marmalade

When Ellie slammed the front door he slowed his cup's approach to the coffee table to glance across his shoulder at the clock on the mantelpiece. Six forty-five? Of course. Monday. Her night for bridge, his for the art class. His coffee made a smooth landing. He sank into his armchair, carefully unfolded his evening paper, looked blindly at its headlines for a while, let it sink into his lap. If only! If only! If only they had had a child! All day she had not spoken one word to him since she said at breakfast, 'May I have some marmalade, please?' And now she was gone for the night.

Which of them first mooted this crazy idea of one night a week apart? She had been sarcastic about it. 'Divorced weekly? A comedy in 52 acts.' He had been sour. 'The road back to celibacy? Act Five.' Probably neither of us began it. Just another Knight's move, another oblique assertion of another imaginary speck of precious bloody personality threatened by some other imaginary attack by one on t'other. *Quid pro quo.* My turn now. Tit for that. Even Stephen. Omens common to every failing marriage? Like her insistence on rising early every Sunday morning for first Mass and his on staying in bed late. His demanding roast leg of lamb on Fridays against her preference for black sole – not that he did not always let her have her way – he liked black sole; or her wanting flowers before her Madonna's statue all through May. It was not the flowers he minded; it was the silent betrayal of her man who had given up 'all that' for . . . For what? At which, as if an earth tremor made the ornaments on the mantelpiece tremble, he heard all around him for miles and miles the tide of Dublin's suburban silence. Out there how many mugs like himself were enjoying the priceless company of their own personalities? He flung the newspaper on the carpet, tore off his grey tie and pink shirt, went into his bedroom, dragged on his old black roll-neck Pringle pullover, groped for his old black Homburg hat and began to brush it briskly. As good today as the day I bought it in Morgan's in Westmoreland Street for the mother's funeral. He curled a black scarf around his neck, felt for his car keys, switched off the Flo-Glo fire and the electric candles on the walls, checked the bathroom taps and the taps of the electric cooker, put out the hall light and slowly drew the front door behind him until he heard the lock's final click. Fog. A drear-nighted February. Every road lamp on the estate had its own halo. He drove with care. Bungalow, bungalow, bungalow. Some lighted, most caverns of television flicker. Exactly the kind of night he had first persuaded Father Billy Casey to doff their Roman collars, black jackets, black overcoats, black hats, put on sports jackets, chequered caps, jazzy ties and set off for some, any lounge bar in the city, in search, Father Billy had said, rocking with amusement, of what laymen call Life.

He was able to accelerate a bit on the yellow-lighted bus route. After fifteen minutes or so he felt space and damp on his right. The sea. The new hospital. Lights in a church for Benediction. Inner suburbia's exclusive gateways. The US embassy. He crossed the canal. The city's moat.

'Whither tonight?' Casey had always said at this point, rubbing his palms. Anywhere west of O'Connell Bridge used to be safe from episcopal spies; the east was less safe, too many people coming and going between the big cinemas, the bars of hotels, the Abbey Theatre, the Peacock, the Bus Arus theatre. There was the same contrast on the other side of the bridge between Dublin's only pricy hub, the cube of Grafton Street, Nassau, Dawson and Saint Stephen's Green on to the east, and the old folksy Liberty's off to the West. Once you got that bit of geography clear in your head you knew the only danger left was the moment of exit from the presbytery and your return to it. Holy Smoke! Supposing the Parish Priest caught you dressed in civvies! As Father Billy once put it a priest in a check cap is as inconceivable as a pope in the bowler hat or, suddenly remembering some scrap of his seminarian's philosophy, if not inconceivable at least unimaginable. He had enjoyed and hated these small risks so much so that he could still groan and laugh at the thought of their hairbreadth escape the night they were nearly spotted by the P.P.'s housekeeper coming home late from what she always spoke of as her Fwhishte Diriuve. That was the night Father Billy had in his Edenish innocence all unknowingly pushed him out of the Church.

'Here's to us!' Billy had cheered from where he lay strewn like a podgy Pompeian on the triclinium of his secondhand sofa, his nightcap of malt aloft. 'To us! Who have at this triumphant moment once more unarguably demonstrated the undeniable truth that privacy is the last and loveliest of all class luxuries. Look at us! Boozing to our hearts' content in peace and privacy and nobody one penny the wiser, whereas all that the most overpaid, socialist, lefty poor working man can do when he is thrown out of his pub at closing time is to take home half a dozen bottles of beer in a pack. In a pub, Foley! That's the key word. In a pub! A public house. Subject to public inspection, permission to drink only in public, get drunk in public, puke in public, under the public eye, to public knowledge. But you and I, Foley, privileged nobs by virtue of our exclusive, élitist rank as officers of the Pope's *Grande Armée* can sit here at our ease, luxuriating in the lordly privacy of Father William Casey's personal sitting-room in Saint Conleth's Roman presbytery and not another soul one penny the wiser.'

He had replied coldly:

'You've got it all wrong, Father Billy. We do not drink in lordly privacy. We drink in abject secrecy.'

One word and he became aware of the duplicity of all institutions, the Law, the Army, Medicine, the Universities, Parliament, the Press, the Church dominated by the one iron rule, *Never let down the side*. There was only one kind of people from whom you might get a bit of the truth, not because they are more moral but because they have no side to let down. Outlaws. Join any organization and Truth at once takes second place. They went on arguing it down to the bottom of the half-bottle of Irish. 'Sleep on it, Billy,' he had said. 'In whishkey weritas.'

The kindled traffic light halted him as he approached O'Connell Bridge. He peered up at the Ballast Office clock, 7.32, and remembered the night – *The* Night – when he had answered Father Billy's ritual 'Whither tonight?' with the dare-devil cry of 'Why don't we try the Long Bar in the basement of the old Met.?' which – bang in the middle of O'Connell Street – spelled maximum danger. He was still chuckling at Casey's reply when the green let him through: 'The Long Bar? The short life! Onward to booze, death and glory.' Poor Billy! Poor in every sense. All a 'booze' meant to him was a large whiskey, or two glasses of ale. He remembered how the two of them had cheered like kids that night when they found a parking spot directly opposite the Long Bar of the Met. And, behold! Here it was waiting for him again. He slid smoothly into its arms, sighing 'This is what I should be doing every night instead of staring into bloody TV or an electric fire!'

He halted at the foot of the stairs, pushed open the glass door, three semi-circular steps above the floor of the saloon, and surveyed the babble. He saw one vacant table and his mistake. A mob of youngsters. Mere boys and girls. Pint drinkers. Years of tobacco smoke. Life? Gaiety? Unconventional? Bohemian? It was just any ordinary bar. Or had it changed? Or had he? Or was it she who had transformed it that night? He edged down to the vacant table and gave his order to the bar curate. After two slow dry martinis he surrendered. He took up his homburg – no other man or woman in the rooms wore a hat – felt for his car key, foresaw fog, the drive, the empty bungalow. How Father Billy had stared around that night at all the pairs and quartettes!

'Well, here it is, Foley! Life! And I can't tell you how glad I am to see it because only last night I found myself going through the dictionary to find out what the devil the word means. I was as nearly off my rocker as that! I can now reveal to you Father Foley that Life is, quote, unquote, that condition which distinguishes animals and plants from inorganic objects and dead organisms by growth through AH metabolism, BEE adaptability and CEE reproduction. Look around you. Look at us. They are growing up. I put on seven pounds since Easter. Look at their fancy dress. Look at our fancy caps and jackets. We all adapt. Reproduction? Look at 'em, every single one of 'em with a one way first class ticket for the double bed. All booked!'

'Not all! Or don't I see over there in the corner two unaccompanied young women. The dark one isn't at all bad looking. Four people spoiling two tables who could be improving one? Maybe those two young ladies are in search of Life? Come on, Billy Casey! Let's ask them over for a drink.'

He had not meant one word of it. What they had already done on half a dozen nights was, every time, an act of the gravest indiscipline. Two soldiers of a victorious Empire frolicking in taverns with conquered barbarians? At the sight of Casey's terrified eyes he had leaned back and laughed so heartily that the dark young woman had looked across and smiled indulgently at their happiness. One second's thought and he would have merely smiled back and resumed his chatter with Casey. He spontaneously lifted his glass to her. Her smile widened whitely. His questioning eyebrows rose, his eye and thumb indicated his table invitingly, hers did the same to hers, he said 'Come on Billy, in for a penny in for a pound!' and the unimaginable of five minutes before became reality.

'Ellie,' her companion apologized admiringly for her friend, 'is very saucy'. She was herself a striking redhead, but he thought the dark one much more handsome and she had by her laugh and gesture across the bar suggested a touch of dash and character. As for her looks she had only one slight flaw; her mouth was by the faintest touch awry, and even this was in itself an attraction, that delicate, that charming fleck of imperfection that never fails to impress a woman's looks unforgettably. Her black hair, divided down the centre of her skull, was drawn back boldly like two curtains. Her eyes were as clear as her clarid speech. Their large brown irises, shining like burred chestnuts, harmonized with her willow coloured skin. She was dressed entirely in black apart from the little white ruff on her high neck that somehow made her look like a nun. He confided to himself the next day that her smiles came and went like the sly sunshine of April. He introduced himself as Frederick Cecil Swinburne and his companion, to Casey's grinning delight, as Arthur Gordon Woodruffe, both of them final medicals at Trinity College. She said, 'I am Ellie Wheeler Wilcox, and my friend is Molly Malone'; both of them private secretaries to directors of The Irish Sweep. They passed what any casual observer would have seen as a merry hour, as light, bright and gay as a joking and laughing scene in an operetta. On parting they all four said they might meet again the next Monday night. He said a couple of hours later in Father Billy's rooms in the presbytery that the only thing missing was that those two young women should have been nuns in disguise and they should all have burst out into an Offenbach quartette. Casey's solemn reply had infuriated him:

'I am afraid, Father Foley, we went a bit too far tonight. We deceived those two young ladies. We pretended. We were guilty of bad faith.'

He responded in exasperation with a whisper of 'Well, I'll be damned!'

This restored Father Billy's sense of humour far enough to let him disagree about the damnation bit though, possibly, there might be an extra couple of thousand years of Purgatory in store for them both. All the same he kept coughing dramatically the following Monday morning to indicate the onset of a bad cold.

The corner table was empty. No Miss Wilcox. No Miss Malone. He sat at the table that he had shared the week before with Father Casey prolonging three tasteless Martinis for an hour. Thereupon, cursing his silliness he had clapped on his homburg and risen to his feet and there she was on the platform of the last three semicircular steps of the entrance door, tall and slim, dressed in black, her eyelashes overflowing her cheeks, her hair as closefitting as a cap, her high neck extended to assist her searching gaze. He flung up his hand. Smiling back at him she slowly edged her way between the tables. She sat opposite him though still looking about her, explaining that she had expected to meet her friend Molly Malone, although Molly did mention something today about feeling a cold coming on, but he felt so happy in her presence that he heeded little she said until he got her to talking about herself, her girlhood in the country, in County Offaly, where her father was a National Teacher, her two younger sisters, her brother Fonsy, short for Alphonsus, who had emigrated to England and was now married in Birmingham; not that he attended to her chat half so much as he did to the fleeting mobility of her features, her contralto laughter, her vivacious gestures, though he did heed her carefully when she described her Auntie Nan with whom she was lodging in a little house in Ranelagh, and her friends, working mostly in the Irish Sweep, which led her in turn to ask him about what it is like to be a final medical in Trinity College and about his plans when he became a doctor, a question that instantaneously reminded him of Father Billy's words about bad faith. She listened to his lies with such a transparent expression of belief that he felt thrown down beneath her feet by a whirlwind of shame that kept gnawing at him for the rest of the night, until the moment came when he had halted outside her aunt's little red brick home in that terraced *cul de sac* at Ranelagh. There, drawn up beside the kerb, he gripped her hand not, as she obviously thought and by her warm smile showed, to say a grateful goodnight but to plead for her trust. He must confess the truth about himself.

'Miss Wilcox, I have been deceiving you.'

'The truth? Deceiving me?'

Staring, frightened by his intensity and tone.

'I am not a medical student. I made all that up.'

If only he could have stopped there. Neither, she could laugh, was she Ella Wheeler Wilcox. He had to tell her the essence of him. He kept pressing her hand tighter and tighter.

'I am a clerical student. Trying to become a priest. You have been a revelation from heaven to me. I can't go on with it. I no longer want to be a priest.'

Her eyelids shot open at that last word. While he went on to half explain they opened wider and wider as if she were opening the doors of her soul to him. In the silence that followed she kept staring at him and he at her. In his celibate ignorance he was feeling for the first time the full blast of power that Woman when reduced to one special woman possesses by the mere fact of being female. She in her virginal ignorance was transfixed by the power that Man in the person of this one man held over her by the mere fact of being male. Each was at that moment so evenly conqueror and conquered that if the essential god of all lovers had in that blind alley breathed over them even so delicately as would not have shaken the filaments of a dandelion in full cloud of seed they would have sunk into one another's arms. That they did not, he often thought later, was due less to the gods than to her aunt, or to whatever other hand suddenly lit the fanlight. What she may have said before she jumped from the car and ran up the brief concrete path to the door beneath the light he was never after to remember verbatim except for the petals of her voice declaring with unarguable clarity that they must never meet again, and her 'Very well!' to his wild pleading that they must meet just once more so that neither of them should remember the other ungratefully. So, they did meet just once again, and went on meeting just once again for the whole of the next year, propelled as gently and as irresistibly as a yacht before a summer breeze by sympathy, chivalry and self-immolation until to his astonishment, one gentle May evening in the stodgy bedroom of her Auntie Nan's dim house in Ranelagh, while the old lady was away on holidays in County Cork, a typhoon of passion swallowed them both. After another year, marked by more agonizing and less passion, he extricated himself from his priestly vows. They married.

All that was five years ago and he had long since accepted that he was never to understand what estranged them, he who had so often in his presbytery given counsel and comfort to young marrieds lost in the same fogged wood. All he knew for certain was that that anticipatory year of waiting, of tenderly comforting one another, of trying to decide what he should do had been the happiest year of his life, conjoined by the misery of separation, divided now by the disaster of domesticity.

They had never really quarrelled, never violently confronted one another, though of course they now and again 'had words', the worst being the night he had evaded her clamant desire on the eve of Good Friday, the anniversary of the execution of a great man in whose alleged godliness he no longer believed, and she had spat at him, 'Your very skin is dyed black! You will never wash yourself of your precious stigmata!' to which he had retorted, 'You? You of all people dare say that to a man who has cast off every last trace of what you call black? You with your getting up at dawn, your statues and your flowers and your evening benedictions and all the rest of your pietistic falderals and fandangos, you say that to me?'; all of which she dismissed haughtily with the passionate observation that God's world is one – joy and pain, crocuses and the crucifixion, love and lust, desire and denial, human passion and prayer.

'Dare you deny it?'

Weaponless he did not.

The only clear hint he ever got anywhere about how marriages break had been vouchsafed to him one morning a bare month ago in the little shop of convenience near their bungalow, managed by an ageing man and wife. He had always found each of them normally friendly and loquacious. This day the two were in the shop together. The old man, before attending to him, quietly asked his wife some trivial question concerning their stock, was it about firelighters or washing soda? She answered him in the voice of *ancien régime* courtesy, in the softest voice, with all the formality of a duchess from the good old days before the Revolution. She said between politeness and hauteur, 'I beg your pawrdon?' He had fled from the shop, horrified by the revelation that this old pair were living out their last days in a state of savage war. Passion ends in politeness. After that he added to his 'If only we could have had a child' the wish that they could have one blazing, battering, bloody row.

He jingled his car keys, rose to face the fog, the bungalow, the evening paper already out of date, clapped on his homburg, and saw a vision. His wife was standing on the platform at the end of the stairs, dressed in black, her hair as black as thunder, her midnight lashes enlarging her eyes that roved the rooms in search of . . . In search of whom? He flung up the arm of a drowning man. For a moment she looked across the rooms at him, then her eyelids sank, her eyebrows shot upwards, she looked at him again, she decided, smiled her small crooked smile at him and edged forward between the tables. She held out her hand, with, 'Well, after all these years if it isn't Mr Swinburne! And what have you been doing with yourself all this time? Medicine?'

'Miss Wilcox!' he said and shook her hand. 'You will join me in a drink?' She gave him her sly smile, took the proffered chair and let silence fall between them as she slowly removed her gloves finger-tip by finger-tip. He as slowly extracted a cigarette and lit it. At their first far-off meeting when he had taken her to be an ingenuous miss of about twenty he had been struck by this same air of complete assurance. They both asked simultaneously, 'Do you often come here?' and chuckled into a fresh silence which she quickly took hold of with, 'I have been told that some gentlemen have their pet pubs. Is this one of yours, Mr Swinburne?'

Two seconds' silence during which he wondered if it was one of hers.

'I have no pet pub. I used to come here years ago to meet a girl I used to know.'

'What happened to her?'

'She just disappeared.' The bar curate stood silently beside them. 'Your usual, Miss Wilcox? A Dry Martini? – Make it two. On the rocks.'

'Nice of you to remember my favourite drink, Mr Swinburne.'

'I have a good memory. When you stood in that doorway just now you reminded me very much of my friend. Oddly enough she also liked a Dry Martini. Like you she was tall, dark and queenly.'

She lowered her head sideways to deprecate the compliment, smiled to accept it.

'This is odd. When I saw you just now you reminded me of a man I first met in this bar several years ago. I have not seen him for a long time either. He, as you say, disappeared.'

'What happened to him?'

Three seconds pause.

'I have wondered. My friends and I have never been able to agree about what happens to make these people disappear.'

'Your friends?'

Four seconds' pause during which she slowly turned her head to look towards a large round table, in an alcove which he had not previously noted, occupied by five or six women of varying ages. They were all looking her way. Her left wrist lifted her palm an inch to greet them. Her chin nodded an unspoken agreement. She turned back to him.

'My friends.'

'Your bridge club?'

Five seconds' pause.

'I never play bridge. But we are a club. All married, all botched, all of us working now in The Irish Sweep. We came together by chance. Last summer I got chatting with Mrs Aitch, that is the jolly fat woman in the orange head scarf with her back to us. Angela Hanafey. She is about 46. Her husband was, is, always will be an AA case. She has four sons all but one grown up. She just happened to be walking beside me one evening when we were pouring in our hundreds out of the Sweepstake offices at five o'clock. We had never laid eyes on one another before. "God!" she said to me. "I'm starved for a drink. Come and have a quick one on me at the Horseshoe." We met Mrs King there. She's the slim, handsome blonde, don't let her see you looking. She is still bitter of her ex. He left her holding three children and slid off to get lost somewhere in England with a slut of seventeen. It was she brought along Kit Ferriter, the baby of the bunch, six months married and glad to be living alone again in her virginal bedsit. Kit studied sociology for three years at Trinity. She says she learned far more about it in six months of marriage. Three or four others drop in and out. All sorts. One is married to an army captain who batters her. Another to a briefless barrister. Mrs Aitch calls us the Missusmatched. Monday is club night. No other rules. No premises.'

'And you talk about men and sex and marriage.'

'Sex? Never. Men? No. Marriage? Occasionally. Not as an important subject. We mostly talk about woman things. Food, cooking, dress, make-up, kids, the cost of living, our jobs, nothing in particular.'

'And in your club's view why do those marrieds have this odd way of disappearing?'

'Why?'

Her eyebrows threw a shrug over her left shoulder. Her eyelids lowered a curtain on the shrug. The corners of her mouth buttoned it down. She leaned back to consider either the question or him. When she tinkled the ice in her glass it sounded like his idea of Swiss cowbells in far-off valleys. When she laughed her contralto laugh it hurt him that he had not heard it for a long long time.

'Yes, why?'

'Why? We solved that months ago when we invented The Seven C's. Every marriage, we decided, sinks or swims on any three of,' right finger, left thumb checked them off, 'Concupiscence, Comradeship, Contact, Kids, Cash, high or low Cunning, and not to give a tinker's Curse about everything in general and anything in particular.'

'Ye have left out Love!'

'Mrs Aitch, our mother hen, dealt ably with that. "I made a fatal mistake" says she, "with my fellow. I led him to think I was the reincarnation of the Blessed Virgin. On our honeymoon I got a sudden, terrible thirst for tangerines. Afterwards we both found out, too late, that pregnant women get these odd hungers. He would have done anything for me, of course, on our honeymoon. He went to a power of trouble to get me the tangerines but get them he did! When we were back home I got a sudden wish for apricots. He rumbled and bumbled about it but still and all the poor devil did get me the apricots. A month later I got an unquenchable longing for nothing less than wild strawberries. Well, by that time I had a belly on me like a major. He told me to go to hell and find out for myself where anyone could find wild strawberries in the month of November and I knew at once that my dear love had vanished from the earth as if the fairies had got him." Kay Ferriter, our expert on sociology, told her she was lucky that he didn't batter the other fellow's baby out of her. The dear child insists that Love, which you say we have omitted from our Seven C's, is a mass-invented delusion with a life-expectation of three weeks.'

She rose, holding out her hand. 'Nice meeting you again, Mr Swinburne. It was very pleasant. Now I must join my friends.' He held her hand pleadingly. 'Can't we meet again? Say next Monday night. Just for a quick drink?' She looked around the rooms, said, indifferently, 'Alright,' and joined her welcoming group. As he walked out he heard behind him again her miraculously joyous laughter.

Back home he kicked aside the evening paper, switched on his fire, sank into his armchair and fell into a stunned sleep. In the morning the only time either of them spoke over their breakfastette in their kitchenette across their hinged tablette was when she said, 'May I have some marmalade please? ... Thank you.' On their way into town to work, he as always driving, he did say that next Monday night he would be as usual at his art class and she with an air of slight surprise replied that she would of course as usual be playing bridge with her friends.

Accordingly, on the following Monday night she again left home before him to walk to the bus, and he, after taut calculations followed her in time to be in the Long Bar before her arrival, seated facing the glass doors. Now and again he glanced furtively towards the women's table in the alcove to his far left. His jury? His judges? His amused witnesses? Again, after two slowly sipped drinks, he jumped to his feet between rage and regret just as she appeared in the doorway. For a moment she stood there motionless, then slowly descended to the level of the bar, edging between the tables towards him with, 'So we meet again, Mr Swinburne,' sat, began calmly to deglove. Of the precious ten minutes she allowed him that night he could afterwards recall clearly only one sequence, which he initiated:

'Did they ask if we were related?'

'No. And I did not vouchsafe. You could be only one of two things.'

He worked it out.

'Or I could be a new friend?'

'Here? So briefly?'

'Did they say nothing at all about me?'

'Mrs King said, "He looks like a priest, all in black, even to the hat." I said that the first time I met you seven years ago, here, you were dressed in the colours of the rainbow. I left them guessing. I said, "Maybe he has become a priest since then."'

Ten seconds' silence, looking at one another. She swallowed her last piece of ice, put down her glass smartly, picked up her gloves and handbag, rose, said, 'Have you?' and turned to go. He winced but held her hand to beg for next Monday. He pleaded for it. They had talked so very little. 'And I have nowhere else to go.'

'Except', she said sympathetically, 'back? Alright. Then they *will* know!', and left him for her beaming friends.

In this fashion he had continued to meet her every week into the first green promises of spring until by early May these extemporaneous meetings took on the character of regular assignations and, since they were never mentioned at home, the clandestine air of a double life. He looked forward to these encounters more and more eagerly; as we say he lived for them, suspected that she enjoyed them equally; he noted with excitement that they extended themselves on occasion to fifteen minutes, even to nearly twenty minutes and on one memorable night to fully twenty-five minutes – this being the night when he asked for her opinion as to which of her club's Seven C's of marriage was the most important of all. She answered promptly.

'The first three of course. Concupiscence, Camaraderie, and Contact. Some people think Camaraderie comes first, but that is just Con disguising itself as Cam. Kids inevitably follow. Then Cash edges forward. Then more and more need arises for High Cunning. But on all occasions thereafter there is the need for not caring a damn, for the indifference of a divorce court judge.'

Naturally they started to argue, and they might have gone on arguing if she had not suddenly become aware of radiations of impatience from across the room. The next morning she said, 'May I have the marmalade please? Thank you.' But then, as lightly as she pasted the preserve on her toast she added, 'By the way I understood you to say some time ago that your art class meets twice a week. My bridge club is proposing to meet on Mondays and Fridays.' He at once decided that their relations had completely changed and on that following Friday the women's alcove contained only two elderly men drinking stout. His chest swelled with triumph. She arrived on time. Unasked he clicked his fingers for the bar attendant and ordered their drinks. Presently he observed with a tolerant amusement at the transparency of the feminine mind that the conversation had returned to last Monday's question about the primacy in marriage of feelings of fellowship or of desire, to which she referred as 'passion' and rather brazenly (he thought) as 'lust'. In the course of their conversation she said:

'Of course in all this one should first agree about the general principle of the thing. I mean is it not all largely a question of what in life does one most believe in, in Poetry or in Prose? I happen to see the world as a complex of things beyond all understanding, far too bewildering to be confined or defined by human laws or rules, shalls and shalt nots. I look at it all as a miracle and a mystery, a place of beauty and horror, a spring flower, a tree in bud, a dead child, a husband dying of cancer— Mrs Aitch's boozy husband is dying that way and she has fallen in love with him again – a lottery like the Irish Sweep, chance, fate, the gods, God, the Madonna, love, lust, passion, a baby at the breast. Everything is one thing. That is why I love to have flowers for the Madonna who had a baby, miraculously according to you, not that it matters how she had it, why I rise in the morning for the first dark mass where they celebrate again the execution of a god, or of God, not that that matters either, why I like to come in the evening for the last benediction before the dark night, why I used to let that friend of mine whom I loved years ago go to bed with me because I thought he saw life the way I do as a poem that anybody can read and that nobody can understand.'

Staring at her, taken again by her passion, yes, he could remember those wild talks during that year of blissful agony before . . .

'Alas!' she smiled her hurt smile. 'When we got married he changed. Looking at him then I was often reminded of the marvellous thing Keats once said about the greatest quality any human being can possess – the power to live in wonder and uncertainty, and mystery and doubt without ever reaching out after fact and reason. My friend turned out to be a man always looking for fact and reason, a law maker, a law giver, a law explainer, a policeman, a judge, a proseman, a prosy priest longing for his pulpit.'

The bar's chatter, rumble, clinking, talk, laughing stopped dead. Silence isolated them. Then:

'Did you never consider, Miss Wilcox, that this friend of yours may nevertheless have once dearly loved you?'

She pounced.

'Once? Yes. Once! One night in my aunt's house in Ranelagh while she was on holidays in County Cork with her sister. For a whole year after that night my wild lover wandered around and around in his head in search of fact and reason. I,' she smiled crookedly, 'was left waiting for the poetry of love.'

Unguardedly he laid a hand on her hand, said 'Ellie!' saw that he had blundered, withdrew. There was a staring silence. Then she looked at the ceiling as if she were listening to a plane passing over Dublin, looked at him once again, drew back her cuff from her wristlet watch with her index finger, seized her bag and rose.

'You have reminded me, Mr Swinburne, I promised my Auntie Nan to keep an eye on her little house in Ranelagh while she is gone to Derbyshire to stay with a niece. Would you mind leaving me there on your way home?'

He threw up his palms. Outside it was raining. They did not speak in their car. She became proprietress of his homburg hat, nursing it on her lap. When they arrived outside the tiny red-brick house he offered Miss Wilcox to wait and drive her to wherever she lived, it was no night for bussing, she had no hope of getting a taxi. She said that that would be most kind of him, 'But do come in! This is real rain,' and clapped his black hat comically on her head and ran through the rain beside the new mown patch of grass. He was relieved to see her laughing gaily at him as he also ran, hatless and stooped, through the rain. She left him in the parlour while she went off to do her checking room by room. He could recognise only two items in the parlour: the aquatint of Christ with the Samaritan woman at the well, its frame painted in ugly commercial gilt (his mind clicked, *They shall not thirst any more*), and the corded old sofa where he had put his arms around her for the first time. He heard her steps on the linoleum overhead. The photograph of a bearded man on the mantelpiece. What relative? He went into the kitchen. Her aunt's kingdom. An antique iron range. A stoneware sink. A crucifix. Tidy. Cold. He wandered to the stairs. On its side walls lithographs of castles. He identified Ross Castle in Killarney. Then Blarney Castle in Cork. He paused longest at Reginald's Tower in Waterford still seeing that corded sofa in the parlour. It had been raining that night too. That, too, had been May. Through a little shower they had raced for the door.

From the front bedroom she called him. 'Mister Ess?' When he reached the half open door he saw through the vertical aperture between the panelled door and its jamb an object that he recalled clearly, and with emotion, a tall mirror so mounted on its mahogany frame as to be able to tilt forward or backward. In this cheval mirror he had, that first night, seen her completely undressed. Now, modestly undressed, in black bikini and black brassiere, she was smiling into the mirror in the direction of the slowly opening door. He entered, became aware that she was deliberately modelling female allurement, his hat tilted on her head, one wrist back-twisted on her left hip, right knee forward, the other hand airily held aloft.

'Well?' she invited him in the mirror with her minx's smile. 'Do you really still love me?'

Between incomprehension and revelation, desire and revulsion, passion and despair he gestured wildly around the room. Over the bedhead Pope Pius X in black and white stared like an intolerant boy from under black eyebrows. His mind clicked: Giuseppe Sarto, that bitter anti-modernist. By the bed on the wall a Holy Water font. Last thing before sleep. His mind clicked: daring seminarian joke – *Here I lay me down to sleep, upon my little bed, but if I die before I wake how will I know that I am dead*? On the dressing-table a tiny Infant of Prague, gaudy, pyramidical, pagan.

'Yes!' he said defiantly. 'I do still love you. But not this way! Not here! Where everything smells of spinster and sanctity!'

She turned to him. She handed him back his black hat. He was prepared for her to spit that there is no other way; or that 'This room was once heaven to you.' If she had said that he would have said, 'Yes! But then I was defying it, now I would be accepting it.' Or she might in memory of lost hope say nothing. She said nothing. She looked from his eyes to his feet, and from his feet up to his eyes, and with one fast swing of her fist she crashed him across the face. Her engagement ring drew a red line in blood across his jaw. He returned the blow, they grappled, swaying and stumbling, screaming bitch and bastard, fell across the bed where her nails tore at his face until he found himself mastering her on her back and suddenly she was kissing his slavering mouth and groaning over and over, 'Give it to me.'

Whether it was the morning sun milliarding through the window into his face or the boom of a plane just taken off from Dublin, or the sound of a neighbouring churchbell that woke him he found himself sitting up in bed bewildered until he was informed by a hand stroking his bare back and her voice soothing him with 'It is alright, Swinny! This is Saturday. Neither of us has to work.' He sank back on the pillow, closed his eyes, remembered, turned his head towards her face on her palm on her pillow watching him quizzically. Beyond her on the floor he saw his homburg hat battered flat.

'I'm starving,' he announced querulously.

'Love always does that.'

Always?

'Can we have breakfast?'

'Here? There's nothing in this house. No bread, milk, butter. Nothing. Water and power turned off. No shave, no shower. Where do you live, Swinny? Let's have brekker in your place.'

At this inane question his eyes widened. His lips tightened. He could say, 'What the hell is this game you are playing?', or, 'I am sick and tired of this falal,' or, 'How long more are we going to act the parts of cat and mouse?' He said sourly, 'I live near Ballybrack. Half an hour away.' While they were hurrying into their clothes she toed his black hat with, 'You might as well throw that out.' He lifted it, dusted it affectionately, punched it, said, 'One never knows' and put it on. 'Hadn't we better make the bed?' he asked in his disciplined way. She waved a paw. 'She won't be back for a week, I'll drop in some day.' He held her wrist when she was unlocking the street door. 'The neighbours?' She ushered him out. 'You are the gas man come to measure the meter.'

He took the six-lane Bray Road. She murmured, 'I am still sleepy,' and leaned back her head and closed her eyes. The morning traffic was floating inward on his right. His outward lane was empty. He would be home in twenty minutes. He pondered on the coming confrontation. Home, she silently prepared breakfast. While he showered and shaved he was phrasing his ultimatum. His cheek needed a slim strip of plaster. Back in the kitchen he found a changeling who spoke silently, as all long-marrieds can, ignoring words, hearing thoughts, interpreting silence, speaking runes. He sat to table and waited for it. Her open palm politely indicated his dish of marmalade. His belly went red with rage. He accepted the challenge. He withheld his marmalade. She looked at him mildly. He yielded the dish and waited. Slowly she stroked his marmalade to and fro. Do come a little early. Before the others. My aunt will not be home until Saturday. He was almost certain that the extreme corner of her upper lip stirred. A speck of marmalade clung to her cheek. It made her look agreeably silly. He rubbed brisk palms, grabbed three slices of toast, surveyed his favourite dish of bacon and tomatoes, poured himself coffee, faced a hearty breakfast. But wait! Hold it! Half a sec.! This woman? His fists closed like castles on either side of his breakfast. Who is she? My wife? Somebody else's? Nobody's? Is she a bit crazy? Does she mean all this? His memory clicked. Who said *Love is a mood to a man, to a woman life or death*? It was Ella Wheeler Wilcox! Without raising her eyes or ceasing to munch her toast she slowly pushed the marmalade back to him. He considered the move, and her. The snippet of marmalade kept seductively moving up and down. He remembered his old Parish Priest saying to him as they parted, 'Once a celibate . . .' Pensively he plastered his toast. Impassively she watched him.

From Huesca with Love and Kisses

A handsome young woman of about thirty, her black hair straight and shining as if it had just been pomaded, her eyes as brown as polished mahogany, her complexion of the warmest, her figure dangerously near to portly, is lying on a deck-chair in the gardens of a small but well thought of Irish rural hotel called, after the nearby village, Carrigduv House. Before her there stretches one of the vast bays, really an inland sea, that the Atlantic has clawed out from between the mountains of this westerly end of Europe. She does not see the bay. Her eyelids are closed tight. When she clinches them more tightly a tear oozes. Her name is Ruth Goodman. She is Jewish. She is in despair.

Ruth had known that the instant she opened her mouth in Carrigduv everybody would think that she was English, which was only half-true; just as they would think when they saw her painting before her easel on one of their blank beaches, or in one of their ragged fields, that she was a painter; and if they had questioned her directly about those things she would not in politeness have denied either, least of all the second, despite her reservations and doubts. Otherwise she had so far truthfully answered every conjecture advanced towards her in the circumlocutory, devious way that an Irish acquaintance had amiably warned her to expect: the jokes about her name, Goodman, Good-woman, Goodgirl, Goodwife, as a delicate way of finding out if she were married; where and for how long had she lived in London, curious about the source of her sallow complexion; would she call painting real work, meaning had she another job; and did she not think that if one can afford it, is it not much easier nowadays to fly to Cork than have to come by train and boat, a way of probing her income. The technique amused her. She was familiar with it from her travels in various remote parts of Europe from her native Spain to inland Greece. In fact she would have liked many more such questions, interchanges (from which she always got as much as she gave), being convinced that nobody can paint anything anywhere, a pig in a sty, a cart in a stable, a lamp in a lane, a tree in a field, a busted zinc bucket being rolled by the wind in a backyard, without first merging oneself intimately into the rustic local life where the humblest household object gradually becomes so familiar as to be no longer seen.

Her obsessive exemplar of this credo was the seventeenth-century Dutch painter Paul Potter whose painting of four bulls had overwhelmed her five years before when she happened to notice it amid a lot of junk displayed in the Flemish-Dutch room of the Galleria Sabaudia in Turin. During the hour or so that she had spent wandering through this old building she found herself coming back again and again to that room trying to make out what it was that had so deeply impressed her about those four bulls, two of them wholly white, one black-rumped and the fourth a Holstein mapped in black and white. Three were standing, one lying motionless, beside an almost defoliated willow in the forefront of thousands of acres of flat land obviously reclaimed from the sea. Otherwise clouds filled nine-tenths of the canvas; that is if the word 'filled' could possibly have any meaning in face of that infinity of light sifted through clouds as chequered as those four tiny bulls down below on their vast pinch of salvaged land.

She had been the last visitor to leave the gallery. That afternoon as she wandered through its once-royal city (modern travellers find it more famous now for motor cars than for kings) she saw only the bulls and the clouds. They followed her even when she extinguished the light in her bedroom. They were her first thought the next morning, so teasingly that although it had been her plan to take the earliest train to Genoa she suddenly changed her mind in order to have one more look at a canvas that implacably challenged her to decide what set it so magically above the hundreds of other pieces of Dutch naturalism that she had admired soberly and tranquilly ever since she had decided in her teens that the one thing she wanted to do with her life was to be a painter. She barely caught her second choice of train, feeling by now thrown quite off her course by those damned bulls.

As she glared out of her carriage window, she pondered on what, she feared, might become an obsession if she did not get some sort of reasonable answer to her question. She was still glaring as the train crept through the Monferrato down to the wide Alessandrian plain manufactured, like the whole series of plains between Turin and the Adriatic, by aeons of river-borne Alpine dust which first became mud and ultimately Venice. Rice country? Cow country? Transformed marshland? Had Time something to say to her problem? If Venice could be based on mud, if beauty could be born of dust ... At which an informing rocket exploded in her dark. She had espied far away across the sunburned plain, hazy under the heat – soporific, shadowless, brutal – a tiny pink campanile right in the middle of the limitless globe of blue sky surrounding it on all sides. Seeing it, defining it, she at first angrily sniffed 'How picturesque!' in much the same scornful voice as she would have dismissed anybody's 'picturesque' explanation of any other equally obvious fact of life, and was the second after suddenly back in London fifteen years ago, a girl of 17, applying for entry to the Slade, listening – she was later assured that it had been a great privilege – to a well known or at least a well established painter chatting to one of the assessors about her 'Examples of Recent Work' as if (she thought furiously) she were stone deaf.

'Oh, not again!' the old painter had sniffed as another of the water colours she had done on the Italian Lakes that summer was placed on the easel. 'You know, Kenworthy, I can never so much as think of those bloody Lakes without feeling that I am back again at a Parochial Sale of Work trying to raise funds for the dry rot in the crypt or wood-worm in the chantry. When I was a youngster you could never go to one of those eleemosynary affairs without seeing at least one water colour of the Lakes on sale. Glass dusty. Frame cracked. Colours faded. Perpetrated by the late wife of the late vicar on their late honeymoon on Lake Como ...'

The assessor yielded him a polite smile; lifted to her apologetic eyebrows! Afterwards he assured her that the old boy always treated new students this way, and a day later could be as kind to them as if they were stray kittens.

'Always the same. See! Here we have it again, sixty years after I was in short pants. The quaint boat moored beside the quaint steps. The quaint garden gate under its quaint arch. The veils of purple bougainvillaea ordered by the yard from Harrods. The good old pretty old pots of geraniums lining the old path from the old boat to the old gate. And of course the inevitable picturesque Swiss mountains as a backdrop to it all. Oh! Well! Never mind! The brush work is vigorous. The drawing is accurate. Time and the Slade will knock the nonsense out of him, or her. Make 'em realize that the picturesque boat was also useful to fish from. That one can get pickled capers from nasturtiums to flavour the perch. That those pretty mountains can send some pretty snow storms all over the lakes when the tourists have all gone home. Why the devil is it that no young person ever realizes that in any part of the world what is picturesque to visitors is a mere fact of life to the natives? Something so familiar that they never see it, not even when they use it. Oh, of course they can feel a presence! Or an absence? A boat, a goat, a dog, a cat, a son, a daughter. If one of these chaps lost his wife he would see with a heart-breaking clarity a face he might not have noticed for forty years. I suppose nothing but experience makes a student realize that nobody can paint anything until he feels it rather than sees it, better still not until he remembers it long after he buried the mere image of it in his memory. He will pass by some place, some corner, some house, some face a thousand times after he first saw it and not notice it in the way a painter notices things until, only God knows why, years and years after he looks at it and at once wants to shove it into a picture. The past is always a bit of the present. After all isn't that the kind of stuff every artist deals in? Scraps found at the bottom of a boot-box, stuck in a book like a marker, or where a fellow I used to know used always keep his cheese, rolled up in a sock in the hot press. I'm sure that is where the Mona Lisa came from. Every Madonna worth a damn. The half forgotten. I must leave you. I have to drop in at the nursing home.'

The old boy's voice trailed away gently, just as he not so much walked away as shuffled to the door while Ruth blushing to her guts with vexation, stood glaring at her shameful water colour, barely hearing the exchange at the door: the younger man asking how was 'she' today and the old man replying, 'Not well. Not at all well', in a bewildered tone as if he were trying to remember some face to which he had not given a thought these forty years.

It was this moment at the Slade that she recalled as the little pink campanile began to move in a slow half-circle to the north. Never looked at by the people living around it? Invisible even to the few who regularly prayed in it? Some presence, some familiar, some memory that if one of those locals were to emigrate to Manhattan or Boston might bring tears; like its one electric light bracket, its one village tree, its old busted zinc bucket they used to be so accustomed to hear rolling in the pastor's backyard of windy nights that they no longer heeded it. Like one of their goats, dogs, cats. Like Paul Potter's four bulls that he had resurrected from his memories not of bulls but of beer houses, of days and nights with the herring fleet, of those boring years when his country seemed to be always at war with Spain, of fat serving girls in fat feather beds, of mornings after when the bells tolling down from the Zuydertorn hammered his sore head. Potter had seen bulls galore but never exactly just like these. And anyway how the blazes could any painter have persuaded four bulls to hold the pose for all the hours during which he recorded them? The man had recreated a thousand moments of his life in a candle-lit attic packed with hastening clouds and infinite space and wandering herds and northern light and called his life-story 'Four Bulls'.

The campanile had floated out of sight, already a nest of memory, and she was open to agree that it is perhaps in that broody nest that all art wherever engendered breaks its shell, opens its yellow maw to be fed by its begetter, and expertly spreads its furry wings for its first flight, already alert, thanks to some ancestral memory, for the magpie and the neighbour's cat.

Ever since that conjunction of a grumpy old painter in the Slade, and Paul Potter's bulls, and a tiny pink campanile seen from a stuffy carriage creeping across a Piedmontese plain, the idea that familiar experiences are the easiest to forget and the most fruitful to recall had nestled in her phylactery. Presently she added to the importance of the familiar a phrase she came on in a poem by Yeats praising 'heart-revealing intimacy'. The words now stayed in her phylactery as things, as ideas never to be exposed, as she had found out when she first tried to talk about her credo in a pub to four other would-be painters. One of them, a woman devoted to abstract art, pretended to assume that by words like 'familiar' and 'intimacy' she meant illicit sexual relations, and two of the other three mercilessly followed her lead. After that she kept her mouth shut about forgotten memories, intimacy and the familiar, excepting only for one of the three others, an Irishman, who seemed to sympathize with her; and after all they were both descendants of lost tribes, conquered peoples ground into the dust, wanderers aware that it takes centuries of forgotten memories to turn a new local habitation into an old home. In all she met him again in their alien metropolis only three times. She heard then that he had weakly surrendered, become first a commercial artist, then moved to Manchester, finally emigrated to Western Australia, married and settled in Perth. She, fortunate to have got a job in one of the well-known, small London galleries, stubbornly held on, now not so much a Sunday painter as a secret painter, as coy about her passion as if art were a glorious young god desirable beyond the reach of all but the barely perceptible few.

Now and again she would get an amiably satirical card from her confidant in Perth (W.A.) signed Liam, she had forgotten his patronymic and he never gave an address nor said anything more intelligible than 'How is your HRI doing?', meaning her Heart Revealing Intimacy. These cards were all aimed to arrive on such self-mocking occasions as Mothers' Day, or April Fools' Day. Once on Saint Valentine's Day he became loquacious enough to claim that the remains of this wandering saintly *Irishman*, that word underlined, are NOT, that word underlined three times, to be found in Rome but under the high altar of the Carmelite Church in Aungier Street in Dublin. She was relieved that he never expected an answer. Her HRI was not doing well, neither in nor out of London. She could paint, yes. So can thousands upon thousands. She could execute a happy design, yes. But the ultimate break through custom and convention to what she still called intimacy (and maybe that sour woman in that pub was right about intimacy being a sexual power) she had never achieved, no matter where or how she sought it. Italy mocked her. To her horror she found that Holland also was picturesque. She did once hear a whisper in Spain. Then last March, she got from Perth a postcard commemorating the common birthday of Saint Patrick and one Bobby Jones. It bore a sketch of an Irishman in kneebreeches, tails, a comic hat with a vast shamrock stuck in it, leading a small pig and waving a shillelagh, saying 'For God's sake send me a sketch of some corner of ould Oireland'. This time it did carry an address, and the full signature, Liam Clancy. It also showed a stain with an arrow pointing to it, saying 'Teardrop?'

So three months later here she is, lying in a deck-chair outside a hotel called Carrigduv House in South-West Cork hiding behind her eyelids. She has been here ten days, is due to return to London inside four more, and every canvas she attempted each day was daubed over every morning after, once spiked again and again in a fury by her Spanish heels. She is not weeping because her holiday has been a failure: she is in a state of terror, because she at last feels certain that she is.

For her first few days in Carrigduv she had overflowed with happiness. 'This', she felt, 'is exactly what I have always been looking for': immediate cognition, doors thrown wide open on Liberty Hall, a fortress of coequality in friendship, tolerance, understanding, warm compassion, a Land of Cockaigne indifferent to, unaware of the venal world beyond the surrounding mountains. After four days her painting informed her that if all this were truly so it did not show in her work. Alerted she began to feel uneasy. She became suspicious. Each new expert, heartless painting, dismissed, denied, destroyed, put her on guard. She presently became inescapably aware of one of those all-too-recognizable flavours that might fling open the eyes of any guest anywhere at the end of an otherwise flawless banquet. Was it instant coffee? Japanese Cognac? Staffordshire port? The peculiar aroma of Scottish cigars? 'All-too-recognizable' because she was by now far from unfamiliar with this experience of betrayal, estrangement, alienation. Had it always been her error to have asked too much? Even though all she had ever wanted was a little of the smell and touch of that familiar experience that so many people call Home? And yet she had to admit that Ireland had some virtues. A certain coequality of feeling between her fellow-residents in Carrigduv House did operate perfectly, even though she had also finally become aware that it worked only after the manner of continental guidebooks that graduate the virtues of hotels by means of crossed forks: five forks for Traditional and Luxurious coequality; four forks for Top Class equality; three for Very Comfortable, two for Comfortable, one for Plain but Adequate, and none at all for places where, like Mimi in *La Bohème*, the visitors did not attend the egalitarian mass even if they did pray a lot to the good Lord.

True, she had had to concede, in her rational Jewish way, that she had noted on her very first night that a priest (a monsignor she presumed from the triangle of purple between his chin and his vest) sat at the head of the long table while she had been seated at the end. However, not being a contentious woman, she attributed this to what she tolerantly called their religion. She had been rather more disturbed by frequent long-distance telephone calls broadcast all over the house by the roaring maids who mediated them. 'Who's that calling? Speak up! Dublin? Louder! Who do you want and what d'yeh want him for? Jamesy, there's somebody here wants the doctor. I'm asking you where the divil the doctor is. Out fishing? Oh, Jasus! Are ye there Dublin? The doctor is gone to Cork on a life and death job. Do that! I'll tell him you'll call again after six o'clock.' Or:— 'Who's calling? London? Who do you want and what d'yeh want him for? He's out. What name did you say? Fiddle and Rich? Riddle and Fitch? Speak up please. Brokers? What message? Cold? Old? Gold? It's what? Roaring? Soaring? I'll tell him. And good luck to you, too.' Whereupon the world would disappear again for a while.

In the end it was the silences that broke the spell. There was nothing, she found, about which she could not talk freely with anybody so long as the two of them were alone and that she or the other were quick to add, at an appropriate moment, a dollop of oily jocosity to soften the salad-dressing of their conversation. If a third joined them the conversation became more guarded. In a foursome, unless the subject mentioned were the weather, sport, fish, drink or politics the talk in hollow murmurs died away. At first she genially thought, 'Oh, well! If they want to live insulated from whatever it is they want to be insulated from why should they not?' But today, so close as she was to total despair, she rebelled. These Irish bastards were just like every other set of bastards whose job was to sell illusions: the Spanish Tourist Board, the Italian Tourist Board, the stolid Dutch, the solid Swiss, the jolly Germans, the fervent Indians, the honest English. These Irish were of all the worst insofar as they believed their own illusions, and at that moment here down the finely-wooded avenue to the hotel there most aptly and appropriately came a new bit of their make-believe – a horse-drawn caravan, painted in the gaudiest, jokeyest, gypsyiest, shamrock-green colours trundling between sentries of trees elegantly planted generations ago by some now forgotten English-into-quarter-Irish-into-halfIrish-into-threequartersIrish-into AngloIrish who had in the beginning come here to grab, to settle, to build, to boss, to farm, to nurture, to plant, to live for ever and ever, until their very last generation saw that what had been for three centuries a homestead had become a mere Departure Lounge and took off for the England they must for centuries have considered their more real home.

As the caravan drew to a halt before the hotel joyous screams from the kitchen preceded the billowing outrush of two white aprons. One apron ballooned to the van. The other, seeing their English guest lying on the deck chair, deflected excitedly towards her. 'Miss Goodman, it is Mister Caraway! All Ireland is out looking for him!' and ran to join her companion who, clutching the gaudy vehicle, was meantime screaming to its driver, 'Mister Caraway, the Guards are out looking for ye!' The daughter-of-the-house came forward to explain sedately:

'It was a police message, Miss Goodman, on the Radio this morning. "Would Mr Roger Caraway of Bristol believed to be touring in the southwest of Ireland in a horse-drawn caravan immediately contact his home in Bristol where Mrs Caraway lies seriously ill, or contact any Garda station." Actually we were expecting him, he telephoned last night asking for a double room and by sheer luck we had had a drop-out, but I doubt if after all this hullabaloo he will occupy it tonight.'

The man who leaped from the caravan was about forty or fifty, smiling widely, sure of his welcome, eyes quizzical, face lean, very much what used to be known as a man's man, the sort who might once have been a boxer, or a reliable hand on the rudder of a yacht, extrovert, born for action in the open air. After him clambered a younger woman, dark haired, shapely enough to wear jeans seductively, her features pleasant but undistinguished. Only a partial friend would call her handsome and only a confirmed enemy plain. Ruth admired the agility with which the manageress defused the embarrassing police message while transferring it to its addressee:

' . . . "contact your home in Bristol where your mother Mrs Caraway lies seriously ill . . ."'

The Englishman looked his dismay at his dismayed companion. She, palms up, indicated that he had no option. He glared back at the gypsy caravan.

'Cork is the nearest airport. Hire a car? Taxi? Bus? With this contraption it would take me four days to get back to Cork. What on earth can I do with the blessed thing?'

From a deck-chair on the lawn a black-haired, brown-eyed, sallow-faced young woman told him.

'You could have it collected. Cost you a lot! Or, if it is any help to you I could take it over from you. I was in any case proposing to return to Cork in three days' time.'

'I would be most grateful. But can you manage a horse?'

'If that were a racehorse I could ride it in the Grand National. My people bred fighting horses, and fighting bulls, for generations in Spain.'

Within hours she had entered into a conspiracy of scandalous laughter with the entire parish. The situation suited them down to the ground. It was a perfect image of their concept of life – a web of illusion and disaster, farce and factuality. Even the monsignor enjoyed their sidelong jokes about adultery. She became singled out by her conspicuous absences from the hotel and her observable presences in the wicked caravan now moored beside the wall of their venerable graveyard; warmly welcomed to the hotel for meals and drinks; identifiable by every local; courteously escorted at night across two dewy fields by never less than two residents of the hotel. It did not accordingly surprise her on her third and last afternoon in the caravan, seated on its steps writing to her friend in Australia to confess her own failure as a painter, that two men should appear behind the portion of the low graveyard wall she overlooked, begin forthwith to dig and, on observing her, wave amiably. In their urban clothes, they looked incongruous among the ancient yews and mossy headstones. Presently two more men arrived with shovels to help with the digging of the grave. They also wore citified suits and pointed shoes. Had they come from England for the funeral? They too gave her such a cheerful salute, which she as cheerfully returned though she also felt so sensitive about her nearness, immediately across the wall, to so gravely intimate a ceremony that she retired to her tiny table by her tiny window to complete her letter. Then, still observing them cheerfully at work and observing that she was so observed, she emerged when the grave was some four feet deep to ask whom were they burying. One of the four, a brawny, blue-eyed, white-toothed giant, handsome in a bullish peasant way, nodded cheerfully towards one of the other three.

'Mick's father-in-law.' His eyes danced mischievously over his companions, and in a tone that revealed that they had been discussing her he went on. 'Jo Canty his name was. Oho! Jo was a wild one in his day, so he was! We were just saying that you'll have good company every night from this on.' Being four feet down his appreciative eyes were level with her legs. 'Jo was a rover in his day. You'd do well to lock your door tight once the dark falls.'

Relaxed, laughing, she sat on her caravan's steps and watched and heard them gasp occasional jokes about the late Jo, smack shovels on clay and stone, sink slowly to their bent backs. At last the grave was dug. It had been hard work, the day hot, they paused, a bottle was produced with a yarn or two about the dead Rover's thirst. The giant fellow held up the bottle and invited her to join them. She agreed eagerly, proffered glasses and the bucket of well-water beside her, cool still under its moist napkin. At once the giant and a fair fellow who was as tall but not so broad, vaulted the wall to help her over. There were no introductions. She just stood glass in hand among the four wiping their foreheads, dusting their Sunday clothes, flecking their

English-looking shoes, exchanging more scabrous memories of the Rover's life. By her feet she noted two big-eyed skulls of older relatives of the deceased culled from the dirt so as not to startle the women of the family the next day when Jo's coffin would be lowered and covered. Presently the giant clambered down into the grave to try it for length. Lying face up to her he asked her, 'Were you ever in a grave?' She laughed, 'Not yet!' He asked her would she like to see how it feels. She said she would, whereupon, helped by the others, he clambered up and she was slowly lowered to lay herself full length on the dry earth, looking up past their four faces at the racing clouds. She had never felt the sky so strongly, nor its dark and white herds passing so swiftly away. No more words were spoken. A hush came over them all as if death had suddenly become real or some tabu broken. She realized this when she heard one of them say earnestly to the others, 'Don't any of ye, for God's sake, let Janie hear one word about this!' She stood, held her hands up, was lifted out. The four gathered their forks and shovels, helped the stranger back over her wall. Then all separated with silent waves.

She at once set up her easel and canvas and began to paint with concentration. She painted first an oblong frame of Vandyke brown to represent the band of crumbling earth that had enclosed the perspective she had seen upward from her grave. She painted at the centre of each side of this oblong a head laughing down at her. She then concentrated on the centre of the canvas, covering it vigorously but accurately with white and dark clouds moving swiftly westward across the sky. By the time she had finished she was hours late for dinner at Carrigduv House, had not eaten all day, was unaware of hunger, kept raising and lowering her eyes between the twilit clouds and her twilit picture like a woman in prayer. She was aware that something had happened inside her that never had happened before. She looked dazedly around her. It would soon be dusk. Her grey horse head-bowed stood as motionless in the middle of the field as if it had been let out to grass a hundred years ago. The dusk was as silent as that grave behind. She went into her van, found the remains of a packet of biscuits, ate them, drank a glass of water, lay on the bed and became unconscious.

She woke at six to full sunlight. It was time for her to depart. She delayed. She set up her easel to sketch a quick reminder of her clouds, vertically this time, above a foreground of beach slit by a fish-shaped pool placidly reflecting the floaters above it. This one would be a beauty. A copy of it would be the envy of Australia. She was presently startled by the funeral bell from the village church but insisted on one last record: a cumulo-nimbus of whiteness erupting tower upon tower from the volcano-peak of a mountain the colour of a bruise.

A basso roll of thunder made her turn her head to the east. The sky had darkened. Rain was coming. She barely had time to tackle her horse and start on the road for Cork before the cloud burst. It battered her roof like hailstones. She could see little between her horse's ears but the fog of rain dancing madly on the tarmac, and she saw this only by constantly wiping her eyes, but not this time to efface tears: she was laughing joyfully at the memory of how her father back in Spain used to laugh whenever he remembered his father's laughter at the memory of the way her great-grandfather used simultaneously pray and curse whenever a thunderstorm came rolling down the Pyrenees over his woods and crops, shaking his clasped hands to plead with God in the bewildered words of Job: 'Who can master the clouds in wisdom? Who can stay the battles of heaven? Who maketh the clouds his chariot?'

From this on she would watch them from her high Hampstead windows sailing in over London before the south-easters, slanting misty rain on the city's million roofs and parks, or unloading downpours as straight as stair-rods, or blowing white and sun-polished out past Land's End to the Atlantic, there at the last drawing their light shadows over that grave where she had been ravished by Huesca.

The Wings of the Dove

A Modern Sequel

(To rewrite a great novel as a short story can only be regarded either as an impertinence or an experiment. I have made the experiment with The Wings of the Dove *to find out what is gained or lost by writing fiction briefly or at length. I have made no great discoveries, and it is more than possible that my reader will have made them all long ago without going to any bother at all. They are: that the writer of a short story does not travel – he is content, like an astronaut, or somebody on a package tour, to be shot to his destination; that he then, unlike the gregarious novelist, can proceed to operate quite successfully with as few as two or three characters; and that the novelist, again like the astronaut or the package tourer, does not always arrive at journey's end. Stendhal's* Charterhouse *is a famous example of a delightful journey some of whose travellers are to this day floating loosely in the air. It seemed to me that* The Wings of the Dove *cries out for a sequel telling us what happened in the end to its two lovers Kate Croy and Morton Densher, whom James ruthlessly abandoned to the elements when he considered that he had squeezed them dry.*

To bring the characters closer to our cameras I have dated my sequel in or around 1970 and everybody in the novel may be taken as rejuvenated accordingly. When the sequel opens Densher is seated beside his wife dining in the old Café Royal – which has also been rejuvenated accordingly.)

'Well? What pretty girl are you staring at now?' Densher's wife asked him with a frown half way between amusement and suspicion.

No man a hero to his wife, nor even, the sudden memory warned him, to his mistress. His eyebrows directed her attention across the restaurant to an elderly couple of about his own age squabbling with the head waiter over their bill. Kate Croy, forty years after he first laid eyes on her in this same restaurant! It was her throat that had alerted him. 'Thy swan's neck and dark abundant hair.' Tower of ivory. Or it used to be a tower of ivory, as smooth as her roll of black hair falling over her white shoulders.

'You who know everybody who are they?'

'Read Morton Densher the best-informed social columnist in London. The Man who Knows Everybody. They are Lord and Lady Macbane. She was once a much photographed beauty. Clever too. Marked out for success, which, as you see, she achieved.'

'She has also achieved a stoop. Who was she?'

'That is a rather more delicate question. She was what people used to call A Nobody in the good old days before the '39 – '45. Bonny Prince Churchill and all that. When every man and woman knew his/her station in life. Those happy years before the Revolution. Sic., as we say in the trade. A *sic.* joke. She was not only A Nobody but a penniless Nobody. Name? It escapes me. Crew? Craw? Croy! That's it. Katherine Croy. Irish originally, I believe, her father had been a quartermaster-sergeant or something. In charge of military stores. Got into trouble, fired, cashiered. Some dark shadow. In fact I may have been the first man to talent-spot her when she cannot have been more than nineteen, one wet day during the war, here in this Café Royal, taking in umbrellas, mackintoshes, gas masks, handing out numbered tabs. That evening I gave her a couple of lines of accolade in my column. 'They Also Serve.' Even then she was ravishing.'

From the Latin *rapere*: rapture; also rape. The film whistled backwards until its tail flipped off the white screen. Seeing her home to grubby Chirk Street. Meetings in pubs. Discreet approaches in parks. That garret he got her in Paddington. His bachelor flat on the King's Road. Jesus!

'From taking in parcels to taking in peers? She must have learned fast.'

'An Irish gift? Or just the usual colonial gift? Indians do it. Blacks do it. Australians do it. Jews do it. Let's fall in love. I swear Becky Sharp was some little copy-cat adventuress Thackeray met in Dublin or Glasgow or Aberystwyth, which is the only word I know that has eight consonants in a row. The only other time I saw the future Lady Macbeth – I beg her pardon, Lady Macbane – was two or three months later, in a B.B.C. canteen dishing out cups of wartime tea made of sawdust. She was doing it as loftily as a lady to the manor born. Feeding starving refugees. Practising?'

He should know who had by then already started to lead her through the golden mirrors of this old Café, or of what was left of its original old Anglo-French rococo pillars, painted ceilings, velvet benches, marble tables, emanations now of a century of painters, writers, scribblers, composers, few of them more than names to him in his twenties, meaningless to Chirk Street. Max, Wilde, A.R. Orage, Koteliansky, Middleton Murry, C. Carswell, K. Mansfield, Augustus John, Acton, Connolly, on down through Roy Campbell, Dylan Thomas, Louis MacNeice to what V. Woolf bitchily called 'the literary underworld'. The lower Brewer Street end was more staid (one of her picked-up words) than the marble-topped tables up front. Back there a sanctity of white linen for diners and lunchers. Learned fast? It took her only one visit to decide that she preferred the quarters aft. 'More solid' had been her decisive phrase. 'More pricey' had been his practical thought. When he said so she pretended she had meant 'more cosy'. And after all there were those masked streets outside, darkness probed by hooded hand-torches, padding feet, perhaps a rare taxi, distant bumps of anti-aircraft fire down river. With a paternal amusement, as time went on, he came to interpret her secret-if-real reason for by-passing the front deck: he loved the catlike way she used to snuggle down among what she once called 'important people', as if all those diners about her had only just emerged for the first time that day from secret underground bunkers humming day and night to conquer the brute conditions of life overhead. Analogues of her own battle in her lofty Paddington garret? He would glance around him with the cynical smile appropriate to his profession and note how lecherously all those spivs, flashers, profiteers, general hangers-on of the actual London underworld kept on savouring her beauty. But would anybody ever be able to resist those wonder-enlarged brown eyes, that midnight cloud, her blend of the artless child and the womanly appraiser, as when her two big eyes would peer at him excitedly when he waved aside such wartime lures as 'Fillet of hake, sir? Very nice, very fresh'; or 'Sirloin of beef, sir?', or 'Jugged hare, sir?', with such sidelong sniffs to her as 'Whale meat, my dear', or 'Horse for certain!', or 'Common rabbit, my darling!', in favour of seagulls' eggs and their moderately decent Australian Moselle. It was this guttersnipe innocence that had first evoked his protective affection. Gradually compassion, then passion, finally admiration for her sheer guts reduced him to complete subjection as he became aware of the dear girl's determination to be free forever of beastly Chirk Street. Inevitably, after a bad bomber's night-raid, a bloody thing that went on for hours, squads and squads of them, he chose to discover in her an ascetic heroine, self-disciplined, will-powered, when she casually mentioned the following morning that she had spent most of the night looking through her garret window at the searchlights sweeping beautifully through the stars in search of the Gerries. 'Well?' she had protested when he protested. 'What else was I to do? Crawl downstairs to that cheery, dreary, beery crowd of men, women, kids, babies singing in a stinking basement?'

Learned fast? Within six months of their becoming lovers she had come to know herself so to a nicety that everyone he casually introduced her to, would sooner or later assure him that she was regularly clever, a lady, as one shrewd woman put it, who would never judge herself cheap. For his part he was delighted to watch her develop, though it would probably have taken one of her own countrywomen to appreciate fully the skill of yet 'another wild wan' smoothly changing gear to match the speed of the emotional traffic around her. How long, by contrast, it had taken him to notice her speedometer! Colleen to climber, dreamer to darer, temptress to huntress, gambler to *grande dame*, artless Kate, admirable Kate, an ambitious, acquisitive, predatory – My God! he had been blind! – adventuress.

'What on earth did he see in her?' his wife asked staring across the white tables. 'Or was she all that pretty then? How could he possibly have thought that she would suit him?'

But, to be sure, if one had understood those changing times properly at the time, had taken their measure coldly, it would not have seemed such a great jump for either of them to ride beside the other. Is there all that difference between gamblers? He did have his ancestral home somewhere in the highlands, and a couple of thousand acres that probably did feed a snipe or two. He was handsome. A gallant soldier. Decorated twice. A member of White's, or the Carlton, or the Burlingham. Holding a seat on the board of a company or two. A man with a fine past, a hopeful future, and no cash.

'What did he see in her? Well, her considerable looks. And it would have helped that by then she had become a model.'

'A model? Only a model?'

His own stupidity to have put it into her head, far-seeing for her, not for himself. Still, the times again! Those extraordinary years after the war ended when life in London became a mixture of austerity and life hunger such as had not been known since the Gay Nineties. In those hungry 'forties and 'fifties a man was not permitted by law to have pockets in his jackets (to save material); everybody virtually ate by meal-ticket; women who for years had been tying kitchen dusters under their chins for scarves, mending torn panties over and over, ferreting for silk stockings on the Black Market, wearing Blitz grey day after day until they could at last at least look at pictures of frills, furbelows, great silly hats, flounced frocks divinely, wastefully, unpatriotically designed by chaps who only a couple of years ago had been shock commandos and kamikaze pilots. 'Only a model?' Only a perambulating sunflower? A fair comparison. Time was when to be a model you could be as fat as a Rubens so long as you wore no clothes. Now a model meant an exquisitely emaciated Botticelli loaded with clothes. Does some post-Churchill Socialist grumble, 'Only a lord?' True; but a lord transformed suddenly into vintage 1880 when both his worse and better off ancestors hung around stage doors hoping to carry off an actress or a dancer, as it were on horseback, to some lost keep in Cumberland, or the Cambrian hills or Connemara. Now squabbling over a bill.

With an inner shrug he told himself that the whole story should be dropped at once; but the barber of Midas had to tell about his master's asses' ears to somebody even if it were only to a hole in the ground; meaning, how the hell could anybody possibly have foreseen that his love's widowed, bloody old Aunt Maud Lowder would, on hearing of her impoverished sister's death, at once have ordered her chauffeur to drive her across the Park to miserable Chirk Street out of her tall, rich, heavy, lonely, empty house at Lancaster Gate – she certainly had never judged herself cheap – taken one astounded look at her exquisite young niece and carried her back forthwith, to live with her in luxury and loneliness. Still, it was a good investment all round: a bounteous new interest for herself, fresh opportunities for Miss Croy, a novelty for her guests, who included Lord Macbane, in short for everybody except this who-ever-he-was Mister Morton Densher, some Fleet Street scribbler by whom the girl, with as little regard for her future as her fool of a mother had ever shown for herself, had apparently (What was the vulgar modern phrase?) allowed herself to be 'picked up'. Mr Densher was nevertheless permitted, very rarely, to make formal calls, either for watchful inspection, or as a demonstration of Aunt Maud's consanguineous tolerance of these extraordinary topsy-turvy post-war years, or perhaps because she was operating some impenetrable sisterly strategy on behalf of her niece. The lovers were otherwise reduced to discreet strolls in the Park, stealthy *billets doux*, exasperatingly brief assignations in his flat. After all he could not in decency expect Kate to push her luck too far, nor did she encourage him to do so.

'That, Merty,' said his wifely hole-in-the-ground, 'was an excellent Fleuris. The old Café Royal never lets you down, does it?'

He raised a finger to the wine waiter for the red, and looked across at Lady Macbane.

'So! A beautiful and ambitious girl, a worldly aunt, a door regularly opened to important people such as Macbane, or interesting chance visitors, like that wealthy young woman from Boston. What was her name? Theale, Millicent Theale. Who took such an enormous shine to our Miss Croy that they became heart-friends, became you might almost say mirror models. In fact that was where our Miss Croy's public career began.' He nodded across the restaurant. 'And there you have the end of it.'

'Have I? You said "wealthy". Was she also pretty?'

'The Theale girl? Oh, quite reasonably good-looking.'

'A helpful aunt? A handsome heiress? A poor but very pretty young woman from Chirk Street? And the noble lord chose the beggarmaid. Well, *good* for him!'

'I'm only guessing you realize? For all I know it may have been as Wellington said of Waterloo a damned close thing.'

'Tell me more about *la belle Americaine*. Did you ever meet her?'

'Once. At some big formal gathering for ... for what I can't now remember. I also heard about her later on from acquaintances of associates of friends who moved in Mrs Lowder's set. Their impression of her one way and another was that she was just a sweet, shining little New England dove with jewelled wings, filled with what somebody described as an embarrassing determination to see everything, meet everybody, do everything, go everywhere, to gleam, to glow, to live. You see, the real object of her visit to London was to consult a famous specialist in Portland Place. In the event her trajectory was of the briefest.'

'That,' his wife remarked with a shrewdness that startled him, 'may have been why our Cinderella over there took such a shine to her. Both dying to live. Life has its meanings.'

The wine waiter had broached the red wine, poured a taste,

proffered, observed. In admiration he raised his glass to his wife, nodded absently to the waiter. Milly Theale.

'True! One of them poor in cash the other in health? Rival backgrounds. The prosperity of Louisburg Square, Aunt Maud Lowder's upholstered house in Lancaster Place.'

La Croy was repairing her make-up in her hand mirror; her rolling eyes were still chestnut brown, her rolling lips were gone thin. Give her her due, it was inevitable that she should have outdone everybody in her attachment to Milly, not only in envy of her new American friend's prodigious position in the world but in admiration and pity of her courage in the face of the oncoming night. Envy. Pity. Admiration. People have done terrible things out of sheer envy. Pity has known its own violence. Admiration can inspire. Like a ghost Lady Macbane had vanished. Kate Croy was gathering up her purple gloves and a couple of elegantly bound packages preparatory to rising.

It stabbed his pride yet once again that for all his efforts over the years he had never been able to say exactly 'That was the moment' when she had floated the seed of her terrible plan into his mind so softly that he became only half aware of its poison three months after it had begun to discolour his blood stream. Even then all he had been driven to say, during one of their assignations in his minute flat on the King's Road, lying on his back, hands clasped behind his head, all passion spent, was 'Have I noticed, Kate, or do I imagine it, that you have begun to be rather cryptic with me these last few weeks? Do tell me why are we two, acknowledged lovers, at least so acknowledged by ourselves,' glancing at their clothes laid across his two chairs, 'temporising about finally declaring our love to the world?' That was all he had said but he was so troubled by the half-memory of a whisper, or a frown, or a suggestive earlier smile about pretty Milly the Millyonaire, and by his agreeing that it must indeed be galling for anybody to be the mere companion of a rich old lady, and his saying 'We were so happy when you were all on your own in that garret in Paddington', that he added firmly, 'We have simply got to make a move!' at which she flung the sheet aside, cried 'We?', rose and dressed. They parted in virtual silence.

It was not until the following day that he weighed between two steps that last word of hers, failing even then to observe that by his use of a mere pronoun he had accepted some involvement, however involuntary, in whatever she was being cryptic about. That he was entangled in some sort of strategy did not truly occur to him until a couple of weeks later, one windy afternoon in the Park, when, under a browning beech, he spoke sympathetically of Milly's falling leaves and Kitty said tempestuously, 'Oh please do *please* let our poor darling have her little adventure,' to which he of course warmly agreed, saying 'She really is prodigious in her determination to live.' They had walked on in silence for a while. Then, tardily he said that he did not see how he particularly could help, or indeed why he should be put forward in her fight for life. They walked on again, Kate now kicking the leaves before her, until at a passionate groan beside him, he clasped his beloved's hand in admiration of her feelings of pity for their poor friend. Kate threw away his hand, halted, faced around, cried that all she was doing was trying to break him into what, in Milly's heartbreaking circumstances, everybody around him must clearly expect of him. He had stared at her in bewilderment laced for the first time by a fleck of fear. 'Expect? Everybody?' He had looked vacantly around the Park. After all Kate had assured him, and on his rare, formally permitted calls to Lancaster Gate he had observed for himself, that Milly was always modestly, shyly undemanding, almost retiring, grateful for any attention, however ferociously she might secretly be importuning the gods for yet another and another sip of the wine of life. Anyway what special relief could he, Merton Densher, a mere journalist, bring to this doomed citadel? That autumn afternoon in the Park Kate had not pursued his portentous question; but within a week the sybil herself answered it in a manner dramatic enough to redouble his mounting fears. Quite simply, casually, gaily in fact, as if it were just one more of her childish 'adventures' she had it conveyed to him, that she had taken over a Venetian palace on the Grand Canal, the Palazzo Leporelli, and was inviting everybody, 'including you, of course,' Kate transmitted unmistakably, to tread its stage.

Coming up as it were out of the *caves* beneath the Café Royal – although he had long since learned that wives also can be sibylline – his echo at his side was saying, 'Darling, why are you so dead set against celebrating our silver anniversary in Venice? You say you are bored with Paris. I am fed up with Florence. Rome is as raucous as a fun fair. The Riviera is a mob. It is odd really that we have never tried Venice!'

'All Venice is good for is a Thomas Mann film about dying!'

But she went on rattling about 'all those exciting plans to keep Venice alive and floating, plans that everybody is always . . .'

In fact everybody loaned a hand to float Milly's Venetian plan: visitors homeward bound for Boston and New York, Aunt Maud's regulars from London, desultory ambassadors from the Home Counties or farther, Kate and Macbane of course, and how could anybody for whatever different reason refuse Milly's invitations? He, however, quite differently to any of all these preferred not to stay at the *palazzo* but in modest lodgings up-canal from the Rialto for the sake ostensibly of memories from his student days, privately to be alone occasionally with his Kitty, most of all in order to be at once sufficiently close to Milly for kindness and good manners yet not so close as to overheat those alleged expectations of him that Kitty continued to press upon him just so near to once too often that he found himself driven brutally to press her to come out into the open once and for all from beyond her vague swayings, suggestions, implyings, encouragements, to speak out, to define exactly what were her hopes for her ailing dove. He gripped her wrists. Her stare forbade him. He stared her down.

'Merty, you must surely see it by now?'

'Is it this then? That you have bit by bit so arranged the condition of things, that she has confided in you that she has come to like me?'

'You cannot be so blind as not to see that she likes you very much. And more. And you know that she is doomed.'

He released her. Quietly, fatefully, fearfully:

'I begin to see. Since she is to die soon you mean that I should show love for her betimes?'

'I have begged you to let her have her little adventure.'

'You? My only love! Say this?'

She slowly lowered her chin but her eyes still fixed his from beneath her brows. He at last unravelled her terrible code, at last spoke it.

'I am to join then in her very last adventure? I am to love her even into marriage? So that when death has taken place you and I shall have her money?'

It struck him as fine in her that even in that moment she had not flinched or minced.

'I mean so that in the natural course of things you and I shall at last be free.'

What did not occur to him until too late was that because he did not then and there turn and leave her he tolerated that word 'free'. He had walked with her in silence back to the precincts of the Palazzo Leporelli. On his way to his lodgings he thought, at every glance that he gave to a passing face, 'Free? Who is free?' Not Kitty certainly, bound by ropes of passion to him, and by her equal passion for the freedom that he had called money; just as he was bound both by his passion for her and his compassion for a dying girl who even as she slowly folded her wings still implored life to yield her the experience of one selfless love.

He stayed on in Venice, loyal to whom or what he would never understand. He tried it, his own phrase, for six weeks, badgered by his London editor, daily counting his pennies, stayed long after both Aunt Maud and Kitty tactfully left this autumnal city of virtually empty hotels where only a few stubborn tourists lingered in hope of one last hour of romance until all their dreams of a Saint Martin's summer collapsed under downpours that leaped back a foot high over the fogged expanses of the lagoons and winds from the Adriatic that rocked the most sheltered *sandalo* in the most greasy gully of this streetless city. He had nothing to do but wander collar up, opened umbrella at the lance, between museum, *caffè* and church, miserably aware that she did not care a jot about this beastly weather so long as she had her dear Merton's afternoon visits to the *palazzo* and his nightly presence alone with her at and after dinner to keep at bay far worse demons than these winds and rains besieging every window in the streaming city outside. His sense of shame and weakness, his futile two-faced pity for a young woman whose beauty gleamed through the frail eggshell of her body not now like a springtime sunrise but like a winter sunset, became final despair, utter defeat on one unusually inclement afternoon as he sought shelter from a cloudburst under the wet, crowded, shuffling arcade of the great Piazza. There he was halted by a familiar face espied through the window of Florian's restaurant. It was Lord Macbane seated by a small table before a neglected glass, not reading the copy of the *Figaro* on his knee, glaring in front of him at the rococo wall.

One glance in through that misty window and he identified a spy. Macbane's astonishing presence was clearly a sequel to some equally fruitless earlier approach in London to the little heiress. He passed on his way through the crowds wandering blindly for two hours before he dared to face the Palazzo Leporelli. Yet, hopeless though he was against the horror that he knew was awaiting him there, he was still, up to the last second after he pulled the chain of the old inward-echoing bell, prepared to enter as usual without being announced. He knew that the game was up when the great door squeaked open just a few inches and he was quite held-off by her x-ray-eyed *major duomo*, her 'great' Eugenio, the personification of Venice's heavy-lidded concept of life as one long clandestine, venal intrigue, informing him through the chained crack politely, which is to say insinuatingly, mockingly, that *la signora padrona* was not receiving today, and slowly closed the door on one who up to a few hours ago had been of all callers the prince.

Standing on the palace steps by the flopping canal he surrendered to the fact. Macbane, unable to tolerate that anybody should win what he had lost had told her, no doubt in the most gentlemanly manner, about her charming Merton's manifest relations with her dear Kate. Milly, upstanding American freewoman, would have gratefully thanked him, graciously got rid of him, then alone with the winds, and the rain, and the waters turned her face to the wall. She was up there now, facing it.

'So?' Kate had greeted him, poised as always and smiling, three weeks before Christmas. 'You have been in London rather a while before calling on me.'

He stood close to her before the warming fire, looking intensely into those lovely brown eyes that looked neutrally into his. He drew from his pocket a long, pale-blue envelope, unopened, franked in Venice, and not ceasing to look into her eyes held up the envelope before them. Almost invisibly lowering her lids she intimated to him that she recognized the hand and foresaw what its frail fingers had written. That there should be no doubt about the matter this time he said it.

'In her prodigious generosity she would have us rich enough to be free to marry.'

Still poised, she stared at him. He crumpled the blue letter and tossed it into the yellow and red fire and said strongly:

'Mind you, Kate, I'd still marry you inside an hour.'

'As we were?'

'As we were!' he answered firmly.

Their silence was not too painfully long. She glanced at the door, went towards it and, with one hand on the knob, said quietly:

'We shall never again be as we were.'

Kitty was leaving the restaurant. Not Kitty! Kitty's back had always been as straight as an undrawn bow. Macbane was bald. As his eyes followed them out he felt a hand, as cool as if it had come out of the night air, softly stroke his. How much had he revealed? How much had she inferred between the white wine and the red?

'Darling!' she murmured. 'I don't really mind if we do not go to Venice. And, after all, she was a long time before me. If life always has its meanings, it also has its pasts.'

'She? Who?' He protested large-eyed. 'I don't follow you.'

She stroked even more delicately.

'But you really were just a teeny bit in love with her weren't you? Any man as kind as I know you are might well be. Alone. Dying in a rainy city.'

He slowly turned the stem of his empty glass.

An Unlit Lamp

When it became known that a woman from Dublin named Goggin was about to open a private nursing home in Ballybun, in that old Georgian house on De Valera Square that had been empty for years, it is doubtful if many of the locals were greatly interested, excepting to be sure our hard core of addicted gossips who are always inquisitive about everything. The sergeant of the Guards may have as a matter of routine made a genial enquiry. One of our seventeen publicans drawing a careful pint may have said to his customer, his eye fixed on the slowly rising froth, 'I hear we are getting a Private Nursing Home now, if you please,' meaning by this last piece of Socratic irony that Ballybun is rising in the world. Or the owner of the Imperial Hotel, a building wizened by the Atlantic mist ever since such hotel names as Imperial, Royal, Continental, Ambassador and the like used to evoke images of luxury rather than, as they do now, of tractors, gas cookers, brassières, motor cars or lavatory bowls, may have said as he looked out at two cows ambling down the Main Street, 'Well, I hope the poor woman will get enough business to fill *her* beds!': a fair remark since Ballybun, according to the official census, contains only 3,426 residents, and lies on the direct road to nowhere, south, north or east and as a local wag has sourly said there is nothing much west of it except the United States of America and more rain.

In this indifferent mood Ballybun's 3,427th resident became generally accepted on her arrival as Nurse Goggin or Miss Goggin. Gradually, that is to say within a year, she became known to some as Judith Goggin, a sure sign of her provisional acceptance as a citizen. After about two years she became known to her very few close acquaintances as Judy Goggin. To the town's gossips, however, she was disparagingly known, almost from the start as Gog, to express their annoyance with her for never coming to the town's café, called *Le Bon Bouche*, never playing bridge, or taking part in the town's monthly Whist Drive, or in any of the many doings of the Ballybun branch of the Irish Countrywomen's Association. Who was she anyway to be so stuck up? Out of what sky did she parachute into Ballybun? Who were her backers in this Nursing Home? Where did she get the cash for all its new shiny medical equipment? They were nettled, felt put down, challenged, and of course in the end they caught their mouse, and caught her in such a neat way that their pleasure in their corporate skill dissipated their annoyance with her as a snobby outsider. Their sense of grievance was also modified by compassion.

What happened was that one of them reported one morning at the round table of the tea shop that a patient in Saint Dympna's Home had mentioned to her that whenever Gog was asked any slightly difficult question she would look up at the ceiling as if seeking advice from another planet, and start to caress the bare first joint of the third finger of her left hand with the thumb and fingers of her right hand. Experimentally the Bong Butchers around the table began to perform the same gesture and at once they pounced. Why had they not guessed it before? But married into which dynasty of Goggins? They knew Goggin families scattered up to Galway, down to Limerick, over into Tipperary. They settled for the Limerick branch: two doctors, one in Galway, one in Gort, an influential Reverend Mother in Kilkee, a chemist's shop in Nenagh, a home-farm near Patrickswell, and had not a Goggin doctor from Athlone been killed in a car crash on the day of his wedding to a Dublin *nurse*? At that everything fell into place: Gog's reticence, retirement, her exile, aloofness, her intense – they did not say, though it was what they meant – 'compensatory' concentration on making a success of Saint Dympna's which, four years after she opened it, was already being recommended by every doctor within fifty miles of Ballybun. Thereafter the gossips lost interest in their Gog, much as a sated cat does with a dead mouse after panting for weeks to lay it low.

Or they did until one day this last winter when, with a lack of discretion quite out of character, Judy casually threw out to somebody, who repeated it to somebody else, who etc.: 'You know! There are times when I really don't know what I am. A spinster, a widow, a married woman or an old maid?' On the spot the Butchers again became, as one of them had the wit to say, agog. They knew her now for a widow, and no spinster, but she had become both so narrowly that they could see how easily she could convey the impression that she was neither absolutely. Was she under that same impression herself? What, otherwise, was this bit about *not* being an 'old maid'? Just exactly how old was milady? They answered it on their finger tips. Say around 40? Whereupon like mice their eyes stole about the table. Around 40. But how round is around? And when does around 40 start being around 50? When does 50...? They sipped their instant coffee and sucked their low-tar cigarettes, unwontedly silenced by a question so fascinating that it would be a crime to dispose of it by answering it: namely, when ought the most reasonably presentable widow or spinster admit that the party is over? It would be fun to let Gog herself answer that question, fun to watch for the slightest sign of friendship, not to mention intimacy, between her and the least likely bachelor in sight. What they did not realize was that the last person to bear witness to what is going on in a battle is somebody lost in the thick of it. If they had read *War and Peace*... Or recalled from *The Charterhouse* that plaintive cry of Fabrizio del Dongo after he nearly lost his life on the plain of Waterloo: 'Was that really a battle? And did I take part in it?' But if gossips were to read such truthful fictions where would they get the time to make up their own? She had, they knew, already found one male friend. But he...

The first time Judy Goggin laid eyes on the Reverend Thomas Tully, C.C., without the slightest personal interest, was on a savagely cold December morning last year when she found him in her best bed, with a temperature of 101°, three cracked ribs, a twisted shoulder and a black eye. This quadruple achievement, Mrs O'Dea her fat old night nurse dryly informed her, was the result of his reverence's unskilful effort to skate down the town's frozen Main Street between midnight and one o'clock in the morning. Dr Cantwell, the clergy's regular doctor, had set the shoulder and plastered up his chest. It had been such a straight-forward job that they had not disturbed her. The patient had had a good night. He had eaten a hearty breakfast. All of which may have been why the somewhat weary night nurse ended her report by whispering as she left the room that Father Tully had been transferred to Ballybun only a few hours before his accident 'Probably for some similar misdemeanour in some other part of the parish.'

Judy, left alone with the patient, observed with professional disapproval that the curve of the bedclothes over his belly implied very little figure skating, or any other exercise, and at least two inches of yellow fat, and she shared every surgeon's distaste for fat. If she had been a surgeon she too would have taken pleasure in cutting through clean muscle. She looked at the card hanging at the end of his bed. Her own age, 39. At her third glance she met two small, blue, piggy eyes glittering up at her like a small boy contemplating mischief, noted his tiny mouth pursed forward like those fat-cheeked cherubs on old maps that are for ever blowing winds of laughter from the four corners of the compass. On the instant she diagnosed him exactly, inspired by his naughty smile, his puppy fat, his gleaming eyes, his puss-mouth and his age: another of those clerical Peter Pans who are a scourge of God to every bishop, vicar general and parish priest, to every layman a bloody good scout, to women a surrogate son to be admired, advised, indulged, protected and sometimes – if (on a fourth glance) he is as handsome as this Father Thomas Tully, in spite of his yellow fat – to be virginally loved by early widows and foiled spinsters.

His first words confirmed her guess. He asked her if she was aware that her Saint Dympna was the patron saint of lunatics. At this she burst out laughing, as he did too with a spasm of pain, confessed that she did not even know that a Saint Dympna existed, and that the only reason she had given this name to her Nursing Home was in the hope that it would 'impress our humbler goodies and intrigue our richer baddies'.

'And are there,' he asked hopefully, also diagnosing a kin soul, 'rich baddies in this bog town?'

It may be a measure of her calm confidence in her knowledge of human nature that she thereupon sat unprofessionally on the edge of his bed and opened up an indiscreet chat the like of which she had not enjoyed during her four years in Ballybun. That frank half-hour chat made bits of the professional barriers between nurse and patient, the proprietress of a Home and a priest without a home. It started a friendship. When he was off the sick list he visited her patients so conscientiously that before July they had become not only trusting friends but . . . Well, what else in the circumstances could they become? Soul friends? Affinities? Conspirators contra Ballybun? Yes! That certainly. Every time he left Saint Dympna's after a sherry in her sitting-room on the top floor she would draw the net curtain an inch aside in the embrasure of her window, look after him as he crossed the square and think, 'What a waste!'

Nevertheless the nearest she ever came to chaffing him in an even slightly intimate way was the July of the following year. After all, business is business, meaning that discretion is also business. He had gone on what she now knew was his annual summer holiday to Italy (he had been Rome-educated) and out of that blue width, heat, noise and wonder of Rome he had sent her a paperback selection of the previous year's Nobel winner, Eugenio Montale. He did it, she knew, because he knew that she had begun trying to learn some tourist Italian on her own in the hope of some day also escaping to 'his' Rome. She smiled patiently when she saw the book. To have sent her this Montale was just the kind of silly, impractical, dreamy, juvenile thing he could always be expected to do. She could not get to the end of even the first poem in the anthology. For a beginner the going was much too tough. To her pleasure, however, she noted (because it made him a bit less silly) that the book had been published in Manchester, edited by a Belfast professor, had notes and a vocabulary in English. With these aids she did, for his sake, partially decode in the first poem, *In Limine*, two lines that hit her across the face like a smack from a wet fish. The two lines said, 'Search always for the weak thread in the nets that so tightly bind us . . .' [Nets of what? Chance? Fate? Memories?] . . . 'And jump! Fly! Escape! Be free! For this, for you, I pray to God.' *Cerca una maglia rotta nelle rete che ci stringe, tu balza fuori, fuggi . . .* She thought for a moment of tearing out the page, underlining the two lines in red ink, and sending the wet fish back to him, but at once thought, 'No! For God's sake! Montale could say that sort of thing to one of his journalist chums in Milan, Florence, Genoa, to himself, to his life, to his mistress if he had one but not, NOT to some poor bastard of a fly caught in the cobweb of an Italian Ballybun.' Nevertheless on his return from Rome to his cloister she did, in all innocence, say something to him along the lines of those words of Montale that made him behave like Vesuvius in a temper.

She had watched him alight from the 5 p.m. Dublin bus and come directly across the Square to Saint Dympna's. She was touched, although she could have wished him a little more prudent, but she excused him knowing that he knew that she was going off for her own modest holidays to Dublin on the same bus in half an hour's time. He brought with him an Italian tan, a dozen tiny papal yellow and white flags to distribute among the boys in his church choir, and a small bottle of the most vulgar scent. She thought his Roman bronze becoming; it went splendidly with the first few grey hairs brushed back from his temples. His holiday had taken years off him, so many that she suddenly wondered if he had not badly needed it. Had he since they

first met, or perhaps long before they met, been under strains unknown
to her? Every priest must at some time in his life find it tough to be cut
off from the warmth of common life, as isolated as a desert monk inside
his mud-hut in the vasty desert. After all, when a young man becomes
a priest he flings all his dearest friendships at the feet of Christ like the
bundle of clothes a swimmer lays on a beach before diving into a lonely
lake to swim to some calm solitude, only to meet on the nearest island
a smiling figure warmly welcoming him, a familiar friendly figure – his
own boring self. She was happy that he had his brief escape from this
Rome in that Rome, sad only because she would have so dearly enjoyed
being shown over his Rome by him; but as she deftly poured him out
a welcoming glass she surrendered to her commonsense. Snatched
moments like this one were the most they would ever share; at which
as if to measure its fragility he happened to mention the name of an
Italian colleague whom he had known in his Roman days but whom
he had in vain hoped to re-meet for a chat about old times. 'Ah, well!'
he laughed. 'That's Rome. The Paradise, the Grave, the City and the
Wilderness as who-was-it, Shelley-was-it, said. Seclusion and Faith.'

She misunderstood that last word, her eye on the clock, and chaffed
him: 'You and your nonsense about fate. Fate is just Chance.'

She had never seen him angry before, wondered a lot afterwards at
this sudden eruption.

'My faith,' his teeth clenched, 'is my own free choice! I chose to be
a priest with my eyes and my mind as clear as the sky. Proud to belong
to a Church that is wide, spacious and open. Room for all sorts in it.
Rome and room enough for all of us. When I stood again last Sunday
in Saint Peter's and looked away up, and up, around and about it, it
came to me that the very size and width and height of it was a symbol
of the liberty, the space, the...'

The compensatory images whirled, transparently. She read them
easily. She clutched her fist behind her back until it shook.

'Ho! Ho!' she jeered. 'Have a bit of commonsense, Tom! After one
week back here you will be singing another tune. Railing at the gossips.
Cursing the prudes. Belabouring the pietists. Growling about the P.P.
I have heard you at it. You see-saw! You great big bundle of
contradictions!'

'Hoho, yourself!' he laughed at her. 'And I suppose you never tilt your
nurse's bonnet this way that way a dozen times between morning and

midnight, and your nightcap after that? Praying to your Saint Dympna to save you from going balony in this madhouse?'

And, to her relief, there he was once again happily wobbling in his fat and she like a kite swaying to the wind on the string of his caprice, delighted to see her smart nurse's cap through his piggy blue eyes lidded with fat, or fate, or faith – she did not give a damn which; although this was the worst of the many exasperating things she had observed about every priestly innocent – that in the pulpit any one of them will appear as steady as an oak tree and be as fickle as an aspen leaf out of it, an overgrown boy all over again, a shrugging fathead, a feeble fool, a child elated by the smallest blessing, hurt by the lightest blow, intemperate as a gypsy, no resting place, up-down down-up, the typical Irish manic depressive, constant in only one thing, his endless power to evoke protection from others. 'Holy God!' she groaned to herself, gathering up her handbag, gloves, small parcels from around and under the feet of and beside her elated traveller back from the blazing sun of Rome, her cheek to the window watching for the bus that would take her for ten days to white-skied Dublin: 'How unjust! Any other priest doing his job as obediently as a circus seal could at the very most count on my sympathy. I would mount the barricades to fight for this fat-bottomed fat-head, waving his sherry glass all over my carpet! Booming away to me about the power and the grandeur of 'my' Rome!' He looked as if he might even lay a condescending hand on her knee, or did she detect a certain (Roman?) look in his eye? If he dared to as much as touch her she would slap his face, and then, God help her, maybe sob on his shoulder?

'All right!' she granted him sourly. 'Room for the whole of Ballybun in heaven! You can stuff them all inside that famous high-walled city in Paradise where Saint Patrick stuffs the Irish so that they can go on thinking they are the only ones who reached heaven. I wish you joy of your fond parishioners. They are still growling at the sermon you gave them last month about their Miraculous Medal being no more miraculous than the pennies people throw into that old fountain in Rome for good luck. And I especially wish you joy of their latest campaign – against the naked Madonna. Good-bye!'

He followed her to the door, touched her arm, said gently:

'What Madonna did you say?'

'Don't you remember? The statue the goodies have been wanting for 20 years to run up on some rock in Galway Bay? That national competition they had to decide on the sculptor? While you were away Foxer O'Flaherty, Ballybun's one, only and therefore greatest-in-the-world sculptor won it. He is using a nude model. I expect he is over there this minute with her,' nodding through her window towards the stables of the Imperial Hotel. 'Working on his masterpiece.'

His eyes became as wide as plates at the idea of a female model in Ballybun.

'A nude model? Of the Madonna? Foxer O'Flaherty? In this town?'

His laughter howled. She did hers remembering by sympathy the sort of sculpture Foxer loved to produce; what she called Giacometti spaghetti, lean, skeletous symbols of starvation. She looked at the frail model of one such on her mantelpiece, bought out of sheer comparison for poor Foxer. Sculptors don't become rich in Ireland. If they choose to live in its wild west they invite Famine. Her hand on the door-knob, she explained rapidly:

'He says he always starts with the undraped figure and moulds the drapery about it. He says sculptors have always done this. He says "I make the flesh vanish into the clay. I finish only when I have produced the shadow of an angel, a female drawn up to heaven like a whistle of air."'

He followed her downstairs. This cultivated Roman did not, she observed, offer to carry her suitcase.

'But where,' he implored her, 'did he get a nude model within two hundred square miles of Ballybun?'

'He got her simply by advertising in that paper in your fist.' He looked unbelievingly at his *Clare Champion*. 'He had them queueing up for the job! And why not? Five pound for doing nothing but stand in your pelt on a box. Times have changed, Tom Tully, since you were a clerical student. Even in this wilderness they see English TV. They read the English Sunday papers. The old prudishness is gone. What's more, he told me he got exactly the sort of woman he wanted, big shoulders, maternal bosom, thighs like an elephant, hips like a mare, muscular arms. Don't ask me why he likes them so fat when they always end up as skin and bones. But I can tell you this, the town doesn't approve of it one little bit. There's my bus hooting!'

She raced for it.

Two weeks later, at five in the evening, she alighted from the same bus, pleased to find him sitting, waiting for her in her office, smoking her cigarettes.

'You've a lovely tan,' he approved. She gave him marks for saying so and took them back on noting that he did not stand up when she came in. Celibacy!

'Marvellously we had sun. I did nothing but sunbathe. That's the advantage of having relatives scattered around Dublin Bay. You still have your Roman bronze. And you have been slimming.' She just stopped herself from saying, 'I missed you'.

He had lost all his tan. He had also lost pounds of fat. His skin looked dry as well as pale. She produced the old bottle of gold and two glasses. She wondered what he had been like as a boy. A rascal? A scamp? A wilder? A little devil? Up to every mischief? His mother's despair? Or pale, slim, young, blushing Tommy Tully? Mother's darling. The morning shadow of a priest? A thin flame drawn up to heaven like a whistle? She banished the happy image with a mock-cheery:

'And how has life been in the wild west since I have been away?'

'I can tell you in five famous words. Out of *Paradise Lost*. Did you know that it was John Milton who first said them? "All hell has broken loose." That is what life has been here since you left. This nude model of Foxer O'Flaherty's has the town in bits. The Parish Priest has thrown it all over to me. "You're young. You can cope. You are the new generation."

'Judy! I need moral rearmament. I need help. Every morning the letter-box in the presbytery stuffed with anonymous letters. A woman without a stitch on her in the Imperial Hotel? Children trying to peep in at the Mother of God naked? Threats to picket the hotel. Two windows of Foxer's cottage smashed one night. Another day he couldn't get out, they had jammed the door. Graffiti on his walls. This morning was the last straw; he called on me in the presbytery with a face like a sheet. He couldn't talk. He just handed me this box.'

He handed her a matchbox. On a piece of paper pasted on one flat side of it was Foxer's name and address, typewritten. The other side bore a tenpenny stamp commemorating some famous Irish nun. She pushed open the little drawer of the matchbox. A revolver cartridge. Brass case. Grey bullet. He annotated:

'It fits a forty-five revolver. You could kill a bull with it. Of course whoever sent it is out of his mind. He would never use it. But still!'

'What did you say to Foxer?' she asked fearfully.

'I said I would protect them both. Him and her. I said, leave this matter entirely to me.'

He spoke like a Napoleon. He collapsed when he glanced across the Square at the hotel archway that led into the cobbled yards to the disused stables that Foxer had rented as his studio.

'There is Biddy Cash now,' he said. 'The madonna.'

She was emerging from the archway, fastening a green kerchief around her head. Young. Say eighteen. No beauty; a splendid image of female strength; a bosom a man could sit on, brawny arms, peasant legs, haunches fit to breed heroes. As she strode she was confronted by the woman who owned *Le Bon Bouche*, given to elegant tropes like 'Ooh, lala!' and 'Commong sa va?' She halted the great creature frontally and said something to her. Biddy Cash at once thrust her fat red tongue between lips that make the contemptuous sound known as a raspberry, and walked on. Judy laughed. 'Well, Father Tom? We don't seem to have much control over our congregation, do we?'

Tully threw back his drink and leaped to his feet.

'I have made up my mind! I will show these bigots that times *have* changed. The Church will show up these prudes for the ignorant slobs they are. Dammit, half the angels in the city of Rome have hardly a rag on them. Baby *putti* flying around every altar in their skins! Countless madonnas all over Italy painted with their breasts bare to the world! Christ crucified like every common malefactor not only naked but stark naked! What's wrong with the body that these ... I am going to visit that studio publicly tomorrow morning. I am going to show the flag. Will you join me?'

'Flag? What flag?'

'Any flag; the papal flag. The green, white and gold, the red, white and blue, the green, white and red, the fifty stars.'

Three minutes too late, Judy knew that she should have immediately replied: 'Look't, Tom! I run a private Nursing Home for the public. I cannot have a private life in public any more than you can. Do you want to make a public scandal out of the pair of us?' Instead, without her volition, obscene words began to pour from her mouth: words like Worldly Wisdom, Tact, Expediency, Diplomacy, Politic, Bread and Butter, Temporize, until she suddenly heard herself saying 'Tricks of the Trade' and in horror she clapped her hand to her mouth.

'Did I say that? I'm possessed. Tom. Exorcise me.'

He said he would call for her tomorrow morning at ten-thirty exactly, and left her to stay awake long after midnight going through what in her childhood, submissive, Catholic, conformist, filled to the gullet with guilt, she used to call An Examination of Conscience. She was now aged 39. A lie! She was 40. A lie! She was into her forties. He was the same. She had a job, a career, a role in life, but she was not tied to one place: if she threw her nurse's bonnet over the windmill here she could start again elsewhere tomorrow. But could he? One o'clock struck from the Town Hall. He had his attractions. Two o'clock struck from the Town Hall. She wasn't all that bad looking herself. Did he ever look at any woman as a woman? Three struck from the Town Hall. She got up, looked across at the hotel, went back to bed, took a Mogadon tablet whose effect was to open her hazeing mind to the beautiful clarity of the unarguably reasonable decision that if a widow married a priest they would accumulate such world-wide publicity that they could run any Horseing Nome at a great Prophet and no schloss, whereupon the Mogadon kindly hit her with its padded mallet.

At twenty-five minutes after ten he was waiting for her at her front door. She knew that he was a priest of Heaven but he looked like Hell. In his white-knuckled fist he held a white and yellow paper papal flag, three inches square, about the size of a packet of twenty cigarettes. He saluted her with it, glared at her, surveyed the empty square as if at one wave of his paper flag his troops would at once pour out from every side-lane and side-street.

The only visible sign of life was the broad backside of a woman on all fours outside the entrance to the hotel scrubbing its steps. Shoulder beside her shoulder, he marched and Judy undulated across the vacant square to the arch and across the cobbled stable yards that were all that remained of the glorious coaching days of the Imperial Hotel. There was nobody in its yard. He led the way across its cobbles, rapped firmly on the door of the particular stable, mews, barn or coachman's house that had temporarily become Foxer O'Flaherty's studio. Presently Foxer unbolted the door, slowly drawing behind him on its curved rail a heavy curtain made, it seemed, of potato sacks stitched together, once dyed red, now approaching the tint of pink potatoes gone dusty with dried clay. His hands were orange with a rather more creative clay, his eyes, enlarged like a man awakened from a visionary dream, looked blankly from one to the other. Somewhere in the town a cock crowed plaintively. Judy felt Tom's elbow jab her ribs.

'Good morning, Foxer,' she said amiably.

'Good morning, Nurse Goggin,' Foxer said, returning crossly to earth.

Her comrade nudged her again.

'Gorgeous weather we're having,' she smiled to Foxer.

'It's all that,' said Foxer, looking towards the archway. Half looking back she saw a small boy of about four looking in. His presence did not suggest any danger of immediate violence. In the silence the distant cock doodledooed again. She got another jab in the ribs from her comrade.

'They'll be cutting the hay soon,' she informed Foxer pleasantly.

At this the Church thrust forward, flung aside the faded curtain and marched through the outstretched arms of the now loudly protesting Foxer. Judy cursing herself, limping after them, beheld with a shock of delight the naked, white buttocked, young Biddy Cash, standing on a low platform, about five foot eleven on her bare feet, angled slightly away from them, maternal, uberous, noble. Tom was still insisting something about 'friends'. Foxer was shouting something like 'God save us from our friends'. The girl's pose was a bit like that of Michelangelo's David: her left thigh splayed to the left, her right hand hanging loose. Her left hand did not however, as in the David, hold a sling-strap over her shoulder. It was a sign of Foxer's genius that he had made her left palm support the back of her head just above the neck thus both indenting a curve in the long black hair that hung down her back, and forcing her to look slightly upward – a gesture that gave to her whole person the moon-staring stance that he considered right for a girl who knows that she is about to become a mother while still a virgin.

Looking at her beauty nobody spoke any further, but the great girl, hearing and sensing their alien presence, slowly lowered her hand from the back of her head and slowly turned to look, saw the rotund black-clothed figure and with the scream of 'A priest!' leaped as lithely as a wild animal for the ladder leading to the loft overhead, her buttocks right-lefting out of sight. Tully roared to Judy. Foxer shouted after Biddy. Judy, vanished after her, knelt by her side where she had thrust herself back into the loose hay, arms hiding breasts, knees updrawn, moaning in horror again and again, 'A priest? A priest?'

'But what about it, Biddy! He's only just a man! Like Foxer!'

In denial the young woman shook her great head of black hair.

'A priest that never seen a woman?'

Judy, silenced, remembered suddenly her own man's astonishment and delight when on their marriage night they stood facing one another naked for the first and last time. She rose, blindly dusted hay from her skirt and arms. Shaking all over she climbed back down the ladder.

They had waited for that night: for eight years, two months and one week. He had been the youngest of his family, the four others had married and had left to him the care of a virtually bedridden father, and a mother soon to become crippled with rheumatoid arthritis, both begging him not to put them into a Home. He had been a second year medico when they met, he twenty, she twenty-two. They did not become engaged until he was still two years short of his medical degree. They waited also for that. They waited again, the old people still on his hands, for two more years while he got his M.D. His father died two years later. Even so Judy could not bear to ask him to put his mother into a Home and anyway few Homes would want to receive her at her age in a now quite crippled condition. The old lady, for her part, used to beg him to send her away, but when she said it there was a look in her eyes that begged him please *not to*. They buried her two years later.

That night in their hotel, at the very moment when they were on the brink of total love there had come a wild hammering on their door and the voice of the proprietress calling for help. A man had come cycling from a cottage a mile away, his wife far gone in labour, a breech birth, a hopeless midwife, for God's sake come. One of the two village doctors was attending a call five miles away. The other was on holidays. He had stared at Judy. She had said, 'You must go'. Years after she came on a line of poetry by Robert Browning that, she felt, condemned them both: the line imputed to every frustrate ghost the sin of 'the unlit lamp and the ungirt loin'. He dressed fast. He drove away fast. She did not see him alive again. When racing his car back to her at speed an hour later, he had run full tilt around a bend into a halted truck.

At the bottom of the ladder she found that Father Tom was gone. The sculptor lifted the curtain for her to follow him. She beheld Tully standing under the arch of the hotel yard, profiled against the morning sun, his head lowered as if in converse with his toes. She watched him raise his head and look northwards towards the open countryside; then look east across the square at her Nursing Home; then southwards towards – she translated with mocking indifference to grammar – Ballybun's *campanili, palazzi, torri, ponti, fontani*. He finally walked their way. As she went out under the arch she saw on the ground at her feet his little papal flag with the crossed keys and triple crown.

In her sitting-room in Saint Dympna's she went directly to her heavy red album of photographs and sat beside her window slowly turning its stiff pages until she came to the wedding group. For a long while she studied his face, felt an impulse to press the page to her lips, resisted, shut the book and shoved it back on its shelf. It was with profound relief that she heard her house telephone's tinkle and Nurse Clane begging her to come quickly to have a look at old Mrs Cronin in Number Six. From that on – it became a ragged day – she was saved from thinking of anything but the job until well after supper.

It was still daylight when she sat before her desk in her bay-window sipping a coffee and smoking her first cigarette of the day. She glanced across at the spire of the church rising above the slates and chimneys about it. It would be a couple of weeks before she got any more signals of distress from that quarter! And would he by then be as full as ever of his jellybelly jokes about Ballybun? And if he were how on earth could she stand him? The night nurse, old Mrs O'Dea, knocked and came in to report her arrival and ask her usual 'All well?' Judy was always glad to see Ma O'Dea, a fat, bosomy mother of seven, with a gusty laugh and full of good cheer. She poured her out a cup of coffee and proffered a cigarette. They chatted a nice little while. Or it was nice except for one remark Ma dropped about meeting Father Tully a couple of hours back in the Main Street. 'A lovely man. Everybody in the town likes him. A funny thing though, I'd swear I nearly thought did I maybe get a smell of you know what?': she raised an imaginary glass to her lips, and winked and nodded solemnly. But, perceiving that this bit of local news was unwelcome she washed the slate clean with a shower of exculpations, and cheerily took herself off to her quarters for the night.

Was the blue of the sky beginning to darken? The evening star above the spire of the church was as clear as a dot over an i. Looking at it she leaned back in her desk-chair, drew on her cigarette deep and slow, and as slowly outbreathed pensive smoke. Venus? Sweet beyond all imagining as friendship and love. Of all mortal promises and pleasures the most fickle. Faithless as a friend, faithful as an enemy. Bitter beyond bearing when it dies. Offering us as Lucifer a brightness that it steals from us before the night. A far from ally, trusting friend,

comrade, pal . . . She picked up her telephone and dialled the presbytery, frightened to hear the empty buzz-buzz, buzz-buzz.

'Hello!' his voice said harshly, impersonally and, old Ma O'Dea was
right, thickly. 'Father Tully speaking.'

'Hello, Tom. This is me. I'm just ringing to say why don't you drop
in here tomorrow evening, say about this time, to visit some of my
ailing patients? We might have a drink and a chat afterwards. Right?
Good. See you. Good night, Tom.'

She replaced the receiver gently. The dusk was gathering. The star
was much brighter. She heard the voices of children playing below her
in the square.

After all! Two of a kind?

One Fair Daughter and No More

For well over a quarter of a century Lizzy Langford, wife of Dr Richard Langford, a – or the – long-established and well-known Belfast physician must (I have calculated in my pedantic Insurance Inspector's way) have struck between 25,000 and 35,000 of her husband's patients as the ideal wife for any doctor. She has always been decorous, sedate, soothing, interested delicately but never inquisitively in every body (not, my joke, everybody) needing Dick's professional attentions. She is not too pretty, meaning that she is not likely to arouse any patient's envy; indeed she is a good deal less than pretty, which could console a female client not feeling up to the mark herself; and lastly she is always dressed so simply, though also so elegantly that even I, a bachelor of many summers, can tell that every frock she wears must have cost at least four virus pneumonias. She may perhaps have one weakness: to be so very correct in every way that it is common Belfast knowledge that some other doctors' wives privately refer to her as Milady Longford.

Last August, therefore, we, the inner circle of the aforesaid 25,000 to 35,000 people who know the Langfords intimately were bewildered to hear that she had begun to berate *in public* none other than her husband Dick's oldest professional colleague and friend, Mr Carl Carson. Mister, not Doctor, he being a surgeon. In fact she had most uncharacteristically begun to behave like a scold, a word which, I gather, means a notoriously abusive woman, saying without regard to the company listening to her such monstrous things, according to the general gossip, as:

'I shall never understand how that nice woman Norma Carson married that ugly man. He must be the ugliest man in all Belfast – hobby-horse nostrils, horse's teeth, piggy eyes, donkey's ears. Oh, he may be a very good eye surgeon, and he has a good physique, we've seen him on the beaches, and there are even people who in their kindness pretend that he has quite a way with him, although I have never seen it, but even if all that were true can you imagine having to face that ugly mug every morning across the breakfast table? Not to say imagine every night having to... And the funny side of it is that when he spotted Norma – she was then just a simple nurse, and it *was* rather a number of years ago – she had just won a beauty competition as the prettiest nurse in Northern Ireland. How *could* she? That ugly, ugly...'

Naturally the first question that occurred to everyone of us was what had happened; what bomb through Lizzy's front window had knocked her elegant manners to bits? Jealousy? Not surely of Norma Carson's frail, pink, girly-sweet, long since faded prettiness? Some social grudge? It is true that we were told that she had called Carl Carson 'common in looks and common in origin.' But Carl never made any bones about being a prole, and a Belfast prole at that. He used to make jokes about it. 'My dad used to say when he'd be cleaning out the Sandy Row sewers...' Was she harking back again to her own aristocratic pedigree? 'My grandfather, the Lord Mayor of Belfast... My dear father, the rural dean... All my people were settled in Ulster since King Billy took possession of this place three and a half centuries ago...' On down to her one chick Anita, studying Baroque architecture in Rome after coming down from Oxford 'with a First'. So? Not jealousy, scorn, envy, certainly not religion, and least of all rivalry; because there is only one single thing in which those two families are not absolutely on a par: the Carsons have six children, the Langfords have only Anita, whom they adopted from her cradle. I did, being unable to think of any other sort of 'difference' between the two couples that I liked best in all Belfast, once let the thought flit past me, like a whiff of smoke from some remote autumn garden, that some childless couples do, sometimes, intimate, half conceal and thereby half reveal... But not those two, surely, after so many years? One cannot, simply, imagine any of those four decent people concocting comparisons. It is true that Carl's skill as an ophthalmic surgeon is so constricted by its very concentration on the tiniest of worlds that no doctor, such as Dick Langford, could rival the wonder of his work; but, then, think of the greater variety of challenges that Dick has to cope with every day. Carl may beat off an immediate dark, but only that. Dick staves off the black-out of life. And Carl has other limitations: he dares have only one hobby, that of playing the violin, which I happen to be able to say authoritatively he does with a sensitivity remarkable in an amateur.

Dick has a tin ear, but, then, Dick golfs, fishes, plays a ferocious game of tennis and he has sailed his *Norma I* to Iceland, rounded the Faroes, nosed into half the fjords of Norway and, I am told, is pretty certain any year now to become commodore of the Royal Ulster Yacht Club. No wonder I crumpled the whole silly gossip into a ball and threw it into the waste-paper basket of memory until the next time I went to Belfast and could smell out the truth for myself. Insurance Inspectors have sharp noses.

I did not get my chance until rather late that October simply because although my visits to Belfast as Claims Inspector have become much more frequent since that unhappy city became a centre of violence of every kind those visits have latterly become much more bustling. So, when I at last drove myself to ring the Langfords it was only to give Dick and Lizzy my apologies, my greetings, and an 'Hello both of you, see you soon – I *hope!*' I was distressed by the pitch and the strain of Dick's voice. I could see him gripping the receiver, leaning across his desk in his surgery, staring fiercely at nothing, begging me to come across and see the pair of them if it were only for ten minutes, they were in big trouble. Please, please... I replied that it could only be for five minutes; I had three more clients to see that day and I wanted to be out of his beastly, bombers' city before night. I was unlucky; held up twice by patrols searching cars, so that I would have arrived in Malone Road in a very bad temper indeed if I had not suddenly recalled on the way that gossip about Lizzy's feud with Carl Carson. Had that blown up again? Dick Langford's strained voice made me think even of libel actions between them. Was Lizzy having a nervous breakdown?

As I stood on the Langfords' sill, being inspected first through the eyehole in the door, and then through the three perpendicular inches permitted by the restrictive door-chain, finally opened by their sixty-year-old housemaid Lena, dressed in the usual Langford canonicals of starched apron, shoulder-frilled, full-busted, cap with tails, I heard what, if I had only understood it at the time, could have given me the key to the whole business. I heard a gramophone upstairs playing some puzzlingly familiar Italian music which I should have been able to identify – I am among my many other accomplishments a bit of a musician. Flutes and harpsichord? Boccherini? Scarlatti? Cimarosa? I kept worrying over it as Lena led me, not as I had expected, into Dick's surgery for our five minutes' talk, but to my dismay upstairs to their drawing-room, which meant Lizzy, explaining to me as she led the way that the Doctor (which, being one of the old, rural Catholic minority, she naturally mispronounced 'Duckthur') had been called out suddenly to attend a girl badly burned by an incendiary bomb. However, she explained further, the Duchesse Oriane de Guermantes was expecting me in her drawing-room whose white door she now opened wide without knocking (well trained) announcing me by my full name as if I were a complete stranger: a little formality at which the two of us exchanged a tiny collusive smile. Nevertheless I could not help admiring Lizzy's insistence, bombs or no bombs, on preserving every possible little punctilio of earlier times in her besieged bit of Belfast's suburban Saint Germain des Près. The music stopped abruptly when my name was announced.

Once inside her white door I turned left, familiar with the geography of the house, leaving to my right the extension known as The Garden Room which could be as it now was secluded by folding doors. It was, I guessed, in this garden-fronting room that the Italian music had been choked into silence on the announcement of my name, meaning, I further guessed, that their daughter Anita was returned from her university studies in Rome and, this being latish in October, returned for good. I also remembered in a flash that I had not seen the girl since the June of the previous year. No! I had not actually seen her even then, I had heard her; or, rather, I had heard that very same slow movement from a *concerto* by – I suddenly identified it – Boccherini, floating through the open window of the Garden Room down to Liz, Dick, Carl, Norma and myself drinking iced champagne on the lawn of the garden below. It had already become an eyebrow-quivering family joke that Anita played this same nostalgic *Andante* three times a day before meals every time she returned on holiday from Italy. Small wonder that the hair on the back of my neck stiffened like a pointer's tail at the smell of game when I observed now that Liz, while glancing over her half-glasses (at me) in poorly-simulated surprise and rising from her escritoire, threw a crumpled ball of paper into her leather wastepaper drum, precisely as I had metaphorically done three months before when I despaired of my guessings about her row with Carl Carson. Shaking her hand I apologized, rather gracefully if I say so myself, for 'interrupting both musical and literary pursuits'. She sat on her chintz-covered sofa and waved her queenly, wrinkling fore-arm towards the opening doors of the Garden Room, snuffling 'You, of course, remember our Anita' with what she obviously thought was a gracious smile, nobody since her schooldays having told her that whenever she smiles she wrinkles her snout in so odd a way that one can never be sure whether she is expressing delight in your presence or disgust at finding you still alive. I turned to greet Anita.

Now I do not think I flatter myself when I say that I am a matured celibate who can appreciate a beautiful female, whether fully dressed in real life or disrobed in art, as a purely aesthetic object. In fact I had already taken notice of the girl in her late schooldays, and more than a couple of times during her college years, always in judicial approval of her good looks and shapely figure. Lately however she had just become a family statistic with its hair up. In astonishment I now saw before me a grown young woman, erect as a statue, breastful if I may invent an apt word, tall, long necked, with two blue-blue eyes so skilfully recessed by Mother Nature as to make them seem at one moment spring blue, at another a rich moonlit midnight. I have never seen blue eyes change colour like that before or since. The effect was hypnotic. Her skin was like warmed marble, such as one only sees and feels in southern latitudes. Her hair was likewise an Italianate black, and so cleverly upcoiled that just one tress sank restfully to her shoulder. My first idea? Naturally: who had her parents been? What genes had given Italy to Ireland? As I reached out my hand to take hers I half-looked back at her mother to compliment her, though instantaneously embarrassed by the awareness that so beautiful a creature could never have come from that progenitor. Before I could fully complete my half-circle from her back to Anita with a cheery 'So we have polished off Rome?' I knew that already, unseen by me, her blue eyes had flashed from light to dark to light again. Implying?

Now, I know I am an odd cuss: a fisherman, a music lover, an Insurance Inspector, a bit of a naturalist, a bit of a traveller with a keen interest in history and especially antiquity, really a bit of everything like a lot of lone bachelors who pass their lives in amassing incomplete collections of information about various segments of life; so much so that I do sometimes astonish my friends with *trouvailles* from my store of universal if, I humbly admit it, incomplete information. My point is that I suddenly realized where elsewhere I had seen that sudden darkening and lightening and at once I had the secret of her beauty in my hand; she was unarguably pretty, but pretty young women are a thousand a penny – she had an extra thing that made her beauty special: she had force, thrust, vibrancy, eagerness, livingness, I suppose what that famous French philosopher whose name I forget, no, I have it, Bergson called *élan vital*. She had in her a powerful will to live. It was this quality in her that reminded me of where I had seen that sudden darkening and lightening of her eyes before. Early of May mornings in the middle of lakes in the west of Ireland, as still and large as mirrors of infinity I had seen away out on the surface of the water a tiny ripple, so tiny that only very keen eyes like mine can spot it, or the eyes of practised fishermen. That ripple reveals what one can only call a shadow of those ephemeridae called may-flies. Some people speak of this shadow as a cloud, but it is by comparison invisible. The ripple is made by a lethal trout. The fisherman aims to simulate the shadow to catch the trout. I had been too slow in turning back to her from her mother to catch her ripple but, by God, I knew that the shadow of a challenge from life and her instinctive leap in response had flitted across her face when I said, 'So we have polished off Rome?' And I saw the proof it in that residual thunder in her eyes. The rest was easy. Any man of my age and experience would have to be a dullard not to understand her response. Two years in Rome. Doing nothing else every day but listen to lectures? Going in and out of Rome's packed wealth of baroque palaces and churches? Really? Every day? Ask any Roman, any Italian, any man at all who has had daughters, especially one so appealing as Anita, and watch his heavy-lidded eyes smile sardonically. I tried hastily to retrieve my mistake.

'But, of course,' I cried heartily, 'there is no real end to Rome, is there?'

'Never!' with a tiny jerk of the head that darkened her lakes again.

Her mother crossed and recrossed her feet and said, 'Don't you think, Anita, you should offer our guest a sherry?' which I cut down at once with my (by now) six people whom I had to see before leaving for Dublin. It was enough. Our lovely smiled at me and the white door clicked to behind her. I said I must go. I said I regretted not meeting Dick. I said she had a pretty daughter. I said she must be proud of her. I said again I must go. I was not heeded. Liz was glaring at the telephone beside her. An extension? Did she want to listen in? She asked me absently where I had spent my summer holidays. I told her I had flown direct to Palermo from Dublin, hired a car there and 'done' the Greek temples around the southern shores of Sicily and the footsole of the peninsula. When she heard the word Sicily she echoed it in such a hiss of disgust that I was hard put to keep from assuring her that all-in-all

Sicily was a safer place to live in than Belfast. Instead I did worse, I asked her, while casually fingering one of her Chinese figurines, where she and Dick had spent their holiday, or were to go for the coming spring. She stared, was lost, gasped, made a contorted face, moaned, 'Us? On holiday?', clasped her hands to her eyes as if to avoid a bomb exploding, sank back into the corner hollow of the sofa and began to wail like a beaten child. In a fright, I slid in beside her, wondering what had I said now, put an arm about her shoulder to soothe her, called out for Anita, begged her again and again to tell me what was wrong, what had I said, for God's sake speak out. She turned, lowered her ringed hands from her tomato-coloured sponge of face, opened her mouth and Milady vanished.

'It's that bastard! That bloody quack, Carson! He did it all, my poor poor Nita, my poor, foolish little girl!'

She should talk about Sicily? Her wails would have done credit to the back lanes of Santa Lucia. What stopped her from wailing merely changed her into shouting – my silence of incomprehension.

'You are a bachelor. You could never understand. You have no idea what she, what all of us have been going through since last June!'

I cannot say that she calmed. She merely shut up; strode to the right hand door of her desk, pulled out from the back of one of its shelves a foolscap wallet marked ANITA, containing presumably every letter she had written since she left for Rome, and dragged out from it helter-skelter to show me from among the general mess of envelopes, picture postcards, letters, tourist folders, telegrams, what I still think of as the remnant papyri of her first and probably unmatchable love affair, or is it another instance of my celibate's ignorance that I hold that the wonder of a first love affair can never repeat itself? Once I was in that kind of love, or I thought I was; I regret to say it came to nothing and that the illusion never repeated itself. For the moment, however, hungrily scanning the papers Liz was passing under my eyes, trying with my fingers to slow their passage, I was far too inquisitive to consider feelings of sympathy or regret for anyone, following a word here or catching a sentence there from three telegrams from Rome, two letters in Italian, a crumpled letter in red ink on pale blue paper partly in English partly in Italian, getting a flash now of a gaudy picture postcard, now of the flying telegram in Italian that repeated its cry of agony so loudly that I still recall its, *Cinque giorni senza notizie devo darmi alla disperazione Giovanni.* 'Five whole days without a word of news must I despair? Giovanni.'

I asked Liz where she got those tell-tale leaves.

'Anywhere, everywhere, they don't care where, forgotten in books, stuffed into shoes, at that stage of madness they despise secrecy, they want to tell the world, scatter their joys and miseries in the streets, write beauty recipes on the backs of them for their friends, add up their debts on them, they are in whatever the hell the bloody goddam words mean IN LOVE!'

The only one of all those pages that I can now record fully is a crumpled one in red ink that she never finished. I have it here on my desk. It obviously got mixed up on that chintz sofa with papers that slipped from my portfolio in the haste of my departure. It is addressed from that house in Belfast and dated a week before. Apart from its *Caro Giovanni* it begins in English, describing the place where she is writing it. She is in the University library. It is a damp, autumnal, northern afternoon. She has come there to get away from 'them', to read something by some 'European'. She had first tried for Giraudoux. Lo and behold! Not one single thing in the catalogue under his name! *Perchè no?* Provincialism? Insularity? He, as a Sicilian, another islander, a sea between him also and the Continent, should know what it means to be cut off from Europe. She searches the catalogue for anything that will carry her mind out of her dreary prison, something by say Gide, something passionate, intimate, say *Et Nunc Manet in Te*, about his awful non-marriage, but of course Gide will not be here either. Lo and behold! They have every single word Gide ever wrote! Here she breaks into Italian which, like any old Susannah-watcher, I translate as best I can with dictionary and the help of my own not half-bad Italian:

'*Clearly this magnificent city of Sodomites . . . I look around me. Green-shaded reading lamps. Pale Irish green faces. Bony Belfast masks. Each in an individual lake of lights. Each an island in an island in an island. Silence. Broken occasionally by small noises, a page turning, somebody blowing his nose. Yesterday when out riding I bit my tongue so I cannot now either eat or speak – the result of which is that I find myself in a state of gentle lethargy. I do not even want to write you a fulminating letter to match your verbal silence. All the same I have it in for you my beloved. You are neglecting me. Are you beginning to forget our love? Or has the Roman post office gone haywire again? Dear, dear Giovanni, remember our pact to say so at once if either of us ceased to feel in love with the other. Would you have the courage to say it? Yes! I am uneasy. I am afraid. My dear one, tell me immediately if it is so. I would prefer a million times to know the truth. Am I boring you? I do know for sure that I love you dearly but'*

End of letter.

The lines of street lamps along the Malone Road lit up. Liz was going on and on and on.

'If you had seen her in June! She had left Rome finally. Sulking and skulking around the house. Playing that stupid Italian record all day long. Hating Belfast, hating us. By July she was unbearable.' Liz shook her jangling wrist over the telephone. 'For long distance calls alone last quarter our bill ran into three figures. In August she was insisting that come what may she was going back to Rome. We said we would not give her the money. She said she would borrow it from her college friends, as she could and would, blackmail us in this small city with the scandal of it. One day Dick was so miserable about her that he confided our trouble to of all people Carl Carson who at once offered to talk sense to the girl. It shows you how desperate we were that we let him try. He drove her out into the country in his car and, we thought it very generous indeed of him, talked to her there for two precious hours. He reported back to us that the only thing to do with her was to let her fly back to Rome just for two days to straighten things out with her *inamorato* but not, *not*, NOT he insisted to let her go alone, have Dick go with her, that as far as violence and terror was concerned Belfast was in the kindergarten stage compared to Rome – the Red Brigade, the Mafia, the *Primo Linea*, Neo-Nazis, and God knows what this boy-friend was. The smarty ass! As if we had not already made contact through the British Embassy to the Quirinal. They comforted us immensely, oh enormously, put us quite at our ease by telling us that this young man in whom our daughter is so interested is on the Italian police lists as a suspected Sicilian left-wing activist. Well, we tried our dear, sweet, good, generous, kind Carl's advice. We told her we would let her go to Rome for two days provided we went with her. If I may make a bright little joke of it her answer was a flat 'No go!' Dick offered to go alone with her, that he would stay at a separate hotel, just be there at hand as a friend that she could contact if she got into trouble. Another 'No go!' The scenes! The arguments! At that point Mister Carson told us that he was due to attend an international congress of ophthalmologists in Zürich the first week in September, and that it had occurred to him that the Dublin-Zürich plane goes on to Rome. If she was agreeable he was willing to go on with her to Rome for just forty-eight hours, keep out of her way, stay strictly in the background, not see her or interfere with her in the least bit, just be there if she wanted help of any kind, and then at the end of the forty-eight hours back with the two of them, he to Zürich, she home to Dublin.'

It was a very old woman who looked at me, and nodded wearily when I asked, 'She went?', and when I said, 'And?':

'And she came home after the two days, beaming, glowing, triumphant. So happy that she revealed to me that on the day Carson drove her into the country to advise her on our behalf – on *OUR* behalf! – he told her he was all on her side, to stick to her guns, that every girl should follow her own star, that he himself was wildly in love with a German-Swiss woman, an eye specialist like himself, living in Zürich.' Liz again put her hands to her face and moaned into their smother, 'I felt like a fly caught in a spider's web of filthy concupiscence.'

Which said, she took a sudden hold of her dignity. Milady rose, wrinkled her tomato nose above her usual ambivalent smile and held out her hand at such a height that it was hard to decide whether she wished it to be shaken or breathed upon. Then, as she started to scoop up her documents from her chintz sofa, I helping, I was taken by surprise to notice the date and location of the post-office stamp on the gaudy postcard. It was *Ottobre X*, and the place of origin was not Rome but Caltanissetta, a name I had noticed last summer bang in the middle of my touring map of Sicily. As I slowly pushed the card Liz-wise I read its message. Four words without a signature. *La mia propria patria.* 'My fatherland.' What had that conveyed to her? It could have been friendly, ironical or dismissive. Was his signature withheld from conspiratorial caution or from coldness? For a moment I dearly wished I had visited this particular *patria* of her lover, remote though it was from my templed coastline, though I would not have needed to go there, I had passed through too many Caltanissettas already not to know what to expect in yet another. Two hotels less remarkable for their comfort than for their declamatory names, a *Zeus*, a *Minerva*, a *Paradiso* or some barbaric oriental name with an X in it or a Z, or a final accented ò or ù; one *trattoria*; a *giardino pubblico*, dusty, parched, flowerless commanding in Baedeker's blurb language 'striking views of the surrounding mountains and valleys'. There might be a decent

Norman church, or a sulphur mine or a salt mine, for there always had to be some explanation for places otherwise distinguished only by some sidelong reference to some quondam Demeter myth or to some Punic War still recorded in the local Museum, meaning a couple of rooms in some public building with shelves of cracked vases, bits of statuettes and other such antiquities displayed in an ambience of dust, graffiti, entwined hearts, cheers for a local football team. Whenever I had paused at such Sicilian townlets I had always assumed that the natives live there in a state of discouraged content, but I had also always remembered that novel of E.M. Forster's about the English woman whose imagination of Italy caused her to marry the local dentist. A wren that ventured where an eagle might fear to tread.

'But do tell me how you find her now?' I pressed Liz, eager to extract the last drop out of my little discovery that at the moment when the daughter was dying of thirst for 'his' sweet Rome, her beloved had already preferred violence in his Caltanissetta.

Before Liz could answer me I saw over her shoulder her drawing room door opening and there was Anita leading in her father and Carl Carson. Liz, to follow my stare, rotated her damp tomato face. When none of the four of us stirred the young woman took command. Young? Certainly by contrast with us her greying elders. For herself in full leaf and flower, though not yet enough so to dethrone her mamma, as she gaily tried to do with, 'Well, well, no introductions necessary here! Right? Elizabeth, a sherry for you I think.' (Did she always first-name her parents like this, or was this a sudden mutiny, a final declaration of independence?) 'Dick? A dry Martini. Right? Carl, something stronger for you, a double Bushmills. Right? And for our Southern Irishman here a double Irish. Right?' Even as a parody of her mother's style it was too much of a bad thing to serve. Liz would have known better than to overdo it. Only hams over-act. She put her daughter down simply by ignoring her.

'Is it a very bad case?' she asked Dick in a voice of such solicitude that she almost sounded sincere. His back-of-the-hand gesture intimated what Carl worded:

'Too soon to say how bad. My interest of course is to protect the girl's sight, if she has any left. The eyes themselves seem okay. She apparently clapped her hands to them at the moment of explosion. Interesting. It is always people's first instinct in the face of violence. The doctors are now spraying what is left of skin and flesh on the rest of her face. Which is not much. Nose gone. Ears gone. Hair of course all gone. The worst of all is the mouth. A few years of grafting and surgery will give her back some kind of nose and ears, but those lips can never really be restored. Thanks, Anita, for your offer of a drink but I am on the job, and I happen to know her father, he lives not far from here, I promised Matron to soften the bad news that they have already 'phoned to him and his wife. That is if I can get a lift.'

'His car,' Dick sighed. 'Rushing into the hospital he forgot to lock it, and you know what "they" are, always on the look-out for cars, especially Cortinas. The spare parts they need. He will never see that Cortina again.'

Liz turned to me.

'Unfortunately Dick ought to be in his surgery by now. Can you possibly give Carl a lift? It won't take you long.'

The four of us started for downstairs. Last out of the drawing-room Dick hastily drew me back to whisper his worry about Anita and also about his wife's unfortunate feud with 'our mutual friend'. I could hear Liz having words with him as they descended to the hall although I was relieved to get the impression that her tone did not suggest a totally broken friendship. When all four of us were together in the hall, amid much searching for hats, scarves, overcoats, medical bags and my own errant portfolio Carl and I kept reassuring the other two about Anita until I realized that I had left my portfolio on the couch upstairs and ran back to get it.

I was halted outside the drawing-room door by that lovely Boccherini. Guardedly I opened the door, so gently that I was not observed by Anita standing before the window of the Garden Room gazing out at a tranquil twilight descending over the lights of Belfast, her palms held out in the posture of a priestess either accepting something with a sigh or invoking it with a tremble; or, I had an old man's fancy to think, like a young goddess balancing two emblems of Time, the human and the immortal; the baroque melody, so elaborate, so civil, so consciously contrived, so adorned, one could even say so full of artifice, and out there the vanishing northern daylight that for a moment seemed, however deceitfully, both pastoral and simple. I was held rigid by the manner in which they enhanced one another and the listening girl. On tiptoe I retrieved the object I wanted and unseen withdrew. Still I paused, on the landing, my fist withholding the door's bevelled click until I might hear the start of that lovely movement which she had earlier choked on hearing old Lena announce me at the door. It came. Again she guillotined it. Why? Unbearable? She wanted the southern sun? Life, not music?

Carl impatiently ran upstairs to call me down. From the pavement we waved and received goodbyes. The door closed. Its chain rattled into place. As I switched on the lights, fastened seat belts, pushed starter, let out the brakes and went into gear I said, 'They can think what they like but if that unfortunate girl does not clear out of that house and this city before Christmas she will go off her head.' Clear out? But to where? To the Leonardo da Vinci airport? Nobody there. Bus into Rome. Ring from the terminal. Nobody she knew answering. Ring another number. Nobody. Ring another number. Nobody. Ring. '*Pronto. Chi parla?* ANITA! *Chi? Ma e andato via.* Gone home. *Sicilia.* Oho, no! He is not coming back *here*! Didn't you know? *E scappato.*' A red light halted us. I looked sidewards at Carl's knotted face. He did not say anything. Then he said: 'She will go. And she will never know how lucky she will have been to get away. Anyhow. Any way. Any where.' He flicked me forwards. The lights had changed. 'Third turn on your left. Number 34.'

It was a quiet *cul de sac* between two level rows of small redbrick houses, each with its tiny garden in front, its brief concrete drive and its garage, each with its own colour of railing. We drew up outside a house whose lighted fanlight bore the white celluloid figure 34. Carl told me not to wait. 'They will want . . .' He banged my door, stepped to the garden gate. As I turned my car to drive away my whirling headlights flooded Carl's back and the faces of a man and woman who had already thrown open their door and were rushing down the drive to meet him with outstretched hands and staring eyes. He was holding out his hands like a priest to comfort them.

A Present from Clonmacnois

It is noon in late May. The only bit of the monastery of Clonmacnois left intact after countless Viking raiders, local Irish robbers, English reformers and over a thousand Irish winters is its tall round tower, bare as a factory chimney. Its other remaining bits and pieces are now in the safe keeping of the Public Works Commissioners under the rubric 'A National Monument'. At this hour the gnomon of the tower casts no shadow. The only sound comes from a lawn-mower man from the Board of Works who is trimming the grass near the river. These last few months have been abnormally rainy, the grass is unusually succulent and thick, the Shannon is unusually high among the reeds along its banks, the surrounding fenlands are sure to be flooded again this coming winter. He halts his engine, takes off his hat, measures the hour by the sun, says the Angelus, wipes his poll whose central bald patch might remind one of a monk's tonsure, and peers up the slopes to where a young man and an old man are picnicking on a flat tombstone. They are the sole visitors so far today. He may advert to his own flask of hot tea and his sandwiches locked in the brown Board of Works van at the entrance to the site, or he may animadvert sourly on the toughness of this accursed grass, or he may be thinking of his wife who prepared his lunch, or of his five children, or of anything at all except the past of Clonmacnois. About this the most learned know no more than a barber does about the past in some grey poll under his scissors.

The younger of the two picnickers glances without interest at him down the slopes as between two large bites of his ham sandwich he mouths passionately, even high-handedly to his elderly companion:

'Owen! I don't know what you see in this bloody place. You have been boosting it to me all the winter and now that I am here it says nothing at all to me. It has no echoes. Its bridge is down. For Ever! That river there has become an ocean. This place is a far away Then. You and I belong to Now. And you know it, Owen! The primitive Church that created this sort of place has lost all meaning for the modern world.

To any rational man all this,' waving his tooth-gapped sandwich, 'is just so much antiquarian nonsense.'

The older man replies placidly.

'This spot has echoes for me. In its hey-day it was a midwife to the Irish imagination. It is one of the sacred places of Ireland. You speak like a young man who might have fallen in love with a girl of an unusual beauty if he had studied her more closely. You have not studied Clonmacnois.'

'My dear Owen, beware! Beware of enthusiasm, above all of patriotic enthusiasm. It could be the ruination of even our finest Celtic scholar!

Our finest Celtic scholar looks admiringly at his companion's head, sculpted by the gods for a prophet or a poet, relishes again the young man's splendid voice that tolls like a basso bell. He pours some more cool Liebfraumilch from his thermos flask into his neophyte's plastic cup. He strokes his greying beard outwards from his chin, looks over the ruins. He replies courteously.

'My dear Donal, beware! Beware of scepticism, above all of patriotic scepticism. It could be the ruination of even our finest Irish poet.'

The young man, obviously flattered by those last three words gulps down his wine, scatters its last drops in an arc over the grass ('A libation?' smiles the scholar) and proceeds with immense enthusiasm:

'I'll tell you, Owen, what we must do. We must exchange roles. You shall henceforth play the part of the sceptic and I the part of the believer. "My true love hath my heart and I have his," as Sir Philip Sidney put it, "by just exchange one for the other given". But that alchemy can't possibly take place in a wilderness like this. My God, even that poor devil from the Board of Works clacking away down there like a corncrake can hardly cut the grass of the place it is gone so wild and thick. Does the air in this place ever dry? A river like the Mississippi! Sodden boglands all around it! I swear half the monks here died of TB.'

'Saints died here. The grass is well manured. The air is numenous.'

'Well, whatever happened here it happened too long ago to break the time barrier. I'm telling you the bridge is down. Only last night I scribbled the rough draft of a poem about that barrier and that bridge. I call it "Rags to Riches". Shall I recite it for you? Mind you it is only a draft. It will take polishing.' And without formal leave he began to bell out his poem:

> Time was, Dark Head, we wore you like a flower,
> Prayed God and Mary nightly to fulfill
> Your longing to be our queen once more.
> For this, for you, for years we died pell-mell
> Until the night we overheard you groan
> 'How many generations more to spell
> My dowry as a queen?' Plainly the dower
> That gave your breath that night a rich-bitch smell
> Of envy was the wealth that taunted you before
> We burned down that town to an empty shell,
> Castles, churches, towers, morgues of power.
> Small wonder that your Wild Geese chose to sell
> Their swords abroad for honour sake, leaving us poor
> To claw barehanded at the citadel
> And free our queen. Ten centuries and more
> Have passed. A happy boy leads to a hill
> An old white-haired woman. Look where she will,
> Only ruins. A roofless church, a quondam tower,
> Tombstones leaning, a fallen bridge long reft and still.
> Laughing joyously he waves. 'All ours!'

The poet ended blushing with chagrin. More bloody rhetorical verse? The old man opened his tobacco pouch and pinch by pinch refilled his pipe, tamping each pinch with his fourth finger. He lit carefully. Then, between tiny puffs, he quoted:

'"Perhaps in this neglected spot is laid/Hearts once pregnant with celestial fire..." Did you know that one of the finest scholars of the eighth century came to this spot with gifts from the court of Charlemagne? The poet Alcuin. And he was not the sort of man who would have travelled far without good reason.'

'Did he write anything that was any damn good?'

'He wrote, my dear boy, what you normally write. Charming lyric poetry. In Latin of course. He wrote about his lost nightingale. About Spring's harbinger, the cuckoo. About his lonely monastic cell.'

'Can you,' his friend asked, a trifle more cautiously, 'quote me any of his verses? Owen, why did we come to this place? The cold of this gravestone is going up through my backside.'

'There is somebody beneath it who is colder. Alcuin's verse? You flatter my old man's memory. Moreover I am a Celtic not a classical scholar. But that splendid North of Ireland woman Helen Waddell, whom I once knew so well, and who translated so many medieval Latin lyrics, did render Alcuin's verse about the cuckoo something like this... I agree that such verses were possibly a common classical convention. "Green branches begin to give their shade to tired men, the goats come to their milking with full udders." It comes back to me. *Tu iam dulcis amor, cunctis gratissimus hospes, omnia te expectant.* "Come, O cuckoo, come! Thou art love himself, the guest on whom all things wait, the sea, the earth, the sky."'

'And man?' annotated the poet, glancing stealthily at his tutor, thinking that he must later enquire elsewhere about this splendid North of Ireland woman whom the old man had evidently once admired.

'Alcuin,' the other went on, 'wrote more than once about the cuckoo. *Carmina deducunt forte.* "Song brings the cuckoo home." *Sis memor et nostri.* "Sometimes remember us, Love, fare you well."'

The old scholar fell silent. The mower stopped. Far away a cuckoo imitated itself.

'Mind you,' the scholar went on, 'Helen inserted that word *love*. All the Latin says is *Semper ubique vale*. She did something similar to Alcuin's lament for his strayed nightingale. "So dim and brown thy little body was./ But none could scorn thy singing./ What a depth of harmony in such a tiny throat!"' He paused, puffed his pipe, looked in a troubled way across the monastery's rotted teeth at a remnant building grandiosely known as the Cathedral. The word implied a bishop's throne. Was there ever a bishop here? 'There is no word *little* in the Latin. Nor is there the word *tiny*. "Tiny throat." *Angusta*, yes. Narrow throat. Helen seemed to like the image of smallness, as if she were writing about a baby. "To thee, O small and happy, such a grace was given." The nightingale is not such a small bird. It measures about seventeen centimetres. Not that she would have known this. The nightingale is not heard west of the Severn.'

His pipe had gone out. He sighed.

'Yes, I suppose it *was* a long time ago!'

The mower stopped again. Silence. 'Cucu!' This time farther away. The poet shifted restlessly.

'Your Alcuin,' he snorted, 'was an Englishman, writing in Latin. Do we know whether even one poem in Irish came out of this place?'

'We cannot know but it is more than likely.'

'How likely?'

'You have, of course, heard of Priscian?'

'By name.'

'A man of no importance, really. A grammarian. A contemporary of that Roman citizen Cassiodorus who became a chief consul in Rome under the Goths. The Marshal Pétain of his day? Well, centuries afterwards some learned Irishman came on one of Priscian's grammarian's texts and started to copy it in an Irish-Swiss monastery near Lake Constance. He got so bored by the grammarian that to relieve the boredom he wrote on the margin of his vellum a little poem that goes like this . . . "A hedge of trees surrounds me . . ."'

The young man became excited.

'I know that poem. I have translated it myself. It goes like this in my version. "Birds chatter above my dull pages,/Trees surround me like a green wall./Over and over the cuckoo counts my wages,/Just now I hear a blackbird call."'

From behind the pair of them a loud burst of laughter. It was the man from the Board of Works.

'By Jiminy!' he swore. 'I must have heard translations of that poem a dozen times. Whenever a bunch of tourists come here there is always somebody who recites it. But the shape you have put on it, young sur, is the besht I ever heard. "Over and over the cuckoo counts my wages." Shtop!' he commanded, finger aloft, ear cocked.

Was it near? Or was it far? That fluting call.

The young 'sur' had become flamelike from pride: a troubadour bonding centuries. His laughter and the rustic's drowned the trailing monastic voice of the scholar:

'We cannot tell how far that Priscian manuscript wandered. Did it come from here? All we can say for certain is that at one stage in its life a wandering Irish scholar wrote a verse on its margin.'

He drained his thermos on the grass. He began to pack their lunch basket.

It was some months before those two amiable inapposites met again, though in the meantime they had communicated through some gay verses from the one and a suspiciously scholarly-looking volume from the other. The young man's first glance judged this volume to be nothing more than an early Calendar of Irish Saints prefaced by about a hundred quatrains in Old Irish which were, he decided after reading six or seven pages of them, the kind of pietistic doggerel to be expected from any unlettered coenobite in any desert in the world under the influence of prolonged mental starvation. Between aversion and puzzlement he fluttered the pages muttering to himself, 'Why the hell did Owen send me this heap of rubbish?' He re-examined the volume. Its Gaelic title was *Félire Oengusso Céli Dé*, translated as 'The Martyrology of Oengus the Culdee'. He noted that the Old Irish text had been 'critically edited from 10 manuscripts, with a preface, translation, notes and indices by Whitley Stokes.' He was aware that Stokes had been a scholar of repute, saw that the work had been published in London in 1905 by a Society with which he was not familiar, The Henry Bradshaw Society, and that it was numbered XXIX of a series.

Culdee? His encyclopedia refreshed his memory. In Irish *Ceile De*. A companion, mate, servant or spouse of God. In modern Irish *Dia. Dieu. Deus.* Zeus. The Shining One? A spouse of Zeus? A bit thick. More likely servant, menial, lay brother, cleaner-up, cook. At best somebody to do with the intoning or droning of hymns in some ruined monastery like Clonmacnois.

He became so bored with his encyclopedia that he returned to his monastery bore, the culdee called Oengus, and was once again on the point of becoming bored by his pietistic verses when, suddenly, as if he had been transformed into a pile of autumn leaves dosed with petrol into which Owen had thrown a lighted match he burst into a flame of enthusiasm at the quatrain following line 209. To anybody else the quatrain might not have seemed of any interest. All that the four lines said, in Mr Whitley Stokes's careful translation, was: '*The cells* (old monastic cells) *that have been taken by pairs and by trios, they are Romes with multitudes, with hundreds, with thousands.*' With a gulping throat he evoked from these four lines a dear image of his childhood in Cork: a tiny, impoverished cottage in a long, narrow city lane that went winding as a goat or a cow wanders, surrounded by multitudes, by hundreds, by thousands of similar cells, and himself and his mother kneeling at night beside the dying fire of her small kitchen, saying the Rosary. As he read again the tears trickled down his face. Poverty. Power. Rome. Empire. War. His pen had of its own will already written:

> Little places taken
> > First by twos and threes
> Are like Rome reborn
> > Peopled sanctuaries.

He hurled back the pages to see at what unperceived point this dreary doggerel had magically turned into poetry and at once found the answer. Two rivals had been at work on this job: a pietistic old (he insisted on the 'old') fool of a pedant, and a superb young artist. His guess was confirmed when Mr Whitley Stokes in his quiet Anglican way blew ashes into flame:

'Heathendom has been destroyed, though it once was widespread, the kingdom of God the Father has filled heaven and earth and air.'

Kings *had* been destroyed! Saints *had* been crowned! Fiercely the artist lashed his racer. Quietly Mr Stokes tapped out the hoof beats of the old tongue. *Múchta*. (Stifled.) *Plághta*. (Plagued.) *Rígtha*. (Kinged.) *Mártha*. (Glorified.) Which, in his Dublin bed-sitter, the poet, bursting with excitement, his voice tolling louder than the buses and the cars outside, transmogrified for the glory of Faith and Fatherland into:

> Sing the kings defeated!
> > Sing the Domhnalls down!
> Clonmacnois triumphant,
> > Cronan with the crown.

> All the hills of evil
> > Level now they lie;
> All the quiet valleys
> > Tossed up to the sky.

That was his winning post, even though the monkish poetaster behind him went on wheezing around the course again and again for 25 rounds more. Not that a great deal of work did not yet remain to be done before he finally winnowed this thousand-year-old celebration of a triumph to which his calmer hours would have given no more than the most transitory belief. Nor would he have been disconcerted if at any moment during those ardent weeks somebody had upbraided him for his inconsistency. 'And how many,' he would have boomed, 'of those exquisite Madonnas of the Renaissance do you suppose were just street girls of Florence or Rome? Think of the most profoundly religious painter of his age, Pietro Perugino, a man,' here he would have pounded his modest breast, 'who was well known to his contemporaries as a villain, an atheist and a genius!'

It was almost September before he was prepared to show his translation and return its source to its owner, his inspiration. To his disappointment he had to leave both with a wizened housekeeper who proudly explained that the 'professor' had gone off to 'speechify' at Clonmacnois. 'About what? About what but the pattern! Doesn't the world know it? Won't the world be there? The feast day of the Saint!'

Still, he thought as he disconsolately turned away from the suburban door, remembered by multitudes, by hundreds, by thousands coming from all over the suckling, Shannon shore in their Cortinas, Ford Eights, second hand Mercedes, to honour the *genius loci*.

But what a letter of praise he got three days later! 'The most superb poem ever composed on the deaths of Wotan and Thunder, of Goll and Manannaan, of all the pagan gods, Celtic and Germanic alike. For this is your very own poem, not to be treated as a mere translation – leave all that to pedants like Stokes and myself – so splendid a re-creation as not to be a translation at all.' The letter went on: 'Alas! My dear friend! How I envy you your faith! So much so that I forgive you for having by one word at our last meeting, beside the Shannon, shaken mine. We spoke then of the poet and scholar Alcuin. He whose great patron was Charlemagne, King of the Franks, Emperor of the West, who came with costly gifts to Clonmacnois, and of whom you said scornfully that he was *an Englishman*. That fatal word stuck...'

'O God!' the poet groaned. 'His patriotism has broken out again.'

'I have not been able to forget it, and I am thereby in your debt for forcing me to consider whether all those costly gifts that Charlemagne scattered among the monasteries of Ireland and Britain may demonstrate not his warm generosity but his cold eagerness to dominate this island and its neighbour. Was Alcuin just another tool in this imperialistic design? Was he first and last an English spy? What *am* I to believe? Whom trust? Could there have been some Irish accomplice in Clonmacnois who . . .'

At this the young man roared with laughter, threw his tutor's crazy letter into the air, following its floating leaves with uplifted hands that slowly sank back on his thighs. Belief? Could it be true that if any man wants badly enough to believe in anything he will believe for the pure relief of belief itself.

'Take that poem of Oengus the Culdee. I translated it. Owen says I did not. That it is my very own. I believe there were two poets at work on it. He makes me a third. Then who did write it?'

At which all his pride in his poem evaporated into the thought that everything created is recreated, that it takes many generations to write a poem, many lives, many grass-grown ruins. All humanity has but one song to sing and that written in many forms by life itself. Was that what Paul Valéry meant by his *La mer, la mer, toujours recommencée*? Life renews itself endlessly. The artist is a mere tiller of ancient soil.

MORE ABOUT PENGUINS, PELICANS, PEREGRINES AND PUFFINS

For further information about books available from Penguins please write to Dept EP, Penguin Books Ltd, Harmondsworth, Middlesex UB7 0DA.

In the U.S.A.: For a complete list of books available from Penguins in the United States write to Dept DG, Penguin Books, 299 Murray Hill Parkway, East Rutherford, New Jersey 07073.

In Canada: For a complete list of books available from Penguins in Canada write to Penguin Books Canada Ltd, 2801 John Street, Markham, Ontario L3R 1B4.

In Australia: For a complete list of books available from Penguins in Australia write to the Marketing Department, Penguin Books Australia Ltd, P.O. Box 257, Ringwood, Victoria 3134.

In New Zealand: For a complete list of books available from Penguins in New Zealand write to the Marketing Department, Penguin Books (N.Z.) Ltd, Private Bag, Takapuna, Auckland 9.

In India: For a complete list of books available from Penguins in India write to Penguin Overseas Ltd, 706 Eros Apartments, 56 Nehru Place, New Delhi 110019.

KING PENGUIN

☐ *Selected Poems* **Tony Harrison**   £3.95

Poetry Book Society Recommendation. 'One of the few modern poets who actually has the gift of composing poetry' – James Fenton in the *Sunday Times*

☐ *The Book of Laughter and Forgetting*
Milan Kundera   £3.95

'A whirling dance of a book . . . a masterpiece full of angels, terror, ostriches and love . . . No question about it. The most important novel published in Britain this year' – Salman Rushdie in the *Sunday Times*

☐ *The Sea of Fertility* **Yukio Mishima**   £9.95

Containing *Spring Snow, Runaway Horses, The Temple of Dawn* and *The Decay of the Angel*: 'These four remarkable novels are the most complete vision we have of Japan in the twentieth century' – Paul Theroux

☐ *The Hawthorne Goddess* **Glyn Hughes**   £2.95

Set in eighteenth century Yorkshire where 'the heroine, Anne Wylde, represents the doom of nature and the land . . . Hughes has an arresting style, both rich and abrupt' – *The Times*

☐ *A Confederacy of Dunces* **John Kennedy Toole** £3.95

In this Pulitzer Prize-winning novel, in the bulky figure of Ignatius J. Reilly an immortal comic character is born. 'I succumbed, stunned and seduced . . . it is a masterwork of comedy' – *The New York Times*

☐ *The Last of the Just* **André Schwartz-Bart**   £3.95

The story of Ernie Levy, the last of the just, who was killed at Auschwitz in 1943: 'An outstanding achievement, of an altogether different order from even the best of earlier novels which have attempted this theme' – John Gross in the *Sunday Telegraph*

KING PENGUIN

☐ *The White Hotel* **D. M. Thomas** £3.95

'A major artist has once more appeared', declared the *Spectator* on the publication of this acclaimed, now famous novel which recreates the imagined case history of one of Freud's woman patients.

☐ *Dangerous Play: Poems 1974–1984*
  Andrew Motion £2.95

Winner of the John Llewelyn Rhys Memorial Prize. Poems and an autobiographical prose piece, *Skating*, by the poet acclaimed in the *TLS* as 'a natural heir to the tradition of Edward Thomas and Ivor Gurney'.

☐ *A Time to Dance* **Bernard Mac Laverty** £2.50

Ten stories, including 'My Dear Palestrina' and 'Phonefun Limited', by the author of *Cal*: 'A writer who has a real affinity with the short story form' – *The Times Literary Supplement*

☐ *Keepers of the House* **Lisa St Aubin de Terán** £2.95

Seventeen-year-old Lydia Sinclair marries Don Diego Beltrán and goes to live on his family's vast, decaying Andean farm. This exotic and flamboyant first novel won the Somerset Maugham Award.

☐ *The Deptford Trilogy* **Robertson Davies** £5.95

'Who killed Boy Staunton?' – around this central mystery is woven an exhilarating and cunningly contrived trilogy of novels: *Fifth Business, The Manticore* and *World of Wonders*.

☐ *The Stories of William Trevor* £5.95

'Trevor packs into each separate five or six thousand words more richness, more laughter, more ache, more multifarious human-ness than many good writers manage to get into a whole novel' – *Punch*. 'Classics of the genre' – Auberon Waugh

A CHOICE OF PENGUINS

☐ *Small World* **David Lodge** £2.50

A jet-propelled academic romance, sequel to *Changing Places*. 'A new comic débâcle on every page' – *The Times*. 'Here is everything one expects from Lodge but three times as entertaining as anything he has written before' – *Sunday Telegraph*

☐ *The Neverending Story* **Michael Ende** £3.95

The international bestseller, now a major film: 'A tale of magical adventure, pursuit and delay, danger, suspense, triumph' – *The Times Literary Supplement*

☐ *The Sword of Honour Trilogy* **Evelyn Waugh** £3.95

Containing *Men at Arms, Officers and Gentlemen* and *Unconditional Surrender*, the trilogy described by Cyril Connolly as 'unquestionably the finest novels to have come out of the war'.

☐ *The Honorary Consul* **Graham Greene** £2.50

In a provincial Argentinian town, a group of revolutionaries kidnap the wrong man . . . 'The tension never relaxes and one reads hungrily from page to page, dreading the moment it will all end' – Auberon Waugh in the *Evening Standard*

☐ *The First Rumpole Omnibus* **John Mortimer** £4.95

Containing *Rumpole of the Bailey*, *The Trials of Rumpole* and *Rumpole's Return*. 'A fruity, foxy masterpiece, defender of our wilting faith in mankind' – *Sunday Times*

☐ *Scandal* **A. N. Wilson** £2.25

Sexual peccadillos, treason and blackmail are all ingredients on the boil in A. N. Wilson's new, *cordon noir* comedy. 'Drily witty, deliciously nasty' – *Sunday Telegraph*

A CHOICE OF PENGUINS

☐ **Stanley and the Women** Kingsley Amis £2.50

'Very good, very powerful ... beautifully written ... This is Amis *père* at his best' – Anthony Burgess in the *Observer*. 'Everybody should read it' – *Daily Mail*

☐ **The Mysterious Mr Ripley** Patricia Highsmith £4.95

Containing *The Talented Mr Ripley, Ripley Underground* and *Ripley's Game*. 'Patricia Highsmith is the poet of apprehension' – Graham Greene. 'The Ripley books are marvellously, insanely readable' – *The Times*

☐ **Earthly Powers** Anthony Burgess £4.95

'Crowded, crammed, bursting with manic erudition, garlicky puns, omnilingual jokes ... (a novel) which meshes the real and personalized history of the twentieth century' – Martin Amis

☐ **Life & Times of Michael K** J. M. Coetzee £2.95

The Booker Prize-winning novel: 'It is hard to convey ... just what Coetzee's special quality is. His writing gives off whiffs of Conrad, of Nabokov, of Golding, of the Paul Theroux of *The Mosquito Coast*. But he is none of these, he is a harsh, compelling new voice' – Victoria Glendinning

☐ **The Stories of William Trevor** £5.95

'Trevor packs into each separate five or six thousand words more richness, more laughter, more ache, more multifarious human-ness than many good writers manage to get into a whole novel' – *Punch*

☐ **The Book of Laughter and Forgetting**
Milan Kundera £3.95

'A whirling dance of a book ... a masterpiece full of angels, terror, ostriches and love ... No question about it. The most important novel published in Britain this year' – Salman Rushdie

ENGLISH AND AMERICAN
LITERATURE IN PENGUINS

☐ *Emma* **Jane Austen** £1.25

'I am going to take a heroine whom no one but myself will much like,' declared Jane Austen of Emma, her most spirited and controversial heroine in a comedy of self-deceit and self-discovery.

☐ *Tender is the Night* **F. Scott Fitzgerald** £2.95

Fitzgerald worked on seventeen different versions of this novel, and its obsessions – idealism, beauty, dissipation, alcohol and insanity – were those that consumed his own marriage and his life.

☐ *The Life of Johnson* **James Boswell** £2.95

Full of gusto, imagination, conversation and wit, Boswell's immortal portrait of Johnson is as near a novel as a true biography can be, and still regarded by many as the finest 'life' ever written. This shortened version is based on the 1799 edition.

☐ *A House and its Head* **Ivy Compton-Burnett** £4.95

In a novel 'as trim and tidy as a hand-grenade' (as Pamela Hansford Johnson put it), Ivy Compton-Burnett penetrates the facade of a conventional, upper-class Victorian family to uncover a chasm of violent emotions – jealousy, pain, frustration and sexual passion.

☐ *The Trumpet Major* **Thomas Hardy** £1.50

Although a vein of unhappy unrequited love runs through this novel, Hardy also draws on his warmest sense of humour to portray Wessex village life at the time of the Napoleonic wars.

☐ *The Complete Poems of Hugh MacDiarmid*

☐ Volume One £8.95
☐ Volume Two £8.95

The definitive edition of work by the greatest Scottish poet since Robert Burns, edited by his son Michael Grieve, and W. R. Aitken.

ENGLISH AND AMERICAN LITERATURE IN PENGUINS

☐ **Main Street Sinclair Lewis**   £4.95

The novel that added an immortal chapter to the literature of America's Mid-West, *Main Street* contains the comic essence of Main Streets everywhere.

☐ **The Compleat Angler Izaak Walton**   £2.50

A celebration of the countryside, and the superiority of those in 1653, as now, who love *quietnesse, vertue* and, above all, *Angling*. 'No fish, however coarse, could wish for a doughtier champion than Izaak Walton' – Lord Home

☐ **The Portrait of a Lady Henry James**   £2.50

'One of the two most brilliant novels in the language', according to F. R. Leavis, James's masterpiece tells the story of a young American heiress, prey to fortune-hunters but not without a will of her own.

☐ **Hangover Square Patrick Hamilton**   £3.95

Part love story, part thriller, and set in the publands of London's Earls Court, this novel caught the conversational tone of a whole generation in the uneasy months before the Second World War.

☐ **The Rainbow D. H. Lawrence**   £2.50

Written between *Sons and Lovers* and *Women in Love*, *The Rainbow* covers three generations of Brangwens, a yeoman family living on the borders of Nottinghamshire.

☐ **Vindication of the Rights of Woman
      Mary Wollstonecraft**   £2.95

Although Walpole once called her 'a hyena in petticoats', Mary Wollstonecraft's vision was such that modern feminists continue to go back and debate the arguments so powerfully set down here.